OLD, NEW, BORROWED, & BLUE

OLD, NEW, BORROWED, & BLUE

BUBBA THE MONSTER HUNTER SEASON SIX

JOHN G. HARTNESS

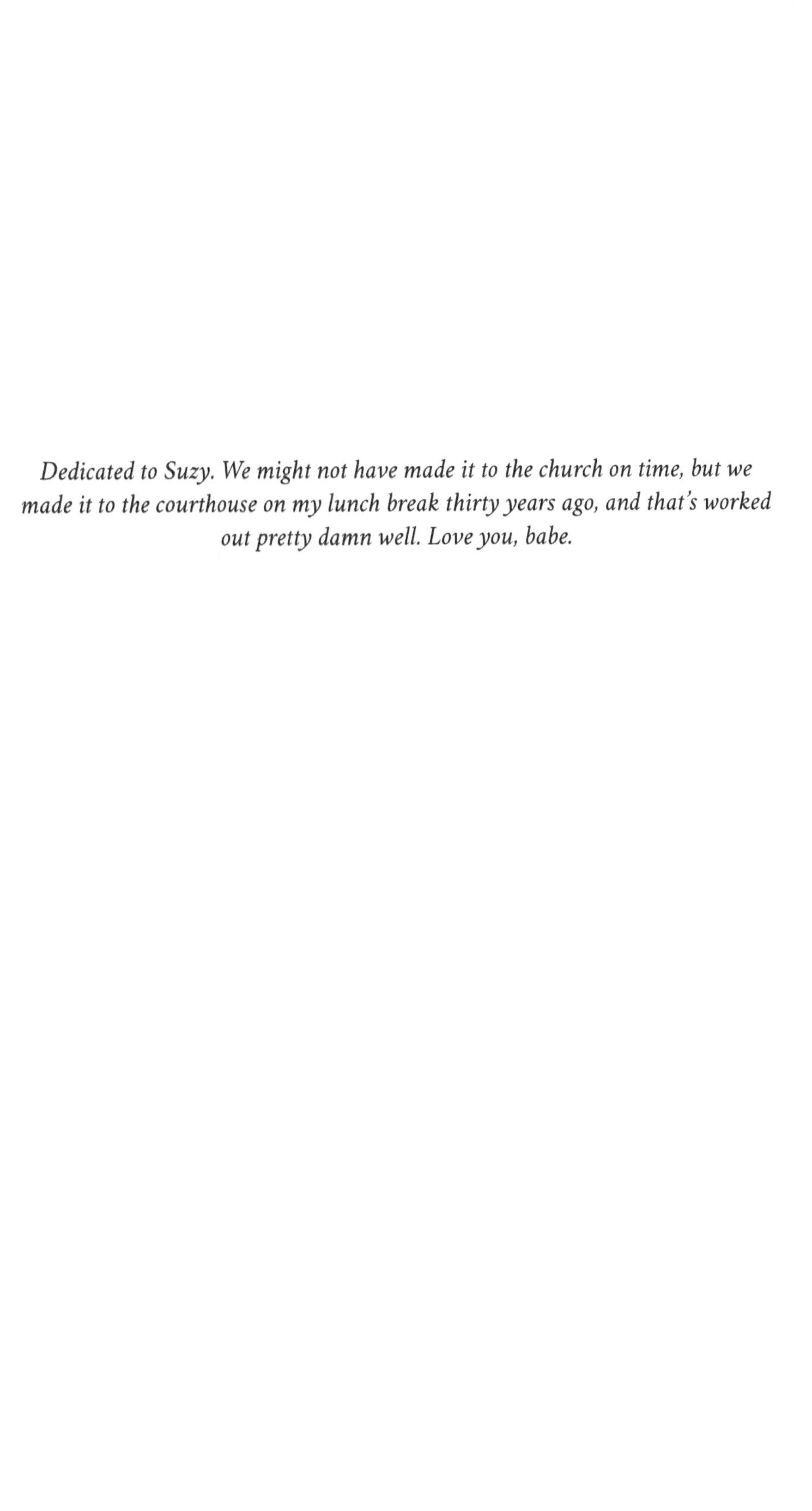

Dedicated to Suzy. We might not have made it to the church on time, but we made it to the courthouse on my lunch break thirty years ago, and that's worked out pretty damn well. Love you, babe.

SWING LOW

A BUBBA THE MONSTER
HUNTER NOVELLA
JOHN G. HARTNESS
SWING LOW

1

I stood in the graveyard in the middle of the night and stared down at the mound of dirt where my friend, and my failure, rested. The little metal stand held a typewritten card with two sets of dates and three names. Joseph Matthew MacIntyre, born then, gone now. That's it. Just a little white cardboard rectangle with the barest of information, a tiny speck of red clay on one corner where a shovelful of dirt had gone astray, the ink faded a little from the winter rain that had been sprinkling for most of a week. Just a name and some numbers to remember a good man.

It wasn't enough. It would never be enough. I couldn't sum up my friend in two lines of Courier font. I half-leaned, half-sat on the tombstone in the row right behind Joe's, just staring at the hump of sod where the ground hadn't settled yet. Uncle Father Joe. The whole name thing had been a joke, a riff on all of us being such rednecks that Skeeter's daddy was also his uncle. But he kinda *was* that, to both of us. Joe was the one who always seemed older than me and Skeeter, even though only a couple years separated us in age. He just carried a maturity with him everywhere, a gravitas that balanced out mine and Skeet's shenanigans.

"Fuck," I said, scooting my butt forward and sliding down the headstone to the damp grass. I felt a lump under one cheek and decided I'd probably plopped right down on a dirt clod and was almost certainly getting red mud ground into the seat of my pants. Amy would gripe a little, but mostly for show. I do all my laundry, so it's not like I'm some

3

Neanderthal who comes in, throws a pile of dirty clothes at his woman, and grunts his way to the living room. Okay, I'm pretty hairy, and I did just describe most of the days when I walk into my house, except for the throwing clothes at Amy part. There's been a lot of grunting and recliner time since we got back from Washington, D.C. and our adventures with Quincy Harker.

"I'm sorry, bud." My words sounded flat, like the oppressive clouds had mashed all the soul out of whatever I thought I was going to say. That fit with how I felt, with how I'd felt every day of the months since Joe died in an explosion in Charlotte while we were fighting Nazis. "If we'da just stayed in our own lane, none of this would have happened. It's my fault, and I'd give anything to take it back." I let my head thump back against the headstone and just sat there looking up, letting the drizzle wash my hot tears away with cold winter rain.

"Wow, you're almost as much of an arrogant asshole as Harker," came a voice from a few feet behind my right shoulder.

"Not interested in your opinion right now, Glory," I said without looking around. I recognized the voice as belonging to Glory, Quincy Harker's guardian angel, who had kinda adopted our group of misfits as members of her flock, which apparently gave her blanket permission to eavesdrop on my grieving and give me crap.

"Don't care that you're not interested," the angel replied, walking around to sit on Joe's grave in front of me. I opened my mouth to say something, and she held up one finger. "Don't start with me on respecting the dead. I get to talk to dead people on the regular, and I know what does and doesn't offend them. Sitting on a pile of dirt six feet above the final resting place of their meat suit? Not offensive. Hiding from your job and sitting around wallowing in guilt instead of doing important work and helping people? The dead, and me, find that offensive as hell."

"You're telling me that Joe wants me to get up off my ass and get back to work?" I asked. "Then how about you get him back here to tell me himself?" The second I said it, I knew it's what I wanted more than anything. Not just Joe. No, if I was going to ask, let's make it a big ask. Let me beg forgiveness from Brittany, who died because she got tangled up in my shit. Let me ask my grandpappy if he forgives me for getting him killed, too. Hell, let me ask my father and my kid brother if they forgave me for killing them. Just one chance, one moment to tell the people I'd loved and lost what they meant to me. Just another second with them, when I knew it wouldn't last but could lock it in my memory forever and hold onto it when they were gone.

"You know I can't do that, right?" Glory said, and I could hear regret in her voice.

I glared at the angel, not ready to let go of anger yet. Out of Elizabeth Kubler-Ross's stages of grief, anger was my favorite. I'm good at anger. A lot of the other stages aren't really my thing, but I've got anger sorted. "So what good are you? If you can't do anything to help, why are you here?"

"Because Amy asked me to look in on you. She's worried. Not just about you, but about Skeeter, too. Have you even seen him since the funeral?"

I thought about it for a second. "No."

"And how long has it been since you went a day without seeing and talking to him?"

That took a longer think. "Jeez, I guess probably since ninth grade."

"Your best friend, who you have spoken to almost every day for over twenty years, hasn't been heard from in almost two weeks, and you haven't gone to check on him?"

Oof. I'd been so wrapped up in my own grief that I never even thought about how much worse it must be for Skeeter. Joe was his safe haven, the one family member whose love never wavered, even when Skeeter came out. I levered myself up off the ground and nodded at Glory. "Okay, you win. I'll go check on Skeeter."

"He might not come to the door," she said, rising from the dirt a lot more gracefully than I managed.

"I've got a key."

"He might have changed the locks."

"I've got another key, this one in a size sixteen."

"Well, then what are you waiting for?" she asked, walking past me toward my truck. I shook my head and followed. She knew I would. She knew exactly which buttons to push to get me to do what I needed to do. I guess you live for millennia and you learn a little bit about how to manipulate grieving rednecks. I didn't mind being manipulated this time, though. I had a purpose, and it was time to get the band back together and go to work.

———

She was right. Skeeter didn't come to the door. And he had in fact changed the locks. Of course, Glory knew that before I drove all the way over there, she just didn't share that information before she *poofed* out of existence and teleported back to Harker's joint in Charlotte, or however the hell she travels.

Skeeter lived just "across the holler" from me, which meant our houses were probably two hundred yards apart as the crow, or in the case, angel, flew. But it was about two miles of twisty, half-paved, narrow-ass mountain roads to get there. Not the easiest thing to navigate in a full-sized pickup, but I learned to drive on these hills, so not much fazes me at this point.

I pounded on the door again. "Skeeter, if you don't open up, I'm gonna kick this sumbitch down," I yelled, knowing full well he had at least two cameras on me and at least one microphone.

"I reinforced the door after the last unwelcome visitor I had." Skeeter's voice came through the little speaker under his doorbell.

That little situation involved a pain in the ass vampire and a lot of people who wanted him dead. And since he was paying me a decent amount of money to keep him undead, I stashed him with Skeeter. Which led to Skeeter's place getting trashed and me footing the bill for his repairs. And some renovations, it seemed now.

"Who said shit about a door, Skeet?" I yelled through what felt like several inches of steel plate. "I need to get into your house, I've got options. I can bust out a window—"

"Reinforced bullet-proof glass set in solid steel frames."

"Okay, I can kick your back door in."

"Same setup as the front. I'm not a dumbass."

"Fine, I reckon I'll unfurl my fairy wings, shrink down to Tinkerbell size, and fly down your chimney. Now you gonna open this damn door, or do I have to get irritated?"

"Since when can you fly?" Skeeter's voice sounded interested, which was better than alternating angry and despondent, which is all I'd been getting out of him.

"If you don't open this door, you're gonna find out the hard way!" I yelled.

"That don't even make sense, Bubba," Skeeter's tinny voice said through the speaker. "How does me not letting you in the house tell me anything about—goddammit, Bubba!"

I barely heard that last bit, on account of me walking off to the back of my truck, yanking an M79 grenade launcher out of one of the storage compartments under the back seat, and firing a forty-millimeter grenade into what I was at least eighty percent sure was Skeeter's living room wall. I was at least sixty percent sure it wasn't load bearing.

Fortunately for Skeeter, and me, I remembered right and blew a massive hole in the wall, rather than taking out the wall of his kitchen or crapper. His kitchen woulda been bad because of the gas range. The bathroom woulda been bad because…well, it's a bathroom. You figure it out.

My best friend stepped through his brand-new front door, right next to the old front door, and glared at me. "You're paying for that."

"Good to see you, too. You should take a shower," I said. "Got some sheetrock dust in your hair. And you stink. Get cleaned up and get over to my place. Amy sent me a text while I was on my way over here. She's got a job for us."

"I'm retired," Skeeter said, turning to go back into his house, where the occasional chunk of wall or tchotchke continued to fall to the floor.

"We don't get to retire, Skeet," I said, wincing as he froze mid-step. This was going to suck. "We don't get to grow old. We don't get to ride off into the sunset, and we don't get to sit back and reminisce to our grandkids about our glory days. We fight, we bust our asses to hold back the shadows and the monsters, and eventually we run into something bigger and badder than us, and then we die. And hopefully somebody else steps up to take our place and keep the cycle going. But we don't retire. We protect, we defend, we fight, and we die. That's the gig, and we both knew it when we signed up."

Skeeter whirled around and ran at me, his hands balled into fists. I felt one thump into my chest, then I opened my arms wide and wrapped them around my best friend, pulling him tight and telling him over and over how much I love him while tears poured down my face into his hair. Eventually he ran out of steam to beat on me, and I let him go.

He took a step back and looked up at me. "You suck at comfort, Bubba."

"Yeah, but I've got beer and a pack of spicy brats in my fridge. Now get a shower and meet me at my place in twenty minutes. We'll throw some shit on the grill and see what Amy's got for us. And don't screw around, Skeeter. If I have to come back over here and drag you out…well, I've got this brand-new door, so I reckon it'll be a little easier, at least."

Two hours later, me and Skeeter were parked in my den in a semi-comatose state brought on by overindulgence in bratwurst and beer that was truly American in its scope. "I think I'm gonna explode, Bubba," he said from the couch.

"If you're bein' metaphorical, you know where the can is," I replied. "If you're being literal, please go out on the back deck. It's way cheaper to pressure wash the porch and the side of the house than to recarpet the living room and reupholster the furniture."

"I think I'm just being a little whiny," Skeeter said. "I ain't ate like that in a month or more."

"From what we've been hearing, you've barely eaten at all in a month or more," Geri said, walking in from the kitchen with a plate of salad and fries.

"You don't want any brats?" I asked. "There's some on the plate next to the stove."

"I know," she said. "I'm trying a vegetarian thing."

"I did that for a while," I said, nodding sagely. "I gave up meat, drinking, strip clubs, and fighting one time. Worst weekend of my life."

Geri just shook her head at me, which was kind of her default reaction. We'd come a long way since her wanting to murder me for getting her big sister killed, but we still weren't what I'd call "tight." Even if she did live in my guest room. She plopped down on the sofa next to Skeeter, her brown ponytail with pink streaks draping over the back of the couch. Her chunky New Rock boots hit the coffee table with a *thunk*, and I winced a little at the spikes digging into the table's surface. Then I remembered that I paid five dollars for that table at a yard sale last year when I was refurnishing my place after some DEMON assholes trashed the joint.

"Okay, Skeeter," I said. "We're all here. Why don't you try to raise Amy on the laptop and we can find out what kind of snipe hunt she's sending us on."

Snipe aren't real. Almost everything I've ever been told will eat you in the woods or under your bed really exists, but snipe are still nothing more than a good way to leave a buddy stuck out in the woods all night holding a burlap sack. And for the last couple weeks, you'd think that all cryptids were snipe, for as many as I'd been able to find. DEMON did a good job of exterminating, imprisoning, or forcibly relocating every supernatural critter they could find anywhere in the U.S., and the ones that survived The Chancellor's purges were either laying *very* low or had moved to someplace way more remote than even my North Georgia mountain house.

"Man, I just got comfortable," Skeeter grumbled.

"No problem," I said. "Hand me your laptop and I'll get everything set up."

That spurred my little buddy into action. "Oh hell no," he said, springing off the couch and grabbing the backpack he had slid under the coffee table. "The last time I let you touch my laptop, the trackpad controls were flipped upside down and backwards, and you changed my keyboard layout to Dvorak. I didn't know you even knew what Dvorak is."

"I don't," I said. "I was looking for porn and pushed some buttons, and the next thing I knew, nothing worked right, so I stuck it back in your bag and used my phone."

Skeeter looked at me like I was drunk or stupid. "You remember I'm gay, right? Like *really* gay."

"Yeah, so what?" I asked.

"Did you really think you were going to find porn on my laptop that you were interested in? Or have you moved a little more toward the center of the Kinsey scale?"

"Skeeter, the only scale I know a damn thing about is the one on my bathroom floor, and I ain't exactly on the best of terms with that lying piece of shit. No, I wasn't looking for porn *on* your computer. I was just going online to look for porn and using your computer to do it."

"Oh," he said. "That makes more sense. But my work laptop is blocked off all porn and gambling websites. Too much sketchy shit on those places. I save all that for the personal laptop. I don't mind completely wiping it every few months."

"As utterly fascinating as this little peek into the workings of the male brain is, can we please call Amy before I learn far more than I ever wanted to know about y'all's porn habits?" Geri said, then shoved a forkful of salad into her mouth. "God, this is terrible. I'm going to get a brat." She stood up and carried her plate back into the kitchen, where I heard a clattering of plates commence.

"Even I lasted longer as a vegetarian than that," I said.

"I remember when you went vegetarian, Bubba," Skeeter said. "You only gave up all that shit for a whole weekend because you got arrested on a Friday night and couldn't get in front of a judge to pay your bail until Monday morning."

"Yeah, you coulda helped a brother out," I said. "Instead of hacking the police computers and getting me sprung, you left me in there to rot."

"Rot? Bubba, the bunks in the county jail are in better shape than your mattress. And you got three hot meals every day that you didn't have to make. Only real gripe you had was that the meat was all mystery and not a lot of meat. That's why you were a vegetarian for two days. Not because you had all this newfound willpower. No, you just didn't know what the hell that hockey puck doused in brown gravy was, so you wouldn't eat it."

"Seems like a reasonable decision to me," Geri said, walking back in and plopping down on the couch, this time with a pair of brats cuddled right up next to her fries. "You got the link up yet?"

"He does now." Amy's voice came from the wall over the fireplace, and my head snapped up.

"Skeeter, you doing that?" I asked.

"Yeah, I'm throwing the feed to the TV so we can see better."

"Alright. As long as there ain't nobody haunting my TV or my internet." Which is not nearly as far-fetched a possibility in my life as it is in most people's.

Amy looked out at us from the sixty-inch screen, and while they say that most people don't look good when they're blown up to humungous, she was the exception that proved the rule. Her blond hair was pulled back in a ponytail that was only doing a medium decent job at restraining her curls, and she looked tired, but was still the most beautiful thing I'd seen in a long time.

"Hey babe," I said.

"Deputy Director Babe," my fiancée and boss corrected me.

"Hey, Deputy Director Babe," I repeated. "You got me hired back?" All my former employers had fired me at some point in the past two years. The Catholic Church kicked me to the Catholic curb when I vanished off to Fairyland for the better part of a year and a half. DEMON showed me the door when they (and I) found out that I'm part faerie, then we got together with Quincy Harker and kinda blew up all their shit and killed all their bosses, so that bridge was well and truly burned. To add insult to injury, the bar where I worked as a bouncer fired my ass just because I set the place on fire a little. And because I had a big fight with a bunch of zombies in the bar, which is what led to me setting the place on fire. Now Amy was a Deputy Director for the Department of Homeland Security's Paranormal Division, but I was still an unemployed redneck who owned a barely self-sustaining CrossFit gym and spent most of his time sitting on his back deck drinking beer and flicking the bottle caps off the side of a mountain.

Amy looked a little chagrined when she said, "Not so much on the hired back thing, Bubba. Apparently, Homeland is still a little iffy on hiring people who aren't completely human."

I opened my mouth to protest, but Geri slapped my shoulder, and I shut up. I was about to make some smartassed remark about her boss, Keya Pravesh, the Director of the Paranormal Division, being a naga and thus a lot further from human than me, but at the last second I remembered that we were probably on a monitored line and that Pravesh might not be out to her bosses as a cryptid, and her fiancé getting her boss fired was not a good look for Amy. Geri managed to convey all of that with a single slap.

I wondered briefly if that was something all women know how to do as soon as they turn twenty-one, or if Amy had been giving Geri lessons. I did not need the women in my life conspiring against me. They were both already smarter than me; if they got organized, I was doomed.

"Okay," I said after a brief pause. "What's the plan?"

"I can still use you as a subcontractor, and I can get Skeeter a position as my offsite tech support, so you won't starve."

"Good thing," I muttered, looking down at my beer gut, which had been fed with a lot more ice water lately. Money'd been tight, and I was starting to be afraid I'd lose weight if this employment dry spell kept going.

"Not much chance of that," Geri said, giving me a grin. I flipped her off, and Amy cleared her throat to draw our attention back to her.

"We need your help," she said, and I could tell by the set of her shoulders that this was "Official Amy." I straightened up in my seat and vowed to focus for at least the next thirty seconds. Sixty if what she had for us was cool or if it looked like I'd get to blow something up. "As you know, cryptid activity has been at a record low since DEMON's recent activity."

"Yeah, well, there's nothing like attempted genocide to keep people indoors," Skeeter said, his voice bitter. He nailed it, too. DEMON's big boss, some asshat called the Chancellor who was on a revenge trip against Quincy Harker, had done his level best to murder every paranormal or supernatural creature he could find, in some of the most horrific ways possible, all the while using skills learned at the hands of Josef Mengele to experiment on cryptids and try to merge their DNA with humans to create super-soldiers that he could sell to the highest bidder, thus funding his new Nazi Party. They killed hundreds, if not thousands, of cryptids and no small number of humans, including Joe.

"But low does not mean non-existent, and some previously peaceable cryptids have been making themselves, and their displeasure at the treatment they've received at the hands of humans, very well known," Amy continued. "Several have attacked individual humans, and a couple have even gone after businesses."

"There's a rogue monster out in the woods somewhere, and you need somebody to deal with it?" I asked. "I'm in." This was way more my speed than breaking up international conspiracies with grudges going back the better part of a century. I'm way better at hunting things through the woods and destroying them than navigating political intrigue.

"First we need somebody, meaning you, to find it, confirm that it's behind the recent spate of attacks on a couple of local businesses, and then either convince the cryptid to leave the humans alone, get it to move somewhere that it won't be a danger to anyone, or bring it into custody."

"Or shoot it," Geri said, a bloodthirsty little smile on her face. Every once in a while, I forget that she used to be an assassin for DEMON before we proved to her that they were the bad guys, and while I'm no saint, I'm a lot less evil than they were. Then she gives me the crazy eye and gets all excited about the opportunity to kill something, and I remember why I sleep with my door locked nowadays.

"If all else fails," Amy said, "then yes, after you have exhausted all other possible resolutions, if the creature remains a threat, you must neutralize it however you see fit."

"Got it," I said. "Talk first, shoot second."

"Or third," Skeeter added.

"Maybe even fourth," I said with a nod. "But where are we headed when we go out not shooting something?"

"Pack your hip waders, boys. You're going to the South Carolina low country," Amy said.

I felt a thrill run through me all the way down to my tippy toes. If she was saying what I thought she was saying, Amy was telling me we were about to go hunt a monster I'd been wanting to chase ever since I first learned that cryptids existed. "Seriously?" I asked. "*Seriously*, seriously?"

"Seriously," Amy said. "There have been a few attacks on fishing boats, and a bait shop was set on fire just last night. Security footage from the scene showed a larger-than-human bipedal creature fleeing into the night just before everything exploded. The last thing on the tape was the monster diving into the water."

"Oh, hot damn!" I clapped my hands together.

"What are you so excited about?" Geri asked.

"He's always wanted to go after this one," Skeeter said. "But nobody ever gave us a reason, and there were too many other things to hunt down that were threatening people. So we left this one alone. Until now, apparently."

"Until now," Amy confirmed. "I've emailed you all the photos and satellite images we have, along with the bait shop footage. Get loaded up and ready to head out first thing in the morning. You're going after the Lizard Man of South Carolina."

3

———————

There's a damn Air Force base right outside of Bishopville, ain't there?" I asked the air as I got back in the truck at a Flying J on I-20 outside Augusta. I needed gas, and I needed to pee, and I wanted a Pepsi and my redneck retirement plan called for the acquisition of more scratch-off lottery tickets, so I settled into the driver's seat to wait for Geri to get back in the truck. There was a line at the ladies' room, surprising no one ever.

Skeeter's voice came through the sound system in the truck, patched in through Bluetooth or wi-fi or LMNOP or some such shit. "Yes, there's Shaw Air Force Base, just outside Sumter. There's also the Sandhills National Wildlife Refuge, Congaree State Park, Manchester State Forest, and Lake Marion, so there's plenty of wilderness to hide a lizard man, even if the Air Force does have a buttload of airplanes and equipment all taking off and landing at all hours of the day and night."

"You think the Lizard Man is real? I always heard it was bullshit," I asked.

"I don't know, Bubba, but I think with the shit we've seen in the last ten years, I'm not gonna be too quick to dismiss anything anymore."

He had a point. Werewolves and vampires and cryptids were bad enough, but when I started dealing with faeries and demons and angels, my life got infinitely more complicated. Now I just wanted to get myself a nice little government job, with nice government benefits, and a nice government pension, and just be a boring government employee for a while. Ah, who am I kidding? There's stuff that needs to be blown up, and I'm a redneck who's very good at blowing shit up. As the man in the movie said, I have a particular set of skills.

Geri opened the door and swung herself in with a thump and a rattle of plastic. She unloaded a pack of Zingers, a bag of barbecue pork rinds, a Dr. Pepper, a Red Bull, and a bag of the big orange circus peanuts. Then she looked over at me, grinned, and said, "Road trip fuel acquired. Let's get it."

"You are not eating that shit in my truck," I said, pointing to the window. "Get the pig skins the hell out of here. The rest is fine, but that shit's gotta go."

"Oh come on, you love pork rinds!"

"I do, but I don't love my truck smelling like pork rinds for the next month. And I know damn well you're gonna drop a couple and then when we stop, it's gonna get hot in here, and the smell of pig skins and artificial barbecue seasoning will be baked into my upholstery forever. Get 'em out of here."

She opened the door and leaned out, pitching the bag of pork rinds into the bed of the truck. "Fine. I'll eat 'em later. If they don't blow out on the highway. But they wouldn't stink any worse than your farts."

"Yeah, but my truck, my farts. That's the law of trucks. It's okay for me to make it stink with my own natural funk. But artificial stink? And somebody else's artificial stink? Not happening."

She sulked but put on her seatbelt. "Fine, but I get to control the radio for the rest of the way."

I gestured to the dash, and Geri beamed as she pulled out her phone and plugged it in. As her fingers flew over the screen, I wondered what kind of hellish bargain I'd just made for myself. It turns out that hellish bargain involved something called K-Pop and a band called BTS. Not bad, if not enough banjos for my taste.

———

"What do you know about the Lizard Man of South Carolina?" I asked around a mouthful of tater wedges.

Geri looked at me from the passenger seat. "You're giving me a pop quiz while I eat gas station fried chicken in your truck? Seriously?"

"One, is this not some of the best fried chicken you've ever eaten? I don't know if it's the mix of diesel fuel and cooking grease, if they literally just boil engine oil and dip the taters in them, or if there's actually spices involved in this shit, but I love it. I will drive twenty miles out of my way to get good gas station chicken."

"I know," Geri said. "I had to listen to your GPS telling you that you were going off in the wrong direction for the first ten miles of this little culinary detour. I never even knew a GPS could get offended at being ignored and shut itself off."

"Skeeter reprogrammed my truck to screw with me. But you're ducking the question. What do you know about the Lizard Man?" I stuck a wing in my mouth, held on to one end with two fingers, and sucked all the meat and sauce off the bone, withdrawing a perfectly denuded chicken bone, with nary a drop of sauce in my beard. Eating wings with facial hair is an artform, one that cannot be effectively practiced in a moving vehicle. Not without getting ghost pepper sauce in your eye, and I promise you that was among my least enjoyable experiences, even surpassing grabbing a Sasquatch by the wiener.

"I'm assuming it's a man that looks like a lizard. Or a man that's part lizard. Or a dude with really bad eczema, which feels bad, like we shouldn't hunt somebody who's already dealing with a painful skin condition."

"So you know nothing about the Lizard Man," I said.

Geri dipped another tater into the ocean of ketchup she had testing the structural integrity of the little cardboard container the taters came in and shook her head. "Not a damn thing."

"Fair enough. I've got a couple podcasts we can listen to the rest of the way there. That oughta get you up to speed."

"Podcasts?" Geri asked. "When did you learn what a podcast is?"

"Hey! I'm tech savvy," I protested.

"You still own a flip phone."

"I like my flip phone."

"You look like a drug dealer on that thing."

"I look like a biker no matter what phone I use. Might as well look like a biker drug dealer." I finished off the last of my wings and held out my hand for her trash. She stuck all her crap into the plastic "Thank You" bag and passed it to me.

When I got back in the truck, Geri had a podcast app called up on the dash computer and looked over to me expectantly. "I found three. Which one?"

"*Arcane Carolinas* did a good episode on it. Let's start there." I backed the truck out of the parking place and pointed the nose of the truck south onto 385 out of Spartanburg.

Bishopville, South Carolina, looks like any small Southern town. Big water tower with the name of the town painted on it, one high school, seven Baptist churches, five Presbyterians, two ARP, four Methodists, and one converted store front with a painted picture window of a white Jesus with blue eyes beckoning everyone to come to the Bishopville United Church of Christ's Everlasting Redemption and Celebration. I half-expected to see the words "and bait shop" tacked onto the end of the long-ass church name. I'm not much of a church guy, myself.

I believe in God, or something that made the world in the first place, but I'm not much for sitting in a pew with a bunch of people wearing uncomfortable clothes while I'm still hung over on a Sunday morning. Most of my adult life, I've kinda felt like I had a more direct line to the Big Guy (or Big Girl or Big They, I don't have any idea if God even has a gender. God's junk is not something I spend a lot of time thinking about. Until literally right this second.). But now that my chief intercessor on the religious front went and got himself killed, I was probably going to have to talk to God all on my own. Pretty sure they didn't want to hear anything I had to say lately. I haven't been in a real respectful mood, to say the least.

One thing that caught my eye was the number of different Lizard Man t-shirts in the windows of stores. The hair salon on Main Street had a couple, the drugstore next door had one, even the storefront church had a sign for their discounted Lizard Man Jesus t-shirt. I slowed down to see if I could catch a glimpse of that design, but the picture was too small to see from the truck, and I didn't care enough to get out and look closer.

"Pull over," Geri said.

"I don't want to know what it looks like that bad," I replied.

"What? I don't care about the t-shirts, but if we're going to find out anything about this so-called monster, it's either gonna be from that bar or those old-timers playing chess." She pointed to a small concrete-block building with beer signs in the window, then to a pair of old men in overalls sitting on the porch of a general store with a chessboard set up on top of an old pickle barrel. They had the whole stereotype working, too, with a pair of giant wooden wire spools turned on their sides for chairs.

"You go talk to the old farts. I'll be in the bar," I said, pulling over to the curb and opening my door.

"Not a chance," Geri said. "I'm taking the bar. You go sing the song of your people to the old white dudes. They aren't gonna be receptive to my charms. Or probably anything about me."

I looked her up and down and decided she was probably right. Geri was an attractive young woman, but she definitely didn't look like she belonged on the Main Street of a tiny Southern town. The neon pink streaks in her hair, the clunky boots, and the tattered red t-shirt with "Where's the Beef" in big white letters made for a decidedly funkier image than most of these folks were used to. I was in jeans, work boots, and a Johnny Cash t-shirt, with a red and black flannel open over it. I blended in better, to say the least.

I was a little nervous about sending Geri in the bar alone, even though at two in the afternoon, I didn't expect there to be enough people to cause any trouble. I got more nervous when she hopped out, opened the back seat, and whipped her shirt off over her head.

"What are you doing?" I asked, turning my head.

"I'm getting into my interrogation uniform. You can turn around now." I did and saw that she'd switched from a ratty vintage tee to a newer t-shirt, this one a tight v-neck that dipped way down into her cleavage. She laughed at the look on my face. "I don't solve every problem with bullets, Bubba. I just haven't needed to be subtle since I've hooked up with your crew. This top is guaranteed to have any redneck eating out of my hand in under a minute."

"Alright but take your backup." There was no way she could hide her regular sidearm, a Glock 17 that she usually kept at the small of her back. I knew she usually kept a little .380 strapped to one ankle, and I hoped she wouldn't need it.

"Got it. Now get over there and get your redneck on while I go unleash the girls on an unsuspecting populace." She grabbed her boobs and did some kind of wiggle or shimmy to get them into the right place, I reckon. I just shook my head and went to talk to the old man, not wanting to see my dead girlfriend's baby sister shimmy, especially since she was something like half my age.

I walked over to the porch and leaned against the railing by the old timers. "How's it going, fellas?" I asked.

"A little better since you brought your daughter to work today, young man," one of the men said. He was a skinny old guy, eighty years old if he was a day, but he had a mischievous grin that told me he wasn't really perving on Geri, mostly just pushing my buttons.

"Not my daughter, Gramps," I replied. "Co-worker, I guess is the best way to describe it."

"You're not hitting that?" the other guy asked. He was younger than the other guy by about thirty years, but still too old for me to backhand for a smart mouth. I wanted to, though. Something about this guy rubbed me wrong. He was a lot bigger than the first guy, balding with a halo of graying hair hanging on for dear life to the skin above his ears. He had a trim goatee and was well dressed for the middle of nowhere in a dress shirt and khakis, all with buttons straining to contain all of him.

He reminded me of the guys I saw at the one and only high school reunion I attended—a fat hillbilly who peaked in high school and spent the rest of his life trying to recapture the glory of his late teens. This dude fit the "former quarterback turned car salesman" stereotype to a "T."

"No, I am not 'hitting that,'" I said. I pitched my voice low, more a growl than anything, and by the look on his face, he got the point. He leaned back and held up both hands gesturing "no offense." I kept my gaze on him for a long moment, then turned and made it a point to address the older man.

"I hear there's a monster in the swamps around here," I said, pointing above his head to the white t-shirt emblazoned with a cartoon image of an alligator walking on two feet and the words "Lizard Man Containment Team" in a circle around the drawing of the "monster."

"Yep," the old guy replied. "Lizard Man running around in the nature preserve and the woods out there. Why? You looking to bag a lizard?"

I pulled out my wallet and flashed my Department of Homeland Security credentials. "Kinda. I work for a division of the government that deals with cryptid and paranormal threats. We've received reports that the Lizard Man is damaging property and threatening the locals."

Baldy snorted. "Man, that's such bullshit. Geraldine ain't no more seen a Lizard Man than I have. We don't need no government idiots down here tramping around messing everything up. You just make sure you stay off any of my properties, or you'll be hearing from my lawyer." He glared at me like I was supposed to be impressed.

"Okay, whatever. People sue the federal government all the time. Only people that get rich in that game are the lawyers," I said, then turned away. Nothing useful was going to come out of that guy. I heard him splutter a little, then stomp away. A few seconds later, a black Mercedes pulled out from beside the building, slinging gravel everywhere.

"Sorry," I said. "Looks like I ruined your chess game."

"Don't apologize. I only play with Petey cause nobody else in this dumbass town knows how to play."

I raised an eyebrow. "I'm not real good, but I know how to play a little."

"You can't be any worse than Petey. You'd think somebody with all his education and money would be able to think more than one move ahead, but he ain't never learned that skill. Now sit down and let me tell you about the Lizard Man of Scape Ore Swamp."

4

"I reckon it was about 1972 when I first saw the Lizard Man," the old man, Merle, started, then held up a hand when I opened my mouth. "Yeah, I know ain't nobody said nothing about there being a Lizard Man that far back. That's because when we saw shit like that back in the day, we didn't tell nobody about it. They'd either have said I was on drugs or that the war had done made me crazy. I wasn't, by the way."

"Wasn't on drugs or wasn't crazy?" I asked.

"Crazy. And I wasn't on many drugs. Sure as hell wasn't on nothing good enough to make me imagine a damn eight foot tall alligator man chasing me through the damn swamp in the middle of the night."

"Why were you out in the swamp in the middle of the night?" I asked.

The old man got a thoughtful look on his face, like he went somewhere else for a minute, and when he came back, it didn't seem like it'd been a pleasant trip down memory lane. "I told you it was '72, right?"

I nodded.

"Well, I got back from Vietnam in '71, and it wasn't the same place I'd left. Or maybe I wasn't the same person who left. I ain't rightly sure which. I managed alright. Better than a lot of fellas that came home. But we all left a piece of ourselves over there in the mud and the blood and the fear that coated everything like cheap paint. So when we got home, there was a hole. Some guys filled it with booze, some with pills, some with women. Hell, some fellas tried all three. Me, I just looked for some quiet. Someplace I could be alone without anybody asking me what I'd seen and done over there. Without anybody telling me I was a hero, or a monster. Whenever the noise in my head got too loud, I just went out into the woods and let the birds and the fish and the water and the peace of being out in the middle of nothing with nobody around soothe me.

"That's what I was doing that day. I was just out in the woods being alone, trying to get back to where I could enjoy walking through the woods without thinking every branch I stepped on was going to get my head blown off. I'd been sitting at the base of an old cypress looking out over Lake Marion, down past the Air Force base, when I heard something walking through the woods. I hollered out, not wanting some dumbass deer hunter to mistake me for a buck and put a bullet through my head. That would be ironic, wouldn't it? Spend two years not getting shot in Vietnam, only to get my fool head blown off twenty miles from home."

"Yeah, that's not the kind of welcome home you'd be wanting," I said.

"No sir, it is not. I yelled to make sure whoever was stomping around out there knew I wasn't what they were hunting, then I realized it was getting dark. My car was off the side of a narrow dirt road about half a mile from where I'd been sitting, so I started walking back, hoping to get out of there before it was too dark to find my car. Then I heard a branch break about ten yards off to my left, and when I turned, what I saw over there was about enough to make me piss my pants."

I leaned forward. "What was it?"

The old man grinned. "Well, that question don't get answered for free, son. Why don't you go on in the store here and get a six-pack of beer from Taylor, then we can be properly lubricated to tell the whole story."

I knew when I'd been swindled, but since I'm not ever one to turn down a friend in need, I went into the store and bought a sixer of Bud Light. I set the beers down between us, popped the top on one, and leaned back as the old man did the same.

"Much obliged," he said after a long swig. He looked around, a nervous expression crossing his lined face. His voice dropped almost to a whisper, and I had to lean forward over the chess board to hear him. "Look, it ain't like I never talked about this, but didn't nobody believe me back in the day, and then after other people started talking about seeing it, folks acted like I was jumping on a bandwagon, trying to get attention for myself. Shit, the last thing I want is attention. All I want is to sit here on this porch playing chess with Petey and anybody else that knows the difference between a rook and a bishop. Ain't too many around here that can play worth a shit, but a bad game is better than no game, like I always say.

"But you don't care about my chess game. You come here all Mr. I'm From the Government, I'm Here to Help, then start asking about the Lizard Man like you know it's real, and I gotta figure you've seen a thing or two."

"Yeah," I said with a nod and a long pull off my beer. "I know there's things out there that we were taught to believe weren't real, and I know some of 'em ain't friendly. You telling me this thing attacked you back in the seventies?"

Merle shook his head. "I don't think it was so much an attack as it was just trying to scare me off. I don't know if I got close to a nest full of tadpoles or what, but when I looked over and saw that big damn lizard standing in the woods, I didn't take the time to ask its intentions. I just ran like hell back to my car, hauled ass home, and spent the next two weeks laid up drunk as Cooter Brown in my cousin Rex's trailer."

"What did it look like?" I asked.

"It was big. Damn big. 'Bout eight feet tall, I reckon. Shaped like a person, only bigger. You know, two arms, two legs, head on top of its neck, standing upright. It was kinda like running into Andre the Giant out in the middle of the woods, if Andre was green and scaly."

"You could see that it was green? I thought it was dark."

"It was *getting* dark," he corrected. "It was dusk, but it weren't dark yet. And I wasn't but about twenty, twenty-one, and I didn't need these damn bifocals, so I could see it as plain as I can see the tattoos running all up and down your arms. You serve, or you just like all them kids nowadays, getting tattoos anywhere they want?"

"I never served, no sir." Not in the military, anyway. You could certainly make a case that I've done plenty in service of my country and the greater good, and there's no doubt that I've seen some wars in my line of work. But Merle didn't need to hear about me. I needed to hear more about him and this Lizard Man. "Now when you started running, did it follow you?"

"I don't rightly know, I if I'm being honest. You know who Satchel Paige was?"

"Black baseball player, right? Played in the Negro League, then for Cleveland, right?"

"Yep. Now when I got to Vietnam, I wasn't nothing but a wet-behind-the-ears private with no more idea how to stay alive than I had how to build a rocket ship. My first patrol, I'm out in the boonies, walking in the middle of the pack, my head on a swivel. One time, I turned around and there was this Black corporal grinning at me. I asked him what he thought was so funny, and he said, 'You, white boy. Ain't you ever heard that old saying? Don't look back, something might be gaining on you?'

"He meant that I was spending too much time looking around, and I wasn't *seeing* anything. Charlie could have walked right up to the edge of the road and I wouldn't have known it because I was looking everywhere but where I was going." The old man wiped at the corner of his eye. "That corporal's name was Rufus Feemster, but we all called him Roof. He was probably the only thing that kept me alive over there."

"Did he make it home?" I asked.

"Oh yeah, Roof was too damn ugly to die," Merle said with a laugh. "He died about ten years back. Prostate cancer."

"Sorry."

"Yeah, me too. Ain't neither one of us sorry as Roof, though!" He threw his head back and cackled, then grabbed a fresh Bud Light and we clinked cans. "To Roof."

"To Roof," I repeated. "So when you saw the Lizard Man, you ran away, got into your car, and drove home. Did you go back and look for it?"

"Yeah, I did. I went back out there the next morning, once I had a chance to get my forty-five. I didn't find nothing except some footprints, but that was enough to tell me what I saw was real. Them tracks were big as a damn bear's, with three toes and what looked like claws on the ends of each toe. When I heard that boy's story later about it tearing up his car, I sure as hell believed it. The thing I saw was big enough to mess up a car, and if its hands are anything like its feet, it had some hellacious claws."

"If I got out a map, could you show me where you saw the creature?" I asked.

"I reckon I could get close. That dirt road got paved and turned into a real road about eighty, eighty-one, so it oughta be on your map. I ain't gonna be able to give you coordinates or anything like that, but I can get you close."

"Close is good enough," I said. "I gotta think the critter might have moved around a little in the last forty-some years."

"Yeah, especially with all the lookie-loos been here ever since word about Lizzie got out."

"Lizzie?"

"What else you gonna call a Lizard Man but Lizzie?" he asked, then laughed. I laughed with him. I liked the old coot enough him swindling me out of a six-pack didn't even bother me. I figured I got out cheaper than Geri, since a mixer of Bud Light was going to cost Uncle Sam less than a single beer in a bar, even a run-down ramshackle juke joint in the middle of the afternoon.

I got the map and Merle circled a couple of places to the south of town. First, where he'd seen Lizzie in the seventies, then a couple of the more recent spots where the cryptid had been spotted. I folded up the paper, not going by the original factory folds at all, just making the damn thing fit back into my pocket any way I could. I stood up and shook the old man's hand.

"Well, Merle, I reckon I need to go gather up my partner and see if we can get out there and meet Lizzie ourselves. Thanks for the info."

"Thanks for the beer," he said, raising his can in my direction. I gave him a little salute and headed back to the truck. I didn't even have to go into the bar to fetch Geri, as she was coming out as I started in that direction. She waved me back toward the truck, her hand making that flappy-flappy kind of movement that told me she hadn't been sipping Bud Light with the geriatric set. She was walking with a very distinct tequila lean to her stride.

Yay. Taking a drunk twenty-something out into the swamp. That doesn't make me sound like a serial killer *at all*.

5

I slid behind the wheel of my truck, then grinned while I watched Geri, usually pretty nimble, navigated the confusing combination of running board, oh shit straps, and truck seat. It took a couple tries, and a piece of contortionism that looked like it fit better in Cirque du Soleil than South Carolina. After almost half a minute of fighting with my truck, she got into the passenger seat and let her spinning noggin drop against the headrest.

"I hate day drinking," she said. "Seems like everything hits harder and faster in the bright sunshine."

"It's cloudy," I said, pointing up through the windshield.

"Kiss my ass, Bubba. Shooting you is not totally off the table."

I grinned. Geri had hunted me down, ostensibly because I'm half-faerie and DEMON wanted to study me, but mostly because I'd gotten her sister murdered. I managed to convince her that I had killed the people who murdered her sister and that she didn't need to murder me to finish out the cycle, and we'd settled into an uneasy truce. I kept her around because if she was in the passenger seat threatening me, she wasn't in a clock tower somewhere with a scope trained on my head. Besides, Amy liked her, and I knew better than to argue with the person I was sleeping with.

"Did you find anything in there other than a worm in the bottom of a bottle?" I asked.

"I didn't eat the worm," she replied. "Just for the record."

"You oughta give it a try. It'll give you visions."

"If I'm gonna eat a worm that's been soaking in cheap liquor, I'd better already be so messed up that I'm seeing things. But yes, I did get information to go with my shots. And it wasn't cheap tequila, thank you very much. I mean, Patron Silver ain't the tippy top shelf, but it's three in the afternoon on a Tuesday in Bumbledick, South Carolina. What the hell do you expect?"

"Okay, so in addition to your good tequila, what did you find out?"

"I'm assuming the guy you were talking to was named Merle, and he had a story about seeing Lizzie way back in the seventies, long before the monster made the national news?" she asked, leaning the seat back and closing her eyes. "Gimme a second. The truck's a little spinny."

"How many shots did you have? You weren't in there all that long."

"I don't know. Five or six. And I was there for about an hour. That's plenty long enough to shimmy a little for the bartender, flirt a bit with the guys playing pool, and then belly up next to the requisite scruffy middle-aged man getting weepy at the end of the bar and pump him for information. Sad guys are the best—they need somebody to talk to, and they usually don't care what they talk about. Ellis couldn't wait to tell me all about his dead wife Barb. He told me about Lizzie. That's the Lizard Man, not his dead wife."

"Yeah, she's Barb. You said that."

"Right. Sorry. Little drunk. Anyway, Ellis said he spent about a month going out into the swamp every night after his wife died, just hoping Lizzie would come along and eat him."

"Obviously that didn't happen," I said, "since he was telling you this."

"Right. But he did hear some weird shit, and I got him to mark where he heard things on a map."

"What map?" I asked. Geri hadn't carried anything into the bar except her phone, and I had taken the only map over to Merle.

She gave me a look that I could only describe as "Skeeter-esque," in that she looked like she was talking to the single stupidest human being on the planet. "I gave him my phone, called up a map of the region, and dropped pins on the map in Google Maps."

"You can do that?" I asked.

"Yes, you can do that. And while Ellis was showing me the places where he heard weird stuff in the swamp, Stan, a scrawny little pool player with a Joe Dirt-level mullet, came over and pointed out a couple spots where he claimed to have seen something weird in the woods while he was not in any way poaching alligators. He was very clear on that point: he was not poaching alligators in the swamp. Because that would be illegal, and he didn't want to admit to anything illegal to the revenuers, as he called us."

I chuckled a little. Homeland Security didn't give a single shit about poaching, and I didn't care enough to alert the state Fish and Wildlife agents, but it was good to know that Mullet Stan was not illegally killing gators. "Good stuff, kiddo. Now we just need to get you sobered up before we head out into the swamp."

"One question, though," Geri asked.

"Shoot."

"What the hell is a revenuer?"

Three hours later we were sloshing our way through a swamp trying to move quickly to get away from the mixed stench of brackish water and tequila puke. "Damn, girl," I said as I tried not to let water slosh over the tops of my boots. "What did you eat?"

"Pork rinds, Zingers, a couple Krispy Kreme doughnuts, and some pretzels at the bar," Geri said, rinsing out her mouth with a water bottle from the truck. She spit into the grass. "But I don't think it's what I ate that's causing problems. Pretty sure it's what I drank."

"I don't know," I replied. "Just listening to that list made me want to vomit, and all I drank was two beers. But I remember what twenty-one was like—all bad decisions and cheap booze."

"I'm twenty-five, Bubba."

"Whatever. Time's gone all wibbly-wobbly since I got back from Fairyland."

"No, you're just getting old and can't remember shit."

"Some of that, too."

"Are we there yet?"

I looked over at her and scowled, but the smirk on her face made me chuckle. Geri was a giant smartass, but she was good in a fight and dependable, so as long as we kept her more homicidal tendencies in check, she could be a good part of the team. Didn't mean I wasn't still locking my bedroom door every night. I might be trusting, but I ain't stupid.

"Not much farther now," I replied.

"You have no idea where we are, do you?"

"Not a one," I said. "But we parked near where Merle had his sighting, and it's starting to get dark, so if we can make enough noise, and manage not to pollute the local flora with gas station snacks and regurgitated booze, something might decide to come check us out."

"Is this how you usually hunt? Just wander around in the woods and hope something tries to eat you?"

"Pretty much." That wasn't me talking. That was Skeeter chiming in, coming across our sat phones to the little transceivers Amy procured for us.

I told her giving me a satellite phone was going to be hard on the budget, given my track record of destroying technology. It wasn't my fault. Not usually. Usually, my stuff gets wrecked because something bigger and badder than me throws me through a wall. It's kinda like an occupational hazard. I shoulda asked Harker how he keeps from breaking phones all the time. Course, that dude probably just wiggles his fingers and talks into a mirror or some such bullshit.

"If we wait on Bubba to find this lizard critter, y'all gonna be wandering around that swamp so long mushrooms'll grow on your butts," Skeeter said. "But lucky for both of you, the Incredible Skeeter is back on the job!"

"Well, does the Incredible Skeeter have any idea where we need to be looking for this Lizard Man, or is he just going to let me splash around out here with all the water moccasins and alligators?" Geri asked.

"I've input all the more reputable sightings going all the way back to Merle's encounter in the seventies, and used that to come up with a likely search area for y'all. You're in the right general area, if the creature hunts near where it lives. If there's anything out there, it oughta be close to where y'all are now."

"I think the part of that I'm getting hung up on, Skeeter, is the concept that some of the sightings are more reputable than others," I said. "What exactly makes a Lizard Man sighting more or less likely to pass the Incredible Skeeter Sniff Test?"

"Quantity of methamphetamine in the sight-er's criminal history, for one. There's a fair number of people who have been stopped in the woods all over South Carolina who used the Lizard Man as a reason why they were out in the middle of nowhere. Usually there was a still or a meth lab found in the general vicinity of the 'crypto hunter.'"

"You gotta love it when they can't even spell 'cryptid,'" I said. "Sounds like a bunch of tech bros out in the swamp chasing NFTs with snipe sacks."

"Bubba, do you even know what an NFT is?" Skeeter asked.

"Dude, I don't think anybody knows what an NFT is," I said. "Last thing I saw on Reddit, somebody made a Photoshop picture of Elmo's taint and sold it for like eight hundred grand. I reckon an NFT is anything you can get some dumb bastard to give you money for, then you can run off to Kinko's and make a shitload of copies and sell it to other dumb bastards."

"That's… not how that's supposed to go," Geri said.

"As thrilling as it is to hear Bubba try to describe technology from this century, if y'all don't get a move on, when you find the Lizard Man, you're gonna have to ask him if he's got a spare bedroom," Skeeter said. "Now you're in the right general area, but it's a couple dozen square miles of swamp to search, and I can't get any decent satellite pictures on account it being a damn swamp and I can't see through the trees. Y'all're on your own. If I see your GPS wandering too far out of the search zone, I can guide you back, but I'm flying blind up here."

"Got it, Skeet," I said. "You point us in the right direction, and we'll go from there."

"Will do. Amy's got a chopper fueled and ready to go out of Atlanta if you get into any trouble you can't handle."

"She won't need it," I said. "We're gonna splash around out here for a couple more hours, then head back to the motel. I haven't seen anything even remotely monstrous out here."

"You aren't walking behind you, dude. Time to invest in some suspenders. Crack kills," Geri said.

"On that note, I'm gonna go get something to eat. Y'all try not to get dead in the next hour, okay?" Skeeter clicked off, and Geri and I continued to trudge through the brackish water looking for a giant humanoid lizard. As one does.

6

———————

We're lost as shit, aren't we?" Geri asked, perching on a cypress root that stuck out of the water. Glad some part of her was narrow enough to sit on that thing. Wasn't happening for me, not in this lifetime.

"Oh yeah," I said.

"Time to call Skeeter?"

"Would be. If there was any signal." I held up the satellite phone, which displayed "NO SERVICE" in big letters.

"I thought the whole point of a sat phone was that you could get signal anywhere?"

"It's close to prime time," I replied. "Maybe Homeland Security rents time on an ESPN satellite or something. The playoffs are this weekend, you know."

"Playoffs for what?"

"I don't know. I watch college football. If it ain't January, it ain't the real playoffs. Do they still do the NCAA tournament in March?"

"It's April, Bubba."

"Then is that a yes?"

Geri just sighed and leaned back against the trunk of the tree. I tried to warn her about the slippery moss, but just shut up and let her do her thing. She was a little irritated with me about the whole getting lost deep in a swamp thing, and if I told her to be careful and not to slide off into the water, it'd just piss her off, and then she'd be more likely to slip off the side of the trunk and go splash, which would make her even grumpier. I don't understand much about women, that much is blatantly obvious to anyone who's ever met me, but one thing I do understand is that if I can see a train rushing right at my face, I should probably get the hell out of the way instead of running right at it. Because I'm way more mature, not because I thought it would be funny as hell seeing Geri soaked through with swamp water.

She didn't fall in, and after we took a five-minute breather, she stood up and asked, "What's the plan?"

"Well, I thought we'd head west and comb the swamp in a grid search pattern until we found trace, but since I was gonna use the compass on my phone, now I don't know which way is west."

"You know the sun sets in the west, right?"

I pointed up. "Yeah, except that happened a while back, and I couldn't see what direction it was in on account of the thick-ass canopy up there." There were slivers of sky visible through the thick mat of branches over-head, gray but moving toward deep purple on its way to full black. Every-thing around us was water, trees, and big clumps of floating vegetation, and it all looked the same to me. Except for a tiny glint of metal off in the distance. "That way," I said, pointing toward whatever was shiny over yonder.

Geri didn't ask any questions, just stepped in right behind me as we waded through the muck. Nothing was too deep, but every once in a while I found a dip that dropped me almost up to my nuts in cold water. I was soaked, between water coming way up over my boots and sweat running down the back of my neck to soak my shirt, and I'm sure I smelled worse than a frat house on a Monday morning. As the light faded around us, I pulled a couple of chemical snap lights out of my back pocket, cracked them, then shook 'em up until a bright yellow light spread out across the water around us and strung them on a pair of shoelaces I carried around just for that purpose. Trust me, when you've found yourself in the dark in some of the places I've been, wearing a yellow snap light around your neck doesn't seem ridiculous at all. It didn't do much more than push the encroaching darkness back a couple feet, but if it kept me from running dick-first into a gator, it was worth it.

"What's that over there?" Geri asked, holding out a hand for one of the lights. I passed one over, then followed as she veered off in a new direction. "I can't quite make it out—hey! What the hell?!?" she yelped as I grabbed her by the shoulder and yanked her backward.

"It's a trap," I said, whipping my head around. I couldn't see anyone, but that didn't make the surprise they left hanging at chest height any less deadly. I stepped past Geri and grabbed what I assumed was a live grenade floating in mid-air. I put one hand around the body of the explosive, pressing the spoon against the baseball-shaped bomb, then I put my other hand over the top and pulled the whole thing back. I felt the fishing line that held the grenade snap, but with my hands holding it together, the pin didn't come out.

"What the actual fuck, Bubba? Why is there a grenade hanging on fishing line in the middle of the swamp?"

I used the bottle opener on my keychain to prise the safety pin apart and spread it out so it couldn't fall out and kill us, then I passed the grenade to Geri. "It's something moonshiners used to do to protect their stills. Nowadays it's mostly meth cookers who do it, or people with a bunch of marijuana to protect. I don't think anybody's growing weed out in the middle of a swamp, so there's probably a meth lab back in here somewhere. The idea is if anybody walks this way, they'll walk through the fishing line, and they use heavy-duty line that will pull the pin out of the grenade rather than just snap. Then it's a really bad day for the poor bastard that's wandering around where they shouldn't be."

"Like us."

"Like us," I agreed.

"Shit, that's hardcore."

"Hardcore money makes for hardcore security," I said. "Now go ahead and walk forward, slowly. Let's see if we can find what they're so protective of. Might be connected to our Lizzie somehow."

"Or whoever is cooking meth and hanging grenades in the swamp might be the real monster, and Lizzie might just be catching the blame for their shit."

"Or that. But we ain't gonna find out which is which by standing here with wet nuts," I said.

"This may come as a surprise, Bubba, but I don't actually have nuts."

"That's okay. Mine are wet and shriveled up enough for both of us."

"You're truly disgusting."

I didn't reply, mostly because she was kinda right. Dudes in general are gross, and middle-aged redneck dudes are grosser than most. And I'm a fat, middle-aged redneck who's used to living by himself for the better part of his life, so I'm the final evolutionary stage of gross. I pulled out my phone and turned the flashlight on, fanning the beam back and forth in front of us as we sloshed forward.

"What's that noise?" Geri asked after a few minutes of splashing.

I stopped moving and listened. There was a definite hum coming from up ahead, a low-pitched mechanical sound out of place in the cacophony of crickets, jaguar calls, and murmuring of running water. "That sounds like a motor of some sort," I said.

"Then we should probably find out what that's about, right? Maybe Lizzie has joined the twentieth century and has a washer and dryer with a nice warm cup of cocoa waiting for us."

"Or it's a generator for the meth lab and whoever is in there will shoot us the minute we get close enough to see," I said.

"Or it could be that," Geri agreed. "If you're a pessimist."

"You spelled realist wrong," I shot back. "You take point." I stepped aside to let her slip past me.

"Why?" she asked. "I don't mind taking the lead, just curious." She pulled out her phone and turned on the light while I doused mine.

"You're the one with the gun, and you can't shoot over me."

"You still aren't packing?"

"Sure," I said. "I've got my sword, my steel fists, and my silver kukri. Just no gun." I hadn't carried a gun since Joe got killed and my favorite pistol, Bertha, got blown up.

"You're gonna have to get over that one sometime, Bubba," Geri said.

"Yeah," I replied. "But this is not that time." In truth, I didn't know if that time was going to come. I felt like I couldn't just go back to the way things were before Joe died, doing things the same way time after time expecting everybody to always come home. People don't always come home, and now that I'd seen that up close, with somebody I loved, it rocked me. I'd lost people I cared about before. Hell, I reckon before I met Amy, I'd lost about *everybody* I'd cared about, but a disturbing number of the people I loved died by my hand, usually because they were trying to bring about a worldwide plague of cryptids. Seeing Joe die right in front of me, and there not being a goddamned thing I could do about it, that messed me up.

But I wasn't much for introspection at the best of times, and slogging nut-deep through a South Carolina swamp at twilight is nowhere close to the best of times. So I packed all that shit up in a little box and shoved it deep into the back of my head, where I'd only take it out and turn it over and over again in the middle of the night where nobody could see me lose my shit.

"Turn off your flashlight," I said.

"We won't be able to see."

"It ain't quite dark, and that little light is a lot more effective at making us a target than it is at keeping us from tripping over a branch or stepping on a gator's head."

Geri tapped the screen on her phone and slipped it into her back pocket. "You had to go and mention gators, didn't you?"

I motioned for her to be quiet and moved up alongside her. I leaned over and pointed at her, then off to the right. I pointed at my chest, then off to the left. Geri nodded and unholstered her pistol. I drew Great-Grandpappy's sword from the sling over my shoulder, and we slipped off into the night with a little less noise than the average water buffalo trying to square dance.

I could just see Geri about twenty yards off to my right, moving toward a small shack perched on a big clump of grass that seemed to have taken root, or had been anchored in place somehow. The shack was smaller than my bedroom at home, just big enough for one person, a bed, a toilet, and a couple of chairs. The hum we heard was indeed from a generator, a small one sitting on the ground beside the shack, chugging merrily along powering a couple strings of clear Christmas tree lights strung up all around the outside of the shack, casting streaks of bright light across the tiny island.

Everything about this operation screamed "small-time." If this was a meth lab, it must have been the only unprofitable meth operation in the world. If it was anything other than a meth lab, then whoever was in that shed needed to take a serious look at their life, because while I've wanted to run away from the world a bunch, this was extreme. And this coming from a guy who lives on top of a mountain. I know about wanting some privacy. But this shit was beyond the pale. Or it was a meth lab.

When the door opened and a skinny dude with skin the color of his dingy tighty-whities came out the door wearing a gas mask and holding a shotgun, all doubt fled the scene. Definitely a meth lab. Not exactly unexpected.

What was unexpected was to have the meth cook reach back into the shed and pull out a chain, then yank on that chain until a giant lizard crawled out of the lab on all fours and started licking the air with its tongue.

"Shit," I whispered. I didn't know if lizards used their tongues to smell, like snakes, but that part didn't matter. What mattered was that the Lizard Man of South Carolina was working for a crystal meth cook in the middle of a swamp, and now I didn't just have to bring a cryptid into custody and make sure it stopped attacking the locals, but I had to bring a meth-fueled cryptid into custody.

Does meth even work on lizard people? Guess I was about to find out.

7

The half-naked meth cook reached down to the collared Lizard Man at his his side, unclipped the chain from the cryptid's neck, and point off into the swamp. "Get 'em, boy! Get out there and eat whoever's sniffing around."

The Lizard Man rose up onto his back legs, looking around the swamp before freezing with its eyes staring straight at me. I mean, it made sense. I'm a big dude, and I wasn't exactly dressed for stealth, in my red flannel and jeans, so I was a little surprised the cook hadn't spotted me himself. Of course, he had a gas mask, lethal fumes, and a history of drug abuse to contend with, so I guess it made sense that his senses weren't the sharpest.

And yeah, I didn't *know* that he was a junkie. I could be putting too much stock into his standing outside a meth lab hidden deep in a swamp to assume that he was a drugged-out loser. For all I knew, he graduated MIT with honors at fifteen and only took up recreational chemistry after he got bored figuring out string theory or quantum computing or some other set of words that sounds like Jeff Goldblum in *Jurassic Park*. But I'm from rural Georgia. I've seen meth heads. This guy had the gaunt body, with dirty underpants hanging off his emaciated hips, and long red scratch marks running up both arms that glowed almost neon under the illumination from the Christmas tree lights strung up around the roof of the shed.

But the lizard dude didn't tear off into the swamp in my direction, outing me to Meth Cooker Ken and starting a fight that would almost certainly lead to something getting blown up. No, he turned to where Geri was frozen with her back pressed up against a tree, then kept turning past her and ran off into the swamp like he was shot out of a cannon, straight off to the left of the cabin far from either me or Geri. We exchanged "what the hell?" looks, but when the cook went back into the shed, I motioned for her to move in my direction. This was weird, and getting weirder by the minute, so we needed to regroup.

"What the hell is going on?" Geri asked in a hoarse whisper as we knelt on a patch of slightly dryer ground and watched the shed.

"Either that's the stupidest, most scent-blind lizard in the world, or he just deliberately went off in the wrong direction," I replied.

"Why?"

"Shit if I know," I said. It was now full dark, and with no cell service, no compass that didn't work off my phone's GPS, and no idea which direction my truck was in, I was getting resigned to spending a night in the swamp. It wasn't the worst thing in the world, and I'd certainly slept in worse places, but I still wasn't looking forward to any bedding arrangements that might involve playing big spoon to a water moccasin. Or little spoon, for that matter.

"So what do we do now? We found the Lizard Man, and he's working for a meth lab. Do we arrest the human? The lizard? How do you arrest a lizard, anyway?"

"It's kinda like how do you keep an idiot in suspense?" I asked.

For somebody who's normally so together and on top of her life, Geri has no defense against dad jokes. She looked puzzled for a second, then sprang my trap. "Huh? How do you keep an idiot in suspense?"

I turned away so she wouldn't be able to see my grin in the darkness, and said, "I'll tell you tomorrow."

There was a long pause, then she said, "You remember that I'm the one with the gun, right?"

I didn't say anything. After all, she did have a gun. After a pause to let the fallout from my brilliant joke settle, I said, "I guess we go after the cryptid and see what we can find out. Maybe it wasn't supposed to hunt us, and it's just out in the swamp hunting, or taking a dump."

"You're gross."

"What? Everybody poops. There's even a book about it!"

"There's more than one book about poop, Bubba. Doesn't mean I want to spend any more of my life than is absolutely necessary talking about it."

"Okay, fine," I said. "But if you step in Lizard Man poop, I'm not letting you back in my truck until you clean your shoes off."

"Lizard man poop wouldn't be the worst thing I've stepped in today," she shot back.

"You'd be right, then, wouldn't ya, love?" A heavily accented voice came from a little ways off to our right, and I swung around, bringing my sword up. Geri spun and drew her pistol in one smooth motion, flicking on the underslung flashlight and sending a tight beam of brilliant white light piercing through the darkness.

"Ow! Shite, lady, turn that thing off, will ya?" The same Crocodile Dundee-sounding voice came through the night. "You're botching up my night vision to a fare thee well, and your own, too. Not that you lot could see in the dark worth a toss anyway."

"Bubba," Geri asked. "Are we hunting the South Carolina Lizard Man or the Geico Gecko?"

"Not sure right now," I replied. "Hey, mate," I called out, putting on my very best Aussie accent. Which is terrible, just to be clear. I sounded a bit like Steve Irwin with his mouth full of marbles, and that's being kind. "You the lizard? Come on out, we won't shoot."

"Well, you won't, at least. Right, mate?"

"She won't shoot, either. Put your gun away, Ger."

She looked at me like I was crazy. I was thinking going back to the pitch dark might not be a terrible idea. At least then I wouldn't be able to see the dirty looks I was getting. "You can draw it again if he tries anything. You're fast enough."

She let her MP-7 fall against her chest, supported by a sling over her head and one shoulder, despite knowing full and damn well she was not fast enough to draw, aim, and fire the 9mm on her hip if Lizzie decided to charge us. See, that's the problem with people. We've all watched so many TV shows and movies that we think we're all Billy the Kid. Spoiler: we aren't Billy the Kid. Who was also a monster hunter, by the way. I know, right? They coulda made a whole different kind of *Young Guns* if they'd known about William Bonney and his curse. I read about it in a book. Yes, I read. I was in the hospital and the TV sucked, so I didn't have a choice.

8

Geri put her gun away, and I pulled the yellow snap light out of my shirt, where I'd tucked it when Meth Cook Ken came out of his trailer. Geri did the same and looked at the lizard expectantly.

"What are you looking at me for, love? I ain't got any silly light, nor any place to hide one if I did have it," Lizzie said. I was thinking that since he was obviously a male, that a name change might be in order.

"I was thinking you might tell us just what the hell is going on out here? Are you playing security for a drug lab?"

"First, I need to know a thing or two. Are you from DEMON?"

"No," I said. I was being honest. DEMON was defunct since Quincy Harker and his bunch of psychopaths had killed pretty much anybody who knew the computer passwords for the place. I might have had a little to do with that, myself. But it was mostly Harker's fault. "We're with the Department of Homeland Security's Paranormal Division. I flashed my badge, then thought how strange my life was that I was showing my federal government identification to a Lizard Man in the middle of a swamp.

"Homeland Security? Isn't that the lot that searches luggage at the airport?" Lizzo asked. Nope. "Lizzo" wasn't going to work, either.

"Yeah, we handle the TSA, too. But I'm not real worried about if you've got a bomb in your shoe," I said. I couldn't see his feet in the dark

40

and with them being a couple feet underwater, but given his lack of any other clothes except a thick leather collar, I felt safe in assuming there weren't any Chuck Taylors hanging out down there. "We got reports of some attacks on local businesses that looked like they came from a cryptid, so we're here to check it out."

"Know anything about that, Insurance Boy?" Geri asked. She was grumpy, which always happens when I make her go too long without shooting anything.

"Oh yeah, that was all me, sweetheart." He looked down at his midsection. "But if you are calling me any kind of 'boy,' you'd better take another peek. Because nobody's telling stories about the Lizard *Boy* of South Carolina."

Well, since he mentioned the elephant in the room...or elephant trunk, to be more accurate. "Yeah, I was wondering about that," I said. "I fought a lizard person in Florida last year, and they had a whattaya call it? A cloaca. But you...don't."

He reached down and grabbed hold of his little Lizard Man and spun it around like a helicopter. "No, I definitely don't," he said. He dropped his schlong, for which I was grateful. I like a good dick joke as much as the next guy, but an eight-foot lizard spinning his pecker around like he's auditioning for a community theatre production of *The Full Monty* is something I can live without. "There are two different types of *homo lacertilia,* or lizard person. All I really know is that it kinda comes down to whether your ancestors came over on a boat with the Spaniards, or walked across the Bering Land Bridge a couple million years ago."

I felt my brow knit in confusion. "I guess that makes sense, but who the hell is doing that research?"

"DEMON, mate," Lacey replied. Yeah, "Lacey" works. It works off *lacertilia* and is gender-indifferent enough as names go. "They done research on all kinds of cryptids."

"Yeah, I get that," I replied. "I just didn't expect them to be sharing their research with the cryptids they were hunting. Shit, they didn't share hardly anything with me, and I used to work with them."

"Sharing is a strong word for it," Lacey said. "I beat the shit out of one of their field agents a couple years ago and stole his laptop. I think he probably retired after that. It wasn't his best weekend. I didn't hurt him too bad, unless you count the mortal wounds his pride took when a lizard kicked his ass."

"God, if Bubba quit every time a monster kicked his ass, he would have retired twenty times by now," Geri said.

"Hey!" I protested. She was right, though. There's a lot of ass-kicking in monster hunting, but it's at least as important to be able to take a licking as it is to be able to dish one out. And I'd taken my fair share. "You say this was a couple years ago?"

"Yeah, two and a half, maybe three. They'd sent agents in over the years, but this one was less of a moron than most."

"So why start wrecking shit in town now?" I asked. "You've been here a long time, right?"

"My family has lived in this swamp a lot longer than you white people have lived anywhere on this continent," he replied. "The natives were cool. They did their thing, left us alone to do ours, and every once in a while they'd leave an offering to us as spirits of the forest. White people are lame. They don't bring presents. Just smelly-ass generators, shitty chemicals that burn my nose, and stinky assholes like Ken over there." He jerked his thumb over a shoulder at the trailer.

"Wait a second, his name really is Ken?" I asked.

"Yeah, why?"

"It's just that in my head I was calling him Meth Cooker Ken, kinda like Malibu Barbie, only strung out. And now I find out his name really is Ken. Kinda funny, you know?"

Lacey the lizard just stared at me. "No. I don't know. Whatever. I started going into town and making sure I left enough claw marks on stuff and three-toed footprints in enough gardens that someone would either call DEMON, or you lot would hear about it and swoop in with your black helicopters and spirit me and mine away from here for research or some shite."

"You want to be locked up in a lab so people can do research on you?" Geri asked.

"Hell no, I don't *want* that," Lacey said. "But if you'd come in and taken me and my family away for research, I wouldn't have to deal with Ken and his bosses."

"Your family?" I asked. I was starting to get a picture of what was going on, and it wasn't pretty.

"Yeah," the lizard said, and I could hear the tension in his voice as he tried to wrestle himself under control. "Ken's asshole mates have my wife and kids. They said that if I didn't play guard lizard for their meth operation, they'd kill Laura and sell Leeroy and Jenkins to a circus. I figured getting the government involved might be the one way I could keep myself from ripping every one of them limb from limb."

"Ummm…why exactly do you not want to rip them limb from limb?" Geri asked. I nodded, thinking it was a damn valid question.

"I try not to murder people," Lacey replied. "Aside from the burden to my immortal soul, too much people meat gives the gators diarrhea. I live in this swamp. You think I want to wade through huge pools of runny gator shit every day?"

He had a point. It was gross as hell, but it was a point. There was a lot to unpack in that explanation, not least of which was the idea that lizard men have souls and are subject to the same rules as humans. It made sense, but I'd never really thought of it before. I was gonna have to ask… well, I guess I didn't have anyone to ask about stuff like that anymore.

I took a deep breath and pushed my emotions back down. It wouldn't do to be crying in the middle of the night standing in a swamp ten feet away from a giant lizard man with claws that could open me up like a Ziploc baggie. Also, there was muck and brackish water all over my everything and I didn't want to wipe my eyes with swamp hands. "So what can we do to help?" I asked.

Lacey's eyes widened, which is a helluva feat for a lizard that starts the day already bug-eyed. "What do you mean?" he asked. Now, I'm no expert on the facial expressions of eight-foot-tall lizards with giant wangs, but I'd bet good money he was surprised by my question.

"I mean, what can we do to get your family back so you can stop busting shit up in town and I can go tell my boss the situation is resolved and I didn't even have to shoot anybody."

"First time for everything, I guess," Geri snarked from beside me. I thought for a second about elbowing her into the swamp, but my upholstery was already going to be in rough shape, I didn't need to make it any worse.

"You mean it? You'll help me?" Lacey asked.

I shrugged. "Well, I'm here, so if I'm not going to wrestle a Lizard Man, I might as well beat the shit out of some meth cooks."

Geri offered up a similar shrug. "I got nothing better to do. The guys in the one bar in town were way not my type."

"It was like two in the afternoon," I said. "Maybe the top shelf talent has jobs."

"Dude, I'm guessing even the top shelf talent in Swamp Ass, South Carolina, is still not gonna be my type. I mean, what's the deal? Do they issue dudes keys to a beat-up Chevy truck along with their driver's license in this dump, or what?"

"Pretty much," I replied. I turned my attention back to the lizard man, whose eyes were brimming with gratitude. Or allergies. It's hard to tell sometimes, and weird things bloom in swamps. "What do you say, Lacey? Want to show us where the douchebros are keeping your wife and kid?"

He grinned at me and spread his arms wide, but stopped cold when I raised a hand, palm first, in his direction. "Let's skip the hugs until neither of us smells like gator crap, okay?"

And that's how I kept from hugging a Lizard Man on the way to rescue his family from captivity and servitude to a hillbilly drug cartel.

9

Ken and his brother Ben run this lab, and this is where they usually keep me as security," Lacey said as the three of us hunkered down behind a cypress tree and looked at the run-down shack where we'd first spotted the Lizard Man and his handler.

"Ken and his brother Ben?" Geri asked. "Seriously?"

"Yeah," Lacey replied, rubbing the back of his head. "They don't have a sense of humor about their names, either. Or anything else, really."

"So are your wife and kids in there?" I asked. The shack was tiny, so unless the hostages really were the size of that insurance-hawking gecko on TV, I didn't see how Lacey, two drug cooks, and three other lizard people could fit in there.

"No, they're at the main lab, deeper in the swamp. This is one of the satellite labs. They move me around, based on where there's been more fishermen, or any cops poking around. I don't know what they expect me to do about a cop. It's not like these scales are bulletproof."

"Any cop that sees an eight-foot-tall lizard hauling ass through the swamp isn't going to be thinking about his gun," I said.

"Nope," Geri said. "But he'll damn sure be hoping he wore brown pants."

Lacey gave her a blank look. "I don't...oh! Because he'll crap himself!" The Lizard Man laughed, a high, wheezing kind of thing that made me expect him to haul out an inhaler at any second. But he managed to compose himself after a few seconds, and we continued observing the shack, which looked like someone hauled a two-wheeled camper trailer into the swamp, cut one side and one end off it, half-built new walls and a pseudo-roof over the bizarre contraption, and then strung Christmas lights all around the place in some weird kind of lethal frivolity. I had to wonder if there were hand grenades strung on the lights, too, or if those party favors were strictly for uninvited guests like me.

"Any more grenades or other booby traps?" I asked.

"Yeah, there's about half a dozen land mines around here, a couple more grenades strung up on fishing line, and a bunch of just nasty little shit, like rusty spikes hidden under the water, or pits dug where you can't see them until you step in them. Narrow, deep holes just big enough around to hold a person, but not wide enough that you'd be able to claw your way out before you drowned."

"That's not sociopathic at all," Geri said.

"Yeah, these aren't nice people," I replied.

"There's not nice, and then there's trying to kill people in a way that insures maximum suffering," she shot back. "Guess which one this is."

"You should see what they do to anyone caught stealing, or anyone who tries to short them on money," Lacey said.

"Let's skip the gory details," I said, motioning for both of them to duck down a little and make even a token effort at stealth. I know, me suggesting the quiet approach is a little out of character, but I was trying new things. "So there should be two guys in there? Ben and Ken?" I was a little proud of the fact that I managed to say that with a straight face.

"Yeah, and they're both gonna be armed to the teeth. Ben has an old-time gun belt that he keeps a pair of six-shooters in, and he likes to act like he's Wyatt Earp or some shit. Ken's more the modern type, so he'll probably have some AK-47 or AR-15 or something like that."

"So what's the plan?" Geri asked. "Assuming you haven't come to your senses and decided to just let me shoot them, that is."

"No, you cannot just shoot them," I said, shaking my head. This kid was more bloodthirsty than some vampires I'd met.

"Pretty sure I'm allowed. I think I still have a blanket kill order from DEMON for any cryptid I encounter or anyone harboring a cryptid."

That was the first I'd heard of any instructions to just randomly murder any cryptid she came across, and I'm sure the surprise showed on my face. But I pushed that to the side and shoved it deep into one of my "deal with this later" boxes in my mind. Those boxes are really handy, but when they pop a top at inopportune moments, they have a nasty way of reminding me that compartmentalizing my shit is not the same as dealing with my shit. Oh well, just another dumbass hillbilly poisoned by his own toxic masculinity. Whatever. "You lost any authorization from DEMON when we kinda murdered everyone that worked for them," I said.

"Murder is such a strong word," Geri muttered.

"And yet accurate," I replied.

"Do you two want to stand out here and gripe at one another like a couple of old ladies in a Helen Mirren film, or would you like to do something about the meth cook who currently has both hands on his dingus and none on his pistol?" Geri and I looked to where Lacey was pointing, and we were…blessed with the sight of Meth Cook Ben, and I know it was Ben because he was wearing a thick tooled leather gun belt with a pair of Colt Peacemakers hanging off his narrow thighs. Unfortunately, the gun belt, a gas mask, and a pair of tighty-whities were all that Ben was wearing, and his undershorts were hanging halfway down his legs, held up with one hand while the other hand swung his member from side to side, spraying piss all over the water just in front of the shack.

"I'm not going in the front door," Geri whispered.

"Same," I said.

"You know it doesn't matter, right?" Lacey asked us. "There's not a pissing section of the swamp. Once his water meets the swamp water, it's all mixed up in there together."

"I know that, but if I don't notice the specific warm spots, I can try to block out the memory of seeing him take a leak right where I need to walk," I said. Ben finished up, tucked his personal inadequacy away for the moment, and stood on the porch scratching his ass and looking out into the swamp. He reached over to a mailbox hanging on the outside of the shack and pulled out a Zippo and a joint, then fired it up, filling the dank swamp with the smell of seriously dank weed.

"Damn," Geri muttered. "I can smell that shit from here. He's got the good shit."

"That's the thing about drug dealers," I replied. "They get the best drugs."

"Are you just going to stand here yakking, or are we going to get him?" Lacey asked.

"I'm not ready to die just yet," I said. "So I'm gonna pass on attacking the man on the porch of the meth lab while holding an open flame." I pointed to the glow of the Zippo. "He drops that in the wrong place, and the whole joint goes boom."

"Or we could help him along," Geri said. I looked over to see her sighting down the barrel of her pistol, a boxy little Glock 9mm. I stretched out an arm for her, but I was too slow. She squeezed the trigger, and everything turned into fire and screaming.

"Oh shit," Geri said a few seconds later, as the three of us slowly stood up out of the brackish water to see the absolute conflagration created by my…protege? Sidekick? Mentee? Pocket-sized Hannibal Lecter?

I didn't spend too much time dwelling on what to call Geri, focused as I was on making sure that none of the flaming bits of shack, lab equipment, or person were on me anywhere. "That seems like a reasonable response to that, actually," I said.

"Huh?" Geri said, sticking a finger in her ear and jiggling it around. I didn't bother telling her that it wasn't water making it hard to hear, it was getting blown up. I've gotten my egg scrambled by a nearby explosion so often my hearing is shot already, so I suffered no new ill effects from the blast, just a little more ringing in my ears than normal.

"I said that 'holy shit' is a logical reply to having a swamp explode around you," I said, drawing Great-Grandpappy's sword and moving toward the blazing pile of splinters that used to be a meth lab.

"Where are you going?" Lacey asked, grabbing my arm.

I pointed to where Ben and Ken were both splashing away deeper into the swamp, their hair and underwear singed but mostly none the worse for wear after having been blown up and hurled through the night to splash down in a swamp. Either luck, stupidity, or mossy water had apparently saved them from serious injury. "I want to look around and see if those morons left any useful evidence before the gators get here and start looking for snacks," I replied.

"Why do we need evidence?" Lacey asked. "Why don't we just go to the main lab and get my family?"

"Do you know where that is?" I asked. "Because if not, we need all the information we can get from these guys and their shack there to find the boss and find your wife and kids."

Lacey looked at me like I was a world-class moron, which on the one hand showed how truly expressive a lizard's face can be, and two, was a little unfair, as I have it on good authority that I'm a national-level moron at best. "Of course I know where the main lab is," he said. "These assholes have had me working for them for months. Where do you think they keep me locked up when I'm not running around like a scaly German Shepherd? In the main compound, with my family."

I stood there for a second watching the meth lab and every tree in a fifty-foot radius burn merrily away in the night and thought that it might be time to rethink my international idiot ranking, because I'm pretty sure I was climbing the ladder with a bullet. Or an explosion.

"Okay," I said, looking at the giant lizard. "So why are we back here at all if you already know where the big boss is keeping your family?"

This time the look I got from the giant lizard told me I'd made it to world-class dumbass, at least in his eyes. "Unless you want to slog through ten miles of swamp in the middle of the night, I thought we'd steal their boat." He pointed to a jon boat currently sitting athwart a fallen cypress with its nose buried in the water and its little outboard motor about eight feet in the air. Seems the boat had been tied up at the shack until the world exploded, then it ended up kinda in a tree.

"Well, that's gonna suck," I said.

"Not a problem," Lacey said, then he covered the yard between us and the boat in two big bounding hops, scurried up the fallen tree, grabbed the side of the boat, rocked the whole thing up on one side to pour water out of it, then lifted the jon boat out of the water completely, turned a little to his right, and dropped the tiny craft with a splash. It plopped into the water and floated there, good as new and de-treed.

Geri and I stood with our mouths open, then we both turned to look at each other. "Holy shit, he's strong," she said.

"Yeah, no kidding," I agreed.

"What does he need us for?" she asked.

"I dunno," I replied. "Cheering section?" I had no doubts that Lacey could kick all the ass that needed kicked to get his family back, so why the hell did he work so hard to get people from outside to notice him? Why did he really want us here?

Yep, I was paranoid that I was being bamboozled by a lizard. And the only thing to do about it was to let it happen and hopefully not blow up anything, or anyone, important in the process.

10

It took about three hours to navigate the swamp before we came upon an island with a cinderblock building dominating most of the dry-ish ground. We left the boat about a mile away and slogged through the waist-high water for the rest of the trip. I was glad I was on the no guns team, since slime and moss, not to mention anything else nasty that might be floating in the water, wouldn't have been good for Bertha. I gave Geri a sideways glance and raised an eyebrow at her just letting her pistol and her MP-7 hang out in the water as she trudged through the cold brown sludge.

"What? If H&K guns couldn't handle a little water, SEALs wouldn't use them," she said.

I opened my mouth to tell her that SEALs don't use H&Ks, they use Glock pistols and M4 rifles for the most part, but just closed it again. Even if the Navy didn't use them, the MP-7 is a good gun, and there's no reason it wouldn't be fine after a little bit in the water, as long as no dirt or whatever got into the moving bits. If so, then I hoped Geri remembered how to use the KA-BAR strapped to her leg. I just focused on trying to be quiet as I sloshed toward the island.

"Island" was me being generous, and I got a real handle on exactly how generous when I reached the edge of what passed for dry land. It wasn't so much an island as it was a big hunk of floating debris, weeds, roots, and vines that had clumped together for decades until it finally became stable. The whole thing was about fifty feet on a side, and most of that area was taken up with a squat, gray block building ringed with bright white LED lights shining out into the swamp. Everything about this mess reminded me of hunting were-gators in Florida, except that trip had Joe with me… I shoved that back into the box it had leaked out of and focused on the task at hand—rescuing Mama Lizard Man and a pair of Lizard Babies from a meth lab.

I spotted two guards walking in opposite directions, just making what seemed like endless laps around the building. One was a big guy that moved like ex-military, and the other was a short fat man with suspenders and a baseball cap. He was probably my size, if I was a foot shorter and the same weight I am now. So basically a sphere with arms and legs. Soldier carried an AR15 with a pair of magazines taped together so all he had to do was pull one out, flip it over, and slam it back into the gun. Looked cool, but all it really did was add weight to his gun in a weird place and throw off the balance of the weapon. He would have been just as fast dropping a mag and pulling a fresh one from a pocket, but who am I to make the bad guys better at handling their firearms? The round guy carried a shotgun and had a pair of what looked like nickel-plated .45s on his hips. Seemed like every idiot in this swamp thought they were gunslingers. His shotgun was a Mossberg with a pistol grip, and I assumed it had the choke out to hold a full eight shells, which would be more than enough to make a hell of a mess out of me, Geri, or Lacey.

I waited until Soldier passed by me, then slipped forward out of the dark water, pulled myself up onto the grassy hummock, and darted the few feet to press myself up against the side of the building. The fat guard came around the corner a few seconds later, and I nodded to Geri, who stood just out of the ring of lights, and she made a big splash just past where anything was visible.

Right on cue, Tiny stepped up to the edge of the island and raised his shotgun. "Who's there?" he called into the night.

"You hear something, Pike?" a voice—Soldier's, I assumed—came from the side of the building.

"There's something out yonder in the swamp."

"No shit, Sherlock," Soldier said. "There's a shitload of gators out there. Why else you think we throw all them chicken necks out every day? We *want* gators. Beats hiring more guards. Now keep walking post. Boss catches us slacking, it'll be our asses."

"Alright," Tiny said, standing on the edge of dry land staring into the darkness. As soon as his finger came off the trigger of that Mossberg, I took two big steps away from the building and wrapped one arm around his neck, pressing the other against the side of his head, trapping my wrist in the crook of my elbow and cutting off his carotid arteries. About ten seconds later, I guided Tiny to the turf and relieved him of his shotgun and his belt full of pistols. I looked around for a place to stash them, but there was nothing. So I strapped the gun belt on and slung the shotgun over one shoulder as Lacey and Geri emerged from the swamp, dripping.

"I don't see why you got to choke the bad guy out," Geri grumbled.

"Because you got to blow up the last ones," I said, not at all serious.

By the look on her face, she took me at my word, because Geri just nodded and whispered, "Okay, that's fair."

"You do remember that there's another one, right?" Lacey asked.

"Yeah," I said, pressing myself up against the cinderblock wall. "And he oughta be coming around that corner right about…now."

As if on cue, Soldier stepped onto the scene, freezing as he saw three people he didn't expect to encounter standing over the one guy he did expect to see. "What the—"

I didn't let him finish. I snatched the shotgun off my shoulder and bashed the butt of it right between Soldier's eyes. He staggered back, arms waving wildly, and before I could grab him and put him to sleep silently, he yelled out and fell back into the swamp with a massive splash. As he flailed in the three feet of water, he yelled for help, and I heard a door slamming from the other side of the building.

"Looks like the cavalry is on the way," I said, drawing my sword.

"Yep," Geri agreed, bringing her MP-7 up and putting a bullet through Soldier's throat. He fell back with a splash, his rifle falling from his hands.

"Was that really necessary?" I asked.

"Only if you don't like getting shot," Lacey said. "That guy was about to put a lot of new holes in your ass."

Okay, then. I guess it was necessary. "Thanks," I told Geri. "But maybe we try not to murder everybody we come across. That's three so far tonight."

"Any of them fine, upstanding citizens?" she hissed at me.

"No," I replied.

"Then shut the hell up and let me do my job," she replied. "I'm sorry Joe's dead. Really, I am. I liked him, and he never looked at me sideways about coming to you from DEMON. But you not carrying a gun isn't going to bring him back, and it might send both of us to join him sooner than later. So, if you don't like the way I operate, why don't you draw one of those shiny penis substitutes on your belt and show me how it's done?"

I didn't say anything, mostly because I didn't have a good answer, and just stepped into the narrow cover offered by the building as footsteps squelched through the wet turf in our direction. Seconds later, a very surprised woman in tactical gear swung around the corner with her rifle held tight to her shoulder, almost running the barrel into my chest as she did.

She caught sight of me and froze, obviously not expecting there to actually be a threat nearby. I was expecting there to be more guards, so I didn't freeze. I grabbed the barrel of her gun, jerked it skyward, and punched her in the nose. I heard cartilage *crunch* under my knuckles and silently apologized to Skeeter's Mama, who taught me never to hit a woman. I'm pretty sure Mrs. Jones never envisioned a situation where I'd need to punch out a female mercenary before she slaughtered me and my friends, so I decided she'd give me a pass on this one.

Ms. Merc dropped flat on her butt, both hands flying to her pulped nose as blood and tears started to flow in equal measure. Getting punched in the nose *hurts*, and it will almost always buy you a couple seconds to deal with a threat. In this case, it gave me a couple seconds to see the next threat, this one a wiry dude with dead eyes in a gaunt face. Scrawny's rifle was on the way up before he even got a good look at me, but Geri dropped him with two rounds to the face.

I knelt down beside Ms. Merc and drew one of the pistols I'd taken off the fat guard. "If you want to see sunrise, you need to ditch all your weapons and get the hell out of here right now."

"But we're in the middle of nowhere," she protested, her words distorted by the busted sniffer.

"And they'll never find your body if I let my psycho little friend over there get hold of you." I pointed to Geri. "Or I could feed you to tall, green, and hungry. I'm sure he'll get over his vegetarian leanings to munch on the people who kidnapped his wife and kids." I had no idea if Lacey was a vegetarian, but it sounded good. "Now, do you want to run, or do you want to die?"

I channeled my inner Quincy Harker and tried to make my eyes look like I didn't care which one she chose. Something in my look or my speech must have been convincing, because she nodded at me, then started peeling off weapons and straps and stuff. When she was unarmed except for a knife at her hip, I nodded and she woke up Tiny. A few seconds of whispering, and the pair of them slipped into the water and started splashing away in the blackness.

"Think they'll get far?" I asked Lacey.

"Depends on how fast her nose stops bleeding. Gators can smell blood for a long way, and if they've really been chumming the water to get gators close, could be a bad day for those two."

I almost felt bad for them, then remembered that they were working as guards on a meth lab for gangsters who had kidnapped Lacey's family in order to make him work for them. That snuffed out any sympathy I might have found. I didn't necessarily *want* them to die, but I sure wasn't going to waste any tears on a pair of mercenaries who would have gladly killed us if they had a chance.

"Okay, we've dealt with security," I said, looking at Lacey and Geri. "Now let's get inside and free Lacey's family."

"Well, looks like we've deal with some security, anyway," Geri said, pointing up.

I followed her finger to see another Lizard Man standing atop the building, also naked, also hung like a damned mule, and looking down at us with an amused expression on his face, if I was picking up on nonverbal signals from cold-blooded cryptids correctly. He was flanked by a pair of half-shifted were-gators, and there was no mistaking the hungry grins they aimed in our direction.

"Well, shit," Lacey said. "Hello, Cletus. I should have known you were mixed up in this crap."

"Hi, cuz," the Lizard Man, who I assumed was Cletus, replied. "I wondered how long it would be before you tried something stupid like coming to the rescue. Didn't expect you to bring along a walking charcuterie board, though. That'll be appreciated. I think Rich and Morrie here are getting a little peckish."

I made a note to ask Geri later what a "shark coochie board" was, but didn't have time in the moment, because just then Cletus and his were-gator buddies jumped off the roof and it was time to fight for my life. Again.

I drew Great-Grandpappy's sword from the sheath slung over my shoulder and stood ready as the first were-gator stalked toward me. He was a big sumbitch, every inch of seven feet tall, with claws at the tips of his fingers and a mouth stretched out by his transition until he looked like a cross between Venom and the Green Goblin. Or Hobgoblin. Or maybe even the Lizard. I'm not too up on my Spider-Man villains. Either way, he was big, with a shitload of teeth, and his arms rippled with muscle under his green-tinged skin.

I'm assuming it was a dude, because thankfully the bad guys, with the exception of Cousin Cletus, wore pants. So it wasn't a cultural thing that had Lacey run around the swamp freeballin', he just liked to feel the breeze on the boys. Whatever. I had bigger things to worry about than the Lizard Man's wiener. That sounded way better in my head. Actually, no, it sounded kinda awful in my head, too.

I heard a splash from my right as Lacey and Cousin Cletus went backward off the island into the swamp, and Geri's MP-7 barked out a quick three-shot burst, but then fell silent for a couple seconds before she launched into an impressive tirade of profanity and threw her gun at the gator's face.

"Jammed?" I asked over my shoulder, figuring the odds of some bit of sand or sludge or moss getting into the works of her submachine gun were high.

"Shut up," she growled back.

So yeah, jammed. I couldn't do anything to help her, because when I turned just a little bit of my attention off the gator in front of me, it charged. In case you didn't know it, alligators are *fast*. Half-human alligators with full-size legs are even faster, so by the time the were had crossed the ten yards between us, it was moving like an Alabama offensive lineman. He had some All-Pro moves, too, using his arms to slap my sword wide and clear a path so when he dropped his head to slam into my sternum, there was nothing in his way. Nothing except a thin layer of Kevlar, which would have been great if he was trying to shoot me but wasn't worth a shit against the impact of nearly three hundred pounds of scaly half-transformed lycanthrope asshole that was currently trying to turn my ribcage into a bowl of Rice Krispies.

I went down, letting the sword fly off to my right. Maybe Lacey could use it against Cousin Cletus, or maybe one of the bad guys would trip over it, but it wasn't going to do me any good against the were-gator that wrapped its arms around my waist, picked me up, and slammed me to the turf like Arn Anderon circa 1987. The breath rushed out of me, and I heard a couple of things in my torso pop, but I got a foot between the gator and me and managed to roll up onto my shoulders a little and push the asshole off me. He took flight, sailing over my head, and crashed to the ground himself, albeit without the added bonus of someone driving their massive skull into his chest.

I rolled to my feet and drew the pair of silver-edged kukris from the back of my belt. Hurt like a bitch to land on those things, but I'd start to feel better just as soon as I whittled a few chunks of gator off into the water. Toothy came at me, more slowly this time, feinting forward a little at a time, then ducking back out of range when I swung at him. I thought I saw a pattern in his movements, then was sure of it, so on the fourth feint, I stepped forward at the same time the gator did, and instead of slashing at his face, I chopped down on his outstretched right arm.

A big green gator paw landed on the damp ground, its fingers twitching as the nerves looked for new instructions that weren't ever coming again. The were-gator let out a screech that almost dropped me to my knees with its piercing volume. I held onto my knives, and my balance, barely in both cases, and spun around the shifter's right side, then slashed down along the back of his legs, severing both hamstrings like they were taut guitar strings. He went down on his back, clutching his right wrist as the stump sprayed blackish blood all over his face and chest. I lowered both kukris to his neck, and a few seconds later, all the blood stopped spurting. Permanently.

My monster dispatched, I turned to see Geri playing with her food again. Judging by the cut over its eye, she'd beaned her gator-man in the face with her submachine gun, and now she had a KA-BAR in one hand and a pistol in the other and was daring her opponent to come at her. It would take a step forward, only to catch a bullet in the top of its foot for its trouble. The normal rounds didn't do any lasting damage, but anytime something creates a hole in your body forcibly, it's not pleasant. A few more steps, feints, and injuries, and the slide locked open on her pistol, pasting a broad grin on the were-gator's face.

"Oh, son," I muttered under my breath. See, I knew what was going on. The gator thought Geri was in trouble now that she didn't have a gun. No, running out of ammo just meant it was time to wrap things up, so she did. As the were-gator let out a roar and came at her, Geri stepped into its charge, turned herself sideways, dropped a shoulder, and flipped the stunned shifter flat on his back on the grass. Then she buried her KA-BAR in his left eye socket, wiggling the handle around a bit to make sure she got his brains good and scrambled.

She stood up, looked down at the body of the dead guard, and said, "Sorry, pal, but I wasn't trapped in here with you, you were trapped in here with me." Then she pulled a fresh magazine from her back pocket, slammed it home, and put a silver-tipped hollowpoint into the gator's forehead.

She looked over at me and grinned. "Oh good, you're not dead. I thought when you threw your sword at me it was some kind of 'carry this when I'm gone' bullshit."

"Not a chance," I said, picking the antique weapon up off the grass and sliding it back into its sheath. "It was more a 'hey, remember where I put this so I don't have to look for it when we're done kicking the shit out of these guys.'"

She nodded. "Okay, I can see how that might be another interpretation. Where's Lacey?"

I looked around, but he and Cousin Cletus were still splashing around in the swamp, their grunts of effort and pain interspersed with all kinds of remarks about whose daddy never liked who, and who was a prime example of what happened with too much inbreeding, and all sorts of other family drama. They were too far out of the ring of lights for us to see, so I started patting down the were-gators while Lacey and his cousin sorted out their familial disagreements.

"Whatcha looking for?" Geri asked, following suit. "This guy's only got like eight bucks on him, but his watch is nice."

"I'm not looting the corpse. I'm looking for keys to the building," I said. But I did notice the one I searched had a new Apple Watch, so I swiped it. Not like he needed it anymore. And I was not looking up his next of kin to return it.

Geri and I found the driest spots we could on the hummock of roots and moss and waited for Lacey to sort out his issues with Cousin Cletus. It took another ten minutes or so, but eventually he limped back to the island, a long cut scoring the left side of his face, his right arm pressed tight against his chest, and a *lot* of blood all over his chest and face.

"Thanks for the assist," Lacey said as he flopped down on his back. His chest heaved as he panted, and he used his more functional left arm to scoop the occasional handful of swamp water up and pour it over himself in a meager attempt at washing off the blood. It wasn't doing jack shit, but I suppose the thought counts for something.

"I did not come out here to become the meat in a lizard man sandwich," Geri said.

"And I've dealt with enough family drama to know I don't want to stick my nose into any that ain't mine. That's a good way to get dead, even without the feuding family members having a shitload of claws," I added.

"Okay, that's fair," Lacey agreed. He lay there for another five minutes or so before he let out a big groan and rolled to his feet. "Did either of y'all find the keys? I can probably rip the door off the hinges, but I'd rather not. My arm's a little banged up."

It looked more than a little banged up. It looked like he was barely holding the thing on, and couldn't lift a feather, much less yank a steel door out of the frame. But I wasn't going to question the giant lizard about his fitness for duty in his own swamp. That just wouldn't be neighborly.

"Yeah, I got keys," I said, standing up and brushing bits of leaves and vines off my jeans. Geri and Lacey followed me around the building to the main door, where I stopped before I opened anything. "Do we have any idea what's waiting for us inside? Are there security cameras out here that we haven't seen? Do they know we just took out the guards and are waiting to ambush us?"

"I don't know," Lacey said. "I'm a lizard, not a Green Beret. It ain't like

I've got the blueprints memorized and know what time every guard changes shift. Give me a break, Jason Bourne, let's just get in there and get my family free."

I almost started to explain to him that I needed as much information as I could get so that we *could* get his family free, but part of me realized that I was just stalling because the last time I went into a strange building full of bad guys, I left a piece of my heart inside when it blew up. It took me another minute, but I managed to shove even more emotion down into that little box in my soul and shut the lid. The more I dealt with this shit, or failed to deal with it, the more I started to think that Amy was right and I should talk to somebody. Somebody professional, not just my long discussions with Jack, Jim, and Johnny. That's Jack Daniels, Jim Beam, and Johnny Walker, in case you aren't a professional drunk.

But that talking shit's tough for me. I was raised a redneck in the 80s and 90s, and talking to shrinks wasn't something men did. Shrinks were for crazy people, not normal people having trouble dealing with the world. Hell, if I'd had therapy when I blew out my knee, I might have stayed in school and gotten a real job instead of spending my life trudging through forests and swamps hunting down mythical creatures that usually wanted to gnaw off important parts of my anatomy. I've seen a couple of psychologists through the years, but most of them start dialing up the dudes in white coats as soon as I start talking about work. Maybe now that Amy was working for Homeland, Director Pravesh could get her hooked up with somebody who knows that monsters are real, and it's the ones *not* under your bed that you have to worry about.

I shook off my hesitation, swore to myself that as soon as we got back to Georgia I was gonna make an appointment with a counselor, and nodded to Lacey. "You take the rear. You're banged up, so I'll go through the door first. I'm going to swing right. Geri, you swing left, and Lacey can run straight up the middle. Try not to murder anything that isn't actively trying to murder you first." That last bit was purely for Geri. She tends to drift toward the bloodthirsty if nobody's looking. Come to think of it, she goes there if people are looking, too.

I put the key in the lock and shoved the door open, charging into the lion's den as it were. And as usual, it was absolutely nothing like what I expected.

12

I t's empty," Geri said, flicking on the light switch and bathing the interior in cool white fluorescent nastiness.

"It's not empty," Lacey said, shoving past and almost flattening Geri against the cinderblock wall in the process. "I can smell them."

"Smell who?" I asked, but Lacey was already sprinting into the building. It was a squat, featureless cinderblock building from the outside, but the interior was one hundred percent meth lab. There were big lab tables with all kinds of beakers and chemicals and stuff, stacks of big freezer bags full of little baggies of yellow crystals, and hazmat suits and gas masks hanging on hooks by the door.

Geri walked over to the nearest table and picked up a gallon bag. "I've heard of this stuff. They call it Goldenrod, and it's supposed to last twice as long as the normal meth high. It's kinda new, hit the scene within the last three years or so."

I opened my mouth to ask where she got all her knowledge of the methamphetamine trade, but she caught my eye and shook her head. "Not now. We've got a lizard family to rescue."

These are not sentences that normal people utter in the workplace.

But she was right. I drew Great-Grandpappy Beauregard's sword and started off toward a maze of shelves where Lacey had vanished. I crept along, doing the heel-toe rolling step thing to try and keep the sound of my footsteps to a minimum, but I'm not known for my stealth. The only sounds I heard over the sound of my own breathing were Geri tromping along behind me, not making any effort at silence, and the *click-thwap* of Lacey's clawed feet slapping the concrete floor.

"Lacey, you got anything?" Geri called out.

I stopped and turned to look at her with an eyebrow climbing for the ceiling. "Aren't you the one always giving me shit for being too loud and giving away any element of surprise?"

Geri looked at me like I was a giant dumbass. I mean, depending on the day and circumstances, I might be, but I didn't think I'd said anything particularly stupid this time. "Bubba," she said, raising a hand to point at the corners of the room. "We are in a meth lab surrounded by at least a dozen security cameras, and we've already killed all their outside security guards. I think the stealth ship sailed a long damn time ago on this one, pal."

I looked up and saw cameras with little red lights shining merrily away from every corner of the room and the center point of each wall. So that was eight cameras that I could see from where we were standing. "Oh. Yeah."

"Lacey?" I called out. "You alive back there?"

"If he's dead, do you think he's going to answer you?" Geri asked.

"In our line of work, it's imminently possible."

"Valid."

We kept walking toward the shelves, making no efforts at stealth now, and when we were almost to the beginning of the maze of chemical containers, office supplies, beakers, and way more plastic baggies than I've ever seen in one place before, Lacey came out grinning like an idiot with a small lizard person child riding piggyback on him and a slightly larger one walking next to him holding the hand on his uninjured arm. I assume he was grinning, at least. It's kinda hard to tell when anyone with that many teeth is smiling and when they're about to rip your face off, but since he was carrying a lizard child, and we were looking for a pair of lizard children, I made the leap that Bubba Face Tartare was off the menu for today.

"Are these your kids?" Geri asked, holstering her pistol and kneeling down in front of the lizard boy's face. I wanted to warn her about not getting her nose bitten off but held my tongue. For one, she's a trained damn professional and should know how to not get her nose bitten off, and for two, if she did, I would have a lifetime of "I told you so" at my disposal, and I'm not one to let that kind of thing slip by.

"Yeah," Lacey said, letting go of his son's hand. He tried to reach up behind his neck with both hands, but one of his arms still didn't work right, so he knelt on the floor and the other lizard kid slid off. "This is Leeroy, and his sister Jenkins."

"You named your kids after a *World of Warcraft* meme?" I asked.

Geri's head whipped around. "You know the Leeroy Jenkins meme?"

"I'm not *that* old," I said. "I know WoW." I don't know WoW. I barely even remember that it's called "WoW." Skeeter, however, has a fistful of Level 80 characters, and when his regular guilds aren't raiding or whatever, he's bullied me into playing with him a few times. I'm terrible at it, which I blame on my giant ham hands being too big for the controllers, but the fact is that I just don't give a shit, so whenever he cons me into playing, I try to cause as much chaos in as short a time as possible. Leeroy Jenkins is my unofficial gaming mascot. So yeah, I know the meme, even if I suck at the game.

Lacey's kids were looking at each other, me, and then at their dad. "Yeah, they were born a couple weeks after I saw the video for the first time, and I couldn't resist."

"You told me it was an old family name!" Jenkins said. "My name is a joke?"

"No, sweetie," Geri said, glaring daggers at me as the little lizard girl started to sniffle. "Your name is from a very famous video game battle, and Leeroy Jenkins is a hero to gamers everywhere. You should wear that name with pride."

I opened my mouth to say something, but without even looking at me, Geri lashed out with one foot and clocked me right in the shin. Impressive, since she was kneeling at the time. I shut up. It was bad enough I was lost deep in a swamp standing in a meth lab with a lizard man and his two children. I didn't need to get shot by my own partner in a meth lab deep in a swamp.

"Okay, so we got your kids back. We're good now, right?" I asked, my mind already back in our boat and headed home. Much more time in this humid-ass swamp and my crotch was gonna be tropical enough to have parrots living in my taint.

I could tell by the look in Lacey's eyes that we weren't good. We weren't even close to good. He let out a low growl, and when his lips pulled back from his teeth my hand drifted down up to the general vicinity of my left armpit, where Bertha, my .50 Desert Eagle, used to live. There was no Bertha there, now, and no gun of any type, so I just absently scratched along my man-boob and watched Lacey struggle to bring himself under control. I could take out one lizard man, but I kinda liked Lacey, so I didn't want to chop him up into gator bites, especially not in front of his kids.

They were cute little things. Nowhere near as big as Lacey, they stood about four feet high and their voices were high-pitched, like some weird anime character. Their snouts were shorter than their dad's, something I didn't know if they'd grow out of, or if it their mom was a short-snouted lizard woman. My education on lizard people was woefully inadequate, as it turns out. So yeah, I'd rather not slaughter Lacey in front of his adorable little lizard babies. Also, they might have been small, but those little baby snouts still had a shitload of teeth in them, and I *really* didn't want to chop up baby lizard people if they decided that Redneck Nagiri was the dish of the day.

"No, we aren't good," Lacey grumbled. "They still have Laura."

"I'm guessing Laura is your wife?" Geri asked. "Or mate. I don't know if lizard people do weddings."

"We don't," Lacey replied. "But you can call her my wife. That's fine. But yeah, Pete and his goons have her in town, as an insurance policy. I don't even know what that means, much less what I'm supposed to do about it."

"It means they're holding her as a control device to get you to behave," Geri said. She stepped toward the pissed off lizard man without an ounce of fear showing on her face. "That means this guy Pete, whoever he is, is a lot smarter than the goons he had out here in the swamp working."

"Low bar, there," I said under my breath. Okay, not very *far* under my breath, judging by the look Geri shot me.

She kept talking, working to keep Lacey calm so he could focus on giving us the information we needed, as opposed to ripping the entire building down. I understood the desire to tear shit up. It's my most reliable coping mechanism when things go sideways, too. But it wasn't going to be useful in this instance. This was one of the very few instances where a situation would not be improved by adding explosions to the mix.

"How do we find Pete and get Laura back?" Geri asked.

"Should be easy to find," Lacey said. "He owns a big place on the outskirts of town, but there's a buttload of security, so getting in and getting Laura back might be harder."

Now *that* sounded like a situation that could be improved by explosives. I stepped forward. "Don't worry about getting in. I haven't found a whole lot of places that can keep out a determined redneck with a truck full of weapons and ammunition."

"That's good, but his guys have guns," Lacey said with a pointed look at the hilt of my sword sticking out over my shoulder. "And you know what they say about taking a knife to a gun fight."

"Only do it if you know you're a bigger badass than the guys with guns?" I asked, grinning. "Don't sweat it, I've fought a lot worse than humans with guns, and had a lot less than a sword to save my ass." I was being partially honest. Some of the things I've fought were uglier, slimier, smellier than most humans. Maybe not Meth Cook Ken, but smellier than *most* humans. But if I was being honest, the most evil creatures I'd ever hunted were the ones that looked the most like me. Human beings are good at a lot of things, but we're absolutely exceptional at being evil.

Fortunately for Lacey and his family, I'm also pretty good at kicking the shit out of evil assholes. It's kinda my entire *raison d'etre* at this point. Whatever the hell that is.

13

So what's the deal with this boss?" I asked as we finally slogged our way up onto dry-ish land a few hours later. Lacey and the tadpoles, which sounds way too much like a pop band with a cute teenage lead singer than I'm altogether comfortable with, were barely winded, and Geri was in good shape after slogging through miles of swamp in the pitch dark, but I felt like I'd gone five rounds with a rock troll. Which I've done before, and it's every bit as much fun as you think it would be.

I dropped the tailgate of my truck, slipped my sword off my shoulder, and flopped down on my back in the pickup's bed. I heard a cacophony of snaps, crackles, and pops from my spine as it tried to contort itself back into some semblance of alignment, and I idly considered the streaks of pink and purple painting the sky with morning as we moved fully out of the night. I'd spent a lot of nights up until sunrise, but they were a lot more fun in my twenties. A lot less likely to get me killed, too. The swamp was strangely silent around us, with every chirping bird, croaking bull-frog, or grunting alligator having fallen silent. I thought for a moment that my splashing around and swearing had scared them, but then I looked to my left where the eight-foot-tall lizard man stood with his two children, and my estimation of myself as the apex predator in the swamp slipped drastically.

"He's an asshole," Leeroy said. His sister reached over and clocked him

65

on the back of the head, and the lizard boy whined. "Ow! He is, though. Even Mom says he's an asshole, and she likes everybody."

"She doesn't like you using that word," Jenkins replied.

"She ain't here, is she?" the belligerent lizard teen said, and I was somewhat comforted to know that smart-mouthed kids being a pain in the ass is a universal truth regardless of species.

"I am, and if I hear you say that word one more time, I'm going to snatch you up by your tail and dunk you in the swamp until it washes your mouth out," Lacey said. He turned to me. "Leeroy's right, though. Pete is an asshole, a rich asshole who owns half the town and thinks he's the second coming of Huey Long."

"Sounds more like Boss Hogg," I said. "Given the lack of economic prosperity around these parts, if this guy is a crime lord, he must not be a very good one."

"He's a lot better than you'd think from looking at the surrounding towns," Skeeter's voice came from beside my head. I turned to the left to look at the tablet Geri had set up next to me on the tailgate.

"What have you got, Skeet?" I asked my friend's digitized image. He was playing with a new piece of software that made him broadcast as a giant raccoon wearing a toboggan. I decided that there was no way I could make a smartass comment about him as a raccoon without being horribly racist, and thus inherently unfunny, so I just let it go. Sometimes I think Skeeter does shit to me on computers or cell phones just to make me really, really want to say something, and be unable to say whatever I'm thinking. He calls it cognitive dissonance; I call it having a flaming asshole for a best friend.

"This dude is like Boss Hogg, Huey Long, and the bad guy from *Road House* all rolled up into one big asshole sandwich. The kid's totally right, by the way. This guy puts the 'ho' in 'asshole.'"

"I told you!" Leeroy cried out, pumping a fist in vindication. His sister smacked him in the back of the head again.

"Okay, so he's a rich asshole in the middle of nowhere, South Carolina. What do we know that we can use to get Lacey's wife back?" I asked.

Lacey looked confused for a second. "Who's Lacey?"

"Oh," I said. "Um…you are. When I didn't know your name, I tried to make up good lizard-sounding names, and Lacey was what I landed on."

"Lacey the Lizard Man?" he asked. If he'd had eyebrows, one would have been climbing the stairway to heaven right about then.

"Yeah…"

"That's awful. Sounds like something you'd put on a gift shop t-shirt at a tourist trap."

"You seen the general store?" I asked.

"Okay, that's true enough. But my name's not Lacey. It's Scott."

"Scott the Lizard Man?" Skeeter's voice chirped over the tablet. "That's lame."

"I'm getting shit for my name from someone named after a swamp parasite?" Lacey/Scott asked.

"My real name is William James MacIntyre Kwame Jones III. Skeeter is just a nickname."

"So…you picked that?" Scott asked.

"Shut up," Skeeter replied. "Our meth kingpin-slash-kidnapper-slash-mayor-slash-postmaster-slash-sheriff is named Peter Drowling. He's forty-three years old, and has lived in Bishopville since he got out of the Army."

"What did he do in the Army?" Geri asked.

"Supply clerk. There was some suspicion when he left the service that he had been shipping some…illicit supplies home from Iraq, and apparently his taste for illegal activities didn't stop when he re-entered civilian life. About a decade ago, he came home, where his father had been mayor for thirty years, and within five years had taken over his father's legitimate business interests, added some less legitimate enterprises to that, and then ran for mayor after his father died in a boating accident four years ago. He ran unopposed for re-election after his replacement term ended and appointed himself sheriff and postmaster within nine months of taking office for his full term."

"That's all great, Skeeter, but how many men does he have guarding his house, do we have any surveillance on the place, and do we know for sure that Laura is there?" Not only is Geri very mission-focused, she's also way better with names than me, so she was able to remember that Lacey/Scott's wife was named Laura.

"I've done a few drone flyovers and had them send footage back. It looks like there are eight to ten guards around the house and the grounds, plus at least two guard dogs. I didn't catch sight of Laura, but there is a heavier guard presence around one particular outbuilding behind the main house," Skeeter replied.

"Drones?" I asked. "Where the hell did you launch drones from?"

"Your truck," came the reply. I watched Skeeter tap a few keys on his computer and heard the sunroof of my pickup slide back. A pair of small drones lifted up from my back seat and hovered over me, waggling their wings down at me.

"You built a drone escape hatch into my truck?" I asked.

"Well, technically I just hacked the sunroof controls of your truck and launched drones through it. But I guess I did build a secret floor into the back seat of your truck big enough to hold a pair of drones, so…yeah, I kinda did."

Normally, the very idea of somebody touching my truck without permission would be enough to make me rethink both my anti-gun stance and my stated goal of not killing humans, but the idea of having a fleet of drones just randomly rising up out of my truck was so cool I figured we could let it slide, just this once.

"So we need to roll into town with two humans, one lizard dude, and two lizard kids, against a dozen armed guards, attack dogs, and…Scott, do you have any other cousins that might be on Asshole Pete's payroll?"

"Yeah, if Cletus is working for him, then probably his whole family is running around there. That'd be Cletus's brother Jethro, Jethro's wife Maisie, and their two kids Repeat and Repeater."

"Skeeter, I am officially never going to give you shit about your name again," Geri said.

"Don't make promises you can't keep, sweetcheeks," Skeeter replied. "That's four lizard people in addition to a dozen human guards. Yeah, you're gonna need a bigger boat."

"We get to ride on a boat?" Leeroy chirped excitedly. "I like boats!"

His sister clobbered him on the back of the head again. "Ignore him," she said, her tone dryer than any place amphibious lizard people should ever experience. "He's an idiot."

"Well, the nearest other DHS teams are at least eight hours away, even with Harker's magic," Skeeter said.

"I thought Harker lived in Charlotte?" I asked.

"He does, but he and his lady are on vacation in the Outer Banks, which is one of the few places on the east coast more remote than the swamp you've been sloshing through."

"Sounds like no backup," I said.

"Any chance of getting any help in town?" Skeeter asked. "And by that, I basically mean is there anyone in town that doesn't hate you both already?"

"Everybody in the bar wanted to bang Geri, but that isn't exactly conducive to running into an armed enclave with us," I said.

"No, but it does mean we could probably get information on the boss's house without too much effort," Geri said. "Let me get a quick shower and we can go ask these gentlemen nicely to share everything they know about the boss and his security."

Jenkins' eyes were wide as she leaned over to her brother. "How is she going to get the bad guys to tell her what she wants to know? Is she going to use her gun?"

"Oh, she's got something way more dangerous than her pistol," I said with a grin. Geri, knowing full well what I was about to say, just shook her head and smiled at my sophomoric sense of humor.

"What does she have that's more dangerous than a gun?" the little lizard girl asked.

"Boobs," I replied. "The greatest weapon any woman has ever wielded, Jenkins. Geri has the one thing men are almost always completely helpless against. She has boobs."

<h1 style="text-align:center">14</h1>

We left the lizard family on the outskirts of town when we headed for the bar. I'm not exactly stealthy, but it's pretty much impossible to be inconspicuous when you're walking along *Reservoir Dogs*-style with a giant redneck, an attractive young woman, an eight-foot-tall gecko, and a pair of cute and potentially murderous gecklings. No, I don't have any idea what you call lizard man kids, but I'm sticking with gecklings. I'm also still calling Scott the Lizard Man Lacey in my head canon. Don't ask where I learned what "head canon" is. It involved me reading a lot of Morgan Brice books and watching *Supernatural* reruns.

I let Geri go in ahead of me, because it felt like us walking in together would give all sorts of wrong ideas. Either the guys inside would think she had a weird daddy fetish, or they'd think I was a creeper, or they'd think we were cousins. And since all of those meant they'd think we were sleeping together, I figured it would be better for her chances to recruit muscle if they thought they had a chance with her. So I stood outside the door for a couple minutes, then pushed my way into the dark, loud, smoky dive bar.

It's hard to have a dive bar when it's the town's only bar, but they managed. Everything smelled like stale beer and bad decisions, and most of the people there looked like they had survived the last time someone yelled "Hey y'all, watch this!" in their vicinity, but only barely. Alan

Jackson was blaring from the jukebox, cigarette smoke hung in the air like the fog of war, and my feet didn't quite stick to the floor, but only just. I walked over to the bar, where a distracted lunk with a mullet, chin beard, and muscle shirt leaned on the polished wooden surface leering at Geri. I was pretty sure he couldn't see down her shirt from there, but if he managed, I hoped he didn't catch too good a glimpse of what was hiding in there. I knew for a fact there was a little .380 in a custom holster in her bra, because I gave it to her for Christmas. I had Amy tell me what size because that is not a question I'm asking the little sister of my first love, who was murdered by my psychotic father at the behest of my even more psychotic brother.

I have a complicated family at its best. It should surprise most of no one that walking around town with a bunch of bipedal lizards and a woman who was initially hired to kill me felt downright normal compared to most of my life.

"Hey pal, can I get a Bud?" I called to Mullet the Bartender. He straightened up and looked around, like he couldn't figure out who was talking to him, then his eyes settled on me and he walked over.

He reached into the cooler under the bar and passed me a Budweiser. He didn't even offer a glass, which was good. I had some modicum of faith that the beer itself was mostly safe, but there was no way I was drinking from a glass in that joint. I could almost guarantee that the same rag used to wash dishes was also used to wipe up blood and puke from the bar most nights. "Eight bucks," he said. "Cash only."

"Eight bucks?" I exclaimed. "For a Budweiser? Jesus, son, does that come with a lap dance, or do I at least get to see your boobs for that kind of money?" I was expecting three or four bucks at most. I'd never paid that much money for a crappy domestic beer in a place where no one stuffed dollars in garter belts before.

"You're funny. Taxes are high around here, dude. Eight bucks." I handed him a ten and told him to keep the change, then waved him a little closer. "You know where I could get anything to help me keep the party going a little longer, know what I mean?"

"You want to keep a private party going longer, like a blue pill kinda longer, or you just want to take the edge off and chill a little bit, or you want to throw down at a hoedown and party hard for hours?"

I am not well-versed in the lingo of drug dealers. I've always been a booze guy, and sometimes THC edibles when I can get them legally, but I only understood about half of what he said to me. I think he was asking if

I wanted boner pills, downers, or uppers, but apparently it's not cool to call them uppers and downers anymore. "I just want a little energy boost, so I can party harder and feel more…everything. No need to chill out, and I don't have any problems with the ladies." I leaned on my elbows on the bar and felt myself slide forward a little in the slime that had built up a permanent residue on the disgusting surface.

"There's a dude in the parking lot. Blue panel van with no windows. Knock on the sliding door three times, then tell them Mick sent you." I slid Mick another ten-dollar bill and sucked down my beer in about three swallows.

"Thanks, dude," I said. I turned around and headed for the door, feeling very safe in Geri's ability to handle herself against a half dozen drunken rednecks. I'd also noticed one of Skeeter's drones zip in when we opened the door and flit up to the ceiling where it hovered just above a ceiling fan, invisible through the smoke and inaudible over the country music if you didn't know what you were looking for. If anything went sideways, I'd get a heads up, whether Geri thought she needed help or not.

The gravel in the parking lot crunched under my boots as I walked out into the night. The streets were deserted, and I was surprised by how crowded the bar, and its parking lot, were. It was well after what reasonable places deemed last call, and the owner must have been either bribing, or sleeping with, someone in the Sheriff's department to be able to stay open without getting hassled.

The blue van was out on the edge of the parking lot, with nothing around it for a good ten yards in any direction. As I walked in that direction, the wind shifted, and I understood exactly why there was plenty of parking available near the local drug dealer—the stench coming off that thing was almost a physical assault. I caught a blast of the cat piss smell of meth and the human piss smell of meth users, and it was enough to make my eyes water.

I blinked away tears and tried to breathe shallowly through my mouth as I approached and knocked three times on the van's sliding door. The whole thing rattled with the *boom-boom-boom* of my knocks, and I realized that maybe I'd been hanging out with Amy and the rest of the federal friggin' government too long because now I knock like a cop.

"Whattaya want?" a muffled nasally voice called from inside the van. I'd assumed whoever was inside would be sleeping, it being the middle of the night and all, but apparently sleep wasn't something meth dealers did.

"Mick sent me. Told me this is the place for party favors."

The door slid open, and a wild-haired skinny white dude knelt on the floor of the van in a pair of bike shorts and nothing else - no shirt, no shoes, just spandex. He stared at me with wide, red-rimmed eyes that peered out at me from the tiny patch of visible flesh between his mop of white-boy dreadlocks that fell to his shoulders and a beard rivaling Tom Hanks in *Cast Away*. I tried to look past him into the van to see if he had a volleyball with a face drawn on it, but it was too dark in there.

"Party favors? What the fuck are you talking about, dude? You want a kazoo or something? I got meth, Viagra in pill or powder, and some shrooms. I'm all out of molly. Carload of guys from The Citadel drove up last weekend and bought my whole supply. Now I'm stuck waiting on a delivery. Supply chain issues, am I right?"

I nodded like I had any idea who or what "Molly" was. "Yeah, man. Things are dry all over. Even in the swamp, I reckon. You say you got meth? Is it from the local guys? I hear there's something special in theirs that makes it better."

His eyes narrowed further under all the hair. "You a cop, man? You know you're not allowed to lie to me about being a cop if I ask you, right?"

I nodded. "I know. And I'm not a cop." But if I was, I totally would have lied to him. There's no rule against lying about who you are if you're a cop. You have to tell people you're a cop if you're actually arresting someone, but the guy buying meth in a dive bar parking lot in the middle of the night does not have to tell the probably armed drug dealer that he's a cop.

Wilson (the name I picked for him because of his resemblance to *Cast Away*) nodded. "Alright, man. I got some stuff, and yeah, it's local. I don't know what they put in this shit, but it seems like it's more potent than normal stuff. Like, it's real easy to get straight hooked, so be careful."

Yeah, because he's the conscientious drug dealer. "How much you got? I'm throwing a big party this weekend, couple hundred people, and I want to hand this stuff out to everybody who comes. Like party favors, you know. Only better than a kazoo."

He laughed. "Yeah, man, way better! I feel ya, bro."

I really hoped he wouldn't feel me. He looked really dirty, and slimy hippie drug dealers were not on the list of people I liked feeling me. "So, can you hook me up?"

He shook his head, sad. "Nah, man. I can't do that kind of quantity.

Maybe if you had a couple dozen people, I could hook you up, but I don't keep that much on hand."

"Is there anybody else I could talk to?" I asked. "Your supplier, maybe?"

Wilson scooted back in his van a little, his eyes darting from side to side like he was afraid of something. "Nah, man. I can't get you in touch with him. He don't know you, and he—*URK!*"

That last bit is the sound a skinny meth head makes when a giant hillbilly reaches into his van and snatches him out by the throat. I dragged Wilson out onto his feet and slammed him into the side of the van a few times. When I felt like his teeth were sufficiently rattled and his loyalty to his supplier sufficiently shaken, I lowered him until his feet once again touched the ground.

I leaned forward. "Now here's how the next five minutes are going to go. You're going to tell me everything about your supplier, including every single detail you've ever seen about his house and the security there, then I'm going to let you go. When I let you go, you're going to reach into your little traveling pharmacy there, grab a change of clothes, your ID, and any cash you have, then you're going to start hauling ass out of town. Then I'm going to drive your van to your boss's house and set it on fire."

"The house or the van?"

"That's what you're focusing on right now?"

"Just wondering, dude."

I hate threatening stoners. It's always really hard to get them to understand the level of harm you're about to inflict upon them. At least for me, since I try not to kill humans and I can't just randomly throw fireballs at people. I bet Harker has it easier. "Probably both. It's entirely possible I'm going to set your van on fire, drive it into the house, and then set that on fire, too. But you won't care, because you're going to be walking west until your damn hat floats, and if I see you again within two hundred miles of the South Carolina state line, I'll shave your head and hang you from the tallest tree I can find, and I'm gonna use your own dreads to do it. Do I make myself clear?"

"Yeah, dude," he said. "What do you want to know?"

And of course, because it's me and my life, just as I opened my mouth to start interrogating the moron, some other jackass broke a two by four across my back, and my night really went to shit.

15

Something to keep in mind about the physics of being a big dude—if you hit us in the back really hard, we move forward just as hard. This was...not good for Wilson, who ended up between a rock and a hard place. Well, more accurately between a redneck and the side of his van, but it might as well have been a rock as hard as I slammed into him.

The air went out of him in a loud *"OOF!"* and I suddenly had something else to be annoyed about. Not only had some jackass blindsided me with a two-by-four, he'd also made me run into a smelly-ass meth dealer and get a face full of the rancid breath that only comes from someone who once watched a TV commercial about brushing his teeth, but was never really down to try it.

I pushed myself off the van, and Wilson, and turned around. Behind me was a round little man who looked like either an oompa-loompa in a trucker hat, or maybe somebody finally managed to put Humpty Dumpty back together again and get him into a pair of dirty jeans with red suspenders, battered cowboy boots, and a Florida Gators t-shirt. That was the part that got me seeing red. Not the part where I got the shit knocked out of me by a cowardly fat fuck who didn't have the testicular fortitude to jump me when I could see him coming, and not even the part where my beard now smelled like cat pee from being too close to the meth dealer. Nope, the part that really boiled my turnips was the fact that I got clocked by a sneak-attacking, chickenshit, no-count, dirty Gators fan.

I don't like the Gators. Never have, never will. Even before I literally fought were-alligators in Florida, I hated the Gators. I'm a Georgia Bulldog through-and-through, and my loathing for all things Gator Nation is deep-seated and unwavering. I don't like UF, I don't like Tim Tebow, I don't like Urban Meyer, and I have a significant dislike for the entire city of Tallahassee. Except for Mo-Betta BBQ. They're alright. Wish they'd move to Georgia, but whatever.

So when I saw that I'd been ambushed by a walking sphere in a Gators shirt, I did what any self-respecting redneck would do. I snatched the lumber out of his hand, tossed it to the side, and slapped the taste out of his mouth. Now this wasn't some slap like your prom date gave you when you tried to steal second base. No, this was a full-barreled, from the hips, my whole hand laid across this idiot's face palm strike. Gator Boy spun around like a top and dropped to one knee facing away from me, and I planted a foot right in his ass and shoved. He sprawled face-first in the gravel, and I turned around to Wilson, who sat on the ground looking dazed as he tried to catch his breath.

"Don't move. I ain't done with you." I stepped over to Gator Boy, who had managed to make it back up to all fours, then I bent down and slapped him on the back of the head. I didn't hit him quite as hard this time, because I didn't want to concuss the little shit, I wanted to interrogate him. And maybe concuss him just a little bit.

"What the hell are you tryin' to do?" I asked him, grabbing the collar of his shirt and yanking him to his feet. He scrambled up, but not before I heard a satisfying *rip* from the threads popping in his shirt. Any day I get to defile Florida merch is a good day to me.

"Y-you was asking about the bossman. He don't like people asking about him. I figured if I knocked you out and took you to him, I'd get a bonus or something."

Okay, I had to admire the initiative. It's not something you usually see in a henchman, or a minion, and no, I don't really know the difference. But you very seldom see idiots like this doing anything they weren't specifically told to do, and even less often do you see them try to jump a larger opponent alone.

And that thought occurred to me just as I heard the crunch of gravel behind me, and I turned to see a skinny guy with a pistol wearing an Alabama hat smiling at me. "Hey," he said, in that tone where you know the person talking thinks they have got everything completely under control because they're the one holding the gun.

So I took it from him. He didn't have the thing pointed at me, just down at his side where I could see it, and he was about three normal-sized steps away from me. Which meant he was way too close. I took one long step and reached out my hand, wrapping it completely around his wrist and squeezing. I felt things grind together that shouldn't grind, and he dropped the pistol. I didn't waste time expressing my near-Florida-like loathing of the Alabama Crimson Tide, Nick Saban, and the entire population of Tuscaloosa. I just punched him right between the eyes, then let go of his wrist as he slumped to the ground, out cold.

I turned my attention back to Gator Boy, who was about ten steps away from me, moving as fast as his little legs would carry him. The problem was, that much mass isn't easy to get rolling when you're six and a half feet tall, much less when you've got shorter legs and even more wind resistance. I caught up to him long before he got to the door of the bar, and dragged him backward by his belt, which I noticed had the name "Milo" embossed right above his asscrack. I also noticed, much to my disgust, that his shirt had pulled out of his pants while he was running, and I now had a horrifyingly good view of the aforementioned asscrack. I had just spent hours slogging through a swamp, blowing up meth labs, chilling with nudist lizard men, and somehow managing not to become an appetizer for a crocodile or a water moccasin, but the fish-white crevasse that peeked out of the top of Milo's britches was the nastiest damn thing I'd seen in a long time. The worst part was the hair. It looked like his ass had a goatee, except it was growing *up*. I shoved my revulsion down and dragged Milo back to Wilson's van.

Wilson had closed up shop, but I wrenched the sliding door open with no problem. That's one of the upsides to dealing with stoners—they frequently forget to lock their doors.

"Dude! We're closed!" Wilson said, sticking his head out the door.

"I don't give a shit," I replied, snatching up a fistful of dreadlocks and dragging him out into the parking lot. I dropped him on the gravel and flung Gator Boy down next to him. "You two are going to tell me everything you know about whoever is running this meth operation, his house, the grounds, security, and anything else I need to know to keep from getting my nuts shot off going in there. Do you understand me?"

"I-I-I can't," Gator Boy stammered. "If I tell you, he'll kill me and feed me to the alligators."

There was an irony inherent in a Gators fan being afraid of gators, but this wasn't the time to give that any more than a fleeting thought. I leaned down but felt a massive hand on my shoulder holding me back.

I turned, and there stood Lacey in all his scaly glory. And given that both these dudes were sitting on their butts on the ground, his glory was swinging in their faces and was at least as intimidating as the rest of him. Until he opened his mouth.

"He's going to kill you?" Lacey asked, with a sibilant hiss that I hadn't noticed before. "What do you think I'm going to do?" He leaned forward now, opening his mouth wide and hissing at the terrified men like a pissed off velociraptor or something. Maybe I should make it a point to not screw with his name, at least not where he can hear me.

The acrid smell of human urine overwhelmed the smell of dank weed and cat pee that surrounded Wilson like an almost palpable fog. I looked at Gator Boy. "Really?"

He looked down at the dark stain spreading across his crotch. "I couldn't help it. He scared me."

"Well, then I hope he scared you enough to tell us what the hell we're walking into, because otherwise your pants are going to be stained with something a whole lot worse than pee."

"Oh, I went number two before I left the bar, so I probably won't poop my pants."

"I meant blood, moron."

"Oh."

"TALK!" Lacey hollered, dragging the word out as long as he could to give Gator Boy a nice, long look at his teeth, which glinted in the parking lot lights like little daggers.

"He ain't gonna talk," came the voice of the skinny guy I'd cold-cocked. "And you ain't gonna sucker punch me again, neither."

I turned, and this time he at least had the gun pointed at me. I thought his threat assessment might be a little off, pointing the gun at the human instead of the giant lizard threatening his friend, but it wasn't my job to teach him how to be a bad guy. It was my job to take advantage of every mistake he made and hopefully beat his ass for making them. "You want to put that away, or am I gonna have to whip your ass again? And for the record, it ain't a sucker punch if I'm standing right in front of you when I lay you out with one punch, you glass-jawed pansy."

"Oh, that is it, asshole. Pete says I can't kill the lizards, but he didn't say anything about needing you alive." He pulled back the hammer on his revolver, the distinctive *click* sound echoing through the suddenly silent night.

"Yeah, we might not *need* him alive, but I've gotten kinda used to it, so why don't you put the gun down and sit over there next to your buddies?" I looked over Alabama Jerk's shoulder and saw Geri standing there holding her pistol. Alabama Jerk didn't move, so Geri made a distinctive sound of her own by racking the slide on her pistol and chambering a round. Another round, actually, because there was one in the chamber, which flew out onto the ground, but I guess she wanted to make the sound. More intimidating if you make the sound, I reckon.

It worked. Alabama Jerk turned around, swinging the barrel of his gun to point at the sky before he slowly bent over and set it on the ground. "Alright, alright," he said, walking backward over to where Gator Boy and Wilson sat. He looked down at Gator Boy and wrinkled his nose. "What the shit, Jimmy Lee? Did you piss your pants again? You remember what the boss man did when Greg did that hunting the lizard people, don't you?"

Apparently, incontinence was an issue among minions in this town. I decided that we needed to get the hell out of there before it infected us. We had too long a drive home for me to want Geri getting a weak bladder, and since she was the one with the guns, I didn't think suggesting she ride in the bed of the truck would go over well.

Alabama Jerk sat on the other side of Wilson, giving a wide birth to his pee-stained cohort. "Alright, asshole. What do you want to know?"

"Well, for one thing, I want to know if you dipshits really think you're going into Petey's place without ol' Merle." The voice came from in front of Wilson's van, where Merle stepped out with a shotgun cradled in his arms. He looked every one of his years, but he handled that shotgun like it was a part of himself. "I been waiting a bunch of damn years for proof the Lizard Man was real, and now that I got it, I ain't letting y'all go get him killed by Petey and his dumbass crew of shitheads and morons."

"Hey!" Alabama Jerk and Gator Boy both protested.

I looked down at the pair of them and said, "Y'all figure out between you who's the shithead and who's the moron, but one of you better start talking, and fast." I looked over at Merle. There was a determined look on his face, a look I'd seen on my own grandfather's face when he was first teaching me how to hunt monsters. This was an old fart with his mind made up, and nothing in the world was going to steer him off the course he'd chosen. I might as well accept it, because the old man was here whether I wanted him to be or not.

"Well, Merle," I said. He tensed up like he was getting ready for an argument. If I was even a little bit sane, he would have been right. But nobody's ever accused me of being particularly stable, so I surprised him when I stuck out my hand and gave him a shake. "Welcome to the team. Let's go blow some shit up."

16

A redneck, a millennial, a septuagenarian, and three lizard people walked into a house, and that isn't even the beginning of a joke. Geri took point, with Merle following behind them. The "don't stand in front of the people with guns" rule still applied, so I was about a yard back. I'd never seen Merle shoot, but if he was at least a little bit better than Skeeter, I was safe directly behind him.

Petey's house was as much a monument to old Southern faux heritage as anything I'd ever seen. It was a total knockoff of Tara from *Gone with the Wind*, complete with long, curving driveway and a massive wraparound porch. The weird part was the lack of security. There were no guards, no dogs, not even a real fence. I get that he thought he had the town completely subjugated, but this level of confidence bordered on hubris. If that's what hubris means. It was on the Word-A-Day calendar Amy gave me last year, but I only skimmed the page it was on because I had forgot to flip the thing for a week, and when I ripped off a stack of pages at one time, I didn't exactly absorb the definition.

"Where is everybody?" I asked, keeping my voice to a whisper as we walked up the long driveway.

"Pete don't think anybody's got the stones to make a run at him, so he only keeps a few of his boys at the house. Half a dozen or so. They're probably all drunk and passed out by now," Merle replied.

I didn't buy it. That was way too convenient, and he had to know we'd blown up one lab and ransacked another by now. There's no way this wasn't a trap. Well, it ain't like it was the first time I'd ever walked into an obvious trap. At least this time I knew it was an obvious trap, for whatever good that was going to do me.

"Any idea where he'd be keeping Lacey's wife?" I asked Merle.

"I swear to every god in every heaven if you don't stop calling me Lacey, I'm going to eat your spleen," Lacey/Scott said. "After we save Laura, of course."

"Well, after we save Laura, I promise to stop calling you Lacey. Eventually," I replied.

Merle looked between us and shook his head. "Is he always like this?" he asked Geri.

"Nah," she said. "Sometimes he's hard to deal with. This is a good day."

"Goddamn, girl," the old man said with a sigh. "You got the patience of Job, don't you?"

"Yeah," Geri said. "So, any ideas about where Laura would be in the house?"

"I've only been in there a time or two, when Pete would have townwide barbecues or something like that. It was better to go and drink his beer than to not go and let him know you think he's an asshole."

"But he is an asshole," I said.

"Yeah, but if you tell him he's an asshole, then he gets mad. Then you've got a pissed-off asshole sending his shithead goons out to have a 'conversation' with you about proper respect and all that bullshit." The old man hawked up a big loogie and spat it onto the grass. I got it. This dude was obviously a tinpot dictator who set himself up as lord and master of this little town, and he'd been using Lacey…*Scott* as his muscle. Then Scott got tired of his shit and decided to bail, and Pete the Peckerhead used his family as leverage. I was really starting to dislike this dude.

"Okay, back to the part where you have an idea of where La—Scott's wife would be?" I asked.

"Oh yeah. I don't know. If I had to make a guess, probably the trophy room. It's a little on the nose, but Pete ain't known for being terribly original."

"Okay, how do we get there?" Geri asked.

"No idea," Merle said. "Only time I ever been in there was at a New Year's Eve party about five years back, and I was a little over served, if you get my drift."

"You were drunk," I said by way of clarification.

"Oh yeah, son. I was God's own drunk and a fearless man."

Anybody that can quote old song lyrics before going into a gun battle to rescue a lizard person from drug dealers is somebody I'm good hanging out with. Merle cemented his status as being good in my book right then. "Alright, then," I said, and drew my sword. "Let's go save Laura."

And then I stepped onto the porch, planning to open the door so Merle and Geri could go in and clear the room, but froze as floodlights blazed to life, bathing the porch in bright, white light.

"Get the hell out of here!" came a tinny voice from the doorbell camera. "You get off my property in the next five seconds, and I won't have to shoot nobody!"

I looked around, then leaned over and pressed the button on the door-bell. "Dude, I don't know if you can hear me, see me, or what, but if you got any kind of camera on that thing, you can tell ain't no way I'm getting my fat ass down that long driveway in five seconds, even if I wanted to run away."

"Okay, ten seconds, then!"

"How about one?" I asked, then kicked the front door in.

At least that was the plan. What really happened was I reared back, lifted my big ol' size sixteen boot, and slammed it into the door just to the right of the deadbolt, about as hard as I could manage. And it gave not at all. But all that force had to go somewhere, and that's how I ended up flat on my back staring up at the ceiling of the porch. He had a couple of nice fans up there, and I wondered if that was something Amy might like us to put on the back deck. Then I rolled over and struggled to my feet.

"The door's reinforced," I said, looking at the rest of the crew.

"Yeah, we noticed," said Scott. "Would you like me to try?" Without waiting for a response, the giant lizard man stepped over me, dug his claws into each side of the reinforced steel door, and yanked the whole thing out of the wall, frame and everything. He turned and chucked the door, frame, and some chunks of wall still stuck to the frame all out into the yard. He waved to the hole in the wall and bowed. "You may enter."

With stealth completely out the window, or more accurately out in the front yard, I drew my sword and charged in first. It would have been smarter to send the people with guns into the building where we expected to find people with guns, but I'm not real used to fighting humans, so cut me a little slack. It's different when you really don't want to kill whoever you're hunting.

I mean, I never *want* to kill cryptids. Most of the time if you can keep people away from them, they're fine. They're just like other animals. They want to eat, sleep, and make new cryptids. It's only when we encroach too much on their territory that they get mad enough to go after humans. But if they do go after humans, then I take them out. And I don't feel the least bit bad about it. In my book, the difference between a cryptid and a monster is the body count.

People are different. I've killed humans, a couple of times, and it's never felt good. Even the intentionally mutated mercenaries we took out in Raleigh still pop up in my nightmares now and then. I really didn't want my team to go in there guns blazing and add a whole new batch of names to my list. I guess I thought if I took a sword to a gunfight, the bad guys would be so taken aback by my stupidity that I'd have a chance to punch a couple of them out before they got their sense back.

But there was nobody there. All that moral gymnastic-ing, and the damn entryway was deserted. And seriously, this was no mere foyer. This joint was *insane*, with a dual curving staircase, marble floor, and polished wooden banisters that looked like mahogany. In that it was wood, it was dark, and I could tell it wasn't pine or cedar. So…mahogany.

I lowered my blade and got out of the doorway so everyone else could come in, Scott ducking to keep from smacking his head on the jamb. He looked around and said, "Ostentatious, but at least he went for the high ceilings."

"Where is everybody?" Geri asked. She hadn't lowered her weapon, and her eyes were sweeping the upstairs landing, which would provide a great ambush point. But no ambush came.

"No idea," Scott replied. "And I don't care. If I have to tear this house apart, I'm not leaving without Laura!" He pushed past me, bulled his way through the double doors directly in front of us, and disappeared into the house.

I looked at Geri, then at Merle, and we all shrugged. "Guess we better go after him," I said. "Geri, you're up front. Merle, you get behind me with Leeroy and Jenkins. Cover our rear with that shotgun and keep any of these assholes from sneaking up on us. Let's go." I followed the path Scott had carved through the house, going slowly to avoid getting jumped, but all that went out the window when I heard the flat *crack* of a pistol from up ahead.

"Shit," I muttered. "I hate running. Cardio sucks." Then I started running. Lumbering, really. It's been a bunch of years and several knee surgeries since I did any real running, but I am a lot like a steam locomotive—once you get me moving, it's gonna take a lot to stop me.

I burst out through the back yard and froze, barely keeping from getting bowled over when Geri slammed into my back. I moved to the side to let her see what was going on, and she froze, too, her hands flying to her mouth as her eyes went wide.

Scott was lying on the ground about ten yards ahead of us, rolling over in the grass clutching his midsection. Standing in front of him was Petey, the douchebag I'd met earlier in the day. A boxy little Glock smoked in his fingers, and a nasty smile danced across his face. On the ground next to him was a lizard woman with her hands tied behind her back and a bandana tied around her snout.

"Well hey there, stranger," Petey said, swinging his pistol back around to hover a few inches from Laura's temple. He was dressed much as he had been earlier, except barefoot, wiggling his toes in the manicured grass of his back yard. "I been waiting for y'all. Now I need you to all put your guns, and…sword…on the ground or I'm gonna blow this little lady's brains out all over her husband's dead body."

"Nah," I said. I took several steps forward so that I was between Scott and the grinning drug dealer. "I think I'll just whoop your ass so bad you won't be able to pick up that plastic pea shooter."

"You gonna do that before I shoot her right in the head?"

"Nah, after," I said, staring him dead in the eyes. "Go ahead, shoot her. I dare you. I just hope you're fast enough to shoot her and me before those two kids back there get ahold of you. 'Cause you done shot their daddy, and I expect they're gonna be seriously irritated with you if they lose their mama today, too."

Petey's eyes flicked back over my shoulder to where Leeroy and Jenkins were both trying their best to push past Merle, who was barely holding them in the back door. The second he took his eyes off Laura, I flung my sword at his face and she dove to the ground.

Funny thing about people nowadays. Since there ain't a whole lot of folks running around flinging swords at people, bad guys don't really know how to react when you fling a sword right at their face. Petey's eyes went wide, and I could almost see the options scroll across his eyes. *Duck? Dive to the side? Stand still and hope he misses?*

He settled on Option Two—dive to the side. I didn't care which one he picked, so long as it gave a few seconds for Laura to get out of the way. I was on Petey before he could get to his feet, and I backhanded him as I hauled him to his feet.

"Get up, asshole," I said.

"Gladly," he replied, and held up a little plastic square I hadn't noticed him holding before. It was black, with one button—a garage door opener. He pressed the button, and the door started to roll up on a massive four-car garage sitting off to the right of the house. "Say hello to my little—"

I punched Petey in the face again before he finished his really shitty Al Pacino impression and dropped him to the ground. "Merle, let the kids loose. Get this bag of shit inside and call the DEA. Tell them you're working with Homeland Security and you have a lead on a major meth operation. Don't call the locals, they're probably in his pocket."

I could hear something as I talked to Merle, a low growling coming from the garage as the door finally locked all the way open. "Hey, Scott?" I asked.

Scott stopped writhing on the ground and looked up at me. "Yeah?"

"Show's over. I think we've got a real problem."

Scott stood up and flicked the mangled 9mm bullet off into the grass. The small-caliber round had slammed right into his stomach, but his thick hide was like a bulletproof vest. It probably still hurt like hell, but he wasn't mortally wounded. Made for a great distraction, though, and gave us the idea that even if Petey shot his wife in the head, she might be okay. We didn't want to try it, but it was a risk we'd taken, and we weren't dead yet.

Yet might have been the operative word there, because what was coming around the corner of the house was…not good. Six lizard men, all the size of Scott or bigger, rounded the corner of the house and stopped cold when they saw us. They all had the twitchy, jerky movements of a junkie looking to score, and I realized why there hadn't been any dogs patrolling the premises—Petey was using lizard men as security here, too, and from the looks of things, he was paying them in crystal meth.

This was not going to be an easy fight, and my sword was laying in the grass twenty feet away. That's what I get for throwing away my best weapon, I guess.

"This is a problem," Scott said.

"Yeah, no shit," Geri replied. She had her MP-7, but it fired similar ammunition to the pistol round that bounced off Scott like a Nerf gun, so I didn't have a whole lot of hope on it being useful here.

"No, it's worse than you think. Remember Cousin Cletus, the asshole in the swamp?"

"Yeah," I said.

"These are all his brothers. His older, meaner brothers, who always loved beating the shit out of me when we were tadpoles."

"And now they're all jacked up on meth, and looking to relive their glory days," Geri said.

"Yep. This is gonna—"

"—suck." I finished what Scott was trying to say, because as soon as he spoke again, the lizard men let out a collective roar. *If I get out of this shit,* I thought, *I am never eating another gator bite as long as I live.*

18

The methhead lizard men stopped in a line about ten yards from us, and sniffed the air, like they were looking for something. Forked tongues flicked the air, and they all turned to stare right at Scott.

"'Sup, Scotty Not Hotty," the largest of the cryptids said. "You miss getting your ass kicked, so you decided to come mess with the bossman? That ain't cool, bro. We're gonna have to rip your head off and shit down your neck now, bro."

Great. Douchebro lizard men. I did not need this in my life. I owned a CrossFit gym for monsters, for God's sake. I never needed to hear another "bro" as long as I lived. Now I was a couple hundred miles from Atlanta and still dealing with steroid-fueled assclowns.

"We don't need to fight, fellas," I said. I certainly didn't need to fight. I had no sword, no gun, and no desire to get up close and personal with a passel of lizard men, even if they hadn't been all hopped up on meth and who knows what else.

"We don't *need* to, fat boy," the leader of the douche lizards replied, flexing to show me his bulging biceps. I didn't need the visual, I was plenty intimidated by the fact that he was nearly eight feet tall with more teeth than I had tattoos. I've got a *lot* of tattoos. "But we *want* to. Especially with our cousin Scott, here. See, Scott's always been a little bit of a beta cuck, and when we're done beating his ass, we're going to show his little wife here what a real monster looks like. After we pick our teeth with your bones, of course."

"Y-y-yeah!" chimed in the skinniest of the douche lizards, a hanger-on if I'd ever seen one. "Pick our teeth with your bones!"

"Shut up, Chad," Head Douche said. "Now Scott, if you just go back to work in the swamp like a good little lizard, we won't have to do anything mean to you. We'll even let you come visit Laura every once in a while. If me and the boys decide to give her a night off." The lizards laughed, but Scott let out a massive roar and charged the whole group of them.

I didn't blame him. If they'd been talking that kind of trash about Amy, I'd have dove right into battle, too. I just wished he'd given us a few more seconds warning beforehand, so we could have figured out what weapons Geri had that might do some good.

I didn't need to worry about her. I sprinted for my sword, getting cut off by a pair of douche lizards. I heard Leeroy and Jenkins let out higher-pitched versions of Scott's rage-filled scream, and Merle's shotgun blew the night wide open with its roar. From Geri's direction I heard a thick, beefy *boom* that reminded me of Bertha, barking out her anger in a deeper sound than any submachine gun I'd ever heard. Obviously she had something up her sleeve in addition to that MP-7.

With my team at least marginally taken care of, or at least surviving, I turned my focus to the pair of muscle heads in front of me. I didn't know if lizard people needed to work out, but whether they needed it or not, these goons had a serious iron-pumping fetish. Each a few inches taller than Scott, their upper torsos and arms were massive, with cords of muscle sticking out everywhere. Their massive upper bodies tapered down to narrow waists, and they had lats that spread out across their backs like sails. It would have been intimidating if they would ever shut up and just growl, but they kept a running discourse about reps, sets, and chasing chicks, all punctuated by "bro" at the end of every sentence. It was like dealing with human incels, only a very little bit slimier.

"Let's ice this bro so we can get first in line for the chick, bro," one of them said.

"Right on, bro," said the other. They bumped fists and turned to me. The second one, we'll call him Tweedle-Dumber, said, "Okay, bro. Time to die."

They charged me, but they obviously weren't used to fighting together, because they immediately bumped shoulders and started shoving each other instead of trying to hit me. I didn't look the gift horse in the mouth, just slipped my hands into the big caestae hanging off my belt and stepped up to the first one, clocking him right in the side of the noggin with my metal-wrapped fist. Caestae are like the offspring of brass knuckles and big welding gloves, with more metal attached. They wrapped my entire hands in bands of metal, and there were threaded holes where I could screw various spikes in, depending on what I thought I'd be fighting. I didn't have anything special attached this time, just the normal rounded studs, so I was just pounding on the lizard with a fistful of metal.

It was effective, snapping his head to the side and dropping him to one knee with the impact. It didn't put him down completely, though, and I barely managed to get my left hand down to block the slash he sent toward my midsection that would have spilled my guts all over Petey's back yard. One more solid shot from my right hand, and Douche Lizard Number One was out.

That left Number Two, and he looked like he was going to be Number Two in a couple different meanings. He hadn't budged when I slugged his buddy, just took a step back and watched. He was bigger than Number One, with arms the size of my thighs, and claws that glinted with metal. I paused for a second and looked around.

"Is he fighting you back here? Like a dog fighting ring, or roosters?" The metal-tipped claws would make sense if this was some kind of perverse cryptid fight club, but it kinda made me wonder how many asshole enterprises Petey was in charge of.

"Not for money," Two said, grinning. "But sometimes he lets us play." The grin that stretched across his face was terrifying. "He lets us play with the humans that piss him off. I think you probably pissed him off when you hit him, so I'm going to play with you while Boss takes a nap."

Great. Now I'm the most wanted toy at Monster Christmas. That's all I friggin' needed. I rolled my head around, cracked my neck, and motioned for Number Two to come and get me. "Come get some, asshole."

He did. He came, and he got some. He got some of my chest, he got some of my neck, and he got a lot more of my fists than he'd bargained for. He launched himself at me like a whirling dervish of slimy skin, twitching muscles, and claws. Lots of claws, all tipped with what felt like razors. I covered up as best I could to try and keep him from slicing open anything fatal, but he was flaying me pretty good for the first few seconds. Then I slipped inside his guard and slammed a metal-clad fist into his midsection, right above where his solar plexus would be if he was human.

Two staggered back, and I followed him, slamming an uppercut into his jaw before throwing a big, looping right cross that smashed his eye closed. He fell to the ground and curled up in a scaly little ball, all the fight knocked right out of him. I hit the ground right after him, the absolute snot knocked out of me as Number One, apparently not nearly as unconscious as I thought he was, nailed me with a flying clothesline that would make Brian Pillman rise from the dead and applaud. I was less impressed, mostly because I was the one in pain. I elbowed the prick in the head, wishing that lizards had ears so I'd have something to grab onto and twist, but there was nothing there, so I elbowed him again and again until he rolled off of me and got to his feet, a little woozy.

I stood up, stretching a little side to side to see if he'd broken anything. It didn't feel like it, but I sure didn't want him to hit me like that again if I could do anything to stop it. And it looked like I was going to have to figure out what to do to stop it real fast, since he dropped his head, let out a loud growl, and ran headfirst at me again.

This time I stepped a little to the left and raised my right knee. I had to stretch to get my leg up high enough, on account of Number One being so damn tall, even bent over, but since he was attempting to drive his skull through my spine, he got low enough, and I gave a little hop right as he met me, and his skull slammed into my knee like a car crash.

Seriously. I've crashed a lot of cars in my time, and the impact of a giant lizard running into my knee was as rough as any of them. Except the time I drove my friend Jimmy's car off a cliff with both of us still inside it. That one was worse.

A deafening *CRACK* split the night, and it felt an awful lot like the thunderclap I heard came from my kneecap. But when I came down, I could stand, albeit a little painfully, and Number One was out cold on the lawn. Somehow, I'd managed to come out the better for that exchange. Or maybe not, since I wasn't unconscious and could feel how bad my knee hurt.

I looked around, and Geri had dispatched two of the Douche Lizards, Scott had one's neck in his mouth and was shaking it vigorously, and Leeroy and Jenkins were ripping the last junkie lizard to shreds and quoting video game dialogue while they did. Apparently not only do lizard people have power in the swamp, they play *Borderlands*.

I looked to where Petey was struggling back up to his feet. He still held the pistol in his right hand, but when he looked over to the snarling Laura, he saw a lizard woman who had burst her bonds, standing next to her lizard husband covered in the blood of his henchmen, and a pair of lizard children who looked as if they'd just taken a bath in scarlet paint.

"I called the feds," Merle said, stepping up next to me. I noticed that while he held the shotgun low, it was still pointed in the general direction of Petey and the Lizards, which would be a killer band name if I could play an instrument. "They oughta be here within the hour. Said they were gonna send a helicopter out of Columbia."

"Hear that, Scott?" I said, loud enough for everyone to hear me. "The DEA is going to drop in here within the hour with enough firepower to take out a tank. We oughta all be gone long before that happens."

Scott just growled, his glare never leaving Petey. The kids bounced up and down next to him like they were getting a piece of birthday cake or something. Laura walked over to me and held out her hand. "Thank you, human," she said.

"You can call me Bubba."

"Thank you, Bubba. You have rescued not only my family, but our entire area, from the vile drugs this man was making and selling. I don't know how we will ever repay you."

I opened my mouth to reply, but Geri cut me off. "If you go back to the swamp and return the Lizard Man, er…Lizard *Family* of South Carolina to mythical status, that's all the thanks we need. If y'all need help, Merle's got our number. I'm guessing there's not a whole lot of email in the wetlands."

"Oh, you'd be surprised," Laura said with a smile that showed off a *lot* of teeth. I took an involuntary step back. "Did you say the other agents would be here in an hour?"

"About that," I said, with a steady gaze to where Petey knelt on the grass in front of Scott and the kids. "I reckon as long as y'all head back into the swamp in about forty-five minutes, you oughta be able to miss them all."

I locked eyes with the tall lizard woman, and she nodded. "We'll be sure to be gone before they get here. Along with our idiot cousins. There might be a little bit of a mess to clean up, though."

"Yeah," I said with a shrug. "That sounds a lot like a DEA problem. Looks like Homeland Security's Paranormal Division's problem is all sorted out." Then I turned around and walked away as Petey screamed into the night.

EPILOGUE

I sat with my back to the gravestone, the same mud clod digging into my ass cheek as the last time I sat here staring at Joe's temporary marker. Skeeter sat next to me, just staring.

"You know I ain't been back here since we buried him, right?" he said.

"I know."

"You been here 'bout every day, haven't you?"

"Yeah," I replied.

"Why?"

"I know he can't hear me, Skeet. I know that if there's a Heaven, and I have it on damn good authority that there is, then Joe's there. He ain't hanging around this boneyard listening to my bullshit." I took a deep breath and collected my thoughts for a few seconds. "But it's for me," I finally said. "It ain't for Joe, or for you, or Geri, or Amy, or anybody. I'm working through some shit, and this is about the best place I can think of to do it."

"You good to share your thinking spot?" he asked. I looked over, and Skeeter wore a look I hadn't seen on his face since middle school. He looked…nervous, like he wasn't sure that I'd say yes.

"Hell, dude," I said, throwing an arm over his shoulder. "I've been counting on you to do most of my thinking for close to thirty years now. If anybody's earned a seat in my thinking spot, it's you, brother."

He didn't say anything, but he didn't move my arm, either. We just sat there for a while in silence. I heard a car pull up, turn off, and two doors open.

Skeeter looked at me. "You expecting somebody?"

"Yeah, I reckon I am," I said.

Amy walked past where the two of us sat, knelt in front of Joe's grave, and set a spray of lilies on the ground where his headstone would eventually be placed. Then she reached out and trailed her fingers across the little cardboard placard before sitting down next to me and nestling under my other arm. Geri hopped up on the tombstone behind where we sat and dangled her feet down over my shoulders.

"Hey," Amy said.

"Hey," me and Skeeter replied simultaneously.

"So…there were no bad guys on the scene when the DEA arrived in South Carolina," Amy said.

"Really?" I replied, mock surprise covering my face. "How in the world did that happen? I suppose the head of the redneck drug cartel must have slipped away in all the confusion."

"If he did, he slipped away missing about three quarts of blood, because that's how much the crime scene techs estimate was sprayed out across the back yard, pool house, patio, and the windows on the back of the house, including the ones on the second floor."

"That's a lot of blood. Sounds like someone was angry," Geri said.

"You two don't know anything about this, do you?" Amy asked.

"He was alive when we left, and we made sure to tell the lizard folk that they needed to be back in the swamp before the feds got there," I said.

"You have no idea what happened to him?" Amy asked.

"I could make a few guesses, but I reckon whatever happened to him was better than he deserved," I said.

"What happened to not killing humans, Mr. Monster Hunter?" Amy asked.

"Petey might have been *homo sapien*, but he was no man. He was a walking piece of trash who profited off hurting people and took glee in causing pain. I reckon what happened to him was more justice than anything we could have dealt out to him, and this way we ain't gotta worry about him making parole."

"A little biblical, isn't it, babe?" she asked.

"Could be." I nodded. "But some problems require Old Testament solutions."

"Is that what Joe would want?" Amy asked.

"Not even close," I said. "But I ain't half the man Joe was, and I ain't a quarter the Christian he was. I'm just a big dumb redneck with a sword, a set of oversized brass knuckles, and a good team beside me. And I reckon that's all I need."

"Yeah, I reckon it is," Amy said, and laid her head against my shoulder as the sun rose over the Georgia mountains.

The End

UNHOLY GROUND

1

"You know it's never Satanists, right?" I said, talking into thin air and expecting a real human being to respond, as one does in the twenty-first century. I had just loaded up the truck and was headed out on my first solo run in a long time. Amy was stuck in D.C. working, Geri had gone down to Atlanta to look in on my werewolf CrossFit gym, and Skeeter…well, we try not to take Skeeter out into the field if we can avoid it. I've made it almost forty years without getting shot by friendly fire, and I have no desire to end that streak.

A mostly real human being with an unreal high-pitched squeaky voice replied through the Bluetooth/cell phone/satellite radio/GPS/personal computer/NASA launch controller/ICBM missile launcher/coffeemaker built into the dash of my F-250 pickup. Seriously, I have no idea what all this thing does, but I'm always afraid that if I tap the wrong piece of computer screen, my pickup truck will either eject me through the roof or start a shooting war with Russia.

"Bubba, I know it's never Satanists, but sometimes it's bad people using cryptids and blaming it on Satanists, or sometimes it's demons masquerading as Satanists. Both of those fall under our charter from Homeland Security," Skeeter said, in his "please stop arguing with me and just accept that I'm right, again" tone of voice.

I didn't stop arguing. He's been using that tone of voice on me for better than twenty-five years, and it's never worked once. Props to him

99

for keeping up with the attempts, though. "What do you mean, 'our charter'? We ain't got a charter. We're independent contractors, the racist shitheads. We ain't gotta do nothing but show up, shoot shit, and go home."

I was still barred from working for the Department of Homeland Security's Paranormal Division by some rule about having to be completely human to work there. And on account of my mother being a fairy, I don't exactly meet those criteria. Skeeter, my fiancée Amy, and our reprobate sidekick/teenage ward/hanger-on/resident psychopath Geri are all completely human, so they get regular paychecks and insurance. Me, I'm stuck reporting as an independent contractor and buying insurance off some guy out back of the Dollar General.

"The white guy telling the Black gay guy that a government agency is racist like it's supposed to be news to me might be the most Karen thing I've ever heard you say, Bubba," Skeeter replied, reminding me that I never get into battles of wits with my best friend because I'm usually unarmed.

"Whatever," I grunted. "Where am I going and what am I looking for when I get there?"

"This is a close one. You're headed up to North Carolina, just outside Raleigh, and you're meeting a Brother Zara. Zara has seen some signs in recent news articles and events that seem out of the ordinary to him, and since he's been useful to the department in the past, this got more attention than the average redneck report of Satanists in the Carolinas would get."

I put both hands on the wheel as I bounced down my long driveway to the main road, then turned right to head down my mountain so I could pick up the highway to North Carolina. At least it was a pretty drive, if long. There's just no good way to get from my chunk of North Georgia mountains to that particular slice of the middle of North Carolina, so it ended up taking me most of a day to get there.

Asheboro, NC, is nice, if stretching a little bit to call itself a city. More of a town with aspirations, it's home to the North Carolina Zoo and not much else, besides the GPS coordinates Skeeter had given me for the Church of Christ the Redeemer of All Mankind Fellowship, which turned out to be a prefabricated metal building indistinguishable from the Rhino Linings franchise on one side of it and the small engine repair shop on the other.

Except for the graffiti. Lots of graffiti, most of it really badly drawn, and a lot of it suggesting that Jesus, Mary, and all of the Apostles should do rude and potentially physically impossible things to each other, and themselves. Sides of buildings and business dumpsters sported all the low-rent devil worship signs—upside down crosses, pentacles with the point aimed down, the numbers "666" painted all over the place, crude devil head images with horns and goat faces—if you were a disaffected loner in high school, you probably wore all the symbols on one or more Slayer t-shirts.

A slim man with a massive beard and blond dreadlocks sat on a stump just outside the door with an array of paint cans, rollers, and other graffiti cleanup gear spread out on the gravel lot around him. "Took you long enough. I thought Director Pravesh was sending someone out right away."

"You Brother Zara?" I asked as I walked up. I was unarmed for this encounter, and I felt a little naked without any of my gear, but since this dude was maybe a hundred-fifty pounds soaking wet, didn't look like he took lessons from Jet Li, and smelled of cheap marijuana, I thought I could probably take him. Unless he started throwing fireballs. Recent experience had taught me that sometimes skinny dudes have more under the hood than I expect.

"Yes, I am Brother Zara. You can call me Evan." He stood up and held out his hand.

We shook and I waved at the walls. "So, this looks like vandalism, but nothing to get the federal government involved with. Have they done anything more than scribble on your walls, or did I just drive half a day to be irritated for nothing?"

"Do you know where you are, Agent…?"

"Brabham," I supplied, glossing over the fact that I'm not really an agent. I'm more of a…special projects consultant, as far as the government is concerned, but Brother Skunk Weed here didn't need all the details about my employment. "I'm somewhere between the place with all the golf courses, the place with all the pottery, the place with the lions, and Raleigh, right?"

I spent a lot more time in North Carolina last year than I wanted to, and most of it was pretty painful, but so far nothing in this case had me crossing paths with Quincy Harker, or setting foot in the city of Charlotte. But as far as the rest of the state went, I kinda just looked at most of North Carolina as "places bad football teams come from."

"You're just a little northwest of Harper's Crossroads, and if you get back on the main road and turn left, you'll notice a little pull-off on your right about a hundred yards up the highway. Walk back off the road a bit, and you'll be in a spot known as the Devil's Tramping Ground. Sound familiar?"

Oh yeah, now *that* was a place I'd heard of. I thought it was in the mountains, but I hadn't really spent all that much time thinking about it, just read a *Brotherhood of the Wheel* book that mentioned it once. Supposedly, it's a circle of ground deep in the Carolina woods where nothing grows because that's where Satan paces around thinking up new ways to torture humanity. Now, I don't know Lucifer personally, and I plan to keep it that way, but I can't imagine why one of the most powerful beings in the universe would walk around in circles in the woods of North Carolina thinking up ways to cause trouble when he could just hang out in Vegas playing blackjack or something, but who am I to question the ways of mystical beings?

"Huh," I said, confused. "What does that have to do with your church getting spray painted? Is it demonic paint?"

Brother Evan looked at me and sighed. "No, it isn't demonic paint, Agent Brabham, but the vandalism at my church was undoubtedly caused by the same coven of witches that have been practicing Satanic rituals on a regular basis at the Devil's Tramping Ground. There are Satanists in our community, and the government needs to do something about it!" For a skinny guy, he could get loud when agitated. And he was certainly agitated.

"Well, Brother Evan," I said in my best placating voice, which isn't very good, I'll admit, "if all they're doing is performing rituals, and they aren't actually summoning demons or putting hexes on people, there's not a whole lot the government can do. Freedom of religion and all that, you know."

"But they're obviously doing more than rituals!" he said, gesticulating wildly at his walls. "Look at this mess!"

"Yep, it's a mess," I said. "But until there's something more than vandalism, it's not a *federal government* mess. Right now, it looks more like a local sheriff's department misdemeanor mess." And it looked like I'd just driven almost eight hours for nothing. Maybe I'd stop on the way home and check out some of this Lexington Barbecue I kept hearing about.

"Well, what about this?" Brother Evan asked, reaching into the red Igloo cooler on the ground by his stump/chair. He pulled out the carcass of some indistinguishable animal, literally dripping blood and maggots back into the cooler. I really hoped he wasn't planning on taking that thing to the family reunion this year.

The animal was about the right size to be a rabbit, or maybe a possum or a giant-sized squirrel. I couldn't tell what it was because it wasn't just skinned, it was flayed, decapitated, gutted, and parts amputated until it was unrecognizable. "What the hell is that?" I said, fanning the air as the sickly-sweet stench of decomposition rolled over me.

"This was nailed to my door when I arrived at the church this morning," Evan said. He pointed to the huge spike sticking out of the critter's chest. "This is a nine-inch nail, just like the ones used to crucify Our Lord and Savior Jesus Christ. What do you think about your vandalism now?"

I stumbled a bit over the whole "Our Lord and Savior Jesus Christ" thing. I have no problem with the title, but the way Brother I Wish I Was Bob Marley said it, the words all ran together like it was one big contraction: "Ourlordandsaviorjesuschrist." I kinda wondered how long he had to practice it before he could say it without tripping over his own tongue. "I think it's grosser vandalism, and smellier, but still vandalism."

"This is a hate crime! This is more persecution of Christians by the unbelievers! I want you to go up to those heathen lesbian bitches in Raleigh and tell them to stay the hell out of my town, and to stay the hell away from my church!"

Okay, now it made sense. Brother Patchouli had apparently had a run-in with some Wiccans in Raleigh at some point, and now everything bad that happened anywhere near him was going to get blamed on witches and Satanists because none of this spray paint and dead…rabbit, maybe? could *possibly* ever be the work of anyone not a horrible, devil-worshipping homosexual. It could *never* be done by any of the grease-spattered rednecks laughing their asses off by the roll-up door of the engine repair shop not fifty yards away.

Nope, that collection of coveralls and diesel fuel couldn't possibly have been yanking the chain of their histrionic hippie preacher neighbor. Nope, had to be Satanist lesbians. But just in case it wasn't Satanists (because it's *never* Satanists), I left Brother Homophobia in mid-rant and started walking over to the collection of hillbillies chewing tobacco and watching the fireworks. Just in case they *might* know something about something. Just in case.

2

The leader of the redneck heckler's club walked, or limped, rather, to meet me. He was a big man, even compared to me, and I displace a lot of water, to say the least. The bulge of a knee brace showed through his right pantleg, and he had the kind of face that made you think somebody hit him upside the head with a shovel. A lot.

He wore an unbuttoned blue work shirt over a tank top smeared with engine grease and several substances I didn't want to know the origin of. The name "Phil" was emblazoned over his right breast, which I judged to be a healthy B-cup, if not moving all the way toward a C. He had on those double-kneed twill work pants that only come in colors meant to hide stains, and thick-soled work boots. I was willing to bet that if I wrestled a boot off his foot, I'd probably find imprints of those size fifteens all along the walls of Brother Dank Bud's church.

"'Sup?" he asked when he was about ten feet away.

"Just here investigating some vandalism," I replied, reaching into my back pocket for my Homeland Security credentials. I'd learned the trick of flipping the badge wallet open while holding my thumb over the part of the ID that read "CONTRACTOR." No point in raising questions about my validity as a federal agent in front of the locals.

"Since when does Homeland Security come all the way down to North Carolina to see about some spray paint?" Phil asked.

"Since there has been a string of similar cases of vandalism against small houses of worship all up and down the east coast in the past six months. We investigate cases of religious persecution very seriously." Which was complete bullshit, of course. This was the first case of any kind I'd caught from DHS in the month I'd been back from the South Carolina swamps. I might've been in the doghouse with the bosses on account of the high number of corpses, human and otherwise, we scattered around the countryside. Or they mighta been pissed about the meth lab blowing up in the swamp, which totally wasn't my fault. Or it could be they weren't happy with me basically letting the richest man in town get eaten by swamp-dwelling lizard people. If I had any regrets, it was for the digestive systems of the lizard folk after they ate that dickhead. There is no way meat that rotten could sit well on the stomach.

But anyway. I didn't know shit about any string of religious persecution going on, and I'm pretty sure the only persecuting going on around this joint was Phil and his buddies screwing with the local hippie preacher for funsies.

"Man, I hope you get on up there to Raleigh and arrest them bitches. They been causing all kinds of trouble ever since they started coming down here doing their coven shit out in the woods by the Trampin' Ground," Phil said, looking over his shoulder. "I gotta be honest, man, I didn't think we'd get anybody from the federal government coming down here lookin' at stuff. I thought we was just gonna get more of Sheriff Shithead and his Dingleberry Deputies farting around and not doing nothing."

He stepped up and gestured at himself and his buddies. "If me or any of my boys can help, you just let us know. You can deputize us or whatever. We all got our own guns."

Well, that was not what I'd expected. He actually looked scared when he was talking about the "witches in Raleigh." I was starting to think I might have to talk to this coven after all.

Now, I've got nothing against witches. I've run into a fair number of practitioners since starting this job, and most of them are harmless, just middle-aged women who like to run around outside in the woods and ask their Great Mother for help in making their crops grow, or helping keep mice out of their houses, or whatever. Nothing real serious, except for a couple cases of frostbite I heard about when a Vermont coven decided that a foot of snow was no reason not to conduct their Winter Solstice ritual outdoors, and "skyclad." That means buck-ass naked, for the non-witches in the crowd.

But this was the second mention of this Raleigh coven in five minutes, and while neither Brother Doobie Doobie Doo nor Helpful Phil were the most dependable of sources, just because a lead comes from a dumbass doesn't mean you don't follow it up. A stopped clock is right twice a day and all that.

"Brother…Evan seems to think they are the most likely culprits, too," I said, once I could remember Brother Stonerpants' real name. Maybe I got a contact high just standing next to him. Can people exude marijuana from their pores? Because that guy smelled like he'd been playing Twister with Tommy Chong.

"Well, Evan's a dumbass, but he ain't a mean dumbass. If he thinks they done it, they probably did do it," Phil said.

I took a second to untangle the tenses in his statement, then just shook my head a little and asked, "What makes you think the witches did this?"

"Their High Priestess, or Head Witch, or whatever you call it, got into a big hollerin' match with Brian when he and some of his 'flock' went over and peed on the witches' candles during one of their ceremonies. He said they cursed him and all his congregation."

"Cursed him like cussed him up one side and down the other, or cursed him like turned him into a toad?" I asked.

Phil scratched his head, then said, "Both, I reckon. I mean, talking to Brian, they put a hex on him, and that's why his bus broke down the next week, and he lost his keys, and he fell down and spent a whole night outside on account of he couldn't remember how to stand up. But I reckon they probably gave him a good cussin' too."

"You think any of his problems might could be explained by him smoking a metric shitton of weed and driving around in a VW bus that's older than he is?" I pointed at the bus in question, the one that looked like it had been following the Grateful Dead around since Jerry Garcia was skinny. And alive.

Phil chuckled. "Yeah, that's what I thought, too. But we don't ask Brian a whole lot of questions. You do that, and you're gonna hear a hell of a lot more than you ever wanted to about Judgement Day, and the Rapture, and Whores of Babylon. Does Babylon even exist anymore?"

"Not for a couple thousand years, I don't think," I said. "But is his name Brian or Evan? I'm getting confused."

"His mama and daddy named him Brian. He's my second cousin once removed on my daddy's side, and that whole side of the family's a little too into their Jesus for the rest of us. He decided that he was gonna be

Brother Evan after his mama died and he started his church. But I've always thought he was a little bit of a pretentious shithead, so I still call him Brian to take him down a notch or two and remind him that some of us knew him when he was still pissing his pants at Little League tryouts."

"Okay," I said. That was a little more family history than I was expecting, but that's how rednecks are. You get one talking, and you'll get the whole family tree if you don't stop 'em. "What about your boys? They all think the witches did this, or could they have maybe wanted to take Brother Evan down a peg or two themselves?" I still thought the good ol' boys were more likely to paint Dio album cover art all over the side of a building than a bunch of Wiccans from most of an hour away, so I wasn't quite ready to abandon this line of investigation.

"Nah," Phil said. "They didn't do this. They know my daddy does maintenance for the mean-ass lady that owns this whole industrial park, so if they painted that shit on one of her buildings, and he found out we made him have to scrub spray paint off the walls, they'd be in for the ass-whooping of their lives." The "industrial park" was a collection of six metal-framed buildings in a cul-de-sac, but given that we were in Bumblefuck, North Carolina, that was what passed for massive commercial development. And that made Phil's father's boss a redneck real estate tycoon, definitely not somebody his son's buddies would want to get on the wrong side of.

Looked like I was gonna have to go talk to some witches about some spray paint. Yippee. I like nothing better than going into an unfamiliar business in an unfamiliar town and telling somebody who might actually be able to turn me into a toad that I think they're criminals. That's my idea of a perfect afternoon. I really needed to get into my truck and use the dashboard computer thingamajig to find me a titty bar in Raleigh. I had a serious feeling that I was gonna need some alcohol and nudity after my interrogation of witches.

3

It was almost dark by the time I pulled into the parking lot of the strip mall housing a PetSmart, a Bruegger's, an Ulta salon (or salon supply store, or maybe makeup store. I dunno. I've still got enough toxic masculinity coursing through my veins that I wasn't even able to slow down walking past the window) and a small hole in the wall with a hand-painted window proclaiming it "Mother's Haven Books and Baubles." Between driving up from Georgia, talking to Brother Dankness and the Redneck Mafia out in Shitsville, then making a pit stop at the Devil's Tramping Ground on my way back to Raleigh, most of my day had been completely blown. Add to that the fact that Raleigh was doing its best damn Atlanta traffic impression while I was trying to get from Point A to Point D, and I was a grumpy, sweaty mess with a sore back when I pushed through the glass door into Mother's Haven.

A tiny brass bell jingled as I stepped through, and I was instantly enveloped in the scent of sandalwood, frankincense, sage, and lavender. The combination of scents was soothing, despite my deep-seated loathing of anything in the same time zone as patchouli, and I could almost feel the rage draining out through the soles of my Wolverine work boots. A short woman with dark hair dyed deep blue at the tips limped out from behind a spinner rack of postcards and said, "Oh my! You're a large one, aren't you? I was expecting a strike force of government troops, but I never imagined they would try to fit an entire platoon in one body!"

Well, there was a lot to unpack there, and I stood like Medusa's own prom date while my brain tried to pull the tangle of words into a coherent thought. "You…were expecting me?"

A broad smile split her rounded features and she laughed. "Oh yes! Brother Evan was very clear that he had called in reinforcements from the federal government and that a heavily armed strike force was en route to apprehend me at any moment. He said that if I was lucky, they'd just use a drone to blow me out of existence from a thousand miles in the air, but that I'd probably be carted off to Gitmo instead."

Even more to unpack there. "Um, first of all, we don't send people to Gitmo. I'm not with the Gitmo department." DHS's Paranormal Division might or might not have taken control of some of DEMON's more despicable black sites and cryptic prisons, but I knew for a fact that none of those were in Cuba. Mostly because you don't want to ship monsters by boat or plane. If you've got to transport something with machetes for fingernails that might breathe fire or open a dimensional rift by farting, it's better to do that in a convoy of very large, very well-armed trucks.

"Well, that's a relief," the woman said. It was tempting to think of her as a fairy godmother type, but so far, she was a lot nicer than any fairy I'd encountered, and given my heritage, I probably *have* a fairy godmother and will be much happier if I never meet her.

"We also don't do drone strikes." I don't think we do drone strikes, anyway. "And I'm just here to ask you a few questions, not storm Normandy."

"Good, because I think Normandy has already been well and truly stormed. Please come in, Mr….?"

"Brabham," I said, pulling out my credentials.

The lady took my badge wallet rather than letting me hold it up to her, and I saw her eyebrow go up as she noted the red "CONTRACTOR" stamp on my ID. She didn't ask, and I didn't volunteer any information. That was something I picked up watching Harker work. The less he talked, the more the bad guys were willing to talk to him, and he gave away almost nothing while they spilled their entire plans right in front of God and everybody. After a few seconds of study, she handed my credentials back to me.

"I don't know why I bothered looking," she said. "I wouldn't know a real badge from a fake. I'm Wanda, and this is my shop. I'm also the High Priestess of our coven, so I expect I'm the person you want to speak to. I found the 'contractor' designation on your badge interesting. Why are you a contractor, Mr. Brabham?"

"The agency and I have some differing views on who exactly should be allowed to handle the cases that fall under their purview." That specific line of bullshit was taken directly from an argument I had with Director Pravesh. "Argument" might be overselling it a little. It was more like I yelled at her about their speciesist policies, and she nodded while doing exactly jack and shit about it.

"You mean they won't hire you because you're not human?" the little shopkeeper asked, stopping me in my tracks. "Oh, come on, Mr. Brabham. I'm a witch. You don't think I know what a fairy smells like? Not to mention you set off every detection charm in the building the minute you touched my door."

"Let's back off the whole 'not human' designation a little," I said. "I spent the first thirty-something years of my life being human, and as far as I can tell, I still am." My mom's a fairy, sure, but I don't have wings, I can handle iron, and I'm way too big to run around cosplaying Tinkerbelle.

"One drop is all it takes, remember?" she asked. "For the government, at least. It's why I check all the boxes on the 'race' section of forms. Because there's so many different people all piled together in my gene pool, there's no way you can pick just one. I'm like an ethnicity Chex Mix. I've got Asian, Latino, Black, and Jewish in the last two generations, and further back than that, there's some Native blood. Of course, it's all diluted by my parents, both of whom were pale enough to pass, so I've only ever gotten the religious discrimination, not the racial stuff. Well, and the lesbian thing, too. But you spent your whole life as a white man, then found out you're not just not completely white, you aren't completely human. What did that do to your sense of self?"

By this point, she had masterfully steered me through the narrow shop, winding between shelves of New Age books, apothecary cabinets bursting with herbs and strange powders, and shelf after shelf of candles. Good lord and butter, the candles. Short candles, tall candles, skinny candles, fat candles, all in varying colors and scents. It was like sticking my head into a perfume counter, only somehow not the least bit cloying. She walked around a small card table draped in a colorful fabric and sat down in a folding chair. She gestured toward another one for me, but I took one look at it and decided standing was the better option. It's real hard to pull off the "intimidating government agent" look when you're flat on your ass with a folding chair bent into a pretzel beneath your ass.

"I don't even know where to start responding to that question, but can we circle back around to how you knew I was part fairy? I mean, I made it three decades without having a clue, and it didn't take you three minutes to figure it out."

She smiled up at me from the table and gestured toward the chair again. "Sit down, Mr. Brabham, and I'll explain. I promise, the chair is sturdier than it looks, and I'm not going to read your cards with you looming over me like some low-rent Andre the Giant."

I sat down. I didn't think I had a choice. This woman had so thoroughly owned me within minutes of our introduction that my head was spinning a little trying to keep up with her rapid-fire speech. "Okay, I'm sitting. Now how do you know I'm fae?"

"I can smell it," she said simply, pulling a deck of Tarot cards and shuffling them idly as she spoke. She didn't put any kind of ceremony to it, no flashy mumbling or making all kinds of mystical noises. She just shuffled the cards and kept on talking. "Every supernatural creature gives off signals to their nature. There are differences in auras, for those who can see them, different ways they appear in Second Sight, if you have that, and there are certain scents that accompany most creatures. Sasquatches tend to smell a little skunky, which is where the name 'skunk ape' came from. Vampires smell like churned dirt, which is where the old wives' tales of them digging their way out of coffins and sleeping in the dirt of their homeland came from."

"And fairies? What do I smell like?" That's a pretty loaded question on a lot of days, but I'd had a pretty bland diet so far that afternoon, so the immediate answer was unlikely to be "stale beer and farts," which was not an uncommon aroma in my vicinity.

"Fairies smell like pine trees and cinnamon. It's quite a pleasant odor, actually, which is how many of your kind get close enough to prey to disembowel them." She paused, her eyes flicking up to mine with a moment of concern. "You aren't here to disembowel me, are you? I just had the floors redone last summer, and I'd hate to ruin them with viscera."

"No viscera-ing here," I said, making a mental note to look up "viscera" on my phone when I got back to the truck. "I just need some information."

"About Evan and his vandalism?" she asked, laying the cards out in a pattern on the purple cloth she had spread across the card table.

"Okay, I'm pretty sure I don't give off some kind of 'I'm going to ask you about a dope-smoking preacher forty miles away' scent, so how the hell did you know I was gonna ask about Reverend Rasta?"

"I told you as soon as you walked in. He called me crowing about my imminent rendition, remember?"

Oh, yeah. She got me so turned around with the fairy thing I'd plumb forgot about that. "Okay, then, did you?"

She looked puzzled. "Did I what?"

"Did you vandalize Brother Evan's church?"

"Oh, Lady," she said. "No, neither I nor any member of our circle had anything to do with painting badly drawn Satanic symbols on Evan's walls. He's an idiot, but a harmless idiot. He runs like a scared puppy if we just wiggle our fingers in his general direction, but he's never caused us any problems."

"What about his congregant taking a leak on one of your candles during a ceremony?" I asked. "That's a pretty good motive. I've seen people do a lot worse over a lot less."

She laughed. A big, lean back in her chair with her bright blue hair cascading over her shoulders and back kind of laugh. The kind where the laugher can't even talk for a few seconds until they get themselves back under control. "You mean the ceremony where Evan brought a pair of terrified teenagers out to watch us performing our 'heresy' in the Devil's Tramping Ground and when he got there all he found was a bunch of women in a circle singing songs and trying to consecrate the ground that has been very obviously defiled by something big and nasty many years ago?"

"Yeah, I reckon. Way I heard it was some of his guys peed on your candles during a ceremony, and you yelled at Evan about it."

"Well, one of the boys definitely peed himself, but he had his pants on when he did it. Evan had those boys convinced that we'd turn them all into toads if we saw them, and of course we saw them. The woods around the Tramping Ground are thin, and nothing grows in the circle itself. Not to mention that Evan smells like dank weed from twenty yards away. They tried to spy on our ritual, probably because they heard a rumor we do our rituals skyclad, and when they didn't see any boobies, they got restless and made too much noise, so I shouted at them to leave. One of the boys got turned around trying to run back to their car and stumbled into the circle, knocking over the West candle. He had already peed himself by that point, so I suppose it's possible he got some on the candle, but I don't really know. I was so busy yelling at Evan for scaring those poor children I didn't notice."

"You were yelling at him for…"

"For dragging those boys out into the woods on a school night and scaring the crap out of them when they should have been home studying. Or at least somewhere doing something interesting, not sitting in the woods watching a bunch of old ladies chant and dance around in a circle. Inasmuch as our arthritis lets us dance much anymore."

I took a good look at the woman in front of me, who didn't look like she did a whole lot of dancing. She walked with a cane and had a list to one side when she walked. She looked to be around sixty but dressed like a twenty-something flower child in flowing jewel tones, Birkenstock clogs, and more rings, necklaces, and earrings than I've seen on anyone outside a sci-fi movie.

"Yeah, I can't speak to the rest of your coven, but you certainly don't look like anybody who's dancing with the devil in the pale moonlight," I said.

"Well, if you'd like to check out the dancing shoes on the rest of the girls, they should start trickling in any minute. It's Thursday night, which means *Supernatural* reruns and homemade peach brandy in the back room. If you're interested, feel free to stick around and talk to the ladies."

And that is how I ended up shitfaced drunk in the back room of a witch's supply store on a Thursday night.

4

There are very few things I hate more than being woken up by a cell phone. Income taxes, dry counties, quarterbacks escaping contain, the Florida Gators, speed traps, and remixes of songs that aren't as good as the original are a few that leap to mind. Okay, so maybe there's a bunch of stuff I hate more than a cell phone waking me up, but all that stuff sucks, too.

Regardless, I managed not to throw the phone against the wall of my hotel room, which was a good thing since as I looked around, I realized that I wasn't *in* my hotel room. I answered the phone, needing to solve at least one mystery before I moved on to the one about where the hell I was.

"Yeah?" I grunted, which is pretty eloquent for me pre-coffee. And pre-Advil, this morning, now that I was awake enough to realize exactly how hung over I was.

"Where the hell are you, Bubba?" Deputy Director Amy Hall, my fiancée and boss, sounded like she was annoyed with me. Made sense, given the fact that being my boss was probably even more irritating than being my fiancée, and without the dubious upsides of sleeping with me.

"I'm…not real sure," I replied, looking around. I was in a dark room, but whatever I was laying on was pretty comfortable. I reached over and found a lamp, then flicked it on to reveal the screening room/parlor in the back of Mother's Haven, the New Age bookstore/witch's supply store where I'd come to interrogate the owner and ended up bingeing *Supernatural* and drinking way more peach brandy than I probably should have.

Nope. Make that *definitely* more peach brandy than I should have drank. "I…might be a little drunk, still." Note to self: witches brew their brandy *stout*.

"I can't let you go anywhere without adult supervision, can I?" Amy asked, and I was pretty sure I heard that same rueful grin in her voice that I had grown accustomed to seeing on her face.

"Yeah, that's a negative, Ghost Rider," I quoted back to her.

"Okay, we're outside your hotel, and when I didn't see your truck outside, I got worried. I'll get Skeeter to track your phone and we'll be there soon. Try not to get in any trouble before we find you, and there had better not be a hottie curled up next to you when I get there."

She clicked off before I could ask her if calicos counted as "hotties," since the shop cat was currently making biscuits on my left thigh. "Sorry, Miss Kitty," I said. "I gotta pee." I stood up, wobbled a little, then smoothed my rat's nest of hair down and looked around for the can. I found it, took care of business, and stumbled out to the front of the shop, where Wanda the Iron-Livered stood behind the counter, humming along merrily to what I could only assume was the latest Zamfir, Master of the Pan Flute, CD.

"How are we feeling this morning?" Wanda asked, a laugh in her voice.

"Well, I don't know about you, lady, but I feel like I've been shot at and missed and shit at and hit."

"Have a cup of tea," she said, pointing to a pot on the counter. "It cures hangovers."

I did as I was told, sucking down a cup of tea like it was water in the desert. I immediately felt the pain in my head lessen, whether from a placebo effect or magic, I didn't care. "What the hell was in that tea?" I asked when I could stand to hear the echo in my skull again.

"Just my normal Thursday night brew—a little hemp extract, some CBD oil, ginger, Jägermeister, Fireball, Earl Grey, and hot water."

My mind boggled at that mix of ingredients. "You gave me weed tea spiked with Jäger and Fireball?" Despite her kindly appearance, this was *not* a witch to fuck around with, as I was finding out.

"Pretty much," she replied. "But your hangover's gone, isn't it?"

It was, in fact. "Yeah, you win. Sorry I passed out on your couch," I said, embarrassed. It's been a long time since anybody drank me under the table, and I felt an overwhelming need to bench press a car or something to prove my worth. I decided to just sit down like a good boy and wait for my ride. "Did anything…happen last night?" I asked.

Wanda laughed. "Oh, my dear boy, no! You're very sweet, and a cute drunk. But you're not my type. I like my men a little older, and to not be men."

I blushed even more. "Um, thanks, but that's not what I meant. My boss just called, and she's here. Which means she flew in first thing this morning, and I don't know why. So did anything bad happen last night? Like, newsworthy bad?"

"Oh! Not that I know of, but I stopped taking the paper around here when they let the Baptists run a full-page ad condemning our coven and urging people to run us out of town. That's when I had to get those installed." She pointed to the bars on the door and window.

"Wow, that sucks," I said. I'm not all that eloquent at my best, and even less so when the room is spinning. "I'm gonna go outside and wait for my ride. I think I might need a little Vitamin D after last night's escapades." That, and I was now genuinely afraid to drink anything this lady gave me. She might not be casting spells on the teapot, but she was certainly playing around with some serious chemistry. God only knew what she was going to make for lunch, roast beef sandwiches with LSD mustard?

Amy pulled up half an hour later in a stereotypical black Suburban, the car of choice for federal agents everywhere, and she and Geri slid out. She walked toward where I was sitting on the sidewalk outside the shop and stopped about ten feet away. "Jesus Christ, Bubba, what did you drink? I can smell the booze from here."

"Which time?" I asked. "I drank way too much peach brandy last night, and my host apparently thinks the cure for a hangover isn't the hair of the dog that bit you, but the hair of every dog within two blocks, because she dosed me with Jäger, Fireball, and weed."

"Not to mention ibuprofen, caffeine, and pseudoephedrine," Wanda said, poking her head out the shop door. "Would you care to come in and have a cuppa?"

Amy held up both hands, palms out. "I think I'd better pass. I'm actually employed by the federal government, so I can't drink anything that would show up on a drug test."

"Oh, I have teas for that, too," the blue-haired witch replied. Some of the things she was saying made me think she might be supplementing her pan flute CD sales and tarot readings with a little dispensing of the wacky tobacky. Fine with me. Weed never made anybody spray-paint things on buildings, and it sure never summoned any demons. The worst thing it ever caused was a serious case of the munchies.

Speaking of munchies. "Hey, can we get breakfast?" I asked Amy. "Whatever sucks bad enough to bring you down here is probably something I shouldn't deal with on an empty stomach."

"Bubba, the only way to deal with the shit we're in is on an empty stomach," Amy said, gesturing to the Suburban. "Get in. Geri's driving your truck."

"The hell she is!"

"The hell she isn't. You can't even stand up straight, and you smell like a distillery. A citrus-scented distillery, but a distillery nonetheless. And you just told me you drank herbal tea with magic herb in it, so there's literally no way I'm letting you drive right now. If you get in the truck, I'll drive through Bojangles on the way back down to Asheboro."

"Oh dear," Wanda said, her face taking on a worried expression. "Something bad did happen, didn't it?"

Amy turned to her. "Yes, ma'am, it did. Someone was killed last night at Brother Evan's church."

"Who was it?" the witch asked.

"We haven't made an identification or notified next of kin yet, so we can't disclose who we think the victim may be."

"And you think this murder is somehow connected to the vandalism?" Wanda asked.

"There are…certain indications at the crime scene that make us think that, yes." Wow. Amy was being circumspect as all get-out. Like, I'd never seen her dance around a topic like that before. I wasn't sure if it meant Madame Wanda was still a suspect, or if whatever happened at the church was so bad she didn't want to screw up the poor woman's dreams for the rest of her life.

I wasn't looking forward to the photos I knew I was going to be looking at as we headed to the crime scene. Anything bad enough to drag Amy down here from DC must be pretty awful. Even with that, I was glad she was there. Ever since she went to work for DHS, we don't see nearly as much of each other as we'd both like, so if it took one redneck getting murdered for us to have some time together, well…there's a lot of rednecks. The world could spare a couple.

I heaved myself to my feet, a troublesome enough proposition when the sidewalk stays where it's supposed to be. When the damn thing keeps rolling like a surfboard, it makes it even harder. I held out a hand to

Madame Wanda, and she shook it. "Ma'am, thank you for the hospitality, and the tea. I apologize again for passing out on your couch, but that was some damned fine peach brandy. As much fun as this all was, I sincerely hope that I don't have to see you again on this trip, because if I do, it means that some other dumbass is making accusations that force me to drive an hour each way to find out that y'all ain't running around the countryside spray-painting buildings."

"But look on the bright side, Mr. Brabham," Wanda said. "We've got Neria cooking up pumpkin bread for movie night tomorrow. And you don't want to miss Tansy's 'special' cocoa, if you know what I mean."

Stoner witches. This is not what I expected when I came to North Carolina. At least, not this part of North Carolina. Asheville or Boone, sure, but Raleigh's supposed to be a little more straight-laced. So much for my preconceptions.

I spread my arms out to Amy, looking for a hug and a kiss from my fiancée. After all, we hadn't seen each other in a few days, but she wrinkled her nose instead. "We're riding with the windows down. You reek of patchouli and liquor farts. You have got to be the stinkiest fairy in the world." She turned and headed to her Suburban.

I shrugged. "I never knew she didn't like patchouli," I said, following her.

"Pretty sure that's not what she was objecting to," Wanda said as she limped along behind me. She made pretty good time for a woman with a bum knee, so I figured it was an old injury that she'd just grown accustomed to. I had enough of those that my spine sounded like a bowl of Rice Krispies every morning, so I could relate.

"Yeah, but everybody farts," I replied. "Can't get mad about that."

"Everybody farts, Mr. Brabham," Wanda agreed. "But I can say without a doubt that you are in a league of your own as far as flatulence goes."

Well, if you're gonna do something, might as well be the best at it.

5

An hour's worth of application of fresh air, three giant coffees, and a couple Bojangles country ham biscuits, and I was good to go. Or mostly, anyway. I got out of the Suburban, tied back the loose strands of hair that had escaped my ponytail from the wind rushing through the open window, and tried to smooth my bushy beard down into something that didn't make me look like the love child of Rob Zombie and Grizzly Adams.

"I didn't think you meant we'd ride the whole way with the windows down," I grumbled to Amy. "I didn't stink that bad."

"You don't stink that bad *now*," she corrected. "When you got in the car, I swear to God the air freshener broke free of its string and bolted for the door. I think it's still huddling under the back seat in terror."

If we hadn't seen all the weird shit we've seen, I'd call bullshit on the air freshener running around under its own power. But less than a year ago, we stood side by side with Count Freakin' Dracula fighting a hundred-year-old Nazi scientist. So, I reckon about anything can happen, just like Wyclef said.

The parking lot of the "industrial park" was jammed with police cars, ambulances, firetrucks, and every flavor of pickup you could imagine, most with some type of aftermarket red light on the roof or dash. This far out of a major city, most of the first responders were volunteers, which explained the half-dozen men in varying stages of turnout gear standing around the back of one fire truck, surrounding a young fire-fighter who was currently leaning over with his hands on his knees studying an immense puddle of vomit on the ground in front of him. I couldn't tell if he was admiring the pool of puke or trying to decide if he was going to contribute to it, so I just kept walking toward the police tape.

"You can't go in there," said a gaunt deputy, his brown uniform hanging on his frame like a slightly human-looking Jack Skellington.

I held up my credentials and didn't break stride, just ducked under the yellow tape and kept walking. Deputy Corndog bowed up like he was going to challenge me, and in a show of ridiculously poor judgement, put his hand on the butt of his pistol.

Now let's recap: I was hung over as a dog, with my stomach trying to decide exactly how much caffeine and pork grease it could accept on top of the near-gallon of peach brandy I'd dumped into it last night, and I'd just spent an hour getting whipped across the face by my face and beard, when I wasn't pulling it out of my teeth as I tried to eat. My back hurt from sleeping on a couch in a hippie bookstore, I was still in yesterday's clothes, and I needed a shower in a pretty serious way. So, I was not in the mood for some redneck dipshit to try to prove how big his dick was by putting me in my place. That's why I might have made a less-than-prudent next move.

That move was taking two long strides toward the cop, covering his right hand with my left to lock his gun in place, and slapping the piss out of his face with my right. I paintbrushed that dumbass across both cheeks twice, then planted my hand in the center of his chest and shoved. He fell down flat on his over-stuffed ass in the gravel parking lot, and as he drew his gun in shaky hands, I bent over and took it away from him. I ejected the magazine, ran the slide to clear the chamber, and then pressed the button on the side to yank the slide all the way off the front of the gun. I handed him most of the frame back, stuck the slide in my back pocket, and said, "You can have this back when I leave." Then I kept walking toward where a growing crowd of cops, EMTs, and firefighters were standing around chuckling.

It wasn't a good idea, on any level, but like I said, I was already annoyed and didn't feel great. So that was my excuse, crappy as it was. One of the EMTs came up to meet me and held out his hand.

"Thanks," he said. "Herbie's been needing someone to put him on his ass since he got out of high school and joined the force. He's been a shithead since middle school and got nothing but worse when they put that badge on him."

"You just let me know if he goes to his car and gets a shotgun or something," I replied. "It's been a shit morning already, and I'd rather not get an ass full of buckshot if I can avoid it."

"Will do, but once you see what's behind that tarp, you might wish you'd let him keep you out," the EMT said.

"That bad?" I asked the EMT, whose name tag read KENNEDY.

"Worst thing I've ever seen, and I've worked multiple car versus log truck accident scenes," Kennedy replied.

"Should I puke now, or wait?"

"Are you sober?" he asked.

"Mostly," I joked.

He wasn't joking. "Then wait. If you're anywhere near as drunk as you smell, then you won't have a choice anyway. Shit, if you've eaten anything in the past week, you should probably plan on revisiting it here in a minute. I mean, the coroner puked. That's gotta be a record or something, right? Don't they like remove their puke reflex in coroner school?"

"I thought so," I said, suddenly thinking that maybe that third biscuit might have been overkill.

"If you're done assaulting the local constabulary, shall we view the crime scene, *Agent* Brabham?" Amy asked, her voice cold enough to sink the *Titanic*. Kennedy gave me the patented "you're screwed" look and disappeared, leaving me to follow Amy to where a hastily erected set of poles and tarps obscured the front of Brother Evan's church. I looked around, a little surprised that the good reverend wasn't right in the middle of the biggest crowd, screeching about persecution or something. Maybe he was in the woods harvesting his own breakfast or something.

I stepped through the tarps and froze. I've seen some shit in my day, and even worse shit in the past few years, but the scene in front of me was worse than being Guest of Honor in a fairy dungeon, and worse than standing right in the middle of the line of fire when a dragon decided I'd look better barbecued. This was like something out of a Hieronymus Bosch painting, and I'm not talking about the cop Titus Welliver plays on TV.

Brother Evan was, in fact, right in the middle of the festivities, but rather than being the complainant or just generally a stoned nuisance, he was the centerpiece of the morning's crime scene. The good reverend had been stripped naked, crucified on scrap wood nailed together from pallets around the area, and nailed upside down to the front door of his church in the middle of an inverted pentagram. Then he'd been sliced open from nuts to nipples and his innards turned into outards. His guts dangled out of his body cavity and his intestines had been pulled out and stretched into hideous designs on the ground. The only way I could recognize it as Evan was the fact that somebody had gone in after they finished redecorating the ground with his organs and wiped all the blood off his face and moved the dangling intestines to one side so his face would be easily seen.

"Holy shit," I muttered. "This took a *long* time." And it was more than just the mutilation of the body that took a long time. The front door of the church was ringed with a litany of horrific symbols, obscene drawings, and defaced religious symbols. It was like whoever did this went down a checklist of groups they could target and spray painted something up there to condemn all of them. There were upside down crosses, a Star of David with a dollar sign painted over it, a crescent and star with a painted dick between them, the words "FUCK GOD" painted in several places, not to mention swastikas, Norse runes, and half a dozen other symbols I didn't even recognize.

"So it's pretty obviously a hate crime," said a tall man who had been squatting down in front of Evan's face, trying not to put a knee in the gore. He stood up and turned around, holding out a gloved hand to shake.

I took a step back. "Sorry, no gloves."

"Oh yeah," he said, looking down at his blood-spattered glove. "I'm Sheriff Russ Miano. I reckon y'all are down here because since it's a hate crime, it's federal now, huh?" He sounded almost hopeful, which I could understand. This was a gruesome scene, and a county's elected head lawman would sleep much better at night if someone else was responsible for figuring who unleashed this level of awful on his part of North Carolina.

Unfortunately, that wasn't anywhere close to why we were there. "I'm sorry, Sheriff," Amy said, stepping forward and shaking his hand. She had gloves in her pocket, like she knew she was coming to crime scene when she got in the SUV. Not like she'd been sleeping off a witches' house party hangover ninety minutes ago. "But it's going to take a little time to see if it actually *was* a hate crime. Right now, I'm honestly doubtful."

The sheriff and I both looked at her like she'd grown another head, this one in green. "Are you nuts, lady?" the sheriff asked, pointing to the wall behind him. "What the fuck do you think this is, if it's not a hate crime?"

"A diversion, dumbass," came a new voice from behind me. I turned to see Geri, our co-worker, protege, and the kid sister of my first fiancée, who had been brutally murdered in front of me by my father. She'd originally shown up on my porch to assassinate me on the orders of a corrupt government agency, and now we worked together for a hopefully marginally less corrupt government agency. And she slept in my spare bedroom. It was a complicated relationship, but I'd recently warmed up to her enough that I no longer locked my bedroom door and wedged a chair under the knob when I went to sleep. I still locked the door, and the deadbolt, but I left the chair alone. Baby steps.

Geri pushed past me to stand beside the sheriff, putting a hand on his shoulder and turning him back to the scene. "Look at this, dude. It's like a buffet of the persecuted up here. Almost anyone who's been treated like shit in this country in the past three hundred years is represented, *and* the Christians, too. If this is a hate crime, who's the target? Muslims? Jews? Gays? Blacks? There's no logic to this—it's just a shotgun smattering of random hate, but most of these symbols don't even apply to this church or to Evan. He was a white Christian dude. Was he straight?" She looked around.

Nobody answered. The sheriff stuck his head out the tarp. "Hey!" he yelled. "Anybody know if Evan was straight?"

"Yeah, he was," a voice yelled back. "I beat the shit out of him in high school on account of him banging my sister and tearing her favorite shirt."

"Shit, Russell, I banged your sister in high school!" came another voice.

"Yeah, but you didn't tear her shirt!" Russell said to general laughter.

The sheriff pulled his head back in the tarp. "He was—"

"Yeah, we got it," Geri cut him off. "My point is, from the research I did on the trip down here, Evan's church was Christian. A little closer to playing with snakes than I'm comfortable with, but still, you have a straight white Christian male murdered and nailed to the front of his church with anti-everything symbology all around him. Doesn't make sense. I don't think it's a hate crime."

"And you're an expert on hate crimes?" Sheriff Miano asked, his voice dubious.

"She is," Amy replied, holding out her credentials. "Deputy Director Amy Hall, Department of Homeland Security."

"You think this is terrorists?" Miano asked.

"We don't know yet."

"If it ain't a hate crime, it's Satanists," the sheriff said, his voice firm in his convictions. "We been having a bunch of Satanist stuff around here lately, probably them witches up in Raleigh wanting to come down here with their big city lesbian witchcraft and make us into their sex slaves or something."

I didn't bother to ask why he thought a lesbian witch would make a middle-aged sheriff with a beer gut and a skullet into a sex slave. I just said, "It wasn't the witches."

"And how do you know this, fatass?" the sheriff asked, and he puffed out his chest a little as he took a step in my direction.

That was the wrong thing to do, and the wrong thing to say. This was the second dipshit to bow up on me in five minutes, and that was not near enough time for my hangover to subside. Add in the comment on my weight, and I was downright irritable. So I might have behaved in a fashion unbefitting a federal agent. Good thing for me I'm not a federal agent, because the government is a bunch of speciesist pricks and stick me with consultant status, an hourly rate, and no benefits. Good thing, because if I *was* a federal agent, they'd probably have to fire me for knocking a county sheriff out cold by slamming my fist right between his eyes.

But I'm not. So they didn't. But I did. Sheriff fall down. Go splat. I turned to Amy. "I think I might have just contaminated the crime scene."

6

It wasn't the first time I'd been in the back of a county sheriff's patrol car, and it wasn't the first time I had to inform some dipshit deputy that if he insisted on handcuffing me, it was gonna take two pair to make my hands meet in the middle of my back. It *was* the first time I'd had anyone actively arguing for my release when I was in the back of a cop car, all my previous arrests having been on drunk and disorderly charges that were fully supported by everyone within a couple miles of me. Come to think of it, if they gave me a Breathalyzer test, I'd probably get convicted of drunk and disorderly in a brand-new county right now. I wondered where this one sat on my "Redneck Places To Get Arrested In" bingo card.

The sheriff hadn't shoved me in the back of his car. He was too busy taking an unanticipated nap in the middle of the murder scene. Three of his deputies were the ones who took offense at my treatment of their dipshit boss, and after a few minutes of engineering, got the bracelets on me. The sheriff woke up about halfway through this and stormed over in my directions, his Taser in one hand and a hanky full of blood and snot in the other one.

"Boy, I'm gonna—" He cut off at a sound unmistakable to anyone in law enforcement. Or most law breaking, come to think about it. The *chick-chack* of Amy racking the slide on her service weapon froze the sheriff in his tracks.

"Arrest him if you feel it's necessary, Sheriff, but he's subdued. So you put that Taser away and step back from my agent right now, or we're going to have a problem." She looked dead sexy standing there in her crime scene gear of black pantsuit, knee-high boots, and latex gloves holding a 9mm pistol trained on the back of the sheriff's head.

The cop straightened up and holstered his weapon, then turned to Amy. "You think you can shoot the sheriff in the back and walk out of here, missy? What makes you think my boys won't just nail you and your boyfriend up next to Brother Dumbass here and burn the whole goddamn place to the ground? Ain't nobody here give a shit about a couple of Yankee federal agents poking their nose in our business. Now you just put that gun back in your holster like a good little girl, get back in your Suburban, and get the hell out of my county."

"I don't think so, Sheriff," Amy said, although she did holster her pistol. "You see, I've got a job to do, and if you'll check that text message that just came through, you'll see a message from the District Attorney telling you that this is my crime scene now and you are to render all possible assistance to me and my investigators."

"I don't work for that fat shithead DA," the sheriff, not the skinniest supermodel on the runway himself, replied. "This is my crime scene, and if you don't like it—"

Another loud sound of a round entering the chamber of a firearm, but this time it was a lot deeper, throatier sound, and the voice that followed it was almost gleeful at the potential for mayhem before her. "Oh, for fuck's sake," Geri said. "I can't leave you two alone for a minute. Sheriff, get the fuck out of here. Go to your office, or Krispy Kreme, or anywhere that isn't here. You two dipshits finish cuffing Bubba and shove him in the back of a patrol car to cool off until he promises to behave. Then we're going to get to work and figure out who decided to make really ugly wall art out of your local stoner religious leader."

I turned along with everyone else to see Geri standing there with a Tavor 12-gauge semi-automatic shotgun, giving her access to fifteen shells worth of double-ought buckshot in a compact package, and definitely giving her the lead in our little mini arms race. "Hey, Ger," I said.

"Hey, Bubba. What'd you do this time?"

"I punched the sheriff," I replied. "But I didn't punch the deputy."

"Man, if you were anywhere near as funny as you think you are, you'd spend a lot less time in handcuffs or getting your ass kicked."

"Geri, most of the things that punch me are monsters. You know, the things that eat people. The things we hunt?"

"Yeah, but you try to make them laugh, too. Which literally never works."

"She ain't wrong, Bubba," Skeeter added in my ear. Now I remembered why I tried to never get handcuffed anymore. Now I didn't have any way to turn off Skeeter's voice.

"Now if everyone can just dial it back about fifteen percent, I think we can get to work. Sheriff, if you feel like your men need to arrest Bubba, I mean Agent Brabham, go for it. Geri and I are going to get to work. Bubba, try not to do anything to escalate this to a felony."

"Assaulting a peace officer is a felony, missy!" the sheriff spluttered.

"Not by the time I discuss with the DA the excessive force you displayed in the arrest of a federal agent in the commission of his duty. Now you just have your boys shove him in the back of a car until he agrees to play nice, and the rest of us can get to work. Oh, and if you call me 'missy' again, I'll shoot you in the balls and send whatever survives to Gitmo."

The sheriff grumbled about it, but he nodded to his boys and stomped off to his pickup, squealing tires and blowing thick clouds of diesel out of the back of his lifted truck. A pair of deputies helped me into the back of the car, one even putting a hand on top of my head to keep me safe, which I thought was sweet since they were ready to murder me about thirty seconds earlier. Funny how polite the threat of a bullet to the balls can make some people. It didn't look like I was getting out anytime soon, so I laid over on my side and went back to sleep. It wasn't much more uncomfortable than Madame Wanda's couch, but definitely didn't smell as nice. Still, I'd slept in way worse places over the years, so within five minutes, my snores were rattling the windows.

I don't know how long I was out, but it was definitely long enough for my whole left arm to go to sleep. I awoke to someone pulling on my foot, and somehow stopped myself from kicking out with all my force, just in case it was somebody I didn't want to kick the piss out of. And when I turned enough to look at who had hold of my boot, I was right. Amy was trying to drag my unconscious carcass out of the police car, with about as much success as you'd expect, given that she was trying to move somebody more than twice her size.

"If you'll cut that out for a second, I can probably get out of the car on my own," I said. I proceeded to do just that, and she held up a handcuff key.

"Can you promise not to punch any more local law enforcement?" she asked.

"No, I cannot. It is my solemn duty to pop douchebags in the nose at every opportunity, and I will not lay down my ancient quest just because one of the miscreants I must pummel has a badge." I put on the most apologetic, mournful, hangdog expression I could muster, which at least got a laugh and a shake of my fiancée's head.

"I'll try to keep you away from douchebag cops," she said, putting a hand on my shoulder to turn me around.

"That's a tall order, since so far all the ones I've seen in this town are at least borderline douchetastic," I replied. Then I flexed my shoulder, arms, and wrists, snapping the handcuffs and freeing myself. Amy and I both looked at the shattered metal in awe. "I…didn't know I could do that," I said in a whisper.

"*How* did you do that?" Amy asked.

"No damn idea. Maybe since I got exposed to all that magic shit around Harker, I'm stronger than I used to be?"

"More likely something in Wanda's tea," Amy said. "Did you notice being particularly strong when you were fighting lizards in South Carolina?"

"I mean, I did beat up a bunch of lizard dudes, and it probably was a little easier than normal, but I didn't think nothing of it. I just thought they were candy-assed lizards."

"Maybe the cuffs were defective. See if you can crush the pieces."

I obliged, picking up the half-moon chunks of handcuffs and squishing them into a little spiky ball of metal. "If they were defective, they were *seriously* messed up," I said. I bent over and put my hands under the edge of the police car. I heaved, and it came up on two wheels pretty easily, but pain spiked in my back and I dropped it down to rock on its springs. "Ow."

"Yeah, I don't care how strong you are, picking up a car is a big deal," Amy said. "If your whole body isn't more durable, then just being strong isn't really worth much."

"Yeah, what good is it to pick up a car, if my spine snaps and I'm crushed by a falling car? Also, I ain't as young as I used to be, apparently," I said. "But that's not why you pulled me out of Deputy Dawg's back seat. Did you get everything sorted with Sheriff Shithead?"

Amy sighed. She does that a lot with me. And she still said she'd marry me. If we can stop saving the world for five minutes, we should maybe think about starting to consider possibly exploring potential dates for that to happen. But since this was not the time to bring up wedding plans, I just waited as Amy collected herself. "Yes, I got everything sorted out. It took erasing five years' worth of back taxes for that asshat, but he agreed not to charge you with anything. Now will you please come look at the crime scene again so we can see if there's anything supernatural going on or if we just need to call in the FBI's serial killer unit and go home?"

"I looked. It's gross. I don't want to look again." I felt a little less drunk, which meant my hangover was about to really get rolling. Yay.

"The coroner took the body away an hour ago," Geri said as she walked over. "Jesus, Bubba. I think you might smell worse than the corpse."

"You spend a couple hours sleeping in the back of a cop car and see how you smell," I shot back.

"If I punch a sheriff in the nose, it won't be where there are enough witnesses to arrest me," she replied. She was probably right, too. Geri was a sneaky little bugger.

"Alright, let's go look around the crime scene." I noticed that all but one of the deputies were gone, and the lone remaining cop was standing by the crime scene tape keeping civilians back. I guessed he was the lucky bastard who got stuck with crime scene security since he had the giant dumbass asleep in the back of his car. I almost felt bad for the dude, then we stepped back through the plastic, and I didn't feel anything but revulsion.

7

I 'm not the forensics expert that Amy is, and frankly wouldn't put my forensic capabilities up against anyone who's watched more than three episodes of any *CSI* show, but I know bullshit when I smell it, and the fragrance of cow patties was all around the crime scene. There was a shitload of blood, hair, and a few teeth scattered on the ground in front of Evan's church, but all the symbols were really neat, with sharp, crisp edges to all the letters, and practically no overspray, like you'd expect with somebody painting graffiti on the side of a building in the middle of the night. "Does this shit look stenciled on to y'all?" I asked, taking a closer look at a particularly legible "Hail Satan."

"What do you mean, Bubba?" Geri asked, coming over to look where I pointed.

"Well, graffiti is usually messier, at least the kind that's actually graffiti, and not street art. This stuff is super neat, with clean edges to everything. And it's all spelled right. I've seen a bunch of graffiti in my time, and I can't imagine that some dingleberry wouldn't have painted 'Hail Santa' on here at least once. Spelling and grammar aren't usually hallmarks of the kind of people who paint racist shit on the side of buildings," I said.

"Good point," Amy said from where she knelt by a pile of fabric. "Also, nothing was stolen from Evan's clothes, which adds to the idea that this was something more than an attack by crazy cultists. Why would they leave close to five hundred bucks in his pockets, especially if they took the time to strip him before they nailed him to the wall?"

"That stoner goofball had five hundred bucks in his pocket?" I asked. Obviously thumping Bibles was more lucrative than thumping monster noggins. I needed to rethink my business model. Maybe if I started quoting scripture while I beat things up… "Jesus wept" is a Bible verse, right?

"Focus, Bubba," Amy said. "We only have an hour with the scene, so we need to gather anything that would indicate a supernatural presence before the local crime scene techs get here."

"What am I looking for?" I asked. "Ectoplasm? I'm pretty sure Slimer didn't do this."

"I think we're looking for stuff like this," Geri said, holding up a black taper candle. "I found this on the ground over here." She pointed behind her. I looked around and saw several other black candles lying on the ground, like someone had tried to make them stand up in the gravel driveway but couldn't manage it and just left them lying there.

"And this," Amy called, holding up a small furry carcass. I couldn't tell what it was, it was so badly mutilated, but it was the right size to be a really big squirrel or a really small rabbit. It looked a lot like the carcass Evan had in a cooler the day before, but this one was even more messed up. The little critter had been brutally hacked apart, with no sense of saving good meat or the pelt. I felt my blood heat up a little bit. I've certainly killed my fair share of animals, but it was always either hunting, self-defense, or accident (look, possums are stupid and unavoidable sometimes). Just slaughtering a helpless animal for set dressing to make your ritual look better? That was worth an ass-kicking all on its own.

"But there's no blood," I said, then waved a hand at the literal gallon of blood spilled all over the ground. "I know, there's a shitload of blood. But none of this shit was drawn in blood, and there are no symbols for summoning, or any of that weird mumbo-jumbo we usually see. This whole mess is starting to feel less like magic and more like just plain murder."

Tires crunched gravel on the other side of the plastic barrier erected to keep people out of the crime scene, and I looked at Amy. "I thought you said we had an hour with nobody else here?"

"We're supposed to," she replied. "Why don't you go check it out?"

I almost responded with "because I'm the only one of us not carrying a gun," but stifled it when I realized that (A) that would piss off my fiancée, which is never profitable, and (B) it's mostly humans who drive cars in the daytime, and we try not to kill humans if we can avoid it, so sending Geri the psychopath would be less than wise. So I ducked through the thick plastic sheeting just in time to see a second pickup truck joining the one that was currently disgorging three large rednecks with shotguns and baseball bats.

That's not too bad. I can probably handle three guys, especially if I had any increased durability to go along with my newly found magical strength. My optimism faded significantly when four more rednecks got out of the second truck, all of them similarly equipped with implements of ass-whooping.

"'Sup, fellas?" I asked, holding up a hand in a manner designed to both be friendly and to say, "Stop, assholes."

Part of it worked because the assholes stopped walking, but I must have missed something in the friendly part because the redneck in front, a redheaded skinny dude in his late twenties with a scraggly beard and the remnants of acne scars under his John Deere hat said, "Who the hell are you?"

I flashed my credentials. "Agent Brabham, Homeland Security. Now who the hell are *you?*" I pitched my voice a little deeper than normal and straightened up to my full height, thinking this might be one of those days that being the biggest dude in the room could actually prevent a fight.

"I'm Ricky Eaton, and I want to see what them witches done did to Evan's church," he replied.

I took a second to parse his sentence, because every once in a while, North Carolina redneck diverges from my native Georgia redneck, and I have to think about what the hell he just said. When I got it, I just shook my head. "I don't think so, Mr. Eaton. This is a crime scene, and we're still processing it." I've seen a couple episodes of *CSI* myself. Just enough to learn terms like "processing the scene." I like the one with Lieutenant Dan better than the one in Vegas or the one with the guy with the sunglasses. But when Sam from *Cheers* went on the one in Vegas, I gave it another shot. Still like Lieutenant Dan better.

Ricky looked around, confused. "Mr. Eaton? My daddy ain't here, son. I told you my name's Ricky. Now why don't you get your revenuer ass out of my way before me and the boys teach you carpetbagging pieces of shit why the South is gonna rise again for real."

I sighed. Sometimes the stupid is just like a rash. It burns. I took a second to figure out exactly how to respond but finally went with a level of professionalism that I was pretty sure would have impressed Amy if she'd been there to see it. "I'm not going to go over every stupid thing you just said because I've got work to do, but you might want to listen to my Georgia accent before you start tossing around words like 'carpetbagger.' Now get your friends, get back in your trucks, and go sleep it off before you get yourselves in more trouble than you know how to get out of."

See? Professional. I didn't call them dipshits, or tell them to get the hell out of there, or threaten to beat his ass like a swaybacked mule, or any of my usual ways to disperse a crowd. I think it shows growth.

Unfortunately, Beautiful Ricky and his third-rate Midnight Express posse hadn't been watching the same self-help YouTube videos I had. Or maybe they were a few episodes behind me because they just started yelling more profanity and random ethnic, religious, and homophobic slurs, along with plenty of speculation about my having sex with members of my immediate family and most types of farm animals. That didn't bother me. I've walked into Death Valley on a November Saturday afternoon and listened to the roar of a hundred thousand Clemson fans. Dumbass rednecks lost their ability to worry me a long time ago.

But they never lost their ability to injure me, so when a beer bottle flew over the heads of the crowd and *thumped* against the plastic sheeting before falling to the gravel just behind me, I got annoyed. When a big clod of red dirt exploded as it smacked into the impromptu wall, showering me with dust, I got irritated. But when a rock whizzed through the crowd and drew a line of blood across my temple? That's when I got pissed.

"Okay, assholes!" I yelled. "That's enough! Now get the hell out of here, go home, and if I hear a whisper of y'all harassing Madame Wanda and her people, I will personally come to every one of y'all's houses and beat the piss out of each and every one of you. Now git!"

Ricky's mouth fell open when I mentioned Wanda by name, and I realized that I might have made a big mistake. "He knows the witch's name! He's in on it with 'em! Get 'im!"

The crowd surged forward, and I had a decision to make. Should I duck behind the sheeting, get Amy and Geri out there for backup, and maybe let Amy's brains and good looks defuse the bunch of angry redneck assholes? Or should I just suck it up and whoop some ass?

Let's recap—I was operating on very little sleep, had a headache that felt like Neil Peart had come back to life and was hammering on my skull, my mouth tasted like a squirrel took a dump on my molars, and my stomach was doing double-gainers that would have snagged gold at the last Olympics. I was not in the mood to defuse.

So I didn't. I set my feet and squared my shoulders, and when Ricky took the first step toward me, I stuck my left hand out way to the side and wiggled my fingers. "Yoo-hoo!" Then while he was looking at my left, I balled up my right fist and planted an uppercut on the tip of his chin that probably dislocated his jaw, and definitely made his eyes roll back in his head. All the fight flew out of him with the wad of Big Red I knocked out of his mouth, and he went down like a sack of bricks. One down, six to go. I kinda liked my odds. Until I noticed the next guy had a baseball bat.

"A little help out here!" I yelled as I ducked under the dude's wild swing at my head. I punched him in his gut, which was a sizable target area, but my hand felt like I'd punched a wall. He was one of those fat dudes that had a ton of muscle buried under their insulation, so hitting him in the gut was about as useful as hitting him in the head—both areas were too solid and too thick to do any damage. He slammed the bat down across my shoulders, but he didn't have enough leverage to do anything more than annoy me, and that ship had long sailed. I wrapped my arms around his waist and lifted, then drove my knees forward to push us through the crowd of idiots like an icebreaker heading to the South Pole.

Which about ten seconds later resulted in me not being backed up against a wall with a bunch of angry idiots in front of me. No, now I was standing smack dab in the middle of that bunch of idiots, with them completely surrounding me. Sometimes I think my JV football coach was right, that I don't even understand the concept of defense. Oh well, time to whoop some ass. Again.

8

I set down the idiot I was holding, spun him around by his shoulders so he was facing away from me, and shoved him backward, *hard*. My newly enhanced strength decided to kick in then, and he flew back like he was shot out of a cannon. He bowled over three of his buddies, so for a few seconds, I only had two idiots to deal with.

The first one had a tire iron, so he moved to the top of my "To Punch" list. There's an actual list. I keep one on my fridge with a running list of people I want to smack the shit out of. It's multiple pages. Skeeter joked once that I should just hang a legal pad up there, and Amy says it would be a shorter list if I put the people I don't want to punch on there. They're both right. But "moron coming at me with a tire iron" gets to jump the line every single time. I caught his arm and ducked under it, using his own momentum to carry him forward into his buddy, who was trying to sneak up behind me with a…long piece of crown molding? Yeah, any port in a storm, I reckon, but he'd have been more effective beating me with uncooked spaghetti.

With them down, I turned back to the four guys picking themselves up off the ground. One was helpfully on his hands and knees about six feet in front of me, so one good step, a plant of my left foot, and his ribs were introduced to the toe of my boot with extreme velocity. I heard something snap like a twig and just managed to get out of the way before he hurled up everything he'd eaten for the last three days. Then he toppled to one side and curled up in a ball holding his midsection. Two down.

Pain exploded in my back as one of the rednecks slammed a fist into my kidney. I managed to keep from going down as I twisted around to backhand him across the face. Except my hand missed completely because this redneck was maybe five feet tall and build like a fire hydrant. He was thick through the neck and shoulders, and his hands felt like cinderblocks as he slammed them into my middle. I doubled over, engulfing him in my arms as I almost toppled over, but managed to slip one arm around his neck and squeeze, cutting off the flow of blood, oxygen, and anything else important to his brain. A few seconds later, he slumped to the ground. Three down.

But the remaining three had wised up and taken positions in a circle around me. They were exchanging glances and making all kinds of hand gestures, so I decided to preempt their attack by charging the guy in front of me. This had the desired effect of stunning them out of whatever they were planning, but it didn't have the desired effect of me running one of them over and squashing his head like a grape. He danced off to one side and landed a ringing open-handed strike to my right ear as I went past.

That shit hurt on a lot of levels. There was the embarrassment of a dude getting out of the way and slapping you in the process, but more painful was the actual *pain* of it. Homeboy knocked the absolute snot out of me, and I wouldn't have been a bit surprised if the blow knocked all the wax out of my other ear, so great was the pressure against my eardrum from his cupped hand.

A good shot to the ear can screw up a lot, and I checked every box—equilibrium, vision, hearing, and general mental sharpness. Most of those were already shot to shit from my hangover, but the knock on the gourd made everything worse. I staggered to one side, and the three uninjured asshats swarmed me—punching, kicking, gouging. I'm pretty sure one of the sonsabitches bit me on the ear. That one, I managed to dislodge by throwing an elbow into his goddamn face. The only saving grace was that one of them actually jumped on me and started trying to wrestle me into submission, which left less exposed surface area for his friends to kick the shit out of.

Which they eventually realized and pulled him off me. They hauled me to my feet, now back to six out of seven on their feet. The guy with the broken ribs wasn't getting up under his own power anytime soon. All he was doing was lying on the ground wheezing. I was mostly sure I didn't kick a rib through one of his lungs, but at the time, I was more concerned with literally anything in the world than I was one dumbass's ribs.

One redneck grabbed each arm, and one of them planted a foot behind my knee so they could force me down to the ground. I knelt there, with a dipshit on each arm and a bonus jackoff standing behind me with his hand curled around my ponytail, holding my head straight.

Ricky the Asshole-in-Chief walked up and slapped me across the face. Not a head-ringing palm strike like his ninja buddy had done. Nope, he just slapped me like I'd been caught dancing with his boyfriend at a high school prom. I mean, what grown-ass man slaps another one?

My answer came a few seconds later as he nodded to the guy behind me, who yanked back on my hair, then suddenly released all the pressure, not without some pain as chunks of my ponytail came out by the roots. A few hairs may have come out by the roots, but the rest of it got sliced off by the dickhead's pocketknife because he tossed it on the ground in front of me where it lay there, lifeless, like a roadkill ferret or something. Just a hunk of hair about a foot and a half long, with more gray in it than I want to admit, lying in the gravel.

Ricky slapped me again, and I understood that this wasn't about beating my ass, it was about humiliating me. Anybody who thinks they can humiliate me is someone who never played Division I college sports because an unwilling haircut ain't nothing to what I got as a freshman at UGA. I mean, until they yank my britches down and tattoo a bulldog on my butt cheek, they can't touch what the varsity defensive line did to rookies. And I reckon I mean tattoo a bulldog on the *left* butt cheek, to go with the one that got tattooed on the right side in Athens when I was eighteen.

I did worry a little bit when Ricky pulled out his own pocketknife and leaned down to my face. "I'm gonna mess you up, you witch-loving Satanist sumbitch," he said, grabbing my beard. For a second I worried that he was going to slit my throat and the coroner was going to have to make two pickups at the same address, but he just sawed off most of my goatee and threw it in my face, laughing like he'd just told the world's funniest joke.

Now, I get it. Really, I do. There are a lot of people who would consider getting an unwilling haircut and beard trim to be hugely traumatic and a massive violation of their person. And they'd be right. It was worse than my hangover, and my hangover was *epic*. But my hair grows back. Sure, I've worn it long for most of my life since I got out of college, but it's like my truck—something I *have*, not something I *am*. So while I was pissed, I wasn't nearly as traumatized as these doucherockets clearly expected me to be.

They relaxed their grip on my wrists just a little, clearly expecting me to freak out and grab for my face or my scalp, but I went in the opposite direction. I leaned hard to my left, shoving my arm through that guy's grip even as the guy holding my right arm clenched down. From my position on the ground, I couldn't reach the redneck's throat, so I grabbed his belt and pulled him around, breaking his grip on me and slamming him into Ricky. Ricky stumbled into the guy holding my right arm, and that combined with me punching him as hard as I could in the side of his knee with my newly free left hand, sent all three assholes tumbling down in a pile of stupid and vitriol.

I scrambled to my feet, my newly trimmed hair immediately falling in my eyes. I brushed it back and punched the nearest moron right in the nose. He staggered back, his eyes watering and blood fountaining down the front of his shirt, and I turned my attention to Ricky, who was back on his feet.

"Alright, asshole. You asked for this," he said as he pulled a massive Buck folding hunting knife from his back pocket. I mean, I don't know how he sat in a car without this making his ass all cockeyed. It seemed like a recipe for a crappy ride to me, but maybe that's why he was so irritated all the time—poor posture and a sore ass. "I'm gonna gut you like a—"

I never found out what he was going to gut me like because a thunderous *BOOM* split the air, and Ricky went down clutching his gut, knife falling to stick point-first in the dirt. I heard the unmistakable sound of a shotgun racking a shell, and as I looked over to see Amy pointing a twelve-gauge riot gun at the rednecks around me, her boomstick barked again, and I dove for the deck, not wanting to get any stray pellets anywhere in me.

I didn't need to worry. One, Amy's aim is a lot better than Skeeter's, which is why we'll let her play with guns that need to be aimed, not just shotguns. Skeeter is a wide spread or nothing kind of shooter. And two, which I figured out when I noticed that neither Ricky nor the other dumbass she shot were bleeding, she was firing beanbag rounds. They hurt like hell and will take the fight out of pretty much anybody, but unless you're too close or are a prick and shoot somebody in the face or head with them, they're non-lethal.

One more boom, one more downed hillbilly, and the three remaining dragged their buddies over to their trucks. As they were loading the moaning idiots into the back seats, gunshots split the air again, this time rifle rounds as Geri, who had traded her own twelve-gauge for a little MP-7, cut loose on the bed of one of the pickups, putting half a dozen holes in a tight little circle just above the rear tire.

"If you assholes come back, I'll be shooting you next time," she yelled, and my attackers moved even faster, if that was possible. It looked like a clown car in reverse with those morons scrambling over each other to get out of Dodge. I plodded over to where Amy and Geri stood with their two smoking barrels, proving to the world once again that the female of the species is the deadlier of the two.

"Thanks," I said. "Couldn't find the exit before they chopped off my hair? Or were you waiting to see if they were going to give me a mani-pedi?"

"I was waiting to see if they'd throw you in a pond or give you a shower or something," Geri replied without missing a beat. "You smell like a peach schnapps distillery mixed with a boys' locker room, and that's…less than fun."

"I'd been meaning to ask you what you looked like with short hair," Amy said. "I kinda like it."

"Good thing," I said. "Because I ain't into wigs. They itch." I held up a finger to Geri. "Don't ask. I promise you don't want to know how I know that."

"I'm sure I don't," Amy said. "But what I do want to know is why Madame Wanda's business card was inside Brother Evan's wallet." She held up a rectangle of cardstock in a plastic envelope. "There's no blood on this, so it was in the wallet before everything got covered in blood, and we need to ask her how it got there."

"So it's back to the witch's lair," I said. "Can I at least get a shower first?"

"Oh, I was going to insist," Amy said, handing me a keycard. "We have a hotel in Raleigh. The address is already in the GPS in your phone. Go get cleaned up and we'll meet you at Madame Wanda's in a couple hours. I need to go smooth things over with the local sheriff for running his guys off and check in with the coroner, not that I expect him to be done with his autopsy yet." I stepped toward her for a goodbye kiss, but she planted both hands on my chest to hold me off. "Not until you get a shower. And if you ever want me in that pickup again, you'll ride with the windows down. Geri's right, you reek."

That's true love, folks. True love.

9

It was good three hours later when I pulled up in front of Madame
Wanda's store, showered, shaved, and my hair and beard salvaged
the best the stunned little dude at Supercuts could manage. He did
an alright job trimming me up, but I've worn a ponytail for nigh on
twenty years, so when he started talking about "product," I started
thinking about ball caps. Problem was, given my location about my only
collegiate options were Duke, Carolina, or NC State, and there was not a
chance in the world I was gonna rep an ACC school on my SEC head. So I
stopped at a Sheetz gas station, which is kinda like a miniature Buc-ees,
and bought a Carolina Hurricanes hat. It was at least close to Georgia red,
if I squinted a little.

I got out as Geri and Amy walked over to meet me by the front door.
"Sweet of y'all to wait on me."

"We figured since you established such a rapport with Madame Wanda
last night, we should make sure you were with us when we had our little
chat with her," Amy said.

"You make it sound like I danced nekkid around a maypole or something with her," I protested. "All I did was drink too much and make off-
color comments about Jensen Ackles' butt."

Geri let out a little sigh. "The ass that broke Amazon. I love that ass."

"See?" I said, pointing. "That right there is why I have to make the
jokes. Everybody knows that Chris Evans has America's ass, but now here

comes Soldier Boy with his substitute glutes, and everybody forgets the sacrifices Steve Rogers made for his country."

Amy and Geri exchanged glances, and I held up a hand. "Skeeter made me watch all twenty-something movies leading up to *Endgame*, so I mighta got a deep dive into the Marvel Cinematic whatever. And I love *The Boys*. Karl Urban is awesome."

"You just like that they cuss more than you," Geri said.

"Nah, he thinks Urban reminds him of his pal, Quincy Harker," Amy countered.

"Shit," I replied. "Harker could out-cuss about anybody, but Urban's an Aussie. He can hang."

"Kiwi," Geri corrected.

"Huh?"

"Karl Urban isn't from Australia. He's from New Zealand. So he's not an Aussie, he's a Kiwi."

"Huh," I said, scratching my chin with its much shorter covering of graying hair. "Who knew?"

"Literally everybody," Amy said, pulling the door open. "And since when do you like hockey?"

I followed her in. "I don't give a shit about hockey, but it was buy a ten-dollar hat at the gas station or spend twenty bucks on hair stuff at the strip mall barber shop that trimmed up my noggin. Pure economics. Once I get back to a civilized part of the world, I'll get me a Bulldogs cap."

Madame Wanda stood behind her counter, looking sad. "I suppose you're here to ask me about Evan," she said as we walked up.

"Yes, ma'am," I replied. "Your business card was found at the crime scene, Madame Wanda, so we need to ask you some questions about that."

"Was my card on the body, or was it in Evan's pocket?" she asked. Smart lady. If the card was just laying around, maybe somebody dropped it, but if it was in the dead guy's pocket, he mighta had it before everything got messy.

"It was in his shoe, actually," Amy said. She and Geri had pretty subtly spread out from me to make a large triangle around Wanda. I wasn't really sweating a sixty-something woman with a limp trying to run on us, but if there was any power to her witchiness, it was better if we weren't all clumped up. That way the fireball might not get all of us. I learned that listening to this podcast where a dumbass bard keeps setting his friends on fire with magic.

"That makes sense," Wanda said. "Evan wouldn't want my card falling out of his pocket if he needed to get to his wallet. It wouldn't do him any favors if people knew that we had a more friendly relationship than most folks would understand."

"What does that mean, exactly?" Amy asked, leaning on the counter to her left.

"Evan was my nephew," Wanda said, wiping a tear from one eye. "He was my sister's youngest son, and while he and I didn't see eye to eye on, well, much of anything, if we're being honest, he was still family, and I loved him. Even if he was a zealot. After Rhonda died, Evan went deeper and deeper down his fundamentalist rabbit hole, and I found solace in the arms of the Goddess and in nature. It drove a wedge between us that I've been trying to repair for five years."

"I'm really sorry," Geri said. "I know what it's like to lose a sister. It's… hard isn't even the right word for it."

"Thank you," Wanda said. "But I never gave up on Evan. Even though he started calling the police on me any time I got within a hundred yards of his church, I'd go down there a couple times a month and stick my business card in the door, hoping one day he'd have a change of heart. He was all I had left of Rhonda. And now…" Her voice trailed off, and she reached under the counter for a box of tissues. She blew her nose loudly and gave us a watery smile. "Sorry. I know you're got a job to do, but…he was my nephew, and that sheriff from down in Asheboro couldn't even have the courtesy to come tell me to my face that my last living relative had been brutally murdered. Little shithead."

"Can confirm," I said. "He is a little shithead." I looked at Amy and Geri, silently trying to communicate that we should take the witch off the suspect list. "Do you know anyone who would want to hurt Evan? Anyone with a grudge against him, or maybe someone who wanted to take over his church or something?"

Wanda let out a bitter bark of a laugh. "Take over that thing? No. It was a financial albatross around his neck, and I kept begging him to take the buyout."

"What buyout?" Amy asked, her eyebrows perking up.

"His landlord came to him a few months ago offering to buy him out of his lease. Something about widening Highway 74 and the landlord needing to do something different with the property. I told Evan the last time we talked that he should just take the money and move up here, start a small church in one of the strip malls if that's what he truly felt called to do. But he wouldn't hear of it. Said he couldn't abandon his flock." She let out that bitter laugh again, and the pain in the sweet but slightly dotty lady's voice was heart-wrenching. "Flock. If they had fifteen people in the building, it was a huge crowd. That boy didn't have enough of a flock to build a pen in the back yard for."

I exchanged looks with Geri and Amy. We were all on the same page, and it wasn't in the "Madame Wanda is the bad guy" chapter. I reached out and patted Wanda's hand in that way we all learned from our Southern grannies. "Miss Wanda, I'm really sorry for your loss. We'll do our very best to find who did this, I promise."

"And then we'll fuck them up for you," Geri added. That's our girl—always with the absolute less-than-perfect thing to say in any situation. But Madame Wanda took the threat of incredible violence in the manner in which it was intended and nodded.

"Thank you all," she said. "If there's anything I can do to help, please let me know."

"Just keep Bubba out of the liquor cabinet," Amy said.

Wanda laughed. "No worries there. After his last visit, we're slap empty!" We all laughed, but there was a tinge of bitterness and grief coloring the edges of the sound.

Half an hour later, we were settled in at a little meat and three restaurant a mile from Madame Wanda's shop. It was the kind of place where the linoleum was a little yellowed, the vinyl seats on the chairs were cracked, and somebody my size had to make the difficult decision between trusting one of those ancient aluminum-legged seats or squeezing my bulk into a booth that was factory formed for somebody about half my size. I chose violence, in the sense that I took my chances at a table and moved chairs around until I planted my big behind in the one that groaned in protest the least when I sat down. I thought there was a better than even chance that one would survive the meal.

I ordered a massive lunch, since the Bojangle's had long since evaporated and it felt like I hadn't eaten in a week. Amy and Geri ordered normal portions of food, probably in an attempt to make me feel fat. Joke's on them, I know exactly what fat feels like, because I live here.

"You keep eating like that, Bubba, and there's no way you're living to see forty," Geri said when my first plate arrived, a heaping mass of scrambled eggs, grits with butter and cheese, and bacon.

"Don't worry, I got veggies for lunch," I replied.

"All of which are fried," Amy pointed out.

"Well, yeah," I said. "You don't expect me to eat vegetables that taste like vegetables, do you?"

Amy sighed and pulled a tablet out of her bag. "Okay, according to the county tax records, the entire industrial park is owned by a Leigh Boros, LLC, with an office in…Pittsboro."

"Let me guess, another pissant little town somewhere around Raleigh?" Geri asked.

"Pretty much," Amy said. "Not the pissant part, it looks like a decent little town, but yes, it's roughly between Asheboro and Raleigh."

"So, we need to go talk to this Leigh fellow and see if he knows anything about the goings-on at his industrial park, or if he had anything to do with gutting a stoned preacher and dressing him like a deer nailed to the front of his church, is that the plan?" I asked.

"Mostly," Amy said. "Except for the pronouns." She turned her tablet around so I could see the image on the screen, and Leigh Boros was very much not a "he." The screen showed a trim woman in her mid-thirties with high cheekbones, striking eyes, and a mass of black hair cascading in waves over the shoulders of a tailored blazer. She looked like class and money, not things I typically associate with people who make their fortune renting out prefab aluminum buildings to mechanics and broke-ass churches. I expected somebody with a little more Boss Hogg in their image.

"She's pretty," Geri said.

I nodded. "Yeah, not what I expected out of a redneck slumlord."

"There's something else," Amy said, spinning the tablet around and making a couple of circles with her stylus. "Take a close look at the area I circled."

I leaned forward until my nose almost touched the screen but couldn't see anything out of the ordinary, just a couple spots circled in red on the picture. Geri put a hand on my shoulder and pulled me back, then did that weird little pinch/unpinch thing with her fingers and the image zoomed in.

"Oh yeah," I said. Technology is not my strong suit. It's not my weak suit, either. Hell, technology isn't really even in my clothes closet. "You seeing this, Skeeter?" I asked the air, drawing a confused look from the waitress, who was dropping off my second plate. I kinda figured if the first plate was breakfast, then on the second run, I should focus on lunch.

So this one was piled high with a thick-ass roast beef sandwich on white, with bacon, pepper jack, and yellow mustard, with a bag of Zapp's Voodoo potato chips to go with it. I reckon "house made" chips were just a myth of the menu. Oh well, Zapp's chips rock anyway.

"You're eating that, too?" Geri asked.

"I'm a growing boy," I said.

"Not in any direction that matters," she shot back.

I aggressively opened my bag of chips beside her ear in a display of the most middle-school behavior I could think of on short notice. I might have to give her a wedgie later to make up for it. Then I turned my attention back to the screen. "What am I looking for, Amy?"

"The cufflinks," Skeeter said in my ear. "And earring."

"Yep," Amy agreed.

I stared at the screen, but all I saw were silvery blobs. "Sorry," I said. "I don't see it."

"Here," Amy said, handing me a pair of lavender reading glasses. "Try it now."

"I don't need cheaters, I…" I shut up as I dropped the lenses over my eyes and the details in the photo slammed into focus. "Okay, I reckon I'm stopping by a Walgreen's when we're done here. I see it now. There's some kind of symbols on her jewelry, but I don't recognize them."

"If you'd spent more time reading and less time drinking and watching reruns with the witches, you'd probably know you were looking at occult symbology," Skeeter said, and by the smirks Amy and Geri were giving me, his words weren't on a private channel. "That's a symbol of Mammon, historically one of the most powerful demons of greed."

"I read about that guy," Geri said. "He's supposed to be able to influence people from afar and really ramp up their normal, mundane levels of greed to do awful things."

"So now we know who Elon Musk-ette works for, but why do we care if a landlord in Horseballs, North Carolina, worships a demon of greed? It kinda seems right on brand to me." I was pretty sure I'd used "on brand" correctly in a sentence, which was a big occasion for me.

"Because if we look at her real estate holdings on a state map, it looks like she's developing properties all over the area, with one specific place at the center of her ring of construction," Skeeter said, as the image on Amy's tablet changed. "I sent a picture marking where her newest developments are."

"Well, son of a bitch," I said as the picture came clear.

"Yeah, pretty much," Skeeter replied.

"I don't know if that answers a bunch of questions or launches a bunch of new ones," Geri said.

"Both," Amy said, using her stylus to trace the lines Skeeter had drawn through four of Ms. Boros' most recent housing developments and running her finger across the screen back to the site of Evan's church and murder. Now there was a new image on the screen connecting all five sites—a five-pointed star. And smack in the center of the pentagram was one of North Carolina's most famous, or infamous spots—the Devil's Tramping Ground.

10

W ell, now what?" I asked. "I'm not the expert on busting up magical mystery tours; I'm the punch things until they fall down guy." We were standing outside the restaurant, where we'd been asked to leave after I belched loud enough to rattle the panes in the picture window beside our table. The waitress didn't seem to believe my protests that it was considered a compliment in some places, just griping that she didn't think her short order cook needed to be complimented with such volume. Or with pieces of egg sprayed across the table.

"We're gonna need an expert on the occult," Geri said. She dropped the tailgate on my truck and sat on it, swinging her purple Doc Martens and popping bubble gum. It was hard to take her seriously when she acted like a kid, on account of her being nearly two decades younger than me, and on account of me first meeting her when she still wore pigtails and jumpers. It didn't take too many times watching her shoot monsters in the face to learn to ignore the Rainbow Brite image. She was the most bloodthirsty out of all of us, and probably the most unbalanced. And that last one was a pretty high bar to clear.

"You know what that means," Amy added. She leaned on the back of the truck with her tablet in hand, probably typing out a message to her boss, Homeland Paranormal Division Director Keya Pravesh, a gorgeous Indian woman with long dark hair, beautiful brown skin, and a lot of scales and fangs hidden under her human suit. Pravesh was a lamia, some kind of ancient snake person monster thought to be extinct for a century or two. Apparently rumors of her extinction had been seriously exaggerated.

I knew where they were going with this, and I knew they were right, but that didn't mean I wasn't going to bitch about it. "Come on!" I protested. "That guy's an uber-dick."

"Yeah, but he's been around a long time, and he knows his stuff," Skeeter said, thereby violating the bro code of not taking the woman's side against your male best friend. I mean, they were all a thousand percent correct, but that didn't mean it wasn't a Benedict Arnold-level betrayal of dude solidarity.

"But I don't wanna deal with Harker again," I whined. I knew I was whining, and I didn't care what it looked like for a man pushing forty who's bigger than most professional wrestlers to be pissing and moaning in the parking lot of Bob & Tom's Family Diner on the side of Highway 64 in the middle of the afternoon. Amy had picked the restaurant not for its look, or for its reviews, which were actually pretty good, and accurate, but for the fact that the tiny town of Ramseur was just outside the lines drawn between places of power on her map. If the pattern was complete, according to Skeeter, there wouldn't be any place in the Carolinas, and maybe not on the East Coast, safe from Mammon and his power, but for now, until the pattern was finished and whatever was supposed to come up in the middle was still locked away, we were safe. We still decided to eat somewhere a little outside the area of the spell, just to be safe.

"You don't have to deal with Harker," said a new voice from the roof of my truck. "After all, you need a subject matter expert, and unless the subject is mass destruction, rampant chaos, or creative profanity, Harker won't do you any good." A gorgeous blonde sat cross-legged on the top of the cab, and I was certain she hadn't been there ten seconds before.

"Hey, Glory," Amy said as the new blonde jumped down and hugged my fiancée. That was a lot of blonde hotness in one place, and I'll admit that my mind went to some downright slash fiction kinda places for a minute, before I wrestled my thoughts back into a line more acceptable for dealing with federal agents and angels.

Glory was Quincy Harker's Guardian Angel, although there was some question as to whether her job was protecting Harker from the world, or the world from Harker. I think most days it was a little Column A, and a little Column B. Either way, as a mystical being who'd been around since the War in Heaven (yep, totally a real thing that happened—surprised the crap outta me, too. I always thought it was just a story from Sunday school), she was more qualified than literally anyone born on the planet to talk about magical stuff.

"So what's the deal?" I asked. "Is this Boros woman trying to summon Mammon to Earth?"

Glory looked me up and down. "New look. I kinda dig it. It's like when Triple H cut all his hair off. Only a little grungier. But lose the hat. You should just learn to use a little hair gel. It won't kill you."

"There's no proof of that," I said. "And it ain't a theory I'm looking to test. So back to Boros?"

"I don't know what she's up to, and I couldn't tell you too much even if I did. I'm…kinda on probation after you and Harker's little adventure last year."

"You mean when we stopped a bunch of Nazis from creating human-cryptid hybrids and selling them as super-soldiers all over the world to sow death, destruction, and hatred all over the world? *That* got you in trouble?" I asked. Man, I knew angels could be dicks, but if the heavenly bosses were benching Glory because she helped us kinda save the world, then they were bigger asshats than I ever knew.

"No, that was fine. The very public fight on the lawn of the Washington Monument with hundreds of civilian witnesses who had to have their memories wiped afterward was what got me in trouble. That and the burrito truck thing."

"The burrito truck thing" was Harker blasting some dickhead wizard named Liang through the side of a Scalzi's Burritos food truck and causing a pretty sizable explosion. I guess that was a lot to cover up, especially with insurance claims and all. I had a thought, and it made it past my lips before I could stop it.

"Are insurance adjusters all demons? Is that where the trouble came from?" I asked.

Glory looked surprised. "That's pretty sharp, Bubba. See how much smarter you are when you don't have all that hair dragging on your brain? Not all insurance adjusters are demonic, but all insurance companies are run by demons, and when divine entities do things that make mostly normal humans interact with demons, it's…not a good look. Not that it was the first time that Scalzi guy had to deal with a demon. I mean, did you see the guitar he was carrying? Nobody can play that thing without some infernal assistance."

"That kid Johnny did okay in the song," I pointed out.

"That was a fable, it never really happened, and if it did ever really happen, not that I'm confirming it, he played a fiddle, not a ridiculous seven-neck guitar. Regardless, because of Harker's fight, a human had to work with a demon, *and* we brought a lot of unwanted attention to the mystical world, so the bosses are pretty annoyed with me."

"What were you supposed to do to keep that from happening?" Geri asked. "Kill Harker? Because that's what it would have taken to stop...oh." She stopped talking as she came to understand the look in Glory's eyes. Apparently, that was exactly what she was supposed to do.

Yep, Archangels are assholes. That sealed it right there. I'm a long way from a member of the Quincy Harker fan club, but he usually tried to do the right thing, and to murder him just to keep a low profile seemed pretty shitty to me. I decided it was time to change the subject, before Glory got really annoyed. I've seen her fight. I don't want to be anywhere near her when she got pissy. "So what can you tell us?" I asked. "Are we even in the same zip code as the right track?"

"Oh, you've pretty much nailed it. Boros is building developments at the points of a pentacle, with the Devil's Tramping Ground in the center. I don't know what her ultimate goal is, but that design was created to harness and focus power, and if someone were to build a sixth structure in the center, on an already powerful place...let's just say it wouldn't be good for the home team. Or home planet. Actually, it might end up being really uncomfortable for the whole home dimension."

"So...we should try to stop this, huh?" I asked.

"Yeah...probably a good idea," the angel agreed.

"Any hints you can give us?" Amy asked.

"Sorry, this is one of those that you're going to have to handle on your own. I have strict orders not to get directly involved and am certainly under orders not to mention that out of all the places Ms. Boros has begun developing, the Devil's Tramping Ground is probably the most crucial piece of the puzzle. So, since I didn't tell you any of that, and I'm not allowed to give you any direct assistance, I suppose I'll just head home. Later!" And with a wave of her fingers, she was gone. She didn't vanish in a flash of light, or a puff of smoke, or anything like that. One moment she was there; the next she was gone. It always seemed like there were weird rules about how angels could travel, and I didn't understand any of them, but it sounded to me like we had a plan.

"So, next stop, the Devil's Tramping Ground?" I asked, looking at Geri and Amy.

"Sounds like it," Amy said. "Let's head out there and see if we can pick up a clue as to what Boros' next move is."

"And then shoot her," Geri added, patting the bulge under her jacket where I knew she kept a pistol. At least one pistol.

"We're gonna have to have a talk one of these days about your impulse control," I said, walking around to the front of the truck. "And if I'm the one giving that lecture, either you've got some serious issues, or we've already seen the end of the damned world."

"My money's on both," Skeeter said in my ear, and I couldn't disagree with him. So we left the DHS Suburban in Madame Wanda's parking lot to deter any of Evan's redneck friends from causing trouble, then the three of us piled in my truck and headed to one of the creepiest places in the United States. Yippee.

11

It took us about an hour to get to the Devil's Tramping Ground from the diner around the corner from Wanda's store, and when we pulled off the road in the middle of absolute nowhere a little bit north of a tiny place called Harper's Crossroads, which was nothing more than another meat-and-three restaurant, a gas station, and a couple of auto repair shops, all arranged around a five-way intersection. A little on the nose for my taste in naming stuff, but I couldn't fault the accuracy.

We pulled off the road onto a gravel area that seemed like it was made just for that purpose, probably because the highway department got tired of people parking on the side of the road and digging big mudholes with their tires. A pretty wise municipal decision, I had to admit. Sometimes it's better to just bow to the will of the idiots around you than to fight them. Instead of coming out every couple months to repair the damage from lookie-loos like us, they just dump a truckload of gravel on the side of the road every couple years.

We could see through the scrubby undergrowth and trees a narrow path leading through the woods to a wide area of open earth. "That must be where we're going," I said, starting off toward the trail.

"Hold on, there, Speedy," Amy said, putting a hand on my arm. "Let's gear up."

"We're just going to walk a hundred yards off the road, in the middle of the day, to look at a patch of dirt. What's the worst thing that could happen?"

Geri rolled her eyes and groaned, Skeeter sighed over the comm in my ear, and Amy looked at me like I was at least five of the stupidest people she'd ever met. Which was unfair. I know a lot of the people she's met, at least for the past ten years or so, and there's at least ten that are stupider than me. Eight of them are dead, but that's beside the point.

"Bubba, you're the one who went to Faerie hunting teenagers who were kidnapped by a rogue video game on their cell phones. Do you really have to ask what the worst is?" Amy asked.

"Dude, you were hired as a bouncer and within a month burned the bar down in a zombie attack," Geri added.

"Bubba, you turned a trip to the ballet into a vampire bloodbath, scarring hundreds of children forever, insuring that every therapist in North Carolina could afford a new boat, and got yourself banned from the city of Charlotte in the process," Skeeter said, piling on.

"For the record, that ban was lifted," I said, the only thing I could think of in my defense. "But I get the point. Weird shit happens when I'm around y'all, so I should take my sword."

Amy opened her mouth to speak, but I held up a finger. "We met over the corpse of a cow slaughtered by a vampire family who refused to drink humans, remember?"

"Okay, valid," she agreed. I opened the rear driver's side door to my truck and flipped up the back seat. Underneath was a storage locker filled to the brim with pistols, rifles, ammunition, and my own gear, lying right on top of it all. I grabbed my caestae and my sword and got out of the way as Amy and Geri started to gear up. I slung the sword, an inheritance from my Great-Grandpappy Beauregard, over one shoulder with its strap running diagonally across my chest like a seatbelt, its hilt over my left shoulder to make it easier to draw across my body. The caestae, thick padded gloves with metal bands across the knuckles that I could screw various studs and spikes into depending on what I needed to punch, were hooked onto my belt.

If it was a punching thing, I had my fists of steel. If it was a cutting thing, I had a giant cheese knife strapped across my back. If it was a shooting thing, well, that's what the women were here for, because they were loading up like we were making a new *Rambo* movie or walking headlong into a trap. I wondered if they knew something I didn't, or if they were just always more prepared than me and I'd never really paid attention to it before. Probably that second thing.

Amy had her pistol in a holster on her right hip, with a long silver-edged dagger on the other, and an AR-15 with an underslung grenade launcher on a sling across her chest. A few grenades rode along her belt, and the rifle had two magazines taped together so all she needed to do was eject one, flip it over, and jam it back into the gun. If we ran into something she couldn't put down with sixty rounds, then no amount of ammunition was going to matter.

Geri was similarly kitted out but had small throwing knives strapped to each forearm and calf, along with a second pistol in a paddle holster at the small of her back. I was pretty sure she also had a holdout piece in an ankle holster and at least one more knife hidden somewhere, but I was *not* going to ask. Odds are I would have found out—the hard way.

"Y'all ready?" I asked after a couple minutes of watching their Hot Chicks with Guns montage. "'Cause this Bastille ain't gonna storm itself."

"What the hell do you know about storming the Bastille, Bubba?" Skeeter asked. "I know for a damn fact you slept through European history in both high school and college, because I sat behind you in both classes."

"Yeah, but I've seen *History of the World, Part I* at least four times. And Mel Brooks is a better history teacher than Coach Legrand," I replied, mentioning our high school defensive coordinator/history teacher, who spoke in a monotone guaranteed to put anybody to sleep, not just football players who couldn't possibly give less of a shit about Louis the whatever and just wanted more pictures of Marie Antionette's cleavage.

I turned back to the woods and headed in, trusting Amy and Geri to follow. The sound of feet on the trail behind me was reassuring, because even if it was the middle of the day, I didn't want to wander off by myself into a place called the Devil's friggin' Tramping Ground. That was just asking for trouble.

As an occult landmark and bastion of spookiness in the North Carolina midlands, the Devil's Tramping Ground was…unimpressive. It was just a big open area of red dirt ringed with pine trees and a little trail leading to it off the main road. There were a couple of discarded beer bottles, a few condom wrappers scattered around, and what looked like a pair of abandoned tighty-whities balled up at the base of a tree. I didn't investigate that one too closely, deciding that even it was somehow relevant to our investigation, I didn't care *that* much.

We stood in the center of the roughly circular patch of dead grass and dirt, looking around for something that would indicate why this place was such a big deal. I turned slowly in a circle, closing my eyes and letting the aura of the place sink in, trying to hear, smell, or otherwise sense something out of the ordinary. I was part fairy, dammit, that oughta be good for something more than the occasional super-strong punch.

Nope. Smelled like red dirt, pine needles, and cheap beer. The only thing to differentiate this place from a million other random spots in the middle of the woods where kids get together to drink beer and fool around was the sign driven into the ground at the edge of the circle. "FUTURE HOME OF THE HOUSE OF THE BLESSED ETERNAL FATHER - ANOTHER BOROS-BUILT MIRACLE."

"So...this Boros person wants to build a church on the Devil's Tramping Ground," I said. "Now, if this really is what legend says it is, which is supposedly where Satan comes up out of Hell to pace around and think up new and nastier shit to unleash on humanity, isn't building a church right on top of his favorite thinkin' spot the kind of thing that would normally piss Lucifer off to no end?" I asked.

"Um, I dunno," Geri said from where she knelt in front of the sign. "I think that depends entirely on who or what is supposed to be worshipped in the church they're building."

She pointed to the decorative border of the sign. "This isn't just flowing scribbles, this is script, just squished and stretched until you can barely read it, but it's definitely words. And I think it's Latin. Maybe something else, but it's a hundred percent a language I don't speak, but I'm pretty sure I've seen it somewhere. Maybe in a book or something."

"Not my department," I said, holding up my hands. "I don't do the whole book thing, especially not old ones in foreign languages. I don't even watch anime with subtitles."

"He's not kidding," Amy agreed. "He watches overdubbed anime. It's an abomination."

"Spare me your nerd gatekeeping and come take a look at this," Geri said. "I know Bubba can barely read, but you've seen some of the stuff DHS confiscated from DEMON headquarters. Doesn't this writing look familiar?"

DEMON was the shadowy government agency Amy and I worked for until it became corrupted by a Nazi with a series revenge jones for Quincy Harker and some Final Solution-style plans for every cryptid or magical being on Earth. Including yours truly. We kinda murdered most of them, and Homeland Security took all their toys into some giant warehouse where I reckon Eddie McClintock and his crew would spend the rest of their lives cataloging it and keeping it from falling into the wrong hands. Which would be any hands, by the way. Some of that crap was nasty enough that even if fell into Gandhi's hands, I wouldn't feel safe.

Amy knelt in front of the sign, then straightened up and pulled Geri back. "Oh yeah, I recognize it, but it's not Latin. Now let's head back to the truck because I've seen everything I need to see here. And we really don't want to be here after dark."

"Why?" I asked, looking around. We were a big bunch of hours before the sun even started to set, but if Amy was spooked by that sign, she probably had good reason to be nervous, and I didn't live this long by ignoring warnings given to me by smart people.

Actually, that's a load of crap. I lived this long despite my almost always ignoring the warnings given to me by smart people, but I was trying to get better about that. So I put a hand on the hilt of my sword and started back toward the truck, my eyes scanning the woods with every step. I'd run into monsters that could dish out illusions before, and I wouldn't put it past Puck or some other trickster assclown to trap us in a weird loop where we walked through the same patch of woods for hours until it got dark enough for the real bad things to come out and play.

But nothing like that happened, and a couple minutes later, we were back in the truck with our weapons stowed. Well, most of them, anyway. Geri insisted on keeping an MP-7 in the footwell of the back seat, and Amy's hand never left the butt of her pistol except to fasten her seatbelt. Okay, so my weapons were stowed. It's hard to drive with a sword strapped across your back. Not impossible, but really, *really* not recommended.

"Okay, babe," I said as I pulled back onto the aptly named Devil's Tramping Ground Road. "What the hell got you so scared back there?"

"I'm guessing that you could read the writing around the sign?" Geri asked from the back.

"Not all of it," Amy said. "What I could decipher was that the new temple wasn't to any god I've ever heard of, or even to Lucifer."

"So…what spooked you?" I asked.

"It was the fact that it was in fact dedicated to Mammon, the demon of greed, and it was most definitely not written in Latin. It was Enochian, the language of angels and demons. I can only recognize a few words, and I've studied it for years. Anyone who can inscribe the entire sign like that is either a magic user on a level probably passing Harker or has a conduit straight from their brain to Mammon himself."

"So…it's a demon," I said.

"Oh yeah," Amy said. "It's a demon. And Glory was right, it's a bad one."

"And this temple is going up right in the center of a mystical symbol drawn by connecting the points of a bunch of property Boros Corp. has been trying to buy," Geri said. "Which means…what, exactly?"

"That either Boros wants to build a temple to worship Mammon right here in North Carolina," I said.

"Or they're trying to summon him," Amy added.

"I was really trying not to say it," I grumbled.

"Well, I've said it," Amy replied. "Now we've gotta figure out how to stop it."

I thought for a moment, then summed up the current plan, just to make sure I had it all down. "So we just need to figure out how to keep an evil wizard from summoning a demon of greed, and by the way, she's moved from buying out competitors to eviscerating people who get in her way. So…yeah, this is gonna suck."

12

The offices for Boros Construction, Inc. were pretty nondescript, just a squat brown building with a bunch of white pickups parked all around it. It looked just like every other contractor's office anywhere, except for the part where the owner was trying to summon demons to take over the world.

We pulled up out front, and Amy opened her door, then pulled it shut and turned around to face me and Geri. "How about I go in first and check things out, then if things go sideways, you come in guns blazing?"

"Why don't we just go with you so we can avoid the part of the plan where you're all alone in a building with a demon-summoning slumlord?" I asked.

"Because I'd like to avoid dealing with any other police departments today if at all possible, and I don't trust you not to be a Bubba in a china shop."

"What's that supposed to mean?" I asked.

"Dude, when I'm not the least subtle member of a team, we've got problems," Geri said. "I'll wait here with the big guy."

I unbuckled my seatbelt and turned around to grab my sword off the floor of the back seat, but I just laid it across my lap instead of heading out. "Go ahead, but you'd better keep your comms open every second you're in there."

"Unless I go to the bathroom, you'll hear everything I do," Amy replied.

"Like I've never heard you pee," I said. "We live together. I've woken up to your farts in the middle of the night."

"And every bit of mystery is gone, just like that," Geri said with a laugh.

Amy didn't dignify my fart joke with a response, which was pretty normal, and honestly the best way to deal with my humor. Most of my jokes are in the "ignore it and it'll go away" category. She just got out of the truck, closed the passenger door, and tapped the earwig in her left ear to activate her comm link with Skeeter and my truck.

A couple seconds later, her voice came through the center console. "Comms check."

I tapped the screen on my dash. "Read you five by five," I replied.

"Where did you learn five by five, Bubba?" Skeeter asked.

"*Buffy* reruns."

"I wish we still had those tiny cameras so we could see what was happening," Geri said. "Downside of not having the big boss of the agency on the field trip with us, I guess."

But we didn't have the cool micro-cameras, so I just sat helpless while the woman I loved walked through the front door of a known demon summoner. Or at least a known attempted demon summoner. And a known hippie eviscerator, which also wasn't good. I fidgeted in my seat, trying to get comfortable while I listened to Amy talk to a receptionist.

"Sit still, Bubba," Geri hissed. "I can't hear over the springs rocking while you wiggle your big ass all over the place."

"Heh heh. If the truck's a-rocking—"

"Ew. If you finish that sentence, I swear to God I will drop a grenade under your seat and blow us both to Kingdom Come. Because I do not want to live in a world where that thought is in my head," Geri said, cutting me off cold.

It wasn't a bluff. Or if it was, it was a really good one, because there were a couple of hand grenades in the cabinets under the back seat, and Geri was definitely crazy enough to blow herself to bits if it meant killing somebody she really wanted dead. I'd had that kind of dedication to a fight once. It ended up with me killing my father and my kid brother shoving a sword through my guts. The sword that currently lay across my lap, as a matter of fact. That should tell you how well it ended for my brother, too.

All I was getting from the other end of Amy's conversation was a muted *Waah-waah-waah-waah*, like she was talking to one of the adults in a Charlie Brown cartoon, but it was only about two minutes until she came back out the front door and walked over to the truck. I started to open the door, but she waved me back.

A few seconds later, she slipped into the passenger seat. "No luck. Boros is apparently out surveying the progress on one of her job sites today."

"Is that code for murdering somebody else?" I asked.

"I don't think so. If that receptionist is in on this mess, she's a better actor than I give her credit for because she really gives off the impression of just punching a time clock and collecting a paycheck. I don't think she's involved, and I expect that means she doesn't know anything about what Boros is up to."

"Or she tries real hard not to know," I grumbled. "Now what?"

"Now we head to Pinehurst to the job site Boros was supposed to be checking on. The receptionist wasn't very good with screen security, so I was able to see the calendar open on her desktop. Today's biggest entry was 'LB at Pinehurst job,' so that seems like our next step."

"Pretty good," I said. "You keep that up, we're gonna promote you past Junior Adventurer."

"I hate I ever let you listen to that podcast," Geri said from the back seat.

It looked like a normal construction site. Some big yellow pieces of equipment, a couple bright blue Porta-Potties, a lot of red dirt and white pickups, and one jet black Tesla gleaming in the sun. "I told you she was in cahoots with that Elon Musk dude. See, she even drives one of his cars," I said, pointing to the electric coupe.

"Dude, lots of people drive Teslas," Geri said. "It doesn't mean you're working with the legions of Hell."

"But it doesn't mean you aren't either," I shot back.

She let out one of those sighs that people give when they think I'm being stupid about something, but I knew in my heart that there was some kind of connection between electric cars and demon summoning. Mostly because I still can't wrap my head around the idea of plugging in my car instead of splashing unleaded all over my pants leg when I'm in a hurry. As clumsy as I am with a gas pump, I hate to see what kind of shit I can get into with a high voltage charging cable. If they even use cables. For all I know, they've got a pad you can drive onto that charges your car overnight, like that thing Amy got to charge her phone on the dresser. She never even plugs it in. Something about that bothers me, and I ain't real sure what, but it don't feel natural.

The one thing missing from the construction site was any actual evidence of something being, well, *constructed.* They had all the stuff that people use to build things, but I saw no evidence of anything actually being built. It was like the whole area was just a placeholder, just a barren patch of ground waiting for something to happen. Which was kinda like the Tramping Ground, if I was honest.

"Hey, y'all?" I asked, slowing my walk toward the small trailer sitting in the middle of a big patch of empty red dirt. "Shouldn't somebody be, I dunno, building something?"

"That's what I want to talk to the guy in the trailer about," Amy replied, continuing to head in that direction. "There's a lot of equipment here, and none of it looks to be getting any use. So I'd like to know what's going on."

A big man stepped out of the trailer onto the small set of wooden stairs someone had wedged under the aluminum door. "What's going on is a closed site, miss," he said, his voice carrying much farther than it needed to, what with there only being four of us within earshot. "I'm Jake Henry, the foreman here. Y'all need something? Or you just lost?"

"We're looking for Leigh Boros," Amy said, holding up her badge. "Is she here?"

Big Jake, because there's no way he was called anything else, given that he was almost as tall as me and maybe as big around, shook his head. "Sorry. Ms. Boros don't come to the job sites. That's why she's got foremen."

"Then whose car is that?" Geri asked, pointing to the Tesla. "Pretty sure that's not your typical construction worker vehicle."

Big Jake laughed. "Nah, that belongs to my secretary, Trisha. She likes all that hippy-dippy tree-hugger crap like electric cars. Give me a big-ass diesel any day." He leaned onto the banister, his bulk completely blocking the door to the trailer. If we wanted to see if Boros was inside, we were gonna have to go through Jake. Fine by me.

"Dude," I said, holding my hands out to the side. "We can do this one of two ways. We can stand out here jaw-jacking for a while until Deputy Director Hall gets her people to drum up a warrant and swarm this joint in black helicopters or some such crap, or you can step aside and let her go look around, ask your receptionist a couple questions, and we can get on our merry way, leaving you to get back to your…constructing…" My affable bullshit ran out of steam when I gestured to the lack of any construction activity taking place around me.

"Or I can lock this door behind me, come down these steps, whoop your ass, throw you in the back of that crappy old Ford you rolled up here in, and then send your little girlfriend and her baby sister off to take you to the emergency room. How does that sound for an idea?" Jake said, turning around and locking the trailer door.

He clumped down to meet us, his big work boots making the aluminum stairs ring with every step. He stood in front of the trailer, hands down at his hips, and rolled his head from side to side to loosen up his neck. I never saw much point in that, myself. I kinda want my neck to be tight, that way if I get popped in the jaw, my noggin' don't wobble around like a dashboard Jesus.

"That sounds fine to me," I said, stepping between Amy and Geri. "I ain't beat nobody's ass in at least three hours, and there ain't no cops around this time, so I might even get out of this one without another arrest on my record."

"If you get out of this at all, son," Big Jake said, and stepped forward to sock me in the jaw.

Now when somebody wants to knock the ever-loving shit out of you, there's a couple of different things you can do. You can stand there and take it, which ain't real advisable with somebody who's built like a refrigerator with fists the size of Honey Baked hams. You can run away, which ain't much of an option when you're as fat as me, as slow as me, and got knees as jacked up as mine. I might make three steps before I either get winded or get caught, which would put me right back where I was before I tried to run.

Or you can step into the first haymaker they try to land on your chin, wrap your left arm over their right, trapping their wrist in your armpit, and headbutt the son of a bitch into the middle of next week.

I chose Plan C, which was supposed to end up with me squishing Big Jake's nose like a grape, but really ended up with him pulling back a hair so my head smashed into his open mouth, which he proceeded to chomp down on my gourd with, ripping my forehead open and leaving me with a crimson mask of blood fountaining down into my eyes and face. I looked like I was on the losing end of a cage match in 1983, and the fight had barely started.

Then four more guys, all Jake's size, came around from the back of the trailer, and shit went even more sideways, if that's even possible.

13

So we had five big sonsabitches, most of them carrying either a two-by-four, length of iron plumbing pipe, or a crescent wrench that looked big enough to bolt an aircraft carrier together. I had nothing but a handful of foreman, and not enough sense to have brought my sword or anything else I could use as a weapon, and a pair of well-armed partners who were awesome at shooting things, or even punching normal human-sized things, but all five of these guys looked like they eat defensive linemen for breakfast, so that was going to pose a serious challenge.

Okay, more than a challenge. We were about to get our asses kicked. Then I noticed something about the guy I was hanging onto. He was struggling, and about to break free of my grip, even though I could feel my newly developed magic muscles kicking in, making me way stronger than I would normally be. His eyes flashed briefly red, and I saw all the other goons' eyes do the same, then he yanked free from my hand like taking a toy away from a naughty toddler.

Actually, probably a lot easier than that. Some of those wobbly little bastards have serious grip. But he pulled himself free and planted a fist right in the top of my bleeding forehead. I felt like somebody had hit me in the head with a tree. Not a branch, but the whole goddamned tree. I dropped straight down to both knees, my eyes desperately trying to swim back into focus as more blood poured from my scalp. I knew it wasn't a serious injury, given how bad scalp wounds bleed, but that didn't mean the blood pouring into my eyes didn't suck. I couldn't see through the red haze and my stinging eyes, but I kinda felt the air move as the big man swung his fist toward my face again.

I didn't really dodge. More like I sprawled sideways to keep from getting my skull cracked. Gravel dug into the flesh of my right arm and shoulder, and I brought my left hand up to wipe the blood from my eyes as I scrambled across the parking lot and struggled to my feet. I took a second to survey the area, and it was just about as bad as I could have expected.

Geri was throwing kicks and strikes as fast as she could, barely keeping two guys at bay, while Amy held her service weapon swinging back and forth at two goons as they approached slowly, spreading out so she would have a hard time shooting one without the other one getting his mitts on her. In a couple steps, her back would be pressed up against my truck, and then she'd have nowhere to go. I couldn't spare the attention for long because Big Jake was still stalking me, and I barely ducked another massive punch that put a dent in the side of the construction trailer.

"They ain't human!" I yelled. "This dude's strong as shit, and his eyes glow when he gets pissed off!"

"Heh heh. Nah, that ain't it," Big Jake said. "That's just me calling on my father's strength to help me deal with obnoxious little shits like you."

"Either way," Amy said, "makes me not feel so bad about doing this." And her service weapon barked once, twice, three times as she pumped two in the chest of the nearest goon, then finished him off with one in the head.

I couldn't pay too much attention to what she was doing because Jake decided since I didn't have a gun, he should just go back to his plan of beating me to death before Amy got around to shooting him. He took a big step in toward me, drawing his meaty right fist back for a punch that looked meant to cave in my skull, but I had a little surprise for Big Jake.

I flung a handful of gravel into his face, blinding him for the couple seconds I needed to slip around behind him, wrap my arms around his neck, and start to squeeze. Now I've watched a lot of pro wrestling, but I also know that a correctly applied sleeper hold doesn't take the couple minutes that Brutus the Barber always took to put his opponents out. Since I wasn't trying to build any kind of drama, or murder the big bastard, as soon as Big Jake went limp, I opened my arms and let him slump to the ground. He wouldn't be out long, but hopefully long enough to get this all finished up before anybody else needed to die.

I hurried over to where Geri was still fending off two attackers and clubbed one guy on the back of the neck. He fell face-first onto the gravel lot, and I reared back and planted my massive boot right between his legs. Him laying on his belly meant I got more taint than sack with my kick, but the results were the same. He curled up in a groaning ball and I turned to the other guy, only to see him on the ground holding his throat and gasping for air.

"The hell did you do to him?" I asked.

"Do you really want to know?" Geri asked. "He's alive, so just call it a win that I didn't kill his ass and make you clean it up."

Amy walked over to us with her last attacker cuffed and docile before her. She put a foot behind his knee and shoved his shoulder down so he knelt on the ground in front of us. "If you're not human, what are you?" she asked, aiming her pistol at the back of his head.

"Babe, you got any more handcuffs?" I asked. "We might want to tie up some of these other assholes before we…well, shit."

"Well, shit what?" Amy asked, looking at me, then following my gaze. "Well, shit."

I wasn't surprised to see Big Jake on his feet. I wasn't even surprised to see the pretty woman with an expression black enough to match her tailored business suit standing at the door of the construction trailer. I was a little surprised to see half a dozen cars with blue lights on their roofs heading our way at top speed. At least, I was surprised until I saw the cell phone in the hands of the woman I could only assume was Leigh Boros.

"I expect we're all about to spend a little time in the county pokey," I said. "Because that is not the face of a woman who thinks the police are coming for her."

"No," Geri said. "That's the face of a woman who knows she's already paid off the police. What do we do, boss? Shoot it out with the local cops, or go to jail?"

"Well, I guess since Bubba's already been to jail once on this trip, it's only fair we all spend at least a little time as wards of the state," Amy replied. She still held her sidearm and looked around at the grinning construction goons. "Just remember, boys. Those cars aren't here yet, and I'm still packing. You take one wrong step, and it'll be your very last mistake."

Then we stood and waited to get arrested. Again. If we kept this up, there wasn't going to be a single town in North Carolina where I was welcome. And that would suck, since I really like the Outer Banks.

An hour later, I was sitting on the uncomfortable bench/bed in yet another central North Carolina jail cell, making this officially the most times I'd been arrested in a twenty-four-hour period. I was leaning back with my head against the cinderblock wall listening to Geri swear at the guards from the cell she shared with Amy across the hall. She was creative with her profanity, and I wondered if maybe I needed to get her a gig writing for *The Boys* or something like that.

She finally ran out of steam, or oxygen, after about thirty minutes of non-stop swearing in which she didn't repeat the same curse words even once. I told you—impressive. It was your typical small-town jail, just six cells designed for one or two people in a hallway leading to a large holding cell down at the end. I was situated in the cell farthest from the door, right next to the drunk tank, while Amy and Geri were in one of the cells nearest the door.

It wasn't too uncomfortable in the cells, even if the deputy who arrested me took my shoelaces and my belt, ostensibly to keep me from killing myself while in custody, but I figured it was also partially to keep me from trying to escape. I might be able to fight my way through a few rural cops, but having to hold my britches up with one hand and fight with my other would certainly make things tougher. And trying to run with my shoes falling off? Yeah, that wasn't gonna happen. I'm way past the years when falling down didn't hurt. So I just leaned back and hummed off-key blues tunes while we waited.

"You're awfully quiet down there, Bubba," Geri called.

"How would you know?" I asked. "You been screeching like a potty-mouthed banshee since the second they locked us in here."

"Don't worry," Amy chimed in. "She was doing the same thing in the cop car the whole way here. I think I even learned a few new swear words."

"You're welcome," Geri said, sarcasm dripping off her tongue like honey. Bitter, poisonous honey that would kill you quicker than cyanide. "But seriously, Bubba. What's the plan? How are we getting out of here?"

"The plan is we sit here and chill until our quarry comes to us," I said.

"Quarry?" Geri's voice floated down the hall. "Who the hell are you and what did you do with Bubba?"

"I know big words," I said, feeling just a little defensive. "I did go to college, you know."

"You went to UGA. For football. I'm pretty sure they didn't care if you ever attended a class," she replied.

"Fair enough. But I read a lot when I blew out my knee. Couldn't walk and all that."

"You mean you didn't just lay in your bed pulling your pud while your leg healed?"

"Oh, I did plenty of that, too. But there's only so many times you can do that in a day, even when you're young."

I could almost hear the snicker in her voice. "Sorry to hear that, Amy," Geri said.

"It's more a matter of friction and blisters than stamina," I shot back.

"*Anyway*," Amy cut in. "I think Bubba's right. We just need to hang out, and eventually either Ms. Boros will come to gloat, or the sheriff and his goons will take us out to shoot us all in the back of the head."

"And…then what, exactly?" Geri asked.

"Well, it's the same plan for either option," I said. "We beat the shit out of everybody, get Boros to admit her diabolical scheme, and then we go home, having cleared Madame Wanda's good name and once more bringing light to the darkest corners of our world."

"No more comic books for you, babe," Amy said. "That sounded like bad *Superman* dialogue."

She wasn't wrong. I'd been channeling my most pompous do-gooder superhero voice, too. But I was going more for Shazam than Superman. Whatever. One imaginary dude in tights was as good as the next. I didn't get to consider my superheroes for very long, though, because the door at the end of the hall opened up and a gorgeous woman with cheekbones you could shave with and eyes like chips of ice walked through, flanked by a pair of new deputies, different from the ones who'd brought us to the jail. Looked like the whole department was in on whatever she had planned. I couldn't imagine that was good for us.

"Well, these are the troublemakers the feds have sent down to investigate our little project, hmmm?" she said, stopping by Amy and Geri's cell. "You look official, you look like you're only here for the mayhem, and you…" She turned to look down the hall at me, leaning against the wall as calmly as possible when I was trapped behind steel bars with a demon-worshipping psycho and her bought-and-paid-for constabulary less than ten feet from the woman I loved. "You are the biggest pain in the ass I've ever met."

"I've always been an overachiever," I said, giving her my best "aw-shucks" grin. I've been told it makes me look a little like Jethro from *The Beverly Hillbillies*, and I've never been sure if that was supposed to be a compliment or not. Since Skeeter's the one who said it, probably not.

Her stiletto heels *click-click-clicked* on the concrete as she walked down to stand in front of my cell. "Nobody likes a smartass, Mr. Brabham," she said, making sure to stand well away from the bars in case I made a grab for her.

"I'll have you know I'm very popular in certain circles," I replied.

"Let's see how popular you are when I raise a temple to my lord and master right in the center of the Devil's Tramping Ground and turn this entire state into Mammon's domain on Earth," she said, a broad grin splitting her face.

In that smile I saw something I'd seen many times before, in the face of my brother, my father, the psycho museum nerd down in Florida who summoned demons, that Liang guy Harker blew up in D.C., and more of my human enemies than I cared to admit. Leigh Boros was undeniably bugshit crazy, and if it wasn't bad enough that she was nuts, she was nuts with cops on her payroll, a shit-ton of money, and a book on baby's first demon summoning. I think Grady Hendrix wrote that one.

I let out a sigh and stood up, walking over to the cell door like I had the weight of the world on my shoulders. I guess I kinda did, but more like just the weight of central North Carolina. "I think we've got enough churches in the South," I said, putting my hands on the bars. "So how about we put a pin in this demon temple idea and get back to dealing with the bit where you murdered a preacher and tried to blame his aunt for it?"

"You mean Evan? He was an idiot, and he should have taken my very generous offer when he had the chance. Now his sacrifice will go to pave the way for my master to—"

I'd heard enough. With a silent prayer to my magical mama and whoever upstairs, downstairs, or sideways had been making me super-strong, I squeezed the bars of my cell and yanked back with all my might. Something gave, and it wasn't my shoulders, because I felt raw power course through my body, and the steel cell door tore from its frame like tissue paper. I gently leaned the door against the bars next to the opening and stepped out into the hallway.

"Now," I said, looking down at the insane demon summoner and real estate mogul before me. "Let's talk about this a little."

Her eyes went huge, and she staggered back a couple of steps, flapping a hand frantically in my direction. "Kill him!" she shouted. The cops behind her started drawing weapons, and I just shook my head. Why does nobody ever want to talk it out?

Oh well. Time to punch things. Again.

14

I fully expected to get shot, but apparently the cops, although bought and paid for, were not interested in murdering a bunch of federal agents on the orders of a crazy bajillionaire. Good to know there was a line that money couldn't persuade these guys to cross. That line didn't extend far enough to keep one of them from drawing his Taser, but apparently, he missed the day they taught How to Subdue Giant Rednecks in the academy because one prong fired true and stuck me in my left thigh, but the other one hit Boros in her right butt cheek. That meant that the circuit never completed, and all I got was a little pinprick in my leg, and Boros just shot the cop a dirty look as she turned and ran back toward the front of the station and the half-dozen other cops that I remembered walking past on the way in.

I took three big steps and stopped right in front of the pudgy deputy who was frantically trying to affix a new little cartridge thingy onto the front of his Taser. I cleared my throat, and he looked up at me, a bead of sweat escaping from his thinning hairline and running for the hills. Actually, it ran toward the first of his several chins, where I intercepted it. With my fist. One good, but not super-strong, punch, and the young deputy sprawled flat on his back.

I looked at the other deputy. "We can do this the easy way or the really painful way. You get to pick."

"What's the easy way?" He was rail-thin, with a shaved head and a face that probably wasn't old enough to have to shave every day. A little sprig of peach fuzz darkened his upper lip in an adorable attempt to make him look older, but I bet he still got yelled at by every little old lady he pulled over for speeding. If he was lucky, Granny took the cigarette out of her mouth before she told him to kiss her ass. That's how you can tell a real Southern lady.

"You hand me the keys to that cell," I said, jerking my thumb at Amy and Geri. "Then you turn around and start walking. Stop when you get far enough away that you can't hear the sounds of the fight that's about to start. The really painful way, even though you didn't ask, is where I knock the shit out of you and take the keys, then at least one person probably steps on your unconscious ass while we try to have a fight in a jail hallway. Spoiler alert—it ain't gonna look anything like the fight in that *Daredevil* TV show because I ain't a ninja. It's gonna be a lot more picking people up and smacking other people with them. So, what's it gonna be?"

He stared at me for about five seconds, then just reached down to where a big jangly ring of keys hung off his hip, unclipped them from his belt loop, handed them to me, and headed for the door, stripping off his badge and gun belt as he went. "Screw this, man. I just wanted a steady job and maybe get laid a little on account of the uniform. I ain't in this for crazy woman raising demons and throwing feds in jail." He dropped his gear by the door and vanished while I started trying keys in the cell holding the girls.

"Could you maybe work a little faster, Bubba?" Amy asked, grabbing the bars and trying to jam her face far enough through them to get a better look at what I was doing. "I don't know if our psycho developer was leaving or going for backup."

"I'm betting on backup," Geri said. She stepped up beside Amy and held out her hand. "Gimme those. We'll find the key while you go hold off the po-po."

I wasn't sure how I was supposed to do anything against an entire police station full of armed cops other than bleed a lot and maybe fall down, but I passed her the keys and turned to follow the smarter guard out the door. Then the screaming started, and I decided that maybe running was the better option.

It wasn't better. It was very much not better. I flung open the door and stepped into the main section of the cop shop and stopped dead in my tracks. There was blood *everywhere*. I mean floor, walls, ceiling, windows, every horizontal or vertical surface was at least spattered, if not covered, in viscous red liquid and oddly shaped chunks of things that I really didn't want a close look at.

Leigh Boros was standing in the middle of the room in a hastily drawn protection circle, with the sheriff standing beside her. Outside the circle were two deputies, one with a dark stain spreading out from the crotch of his uniform pants, and the other looking like he really needed his khakis to be a darker brown.

I couldn't blame them, though. The first time I saw a demon, I almost crapped my pants, too. Almost. I might have peed just a little, but not like a full-on whizz, more like a little spritz. And this demon was every inch the pants-wetting, trouser chili-generating nightmare that Pentecostal preachers have built mansions preaching about.

It was barely short enough to stand upright in the bullpen, with unnaturally long arms dangling past its knees, ending in six spindly fingers with clawed fingernails. Its body was gaunt, and its knees hinged backward like a grasshopper, giving it a nauseating surreal appearance that was just undeniably *alien*. Even before I looked at its face, I knew I wasn't going to like what I saw.

Sometimes I hate being right. This thing's face made Deadpool look like a runway model, with gore dripping down its chin, fangs jutting out from the top and bottom jaws, and three red eyes gleaming as it turned to me. "Mmmm…" it said, its voice like rocks rolling around in a bathtub full of vomit. "Lunch is served."

"Bitch, if you think I'm just lunch, you'd better look again. I'm a full seven courses of ass-kicking, so you can either get back downstairs where you belong, or I can unleash some seriously biblical punishment on your ugly mug," I said, channeling every bit of courage I had just to keep from running back into the jail and locking myself in the farthest cell. This thing was frigging terrifying, and I had absolutely no idea how I was going to deal with it.

Fortunately, I didn't have to deal with it alone. Amy and Geri stepped through the still-open doorway, Amy carrying a pistol I assumed she took off the unconscious deputy, since Geri was wearing the other cop's discarded gun belt.

"Holy shit," Geri said. "What the fuck is that thing?"

"Demon," Amy said. "And way above our pay grade. This is not what we're supposed to be handling."

"You wanna tell him, or you want me to?" I asked. "I mean, I don't think he's just gonna go away, no matter what we say, but I reckon if you say 'pretty please,' you might get somewhere."

"By the power invested in me by the great Lord Mammon, I command you to destroy them!" Boros shrieked, pointing at us. It felt a little excessive, honestly. I mean, we were standing in the middle of a small-town jail with a demon literally dripping black saliva all over the floor. I felt pretty confident that this critter was going to do its level best to destroy everything in a five-mile radius, or more. I was also pretty confident that I wasn't going to be alive to see much of its destruction, on account of me being way closer than five miles from aforementioned slavering maw. Cut me some slack; I got a Word A Day calendar for my birthday and I've been studying.

The demon turned its head slowly to face the thin woman screaming in its ear, and while I'm no expert on demonic facial expressions, I'm pretty sure the grin that spread across the demon's face wasn't because it was happy to be there.

"You have meddled with powers beyond your imagining, mortal, and you have done so without proper protection," the demon said, and about a hundred poorly timed condom jokes ran through my head, but somehow, I managed to keep them all to myself, except for a little snort that I tried to pass off as a sneeze.

"I summoned you, demon, so you must obey my bidding!" Boros screeched. She stretched a slender arm in our direction again and repeated, "Destroy them!"

The demon looked at the three of us standing clustered around the door to the holding cells. "Don't worry, mortal," it said, the rasp of its voice making my head hurt with some kind of unearthly pressure inside my skull. "I shall destroy them. But not before I demonstrate the folly of attempting to control a Duke of Hell!"

Boros's eyes widened, and she took a step back from the monster, crossing over the fragile boundary created by her summoning circle and leaving her completely exposed to the demon. It hadn't looked like much of a circle, just a chalk line scrawled onto the tile floor, and I don't know how much defense it provided against the dark arts, but once she was outside of it, the demon was *completely* free to do whatever it liked. And what it liked was murder.

The creature reached out to Boros, completely enveloping her head in one massive hand and lifting her off her feet. All that remained visible of her was the body from the neck down, flailing helplessly in the air as she fought to break free. Wasn't gonna happen. I could see from where I was standing that there was no way in hell she was getting out of the demon's grip without help.

"Should we help her?" Amy asked in a whisper.

"Hell no," Geri snapped. "We need to get our asses out of here as fast as we can while it picks its teeth with her shinbones."

I couldn't argue with her logic, but there was still the matter of a massive demon standing between us and the door. Even if it got distracted tearing the crazy demon-worshipper to shreds, I'm not exactly what anyone would describe as "stealthy." Plan B it was. I took three big steps over to the gun case against the jail wall, smashed the glass with my elbow, and grabbed a twelve-gauge pump shotgun from the rack inside. I slid five shells into the tube, racked one into the chamber, then topped off the magazine with a sixth round, all slugs. I didn't want a bunch of pellets bouncing around the cop shop and maybe hitting Amy, or I guess Geri, plus the slugs would blow a big hole in anything I hit, hopefully up to and including demons.

I turned back to the demon, only to freeze at the sight in front of me. The demon had switched up its grip on Boros' body, now holding her one-handed around her torso while it took bites out of her still-twitching corpse. Her head was gone, and as the sound of Amy retching filled the room, it turned its attention back to us and grinned.

Look, it's bad when a demon grins at you, just as a rule. It's way worse when it's grinning at you from the same room when unbound by a circle or anything else that might keep it from ripping you to shreds. It's even worse than that when it has a chunk of what looks like lung wedged between a couple of its front teeth and an ebon shock of its victim's hair hanging down over its chin. It flung what was left of Leigh Boros, crazy real estate magnate, vicious murderer, and one-time demon summoner, across the room to splash off a wall and slide to the floor in a puddle of blood and viscera.

I was in a bad spot, up against a seemingly invulnerable enemy, without a magical sword, or even a rocket launcher, to my name. I was probably going to die, so I decided to channel a couple of new friends I made in the swamps of South Carolina and die in style.

I turned to the demon, took a deep breath, and bellowed, "LEEEEEEROY JENKINS!!!"

15

Perhaps an internet hoax isn't the best place to draw from for a battle cry, but it's what I had at the time. Actually, what I had was a twelve-gauge shotgun and two women crazy enough to follow me into a fight with a literal monster from the bowels of Hell, each of whom was toting a handgun. I can't imagine any of these things are in the Demon Hunter Starter Kit, but I reckon I can ask Harker next time I see him.

At any rate, the demon was at least surprised by our reckless, if not downright brutally stupid, charge. I fired on the move, which is harder than you'd expect with a shotgun, because it basically meant I had no control over my shots. Amy and Geri were walking forward at a steady pace, squeezing off rounds one right after the other, dropping magazines and quickly slamming home spares like they were trained for this kind of thing. Of course, they *were* trained for this kind of thing.

I was trained to drink beer, chase cheerleaders, and flatten quarterbacks, none of which were skills that translate well to hand-to-hand combat with demons. Okay, there's a little crossover between sacking a quarterback and hitting a demon, but only if it's a quarterback too dumb to get out of the way. So an *ACC* quarterback.

I managed to hit the demon with three of my six shots, which was pretty good. But way too soon, I was five feet away from the giant witch-eating monster with an empty shotgun, also known as a stick. So I did what comes naturally. I flipped the Mossberg around, gripped the barrel as tight as I could, regretting it immediately because gun barrels get *hot*, and swinging at the demon's knees like I was the second coming of Hammerin' Hank Aaron.

And dropped the gun as soon as I made contact, thanks to the vibration running up my arms. The demon didn't even flinch. I was starting to dislike everything in North Carolina at least as much as everything in the state seemed to dislike me. It swatted me to the ground with a negligent backhand, like I wasn't even worth its attention. I smacked into the tile and slid a few feet to the side, then rolled over onto all fours, planting my hand right smack in the middle of something that felt like uncooked sausage. I wiped off the chunk of intestine and hauled myself upright, shaking my head to clear the cobwebs.

"Hey, asshole," I called. "I ain't done with you yet."

That got its attention. The demon stopped, completely ignoring the fact that Amy and Geri were still pumping nine-millimeter rounds into its chest as fast as they could pull the trigger. It turned to face me, a horrific grin splitting its toothy face. "That blow should have shattered your skull, mortal."

"Mama always said I was hard-headed," I said, holding up both fists. I had no idea if some kind of enhanced durability came along with this boosted strength I was feeling, but the only way Amy was getting out of that police station alive was if I could keep this thing's attention on me. And that was all I cared about right then—giving the woman I loved a chance to survive.

That all came to me in an instant. I didn't care whether I lived or died. I hadn't really cared since Joe died. But I cared about Amy living. And I cared about Geri living. I'd failed her sister, and I wasn't going to fail her, too. So if the big bastard in front of me gutted me and spread me all around the floor of the cop shop, so be it. As long as those two women got out alive, that was all I gave a shit about.

There's something very freeing about not caring whether you live or die. Throwing yourself into unwinnable fights trying to die is one thing, and I'd been there, too. Trying to hurt someone or some*thing* else as badly as you're hurting is another way I'd tried to cope with my pain, and it wasn't any better. But this strange calm that washed over me as I stood there about to go toe-to-toe with a demon was like nothing I'd ever felt. I felt...clear. Like everything finally made sense. I was Bubba the Motherfuckin' Monster Hunter, and this son of a bitch needed somebody to open a can of whoop-ass and dump it all over him.

So I did.

I took two big steps in the demon's direction, then jumped up on top of one of the desks and used the height to launch myself right at the demon's face. I slammed into the big bastard with my shoulder right under its chin, and we went down in a tangle of limbs, swearing, and nasty bits of crazy lady. I drove a knee into the demon's chest and heard a resounding *crack* from somewhere in the vicinity of a sternum. It opened its mouth to scream, but I did one of the stupidest things I've done in my life, and that is a *long* list.

I shoved both hands into the demon's mouth, grabbed its lower jaw with one hand, its upper teeth with the other, and started trying to pull its head apart. The razor-sharp teeth shredded my palms, and I felt blood dripping down into the thing's mouth. It flailed at me with its arms, but I was too close for it to get a good swing in, and it didn't have any leverage lying on its back. Seems like physics is a bitch to Hellspawn, too.

I felt lines of red-hot agony spring to life along my back and sides as the demon's claws dug into my flesh and turned to see Amy and Geri standing frozen by the door to the jail. "Get the hell out of here!" I yelled. "Get help. Or call in an airstrike. But don't just stand there while this son of a bitch rips me to shreds!"

I heard something begin to groan and creak under my hands, and the demon's screaming went up an octave, morphing from a howl of rage into a shriek of agony. I kept slamming my knee into its chest over and over again, and it kept clawing at my sides and back until it finally got one hand between us and shoved me off onto the gore-slick floor.

I landed on my side, rolled onto my back, and used my elbow to keep rolling and struggle to my feet. The demon wasn't looking much better than I felt, and I was kinda impressed to see that its mouth didn't close quite right anymore. I'd at least given the bastard something to remember me by. I'd have a bunch of new scars, too, if I lived through the next couple of minutes. It didn't look very likely, but a sharp report yanked my attention away from the demon and into the body of the police station.

The sheriff, who up until a couple minutes ago had been completely in the pocket of the now-dismembered real estate mogul-slash-demon summoner, stood with his feet shoulder width apart, arms extended straight out from his body in a tight isosceles stance, and was emptying his sidearm into the side of the demon's face from twenty feet away. I was impressed. I figured he would have slipped out and headed for the hills once his meal ticket got devoured. All it served to do was distract the demon more than hurt him, but a distraction was exactly what I needed right then. I mean, that airstrike woulda been nice, too, but I'd take the distraction.

I frantically waved for Amy and Geri to run while I looked around for anything that might be useful in fighting a demon. I was just about to give up and wade back in with my bare hands when I spotted a familiar pile of gear lying on a deputy's abandoned desk. They hadn't just arrested us; they'd arrested us while we were carrying all our stuff. Including Great-Grandpappy Beauregard's sword. I snatched up the blade from the desk, turned around to the demon, who had just started moving in the sheriff's direction, and said, "By the power of Greyskull, you son of a bitch."

The demon, obviously not a fan of 1980s cartoon, ignored me. That was fine by me, because it meant the big ugly bastard was still focused on the sheriff and completely ignoring the two women running and one deputy limping for the front door. The digital chime of the door opening caught the demon's notice, and I yelled for the sheriff to run. Then I did something that cracked into my Top Ten list of stupidest crap I've done in a police station, and yes there are more than ten stupid things I've done in a cop shop.

I raised Great-Grandpappy Beauregard's sword over my head and charged the demon, screaming like a banshee and without a single damned idea of what I was gonna do when I got to the thing. Fortunately, I guess, the demon had a plan. Unfortunately, that plan was to murder me.

It raised both spindly arms as I ran toward it, and I could almost hear the air whistle across its fingertips as it lashed out at me. But football wasn't the only sport I ever played; it was just the only one I was good at. I played Little League baseball and church league softball, and even made the varsity team in high school before I had to choose between sports. So, when I saw those Slenderman arms stretching out to unzip my guts, I dropped to the tile and scooted along the floor like I was sliding into home plate. I slashed out with my sword as I zipped right past the demon's legs, hoping to snap its hamstring like a rubber band.

Here's a pro tip—if you're fighting a monster whose legs are hinged backward, the hamstring, if you even call it that, is also in the wrong place. So, while I slashed the monster in the leg with my sword, it was more like I slapped it in the shin with a sharp stick. I mean, it was better than nothing, but it was a lot less effective than I'd hoped.

I scrambled to my feet and spun around to face the demon, who grinned down at me with that mass of teeth. "You wish to be the next to perish, human? So be it."

I held up a hand in a "Stop" gesture. "You've got a chunk of face stuck between your front teeth. It's real hard to pay attention to you when your mouth is staring at me."

The demon drew back a hair, obviously confused. I got it. I'd be confused, too, if somebody who was supposed to be crapping themselves stopped in the middle of a fight to tell me I had something in my teeth. That's kinda why I did it. Because when the demon straightened up and cocked its head to the side in confusion, I lunged forward and stabbed it in the chest with my sword.

The demon screeched in agony as Great-Grandpappy's magic sword slid into its ribcage like it was butter, then it swatted me upside the head, cartwheeling me over a nearby desk and taking out two rolling office chairs as I went down. I also lost hold of my sword, but it seemed to be doing pretty good work right where it was, sticking out of the demon's middle.

"I'll kill you, mortal! You can't harm the Hand of Mammon! I am—"

"Going home, is what you are." I knew the voice that came from the front of the station, but it sounded way calmer than any sixty-something woman with cool blue hair and a mother of a limp should be when faced with a demon in the middle of a police station. I looked past the demon, and sure enough, there was Madame Wanda standing in the hole where the front door used to be, now wearing a long blue robe to match her royal blue hair. She looked regal, carrying an air of calm about her that made me feel like everything was going to be okay, all toothy bloodthirsty evidence to the contrary.

"Who's going to make me, witch?" the demon asked in its gravelly, spine-chilling voice.

"I am," Wanda said, holding her arms out to the side. A warm glow spread from her fingertips to envelop her entire body and bathe the area around her in yellow.

"You and what army, mortal?" the demon asked, its grin widening even further at the prospect of extra snacks for its little topside vacation.

"I don't need an army, demon," Wanda said, raising her hands. As she did, the glow spread even farther, extending from her to a short purple-haired woman who literally had a pair of tabby kittens riding on her shoulder. She was barely visible through the picture window, but I saw a glow emanating from her right hand off past the edge of the building. Another beam of light streaked out to Wanda's left, to the fifty-something woman with kind eyes and red-and orange-streaked hair who rolled into the bullpen from a back door on a jet-black mobility scooter with flames on the front. Energy poured through the woman on the scooter and out the wall of the sheriff's office, to the other witches that apparently ringed the building. It looked like Madame Wanda had brought her own Hell on Wheels Woman, a Crazy Cat Lady, and enough witches to make a big-ass circle.

Wanda looked around the room and gave the demon a calm smile. "Men need armies, demon. I have a coven."

The witches began chanting in unison, and the glow from their hands brightened as more and more light streaked between them. Strands of ethereal gold wove between the women, spinning a glowing web around the ring of barren earth.

"You can't do this to me!" the demon howled. "You do not have the power to banish the Hand of Mammon!"

"You don't belong here, creature," Wanda replied. "Go home and leave this world to those who are of this plane. Tell your master that he has received all the blood sacrifice he will get from this place."

I took a step forward, grabbed hold of Great-Grandpappy Beauregard's sword, and yanked it free from the shrieking demon's chest. The ring of glowing light snapped inward, passing harmlessly through me and making a golden cocoon around the demon, who kept screeching about how we couldn't do this to him and how his master would feast on our entrails. Honestly, I stopped listening after he yelled for about half a minute while not tearing my guts out. He obviously was pretty well neutered by the magical lasso Madame Wanda spun around him, so I just stepped back and watched. I did keep my sword out, just in case.

The screaming lessened in volume as the golden bonds covered the demon's face, then in a blinding flash of light, the yelling, the magical bonds, and the demon all vanished, leaving me standing in the sheriff's department with a bunch of corpses, a *lot* of blood, and parts of at least three bodies strewn around the room. I peeked out into the parking lot, but there was no Emily Deschanel or David Boreanaz coming over the horizon, so I had little faith that anyone was going to sort out what parts belonged to what body.

I looked over at Madame Wanda. "Thanks for the assist. How did y'all find me?"

She chuckled. "A very angry young man called me several times and was very insistent that you needed our help. I think he called me 'Obi-Wan' several times and said I was your only hope."

Geri walked over to me and held out her cell phone. "Dude, you really need to call Skeeter. He's been yelling non-stop since the second I got my earbud turned back on." She tapped the black device lodged in her ear and I looked around, wondering where mine had gotten to. It either got knocked out when I was fighting the dudes back at the trailer, confiscated by the cops, or I turned it off again and didn't remember. Which happens way more often than I'd ever tell Skeeter. Either way, it wasn't in my ear, so I didn't have to listen to him yell at me. Good thing, since my ears were still ringing from a pissed-off demon.

I looked down at her phone, then around at the bloody wreckage of the clearing. "Nah," I said with a shake of my head. "Pretty sure we need to call in some crime scene cleanup first. Honey," I asked Amy, "does Homeland Security have some kind of supernatural janitors or something we can call?"

"Yeah," she replied. "I got a guy. Let's get the hell out of here and I'll call it in."

"Sounds great," Wanda said. "We can go back to my store, and you can explain to me exactly what happened here."

"Okay," I replied. "But no more schnapps!"

EPILOGUE

The next morning saw me and my crew standing in the back of a cluster of people all gathered in front of a grave. It was all too familiar a feeling, even though I'd never been in this particular cemetery before. They all have kinda the same vibe to them—peaceful, but with a layer of sadness winding through every other emotion, kinda binding all the good and bad feelings together into a sense of melancholy peace that's at the same time heartbreaking and consoling. I'm Southern, we get poetic about our graveyards.

Madame Wanda stood in front of the crowd, flanked by Hell on Wheels and Cat Lady, who I'd learned were really named Joey and Carol, but I liked my nicknames better. Carol still had a gray kitten riding on her shoulder, and the longer it sat there behaving, the more I believed in witchcraft. I've met cats, and this one was actually doing something other than being psychotic and trying to eat its owner's eyeballs.

"Evan was a good boy," Wanda said. "We didn't see eye to eye on...well, much of anything, but he was my kin, and I loved him. And he loved me, and he loved his church family as well. He never gave up trying to bring me to what he felt was the salvation of his faith, and I never minded, because as long as he was trying to convert me, it showed he cared what happened to my soul, and by extension, me. I'm going to hold on to that sense of caring whenever I think of him, which is going to be a lot. He was a beautiful little boy who grew into a fine man, and I am proud have called him my people."

Wanda stepped off to one side, and one of the roughnecks from the industrial park came up to the little makeshift podium. He was a thickset man with bristly blond hair shaved to within an inch of his scalp. He took off his Caterpillar gimme cap and twisted it between his hands while he spoke.

"Evan was a little weirdo, but he was *our* little weirdo. We gave him a bunch of crap, 'bout all the time, but he always took it good and never got real mad at us, even when we mighta went too far once in a while. He just went out, cleaned up whatever stupid stuff we done to the outside of his church, and made us feel like right heels for picking on a harmless little church dude. Eventually, we stopped messing with him altogether on account of it weren't no fun when he didn't get mad. Then something kinda weird happened—I started talking to the little dude. He didn't get no less weird, but I started to see where he was coming from with all his peace and love stuff, and before too long, I even believed a little bit. A lot more than my mama making me go to Sunday school all those years made me believe, anyhow.

"Evan was a good little dude, and I wish I'da told him that while he was around to hear it." The big man looked up, and I was surprised to see a tear rolling down his cheek. "If there is a God, and since Evan always believed there was, I hope there is, for his sake. But if there is a God, I reckon him and Evan are up there sitting on a cloud toking up and talking all kinds of philosophy and stuff. I'll miss you, little dude." He patted the coffin awkwardly and walked back to stand with his buddies, who all patted him on the shoulder.

Then the reverend walked back to the front of everybody and held out his hands. "Let us pray." Everybody but me, Geri, and Amy bowed our heads. It's not that none of us are religious, or respectful. It's just that I've been to one too many funerals where ghouls showed up and tried to eat the congregation to ever close my eyes in a cemetery. Admittedly, that only ever happened one time, but that was one time too many, and it made me a little paranoid.

After the prayer, Madame Wanda walked over with her friends to where me, Geri, and Amy were standing. "Thank you all for coming. I really appreciate it."

"It was the least we could do," Amy said, hugging the older woman.

"Yeah, especially since you saved all our asses," Geri added.

"Yeah, we did," Scooter Girl said, high-fiving Cat Lady.

"I'm sorry we couldn't get all this sorted out sooner, so Evan might still be around," I said.

"Don't you feel bad about Evan." Wanda cut me off before my guilt could really get rolling. "He gets to find out which one of us was right, and I'm a little jealous about that. I don't want to die, but it does rankle me a tiny bit that he's going to know the answers we spent so many hours speculating about." She let out a sigh. "I'm going to miss him, but when you get to my age, about the only constant is funerals."

"And faith," Cat Lady said, reaching up to scratch her shoulder ornament under its chin. The cat just kind curled around the back of her neck like a stole, purring loud enough for me to hear it a couple feet away. Yeah, she was definitely a witch.

"Y'all heading home?" I turned to see the sheriff walking over to us. I held my breath, really not wanting to get in a fist fight at a funeral. I mean, it wouldn't be the first time, but usually I only scrap with kinfolk at funerals. I've never beat up a cop in a graveyard before and was hoping I wouldn't have to start now.

"Yes, sir," Amy said. "We're heading out right now."

"Well, thanks for your help getting that crazy Boros lady run out of town," the sheriff said. Amy and I looked at each other as he continued. "She was backing my only opponent in the election next month, so if she ain't giving him money no more, I can probably keep my job. I appreciate what y'all done here, even if you can't tell me all about what you really did."

He held out a wooden box to me. "Miss Wanda said you used to use a big ol' pistol, but you lost it in a fire or something?"

I just stared at the handgun-sized box. "Or something."

"Well, take this as a peace offering. I took it off a couple ol' boys a couple months ago who were hauling pot from Georgia to New York City. Can't nobody in my department tote a hand cannon like this, and I can't sell it on eBay as surplus. So I want you to have it, as a token of my appreciation. And a bribe to stay the hell away from my county. I looked y'all up on the internet, and you leave a mess every damn where y'all go."

I laughed and took the box. "I can't argue with you there, Sheriff. Thanks for this. I'll try to see that it gets good use." I opened the box, a little worried that I'd see a new Bertha lying there. But no, it was a nickel-plated revolver that I recognized instantly.

I took it out of the box and held it up to the light, sun glinting off the polished barrel and making the red dot on the front sight glow like a burning ember. "Damn, that is a good-looking firearm," I said.

"Look under the bottom of the box," the sheriff said.

I did as he said, pulling out a set of leather straps and handing the box to Geri. I slipped the straps over my shoulders and adjusted the length all the way out, then once I had that all sorted, I slipped the Smith & Wesson 500 pistol into the holster under my left arm, and it hung there like I was born with it. I noticed a pair of speed loaders hanging off the right side of the shoulder rig, giving me a total of fifteen fifty-caliber rounds of absolute devastation I could unleash on anything that got in my way.

I was genuinely moved and held out a hand to the sheriff. "Thanks. I'll put it to good use."

"If half what I heard about y'all is true, you ain't gonna have much choice, son," the chubby man said as he tipped his hat to the women and walked over to his car.

I stood there for a minute looking down at the gun hanging under my arm. Amy walked up and out a hand on my shoulder. "You okay with this, Bubba?"

I didn't look at her. Not yet. "Yeah, I think so."

"I thought you were done with guns?" Geri asked.

"No, I think I just needed to do a couple jobs with nothing but my fists and my blade to remind me that there were other tools, other ways to get the job done. All that mess with Harker, it all felt like we were just running into everything guns blazing, because that's what we'd always done. And it got good people killed. I needed to see if I could still do this job a different way, *my* way."

"And you did," Amy said.

"I did," I agreed. "Mostly. I think what I learned wasn't that I can do this job without a gun if I have to, but mostly that I can still do the job at all, and if I'm going to do it, I need to use whatever tools I have to get that job done. So yeah, I think it's time to load up and go hunting monsters again."

"Good to have you back, buddy," Skeeter said in my ear, his voice thick with emotion.

"Good to be back, brother," I replied. "Good to be back."

I looked at Amy and Geri, then said, "Come on, y'all. If we get on the road, we can be in Lexington before they stop serving lunch. I am in the mood for some barbecue!"

. . .

THE END

WAMPUS RUMPUS

1

She moved well for somebody with no formal training, keeping her muzzle down unless it was time to shoot something, eyes flicking back and forth over everywhere a threat could materialize, and gliding along in a smooth step that kept her shots tight and her hands steady. A figure swung out from behind the corner of a building, and her MP-7 snapped up, putting a red dot on the man's forehead before moving off to the left as she saw he carried a bag of groceries, not a gun. Then a pair of shapes lunged into view almost simultaneously, one with a shotgun aimed straight at her midsection, and the other with a pistol pressed to the temple of a frightened child. She put two rounds through the face of the man holding the hostage, then swung her barrel over to the other attacker. Just as she brought her gun to bear, all the lights turned red and a loud buzzing sound filled the air.

"Shit!" Geri yelled as the fluorescent lights flickered to life. "There is no way a human being could have taken down both of those guys! Hell, most *monsters* we hunt aren't fast enough to take them out!"

Skeeter's voice, amplified to almost skull-splitting volume and forced through the crappy intercom system strung throughout the building, came from everywhere all at once. Like that movie, only…more annoying. "You're right. The buzzer is to indicate that you're dead, not that you failed. You made the right choice. Sometimes there is no choice that has you walking out of a situation. When that happens, you save everyone you can and go down swinging."

"Well, that's morbid," I muttered.

"But accurate," my fiancée, and our boss, Deputy Director Amy Hall with the Department of Homeland Security's Paranormal Division, replied. "Now are you going to shoot, or you gonna stand there and gripe about how Skeeter runs the *Hogan's Alley* simulation?"

"Little from column A, little from column B," I said as I picked up the mammoth revolver laying on the bench in front of me. I sighted down the eight-inch barrel, laid the front sight across my target, and squeezed off a quick five rounds. Quick for a gun that fires a fifty-caliber, five-hundred-grain round, which isn't really all that quick.

A normal human-sized handgun, you can hold it in one or both hands and squeeze off rounds one right after the other, throwing an absolute hailstorm of projectiles at your target. For a lot of shooters, that's good, because they can't really hit the broad side of a barn and their only chance of hitting something is to send a lot of bullets in its general direction. I was trying out my new sidearm, a Smith & Wesson 500 X-Frame revolver, so there was no world in which I fired that pistol with one hand and then was still able to stay on target. So I squeezed, reset, squeezed, reset, until the five rounds were gone and my ears rang even through the noise-cancelling headphones I wore.

"Not bad," Amy said as I ran the target back to check my accuracy. Three out of five were in the X-ring, which was pretty good. The other two were still good, center mass shots, which would be enough to take down almost anything that I ran into. As long as they could be hurt with bullets, that is. Not everything can. But if bullets would hurt it, this new cannon would kill it. That was pretty much guaranteed. It was slow, though. Revolvers were typically slower than semi-automatics, and the 500 had pretty serious recoil, so it wasn't as fast as Bertha, my old Desert Eagle. But Bertha was gone, and New Gun didn't have a name yet, so that's where we were.

"I think I'm gonna like this thing," I said, turning the pistol over in my hands. It was a pretty weapon, shiny and new, but it still felt a little strange strapping on a gun again after the better part of a year. But our last mission proved to me that not all problems could be solved with charm and diplomacy. Hell, I've never managed to solve *any* problem with charm or diplomacy, but there are also a lot that can't be solved with swords and fists, either. Sometimes you needed to put large holes in bad things. And this beast certainly put large holes in things.

"You done?" Amy asked, drawing her own service weapon. She carries a much more reasonable Glock 19, one of the preferred weapons of law enforcement everywhere. It's neither as ridiculously large nor loud as my pistol, but in Amy's hands is probably even more dangerous. She put ten rounds down range in a matter of seconds, every one landing square in the head ring on her target.

"Yeah, yeah, you're a better shot than me," I grumbled. "But I still bench more than you do." The eternal defense of a man with a bruised ego —upper body strength.

"We could run the obstacle course after this if you like," Amy shot back, one eyebrow climbing in challenge.

"Not a chance. Those psychos put up some new *American Ninja* shit in the gym, and there's no way I'm getting on that. Besides, I deal with all obstacles the same way—by running right through them." We were practicing in half of the CrossFit gym I owned in Atlanta, in a training facility DHS set up for us. The lease from the government helped cover the money the gym lost every month, and gave me a place to shoot where I didn't have to worry about killing a random hunter or other idiot who couldn't respect the "No Trespassing" signs all over my property.

"Okay, gang," Skeeter's voice came back over the intercom, "unless you want to run through the Alley again, it's almost time for the gym to open for the evening crowd, so let's bug out."

I nodded, not that he was looking at me, and started packing up my gear. New Gun went into a pistol case, then that went into a backpack along with all our ammo and Amy's pistol. Geri came over and dropped her spare magazines, safety glasses, and ear protection into the bag with all our gear, then slipped her MP-7 into a duffel bag. When we walked out into the Atlanta sun, we looked like three normal civilians leaving a gym, not super-secret government operatives who had just sent hundreds of rounds of ammunition into steel and paper enemies.

"Taco Mac?" Geri asked as we piled into Amy's Suburban. We'd taken her ride down from my mountain cabin because her Suburban, even heavily armored with bulletproof glass, run-flat tires, and special hidden cargo compartments full of weapons, explosives, and protective gear, *still* got better gas mileage than my F-250. I kept hinting that Homeland should buy me one of the new electric pickups, but Amy kept stubbornly not forgetting that I'd destroyed half a dozen trucks in the last decade. Maybe spending a hundred grand on a vehicle for me wasn't going to make anyone's budget, but I wasn't giving up. If I was known for one thing, it was for being stubborn.

Okay, I was probably known for being carelessly destructive, horrifically smartassed, possibly psychotic, often smelly, usually rude, and potentially completely unhinged, too. But I'm sure stubborn figured into the equation somewhere.

"I could go for wings," I said.

"Nope!" Amy and Geri said in unison.

"I am not spending two-plus hours in this truck with you and your wing farts," Geri said. "I'll shoot you myself."

"I'll buy the ammo," Amy said. "We're going to Fox Brothers, and you're *not* ordering anything extra spicy."

Good. I wanted barbecue anyway. Wings are awesome, one of my favorite food groups. But dudes with facial hair understand that wings are a constant balancing act between sauce in mouth and sauce in beard. I just wasn't up for all the maintenance wings would require, not after a full morning of training. "Can I get banana pudding?" I asked.

"Does banana pudding give you gas?" Geri asked.

"No more than anything else. I'm a dude, and I'm pushing forty. Most everything gives me gas." With that thought looking heavy over our heads, we rolled out toward the best barbecue in the city of Atlanta, and the best banana pudding. Maybe I'd just have pudding for lunch. A *lot* of pudding.

I woke up from my barbecue coma just about the time we turned off the main road to head up the gravel path to my cabin back in the woods outside Dalton, Georgia. It was a good day. The sun was shining, the birds were singing, I had a belly full of good barbecue, and my Bulldogs were back-to-back National Football Champions. What in the world could go wrong?

"Well, shit," I said, looking out the windshield. Skeeter was sitting on my front porch in a nice wooden rocker with his feet up on the railing. He had a Cheerwine in his hand and a white plastic bag by his feet. I could see the telltale shape of a six-pack in the bag, and that was never good.

Skeeter's my best friend. Has been since middle school. We were a little bit of an odd pair in our youth—the big muscular football player and the gay Black nerd who weighed a hundred twenty pounds soaking wet. But it worked for us. I kept Skeeter from getting his ass beat by racist homophobes who didn't like comic books, and he kept me from flunking Trigonometry. We'd gone to college together, gotten jobs with the government together, gotten shipped off to Fairyland together, gotten fired by the government together, and saved the world at least twice.

And I still never liked it when he showed up on my porch unannounced with booze. It meant something was seriously screwed up, and I was probably going to have to punch a lot of people before it was unscrewed. Or maybe I'd just have to punch one person (or monster, cryptid, magical being, or unicorn—I don't discriminate, I just punch), but I'd have to punch them an awful lot. Either way, Skeeter bringing booze as a bribe meant that somebody was in for an ass-whooping. I hoped it wasn't me this time.

I got out of the passenger seat, blinking my eyes against the bright sun, and regretted once again that I'd never developed a taste for sunglasses. I'm a big dude, and I frequently have to leave places in a hurry. Sunglasses are one of those things that end up getting left places, or flying off my head while I run, or getting squished when I jump into my truck and haul ass out of whatever shitstorm I've found myself in. Regardless, I don't usually have shades, and it was really bright.

I held out a hand as I climbed the steps. "Beer me," I said.

Skeeter reached down beside his chair without breaking the rhythm of his rocking and passed me a bottle of Miller Lite. I twisted the top off and flipped the cap toward a small trash can Amy kept on the porch. Probably just for that purpose, now that I thought about it.

"What's up, Skeet?" I asked. "Can't be too terrible, I reckon."

"Why's that?" Geri asked, clomping up the steps behind me, snagging a beer for herself, and sitting in the rocker by Skeeter.

I held up my bottle. "Domestic beer. If it was really bad, Skeeter woulda sprung for better beer. At least a micro-brew."

"You know I'm not about the hipster beer, Bubba," Skeeter protested.

"You literally have half a dozen craft brew t-shirts in your closet," I reminded him. "And you get beer shipped to you from all over the country. You're the most hipster beer drinker I've ever met. Now what's up?"

"Well, my taste in beer aside, we've got a case," Skeeter said.

"Pretty sure I'm the one who decides if we've got a case or not," Amy said, leaning on the rail beside me. "That whole 'Deputy Director' thing, you know."

"Yeah, but this one's right in our wheelhouse. It's in Tennessee, it's a monster, and there's almost no chance that it involves demons, Nazis, fairies, dragons, or CrossFit werewolves."

"I'm interested," I said, draining my beer and reaching for another. Shut up. I drink fast, but hydration is important, and it was domestic light beer, anyway.

"Then strap in, Bubba, because we're going after a wampus cat!" Skeeter and I high-fived at the idea of chasing down one of my bucket list cryptids after all these years.

Geri, however, was unimpressed. "Um, guys," she said, holding up a hand. "What the hell is a wampus cat?"

2

Five minutes later, we were in my living room and Skeeter had made a laptop materialize from somewhere. Hell, for all I knew, it might have been living under my couch cushions, just waiting for the day when Skeeter needed to hijack my television and give a video presentation on the magical, mythical, wampus cat.

The wampus cat ranges from hilarious to horrifying, depending on the version of its origin and who's telling the story. Some Native tribes have the creature as a woman condemned to wear that shape after hiding under the pelt of a mountain lion to observe a sacred ritual. Other tales have it as a natural creature with a large, spiked ball on its tail, while some say that the creature can teleport, popping into existence, taking a swipe at any idiot who came to close to its lair, and poofing away again. I had never paid too much attention to origin stories, but it was one of the few cryptids native to the Southeastern U.S. that I hadn't been sent out hunting at some point.

Now a fair number of the things I have been assigned to chase turned out to be something else entirely, like the chupacabra attacks that were really vampires who ate cows and not people, or the vampire ballerinas, or the troll under the bridge in South Carolina. No wait, that one was pretty much exactly as advertised. Big, ugly, mean as hell, lived under a bridge...yep, it was a troll, all right. Until it was troll parts scattered all over Falls Park in downtown Greenville. I even felt a little bad about the mess from that one. Not bad enough to help clean it up, but there was a touch of regret there.

But now Skeeter had some doohickey connected to my TV and was beaming drawings, fuzzy vacation photos with weird shapes in the background, and a skipping, out of focus video that made the famous Bigfoot video of the dude in a monkey suit look like Scorsese.

"The wampus cat is generally considered harmless, unless its home is threatened. Or its children. If you come upon a wampus cat with young, you really want to be somewhere else, and quickly. The creature has powerful jaws, razor-sharp claws, and is a hell of an ambush predator, so don't forget to look up."

"What about the spiky ball on its tail? Is that a weapon, too?" I asked.

Skeeter nodded. "Yes. If it's real. It shows up in some legends and not in others, so I'm not sure if the stories are accurate, if they got the wampus cat confused with something like a gowrow, or if there's a random ankylosaurus running around the wilds of North America."

"So no one has ever captured one of these things?" Geri asked.

"Not that we know of," Skeeter replied.

Amy nodded. "There are records of three different Hunters being sent to capture, rehome, or destroy a wampus cat, but they all reported being unable to locate the creature. The last time anyone was dispatched on a wampus cat call was 1984."

"So our tech is way better," Skeeter said.

"And we're less likely to be actively on coke while we're hunting," I added.

Amy shot me a dark look, but I just shrugged. My grandfather was hunting back in those days, as was my dad. Pop was pretty straight-laced back then, but by all reports, my grandfather would definitely be on the list of Hunters likely to be found snorting lines off a stripper's butt in the bathroom of a topless club when he was supposed to be chasing monsters.

"Wait, hunting while high is an option?" Geri asked.

"Not for you," I said. "I'm in your line of fire way too often for me to be down with you imbibing anything that might give you the shakes."

Geri shrugged. "Not an unreasonable concern, I guess. What else do we need to know, Skeeter?"

"Well, this sighting was reported in the mountains around Pigeon Forge, so it won't be too bad a trip to get there," Skeeter said, but something in his expression told me there was more coming, and I wasn't going to like it.

"What else?" I asked, putting a little bit of threat in my tone. It would probably carry more weight if Skeeter didn't know full well I'd never actually beat his ass, but I hoped maybe he'd forget that fact for a second or two and be intimidated enough to tell me what I needed to know.

Not so much. He just looked me in the eye and said, "You ain't gonna like it, but I don't want to hear any bitching. You need the money."

"What money?" I asked. "We're doing alright. The gym pays for itself, freelancing for Homeland covers most of the bills, and if I run short on cash, I just call on my sugar mama." I gave Amy what I thought was a saucy grin, but the flat stare she sent back in my direction told me that she somehow didn't find me as hilarious as I do. That always confuses me. I think I'm amazing, but I guess my sense of humor is just ahead of my time. Like Oscar Wilde, or Gallagher. Misunderstood geniuses, both of them.

"You still have a roof over your head only because you don't have a mortgage," Skeeter said. "Homeland has been decent, but that new pistol uses expansive ammo, and I bet the first time you turn in for reimbursement of that, you're going to get a strongly worded memo about the virtues of the nine-millimeter round."

"I bet anyone who thinks a nine mil is a reasonable sized bullet has never stood toe to butt-nekkid toe with a grumpy Sasquatch," I said. "Because that wouldn't even push through the body hair on one of those beasties, much less their thick hide."

"You know that, and I know that, but I'm pretty sure the DHS accountants don't know that," Skeeter said. "Which is why I wanted to introduce you to our newest employer—"

"Oh, what the absolute hell is this?!?" I asked, coming up out of my chair at the sight of the man walking in my front door. "I did *not* agree to this shit."

"Good to meet you, too, Mr. Brabham. My name is Father Matthew Ortega, and I am your new liaison with the Church. I'm happy to say that after some…shakeup within its structure over the past few years, that you have been reinstated as the official Southeastern Regional Monster Hunter for the Holy Roman Catholic Church. If you want the job, of course."

I gave this new guy a long look up and down. He wasn't very big. Not much bigger than Skeeter, really. So I'd put him at five ten, and skinny, maybe a hundred fifty pounds soaking wet. He was youngish, maybe thirty, with a neatly trimmed dark goatee showing not the slightest hint of gray, and close-cropped dark brown hair cut in a professional style. Now contrast that with my shaggy brown locks hanging down around my ears, courtesy of an impromptu haircut from a bunch of assholes in North Carolina, Skeeter's gleaming black pate, and Geri's purple and pink-streaked black hair. Amy kept her blond hair neatly cut a little longer than her shoulders, the only one among us who looked like she could actually go work in an office. Good thing she was the only one of us who ever had to go work in an office, then. But this dude? Take his collar and cassock off and he could fit right in at an insurance agency or a call center. He just looked…normal.

"You know who we are?" I asked.

"I do," Father Matthew replied.

"You know what we do?"

"I do."

"You know how to say anything else, or are we gonna end up married after another 'I do'?" I asked.

"You're not my type," he said. "Too much body hair and I'm not into tattoos."

"Or dudes," I added.

"I didn't say that," the priest replied.

"I thought you still couldn't be gay and be a Catholic priest?" Geri piped up.

"I'm Episcopalian."

"But you're our liaison with the Catholic Church?" I asked.

"It's a little complicated, but just like you aren't required to be Catholic to hunt for the Church, I don't have to be Catholic to liaise with them for you. The position doesn't actually require a priest of any denomination, but the Church leadership felt that someone with an official title might be more effective in helping you—"

"They thought if I saw the collar, I'd be less likely to beat the shit out of you and throw you out into the dirt," I said, cutting him off with a wave of my hand.

"Yeah, that. Now since I don't want to have my ass kicked, and this cassock looks better without me being thrown in the dirt, do you want the gig or should I just piss off?"

As much as I wanted to tell him to kiss every inch of my massive furry ass, I looked at my friends and could tell they really wanted me to at least hear this dude out. "Okay, how much are you paying? Because I'm gonna need a hell of a raise after the way the Church tossed me to the curb when they found out I'm part fairy. Racist pricks."

He quoted a number, and it wasn't just larger than my last salary with the Church, it was *way* larger. Now he had my attention. "Well, Padre, why don't you have a seat. You want a beer? Wine? Do we have any wine?"

"Yes, we have wine," Amy said.

"No, thank you," Father Matthew said. "But now that I have your attention, let's look at the information we have on this supposed wampus cat."

3

Father Matthew came prepared. He handed Skeeter a thumb drive, and in seconds we were looking at satellite pictures of the woods around Pigeon Forge. He zoomed in, and I thought for a second I could tell where Dollywood was, but he scrolled sideways before I could see any cool roller coasters.

"Where did these pictures come from?" I asked. "Is this one of those super-secret Catholic satellites I've heard about?"

Father Matthew sighed. "Secret Catholic Satellites? Is that like Jewish Space Lasers?"

"I don't know," I replied. "Jewish folk ain't exactly what you'd call thick on the ground in North Georgia, so I ain't had the chance to ask anybody who might actually know. There's that woman up in Cleveland. She might have more info."

"Well, regardless, these images didn't come from a secret Catholic spy satellite. See the little multi-colored circle in the bottom corner? This is Google Maps."

"Oh." Everything about this presentation just got a lot less interesting. I got up and headed for the kitchen to grab another beer, thought about it for a second, and just grabbed the whole six-pack. I didn't know how many PowerPoint slides I was going to have to sit through, but I wasn't doing that shit sober.

"As you can see," Father Matthew continued, just as though I hadn't wandered off in the middle of his dog and pony show. "There are hundreds of acres of heavily wooded mountainous terrain in the Pigeon Forge area, giving the wampus cat, if that is in fact what we're looking for, plenty of places to hide."

He tapped his phone, and a string of red dots appeared on the map. Another tap, and a series of yellow dots popped up. "These are confirmed and potential sightings that have been reported in the region within the last eighteen months."

I leaned forward to get a better look. "Yellow are the maybes and red are the definite sightings?" I asked.

"As definite as cryptid sightings get, yes."

"Looks like they're running east from something." I pointed at the TV, and Father Matthew passed me a laser pointer. I mean, I don't know what kind of bag of holding he had sewn into the pockets of his robe, but who the hell runs around with a laser pointer in their pocket? Unless you're a middle manager or a cat person, why do you even own one of those things?

Regardless, I took the pointer from the priest and aimed it at the screen. "See how the yellow dots make an arc behind the red ones? I'm gonna guess that all those sightings took place far from any town or even a trailer park. Probably way back in the woods somewhere, and the critter was spotted by a hunter or a fisherman. Or maybe teenagers looking for a place to hook up or get loaded."

"Yes, the unconfirmed sightings are older than the red dots," Matthew confirmed.

"So these red dots are in more populated areas, and the people who saw the wampus are less likely to be stoned out of their gourd or straight up crazy," I said.

"I probably would have used different words, but basically correct," Father Matthew said. I thought there might have been a hint of a smile, but just a hint. This dude was wound pretty tight.

"Okay, so is there a plan in that slideshow of yours?" I asked. Geri and Amy were just sitting on the couch watching while I tried to see if I could push the skinny priest off his game.

"Not really," he admitted with a hint of red creeping into his cheeks. "I've never done any kind of field work. Honestly, I'm pretty new to the job. I understand that my predecessor left some big shoes to fill, and it's taken the Church a while to find the proper replacement for this region."

"You ain't replacing nobody," I said. "Uncle Father Joe was family, and even if you turn out to be the best monster hunter liaison in the world, you ain't gonna be family. Besides, I thought the Church already had a dude taking care of my territory. That Dallas Hunter dude or whatever his name is."

"Hunter Houston," Father Matthew said with a slight grimace. "He's good at what he does, but…well, you're better. You have more experience, more successful resolutions, and a strong team built in. We will likely continue to utilize Mr. Houston from time to time, but the Church feels that it's time to…"

"Get the starters off the bench," I said.

"Get their heads out of their asses and re-hire the pros," Geri added.

"Call in the big guns," Skeeter finished.

Father Matthew nodded. "Yes, all of those things. There are monsters out there in the world, Bubba. Someone has to hunt them down and keep the world safe for humanity. You're that someone."

Well, shit. I was going to do it. I was going to take the Church's money, and hunt the Church's monsters, choke down my dislike for organized religion, and forgive them for firing my ass. Because he was right. This was what I was put here to do. I hunt monsters. And I did need the money, apparently.

"Okay."

I heard Skeeter let out a massive sigh of relief, with a slightly smaller one coming from Amy. Geri just clapped her hands, jumped up from the couch, and sprinted to her room. I assumed she was going to spend some quality time with her favorite gun. Or her favorite knife. Or maybe her favorite high explosive ordinance.

Father Matthew gave me a relieved smile. "Good. I'm very glad to hear that. I have rooms booked for us at a hotel right outside Pigeon Forge. They're expecting us tonight."

"Pretty sure of yourself, aren't you?" I asked.

"No," Skeeter said. "He was sure of me. You need this, Bubba. And if Father Matt couldn't get you to see that, I was going to bully you into doing it. Now get packed. Pigeon Forge is only a couple hours from here, but y'all all gonna need showers before you spend three hours in a car together. Every one of you smells like gunpowder and sweat."

"Two of my favorite perfumes," I said, raising an eyebrow at Amy.

"Gonna have to put a pin in that one, loverboy," she said. "We're on a schedule, and this time it's not mine. But I'm calling dibs on the shower now that I'm the one with the longest hair." She gave me a saucy grin and hopped off the couch, heading for the back of the house.

I ran my fingers through my hair, shorter than it had been since I blew out my knee playing college football. "That's just mean," I said, but I doubted Amy could hear me over her own laughter.

We got to the hotel, a Fairfield Inn just off I-40, and I raised an eyebrow at Father Matt when he came back to where we waited for him to handle everything and handed a key to Amy, then turned around and started walking toward an elevator.

"Where's Geri sleeping, Padre?" I asked. "Because vow of celibacy or no, I don't think she's gonna dig crashing with you."

Father Matthew stopped and turned around, looking at me in confusion. "I got one room for the men, and another room for the ladies. That seemed to be the most logical and economical course of action."

I laughed out loud in the middle of the hotel lobby. "Dude, I ain't bunking with you when my fiancée is sleeping in the same building. Amy and I room together."

"And as much as it hurts to let these words pass my lips, Bubba's right," Geri said. "I'm not sharing a room with you, Father. No offense, but I know more about Episcopalians than Bubba does. You guys don't take vows of celibacy, do you?"

Father Matthew blushed a little. I reckon there ain't too many days of the week he ends up chatting about his sex life in a public place. "No, we do not."

"Are you gay?" Geri asked.

"I don't know that my sexuality is any of your business," the priest replied.

"Yeah, it wouldn't be most days," Geri replied. "But if you're not into girls, I'd be more likely to share a room with you. Like two percent more likely, because no matter who you're into, I just met you like six hours ago, and I am not all that interested in rooming with a complete stranger."

Father Matthew stammered around for a minute, looking back and forth between Geri and me, then turned to Amy for help. She shook her head and held up both hands in surrender. "Not my circus, not my monkeys, Padre. This is a Church job, so you're dealing with the accommodations. If I plop my DHS credit card down on the counter of an unapproved hotel and it's not a matter of life or apocalypse, I'll be filling out forms in triplicate until Bubba's hair grows back."

"Still mean," I said.

She blew me a kiss. "Babe, we've been together for close to ten years now and these past few weeks is the first time since we've been together that the back of your neck hasn't been covered by long hair. You've always claimed to be a redneck, but it's been really funny to see your neck actually turn red in the sun. *And* when you get embarrassed, usually about not having any hair. So yeah, I'm going to give you shit until your hair grows back."

"It's a good thing I love you," I grumbled.

"Damn right," Amy said, and hopped up on tiptoes to give me a quick peck on the lips. I was a little surprised. We aren't much for public displays of affection, normally, but I was happy to take it.

"Heh," came a voice from across the lobby. "She's got you whipped, boy." I looked over to where a trio of middle-aged rednecks sat in the small "lounge" area, clustered around the remnants of a twelve-pack of Bud, with two more cases sitting on the carpet next to the small table they sat around.

I opened my mouth to reply, but Amy squeezed my arm in that unmistakable "please don't start a fight and destroy the hotel because we'll have to find another place to sleep and I'd very much appreciate it if you would not allow your baser Neanderthal instincts to dictate your actions for the next thirty seconds." Yes, that's a lot to pack into one squeeze of a forearm, but Amy could be very eloquent when she wanted to be.

And I, with the glorious stubbornness of all middle-aged rednecks, even those of us whose necks haven't seen the sun for the better part of twenty years, ignored her completely. "Well, boss," I said, giving the redneck who spoke my best "eat shit and die" grin. "If you had a woman like this, you'd do anything she asked for, too."

And of course that was the opening Tweedles Dumb, Dumber, and Dumbest were hoping for. They all hopped up from the table and stomped over to me, chests puffed out and mock fury all over their faces. "You calling my wife ugly, asshole?" asked Tweedledumber, the lead redneck who first called out to me.

"Nah," I said. "I wouldn't insult a woman, especially not one who ain't here to defend herself." I felt Amy relax a little beside me, like she was relieved I'd finally matured enough not to start a fight with every single idiot that stepped up to me.

And here I thought she knew me. "You, on the other hand…well, you're standing right here, so I can call you a fat, inbred, gap-toothed dipshit with nothing better to do than sit around in a half-drunk circle jerk with your two boyfriends here looking for entertainment in the lobby of a Tennessee Fairfield Inn. See? I don't have to call your wife ugly. I can just imply by everything I say about your dumb ass that she's either so butt-ugly she could only get a husband that no other woman would look at, or blind. Or ugly *and* blind, that's also an option. Hell, maybe she's blind, ugly, and stupid, because if she married you, there's gotta be some first cousins married not too many branches up in her family tree."

I could almost feel Amy shaking her head beside me as I played Antagonize the Morons. I would have felt bad, but I needed some therapy right then. I'd been trapped in a vehicle for three hours with a brand-new priest, who made my whole truck smell like incense and fresh soap, completely overriding the carefully cultivated aroma of Chili Cheese Fritos and Cheerwine that I had built up over months of eating on the road. I needed to punch something, and I was afraid if I didn't beat the shit out of these idiots, I'd do something stupid, like running around in the woods at night looking for a wampus cat.

Yeah, I know running around the woods at night looking for monsters is literally my job, but as far as excuses to get in a friendly little scrap go, that one was pretty good. Either way, it worked. It took Tweedledumber almost ten seconds to sort through everything I said and decide that yep, I did in fact insult him, his wife, and the last few generations of his wife's family.

Then he punched me in the face and the fun really started.

4

I staggered back, neither surprised nor really all that off-balance from his punch, but I wanted it to show very clearly on the security footage that I didn't throw the first punch. That has been important in many conversations throughout my life, all of them involving myself and one or more members of law enforcement. And I was pretty sure we were gonna be introduced to the local constabulary before long.

But like Ke$ha, I was ready to go "until the po-po shut us down." Shut up. I like Ke$ha. How could you not like someone with honest hips? So once I was sure the cameras had recorded the start of the fight, I figured I should try to end it as fast as possible. Not because I was afraid of these idiots hurting one of us, or earning significant jail time, but mostly because I didn't want to give Geri time to really get going. To say she's a little…"bloodthirsty" would be putting it mildly. If one of these idiots got a lucky punch in and actually managed to hurt her, they'd be picking viscera out of the ceiling lights in this lobby for *weeks*.

So I reeled back way more than I needed to, put a hand on the registration desk, and pushed off, tackling Tweedledumbest and taking him to the ground, where I started punching him. Not much, just enough to get his attention. I have to be more careful about hitting humans since I got back from Fairyland a couple years ago. Seems like being exposed to a realm of pure magic jump-started the fairy magic in me, and now I heal better, hit harder, and…well, I probably run a little faster, but I try not to run at all if possible. So I hit harder and heal faster. And since I didn't want to turn this guy's skull into a jigsaw puzzle, I held back with my punches.

Of course, Geri jumped right in and went after Tweedledumb like a spider monkey on crystal meth. She leapt up on the dude, wrapped her legs around his waist, and started punching him in the face while he spun around in circles trying to dislodge the psychotic starfish that was wrapped around his face pounding his nose into hamburger.

What surprised me was that it was Father Matthew who leapt into the fray next, while Amy just stood by the front desk recording everything on her phone. The little priest didn't hesitate; he just stepped right up to Tweedledumber and punched him in the nose. No muss, no fuss, just a straight left jab to the face. Tweedledumber looked flummoxed at being attacked by a slim, middle-aged man wearing a priest's collar. It had to feel like getting mugged by Father Mulcahy.

I turned my attention back to Tweedledumbest when he managed to buck me off and scramble to his feet. I rolled over and pulled myself up using one of the lobby couches, then almost fell over that same couch when he caught me with a massive right hook that made me wonder for a second if I was the only person in the room that wasn't completely human. Dude was *stout*. Then I decided that it had just been too long since I got in a real, fair fight, so I put my guard up and grinned at him.

"Let's dance, dickweed," I said, spitting out a glob of blood onto the lobby floor. We were one hundred percent not gonna be allowed to stay in this hotel, or maybe any hotel in the chain, ever again.

Tweedledumbest came at me with his hands up, bobbing and weaving like he'd watched *Creed* too many times. I like those movies, but they don't teach anybody how to box, much less how to fight in the lobby of a Tennessee hotel. While he ducked from side to side and jabbed the air, I took two steps forward, wrapped my arms around him, pinning his arms to his ribcage, and gave him a belly-to-belly duplex into a coffee table. Glass flew everywhere, wood splintered, and Tweedledumbest let out a yell like a cow woken from a deep slumber by a group of drunk high school football players pushing it over onto its side.

Pro tip—if you're going to do this, make sure you don't tip the only bull in the pasture. They don't take it well.

Tweedledumbest didn't take it well either, writhing in pain on the lobby floor calling me all kinds of names, some of them even accurate. I'll own "fat redneck piece of crap" and "giant dipshit" because those are pretty accurate a lot of the time. But all the stuff he was yelling about my mother? Nah, that's not cool, man.

It was not cool enough that I stomped on his nuts to shut him up. I know, it's not really sporting. But that's the difference between boxing, whether you learned it from Michael B. Jordan movies or from someone who could actually teach you to throw a punch—rules. In boxing or MMA there are all these rules about where you can hit somebody. In a real fight, where the other person, or creature in my case, is trying to you permanently damage or flat-out kill you, there are no rules. You need to kick some dumbass in the balls to keep him from breaking your neck? Kick away. You need to bite some dipshit's ear off so he'll stop choking you? Chomp to your heart's content.

Tweedledumbest was one of those rednecks who has spent his whole life being the baddest dude in the room, and being backed up by the second and third toughest guys in the room. When he ran into somebody who was bigger and badder than him, with friends who didn't give a shit how tough his buddies were, he didn't know how to adapt. Me and mine are used to fighting monsters that would rather rip our guts out and wear them as necklaces than chitchat, so three dumbasses in a hotel lobby were not much of a challenge. That said, the longer any fight goes on, the more likely someone I like is going to get hurt, so it was in our best interests to get everything settled quickly. And stomping on a dude's nutsack settles stuff pretty damned quick.

I looked over to Geri, and she was still riding Tweedledumb like some kind of weird new Dollywood ride, with one arm around his throat and the other one slamming into the side of his head in quick little punches. Father Matthew was dismantling Tweedledumber piece by piece with kicks, punches, and throws. When he saw me stop moving out of the corner of his eye, he stopped playing around, took a step back, and kicked the dude right on the point of his chin.

Tweedledumber was a good six-three, giving him better than six inches on Father Matty, but the skinny priest just stood flat-footed and kicked him in the face. Tweedledumber fell backward and stretched out his full length along the carpet, unconscious before he hit the ground. Father Matthew turned back to me and gave me a little nod, as if to say, "Okay, my shit is handled."

Geri was a little more direct in her finish, but no less impressive. One second she was wrapped around Tweedledumb's torso like moss on an oak tree, and the next she vaulted off his shoulders, flipped over the dude's head, spun around, and leveled a pistol at Tweedledumb's face. I have no idea where she drew the gun from, and am not nearly stupid enough to ask. She reached into a back pocket, pulled out her credentials, and yelled out, "Homeland Security, nobody fucking move!"

And that's when the cops showed up.

And by "showed up" I mean it seemed like every cop within fifty miles must have rolled up into the Fairfield Inn parking lot with their sirens blaring and lights flashing and basically guaranteeing that nobody in the hotel was getting anything like a late-afternoon nap. No fewer than six cop cars of various vintage—sheriff, police, highway patrol—slewed into the lot fishtailing and threatening to trash any vehicle in their way.

"Anybody scratches my truck and I'm gonna have to go back to jail," I yelled to Geri.

"I am *not* bailing your ass out of a Tennessee jail, Bubba!" Geri replied, then thumped Tweedledumb right between the eyes with the butt of her Glock. He didn't slump to the floor immediately unconscious like he would have in a Jason Statham movie, but he did fall to his knees and clutch his bleeding forehead with both hands, removing him from the fight just as effectively.

I lost count of how many cops poured through the front doors of the hotel after eight, but they didn't stop coming for a while past that. All I could really keep track of was the number of guns pointed directly at me, and that number topped out at five—two shotguns and three sidearms from a mix of different uniforms and one fat man in a sport coat with a badge hanging around his neck. I put my hands up over my head and waited for Geri to sort shit out.

Yeah, I know, technically I was probably the senior member of the team, and either Amy or me should have been the one to step up and smooth things over with the local constabulary. But there are a couple of problems with that. First, while I have a Department of Homeland Security badge, it's not worth the tin it's stamped out of. I don't actually work for DHS; I'm a contractor. I don't have any authority to deal with state or local law enforcement. I go out in the woods hunting monsters, and Uncle Sam sends me a check. Interfacing with overblown rednecks who peaked in tenth grade is a job for people who actually get health insurance.

The other problem is my general disdain for most local cops. I'm not saying that the training is substandard or that a lot of the guys working as small-town cops are in it for some kind of twisted power trip, but I might have said that very thing a couple hundred times, usually when I was in the process of telling a small-town cop to kiss my ass. Which was usually quickly followed by me getting arrested. All the charges were always dropped, but I still don't have the best history with defusing situations, so I decided that we might actually be better off with the heavily armed psychopath dealing with the authority figures than with me in that role.

And Geri dealt with them just fine. After Tweedledumb collapsed to the floor clutching his busted gourd, Geri just swung her pistol over to the first cop in line. "Stop right there or I'll put a bullet in your skull!"

That announcement had two immediate reactions. One, every gun that had been aimed at me was now pointed right at Geri. Two, everybody in the lobby froze in place. It was like they were in that really bad Batman movie and Arnold Schwarzenegger had just iced them over.

I stepped a little out of the line of fire and folded my arms over my chest. She obviously had a plan, and I couldn't wait to see what it was.

5

G ood," Geri said, raising the barrel of her pistol so it no longer pointed straight at a cop's face. "Now that I've got your attention, let's all holster our weapons and talk this out like grownups."

"How about you put your gun on the ground and we won't shoot you?" asked a young cop standing right next to me. He had his weapon leveled at Geri, but I could see from where I was standing that the safety on his M&P 22 was on. I reached over to my right, snatched the pistol out of his hand, ejected the magazine, and slid the gun and clip into separate back pockets. Then I turned to the rookie, who was staring at me with wide eyes, and punched him in the nose.

I turned back to Geri. "Pardon the interruption," I said. "Please proceed."

Now we were surrounded by a room full of absolutely confused cops. At one point of the triangle, they had a pretty young woman with multi-colored hair holding up a badge and yelling about being a federal agent. At another point was a giant redneck who just decked one of their buddies. And the third point of the triangle was occupied by some kind of weird hybrid ninja priest, complete with white collar. Yeah, we were not what they were used to.

All the cops put their guns away, and Geri did the same. Father Matthew and I weren't armed, but from what I'd just seen, the little priest kinda *was* a weapon, so maybe he didn't need one. The Tweedle triplets (Dumb, Dumber, and Dumbest) were all still kinda rolling around on the lobby floor like…well, like they'd just had the shit kicked out of them by a bunch of out-of-towners. Which was pretty much exactly what had happened.

"I am Agent Geraldine Stimson with the Department of Homeland Security. We are in the area investigating a threat to national security. These men assaulted my contractor, and we defended ourselves. Now you can either accept this explanation at face value, drive these idiots to the nearest drunk tank where they spend the next twelve to eighteen hours drying out, or you can try to arrest all of us and have the entire weight of the federal government come down on your shoulders. Trust me, you do not want to feel that weight, gentlemen."

I'd never seen Geri put on her "Official Government Agent" routine, and it was pretty impressive. Judging by the low whistle coming through my earpiece, Skeeter was impressed, too.

"You seeing this, bud?" I whispered, trying to move my mouth as little as possible. I probably either looked like a cow chewing its cud, or like a constipated ventriloquist.

Skeeter understood me, though, and said, "Yeah, I see it. I hacked the hotel's security system and am watching you on the lobby cameras. You really don't have a good side, do you?"

"Not as far as a camera's ever found," I replied. "You hacked the hotel? Can you get our rooms comped?"

"One, I might be stretching things to call what I did hacking. The password is PigeonForgeFairfield, all one word, with the first letter of each word capitalized. Not exactly triple-factor authentication. Two, I could get your room comped, but that would screw the small business that owns the hotel, and thus be a dick move. And three, why do you care what your room costs? The government is paying."

"No, the government wants me to turn in receipts for reimbursement, since I'm a contractor. Geri's room is on Uncle Sam's credit card, and Father Matt's got the Vatican black Amex or whatever, but I'm stuck paying out of pocket and hoping I don't lose the paperwork before I file my expense report."

"A monster hunter doing expense reports." I could hear the little shit-head giggling over my earpiece. "What is this world coming to? Fine, your room is comped. But I doubled the rate on Geri's room to compensate."

"Whatever," I replied, turning my attention back to Geri and the po-po. Which would be a really fun name for a bubblegum pop band.

They seemed to have sorted out all their issues, because the cops had the Tweedles in cuffs and the first one was headed for the door. Geri shook hands with a pudgy cop rocking a serious GCM (Generic Cop Mustache), then went over to the terrified desk clerk, who had stood frozen behind the counter throughout the entire fight. I watched as she leaned over the counter, patted the stricken clerk's shoulder, then handed him a flask from her back pocket. The terrified dude took a swig, grimaced, then took another, much longer, pull. He handed the flask back to Geri, who slid it back into her hip pocket and patted him on the cheek, literally the most compassionate move I'd ever seen from her.

She walked over to where I was standing and motioned Father Matthew over as well. "I've got things settled with the cops and the hotel. The cops are going to hold these idiots for a couple days on a drunk and disorderly, which will hopefully give us time to find whatever is running around the woods out there before they get sprung and come looking for us. The desk clerk is going to split the damages between my credit card and yours, Father. It only seemed fair that the Church and the government pay for the mess."

"Can we do that?" I asked. "Separation of church and state and all that?"

Geri gave me a withering glare, and for once I just shut up instead of continuing to poke the bear. If this bear was going to pick up the tab for the wrecked coffee table, busted chairs, and ripped couch that we left strewn around the lobby, I should probably keep my big mouth shut for once.

"In exchange," Geri continued, "we will do our best not to do anything else while we're here that gets the police called to our location, and if we do decide to do anything that requires law enforcement's attention, we promise not to do it here in the hotel. Those are the conditions on which I kept us out of jail and in the hotel. Nod your head if you understand me, Bubba."

I nodded, then held up my left hand, middle finger extended, to the nearest security camera as Skeeter's laughter almost deafened me. "Got it. Don't start any fights where the cops get called, and if I do get the cops called on me, do it away from the hotel. I think I can manage that."

"Good plan," Geri replied. "Because if you get us thrown out of this hotel, we're either sleeping in the truck or driving a long-ass way to find someplace else to crash, because the front desk guy swears that if there's any more trouble out of us that he'll get us blacklisted from every hotel within a hundred miles."

"I'm probably already banned from half of them," I said. "I can't stay in a Holiday Inn or Sheraton anywhere east of the Mississippi anymore. Not since the unfortunate incident with the selkie in the bathtub that one time in Birmingham."

"I don't even want to know," Geri said. "Now can we please go to our rooms, get a shower, and find someplace to eat? I worked up an appetite kicking that guy's ass."

An hour later and we were sitting at a Cracker Barrel two exits away from the hotel. There was a Ruby Tuesday across the hotel parking lot, but they serve booze, and their proximity to the Fairfield was not a plus in this situation, because the likelihood of me punching somebody and/or breaking furniture increases dramatically with the application of alcohol, and I wanted to put distance between me and the hotel before I entered any potentially fraught situations. Like dinner.

So I had a plate piled high with chicken and dumplings, fried okra, French fries, and one lonely little broccoli tree breaking up the taupe landscape of my dinner plate. Amy ordered a hamburger steak with mashed potatoes, gravy, onions, and asparagus, referring to the thermonuclear fart fuel she had on her plate as "self defense" when I raised an eyebrow at her. Geri had a hunk of country-fried steak slathered in gravy with mashed potatoes, more gravy, and a heaping bowl of apple sauce on the side. Father Matthew actually had multiple colors on his plate, since he picked the veggie plate and somehow managed to find three vegetables on the menu that weren't breaded and fried. I was starting to think our new liaison might be a Communist, ordering steamed veggies and unsweetened iced tea in the South. Obviously we were going to have to educate this ol' boy.

"Okay, so our arrival in Tennessee was a little more…eventful than we might have expected, but now that the sun's going down, what do we know about where this wampus might be causing its ruckus?" I asked.

"You're going to make every really awful rhyme with wampus that you can, aren't you?" Geri asked.

"No question," Skeeter replied. We had him conferenced into our meal on Geri's tablet, which we had propped up with a basket of cathead biscuits and a ketchup bottle. "Bubba has never found a joke he wouldn't beat into the ground."

"Well, how do you know a horse is dead if you ain't beat the shit out of its corpse?" I asked.

"Anyway," Geri said around a mouthful of steak-like meat, "all the reports we have of wampus cat sightings are located around water, mostly the Little Pigeon River, with a few mentions north of here around the French Broad River."

"That makes sense," I said. "Wampus cats love water. They swim like otters, and legend says they can stay underwater long enough to drag a man down, hold him beneath the surface until he drowns, then haul the body to shore to eat it."

"How the hell is something the size of a bobcat gonna lug a full-grown human being, waterlogged no less, anywhere, much less up onto the banks of a river?" Skeeter asked.

"Because wampus cats ain't bobcat-sized, Skeet," I replied. "They're big as mountain lions, with an extra set of legs in the middle."

"And tentacles growing out of their backs?" Skeeter shot back. We were starting to get strange looks from neighboring tables for talking to an iPad at the dinner table, but if they couldn't get with the times, that was a "them" problem, and not an "us" problem. "Bubba, you're thinking about a displacer beast."

"What the hell is a displacer beast?" I asked.

"It's a monster from *Dungeons & Dragons*, you big idiot. Now we ain't chasing stuff out of *Volo's Guide to Monsters*, we're hunting down real-life cryptids, so let's keep everybody else's intellectual property out of our jobs, how about it?" Skeeter raised an eyebrow at me, and I nodded. Now that he mentioned it, I did remember displacer beasts. Skeeter got me hooked on *D&D* video games way after our freshman year of college, and I guess some of the ideas stuck in my head through the weed haze we were wrapped in most of that summer.

"Okay, so a wampus cat is smaller than I thought," I said. "Doesn't change the fact that they love water, so around the French Broad is where we need to be hunting."

"Why not the Little Pigeon River?" Father Matthew asked. "It's a lot closer."

"Yeah, but it runs right through Pigeon Forge and alongside decent-sized highways for a lot of its course," I said. "If the wampus cat has a nest, or lair, or whatever, it won't be near where a bunch of people live. The French Broad runs right by a big patch of undeveloped woods not far from here. If the critter's been seen along both the French Broad and Little Pigeon, it stands to reason the nest is somewhere near both rivers, and they meet up not far from this wooded area."

"I've got something else that backs up Bubba's theory," Skeeter said.

"Yeah?" Geri asked. I don't know when we elected the youngest and least mentally stable member of our team Amy's second-in-command, but the more she took on the role, the further away Geri was from wanting to murder me, which was her whole raison d'etre when we first met. So if it meant I didn't have to lock her bedroom door from the outside anymore, she could be Assistant Boss or whatever. I didn't mind. I mean, it's not like I ever listened to what anybody told me to do anyway, so I could ignore her just as well as I ignore anybody else.

"Yeah," Skeeter continued. "There's a new campground being constructed in that chunk of wilderness bounded by the French Broad and Little Pigeon Rivers. It's possible if the wampus lived in those woods, that its habitat was disturbed by construction, and that accounts for the uptick in sightings."

"Okay, then," I said. "We'll gear up and spend a night tromping around in the woods. Again."

"Yippee," Geri said.

"Look on the bright side," I said. "It ain't a swamp this time."

She shot me the bird as I flagged down our waitress, a matronly woman with a lavender rinse in her hair and a scandalized expression at the profane gesture she saw Geri make. I ordered three peach cobblers to make sure we had enough energy for a long night of wampus hunting. Then I got dessert for Geri and Father Matthew, too.

6

Two hours later, we pulled my truck off the side of the road a little northeast of Pigeon Forge, and Amy pulled up behind me in her Suburban. I got out and went to the back seat to start gearing up. Amy pulled her Suburban up behind us, got out, and opened up a laptop using the hood of her SUV as a table. I loaded up a shoulder holster with my new pistol under my left arm and a couple speed loaders under my right. A paddle holster so new the leather still creaked went into the small of my back, and a brand new Taurus Judge revolver slid into it.

I grabbed a web belt with a pair of silver-edged kukris hanging from it, strapped that around my waist, then clipped a pair of spiked glove-looking things to it. The were my caestae, a Christmas gift from Amy a few years ago. They gave my hands some protection when I needed to punch above my weight class, which was almost always, and they had neat little accessories like silver and cold iron spikes, if the monster gave me time to add the appropriate accoutrements to my ensemble before starting our fight.

They almost never did, but the oversized knuckle dusters had served me well, whether I had the spikes in or not. Something about swinging a fist the size of a Honeybaked ham wrapped in steel at someone's face can be very persuasive.

I heard an odd whirring sound coming from behind me, and turned to see a massive antenna with what looked like a collapsed umbrella on top of it rising up from the back of Amy's SUV. She tapped a few keys on her laptop and the umbrella opened up into a black mesh satellite dish, which spun around once, then pointed up at the sky toward the northwest.

"What the hell is that?" I asked. I noticed Father Matthew wince when I said "hell." He might be in for a rough time if that kind of mild swearing bothered him. Either that, or he was about to learn a whole lot of new words.

"This is a new communications rig. After your…adventure in the South Carolina swamp a few months back, I petitioned the department for a portable satellite uplink. When I expressed my belief that keeping you in more constant, consistent communication would lower the amount of property damage the government was on the hook for, they agreed that this was a far less expensive solution than letting you run around unsupervised."

"How much did that thing cost?" I asked. I was trying to figure out if I was impressed that they would spend that much money on keeping me out of trouble, or if I was offended that they thought my good behavior could be bought that cheaply.

"More than your brand-new annual salary from the Catholic Church," Amy replied.

Wow. That was more than the value of all the guns I owned, plus ammunition. Yes, I calculate my salary based on how many bullets it will buy. It's an easier system of measurement than metric, but it is subject to variance based on market forces. And hunting season. "So that thing is just going to beam Skeeter right into our heads? Did I get another implant while I was sleeping?"

Back in the day, DEMON, the super-secret predecessor to the Department of Homeland Security Paranormal Division, the moderately secret division of the federal government I currently contracted for, had implanted RFID trackers in all their agents, including me. My tracker was probably still laying in the woods between Skeeter's house and mine, having been discarded in a heavily armed disagreement I had with some former DEMON agents. Some of whom were now also formerly alive. It was a pretty serious disagreement.

Then Quincy Harker got involved, and it became a disagreement with an impressive body count. I thought I knew how to wreck shit, but that dude takes mayhem to levels I ain't even thought of.

"No, Bubba. Homeland is not interested in putting a tracker in you.

They just want to put a Jiminy Cricket in your ear when you're on the clock, so maybe there's a snowball's chance you'll destroy fewer buildings," Amy said.

She handed me a little earwig communicator that didn't look any different than the ones we'd been using. I stuck it in my ear and was immediately serenaded by the dulcet tones of a middle-aged gay Black man in rural Georgia swearing about the officiating in some football game somewhere. I only follow college ball, and I root for two teams: Georgia and whoever's playing Alabama.

"Skeeter, we can hear you," I said.

"I don't give a tinker's damn whether you can hear me or not, Bubba. That call was a joke and a half, and in the biggest game of the year? I want to find that ref's eye doctor and beat his ass for him." Skeeter was way more worked up about this game than was normal for him. Frankly, the fact that he knew when the big game was happening was strange enough, much less for him to be griping about it a week and change later.

"How much do you have riding on the game, Skeet?" Geri asked as she got her little ear thingy settled.

"I've gotta do the dishes and clean the litter box for a damn month thanks to that idiot zebra and his crap eyesight!"

That made sense. Skeeter's always been pretty chill about money, knowing he can just spend some time on the computer and either earn more or fleece unsuspecting rubes in an online poker room and steal more that way. But cleaning the litter box? That one hit him where it hurt. Skeeter's boyfriend had moved in a few months back, and he brought James Tiberius Cat, a massive Maine Coon mix with a missing eye, one leg that didn't work quite right, half of one ear torn off in a fight, and a few teeth gone. That cat has seen some shit. Skeeter was pretty much in love, but J.T. Cat has not adjusted well to his new living arrangements, and Skeeter has told me horror stories about waking up to a fifteen-pound furball sitting on his chest glaring at him with the hole where his eye used to be, or J.T. Cat opening the shower curtain, taking a swipe at Skeeter's backside with his razor-sharp claws, then running away before the screaming started.

I loved the idea of Skeeter having a cat. And a boyfriend, because it had been too long. But I took a lot of joy in watching this furball turn my best friend's life completely upside down. Male friendship is often based entirely on schadenfreude. Because we're all kinda assholes.

"Lemme guess," I said. "You already do the dishes, and he snuck the cat boxes in on you when you weren't paying attention."

"We were watching the NFC Championship, and he wanted to up the ante. I was good for it, because I was pretty sure I was gonna win, and that meant he'd be doing the dishes and my laundry for a month. But no, it's almost like somebody paid off the ref just to screw with me personally!"

"Hell, if I'd thought I could get in touch with him, I woulda paid a good bit of money to make you have to clean litter boxes, buddy," I said.

"You're a real pal, Bubba."

"Are we going to stand around talking football all night, or are we going to hunt this wampus cat?" Father Matthew asked.

Maybe he was going to be all right after all. I mean, he did give us a choice. "I reckon we didn't bring enough beer for a lengthy discussion of pro football officiating, so we might as well go hunting," I said.

"Not bringing enough beer implies that you did bring beer," Geri said.

"Yeah, there's a cooler built into the bed of the truck, and the rednecks at the hotel left all that beer behind with nobody to drink it. I dumped it into the truck and iced it down before we left."

She just shook her head and finished gearing up. I can't believe she was surprised. It's like she didn't even know me.

It took us about forty-five minutes of walking through the woods to get to the last place a wampus cat had been seen. We'd left any semblance of civilization behind half an hour ago, and couldn't even hear the highway from where we stood looking around. We were on a wooded hilltop with a clear view of at least a mile in every direction, and the setting sun had everything ablaze in brilliant oranges and golds. Geri was a good twenty feet up a live oak that was so big I couldn't even wrap my arms around it, looking for anything that looked like a wampus cat's natural habitat.

"What the hell are we looking for again?" I called up to her.

"Ponds, any kind of creek that looks deep enough for a decent-sized cat to swim in, caves, big brushfalls… Come on, Bubba. You're the Hunter. You're supposed to know this stuff."

"Skeeter's in charge of research," I replied. "I'm in charge of mayhem and alcohol."

"Play to your strengths, I guess," Father Matthew said.

I raised an eyebrow at him, and he just gave me one of those "I said what I said" shrugs that I've learned to recognize after catching a couple hundred of them from Geri over the last two years. Just what I needed—a priest who thought he had a sense of humor. "Anyhow," I called back up the tree. "You see any place that might be worth checking out?"

"Yeah, there's another big hill about half a mile west of here, and it looks like the creek carved a chunk of it away. There are some shadowy caves that might be the kind of place a wampus would like."

"How do you know which way is west?" I asked. I didn't remember her carrying a compass up the tree, and if there was a new phone app that was worth a shit at navigating the middle of nowhere, I needed that pronto.

Geri disappointed me, a little too gleefully for my tastes. She just pointed up at the setting sun. "It's over that way, where the big orange thing is falling out of the sky. I hear the sun sets in the…wait for it…west."

All my friends are smartasses. I'm not sure what that says about me, but I'm sure it says something. "Alright, then let's head west to this hill, see if there's any spots that look like they could be wampus holes, and set up a perimeter around them. Everything I've read says wampus cats are nocturnal, and ambush predators, so it'll probably be hiding until it gets dark, then come out to hunt."

Geri had been clambering down the big oak while I'd been talking, and she dropped to the ground behind me right as I finished. I turned to see her dusting the bark off her hands onto her jeans. She looked up at me and grinned. "Damn, Bubba. You sounded almost like you knew what you're doing there. Keep that up and somebody's gonna think you're a pro."

"He's just trying to impress the new boss," Skeeter said in our ears. "Nobody tell him that the Church gave us a three-year contract whether Father Matthew likes us or not."

"Ahem," Father Matthew said, looking up as though he was talking to a power much higher than my nerdy best friend. "You do know I'm on this comms channel, right?"

"Yeah," Skeeter said. "I know. I just don't care." Then he clicked off and left the four of us looking at one another in the rapidly darkening woods.

"Well, that went well," Matthew said.

"Don't sweat it, Father," Amy said, patting the slender priest on his shoulder. "Joe was more than our liaison. He was family. And for Skeeter and Bubba, he was family for their entire lives. It might take Skeeter a bit to get accustomed to someone filling his role."

Matthew nodded, his face stern. "I understand. And I don't want to take Father Joe's place. But I do have a job to do, and we can't have our tech support going off in a snit whenever he remembers that his uncle isn't the liaison any longer."

I stepped over to the priest and looked him in the eye. "Father Matthew, let me be perfectly goddamn clear. Skeeter is part of this team. He is my best friend, my brother from another mother, and one of very few people on this earth that I trust implicitly. You are none of those things. You *might* eventually become someone I trust, but Skeeter has been my best friend since middle school.

"He was there for me when my mom vanished. He stood with the family when we buried my grandparents, my brother, and my father. He was the *only* person from our part of the world who stood by me when I stuck a sword through my father's guts and watched him bleed out in front of me.

"So if anybody needs to remember anything, it's you needing to remember that we are family, whether we were born that way or not. And you ain't. Maybe not yet, maybe not ever. But if I gotta choose between losing the Church's money and their babysitter, or losing my best friend for better than twenty-five years? Well, I've survived without the Church's money before, and I reckon I can find a way to do it again. But I ain't never walked through the world as an adult without Skeeter by my side, and I don't intend to start now.

"So if you want to be part of this team, you can follow me over to that next hill and hunt some wampus. But if you want to threaten my brother because he's working through some shit, you can fuck right off." Then I stomped off through the woods to the west, not giving a shit if the priest followed me or not.

7

Spoiler alert—Father Matthew didn't follow me off into the rapidly darkening woods a few miles away from anyone who would hear him scream if I was really that pissed off at him. I wasn't. Not *really*. I was annoyed, and it was better to just lay it all out on the table early in our relationship with the new priest than to pussyfoot around stuff and have some big fight when we're in the middle of the shit and it might get us killed. If I'm gonna have to deal with team meetings and the fallout of my temper and other bullshit that I thought I was free from having to deal with by dint of not working in some big corporation, I wanna deal with that shit when nobody's actively trying to murder and/or eat me.

But it was fine that he didn't follow. Amy and Geri were back there to talk him through Dealing with Bubba 101, and I had Skeeter in my ear relaying to me anything important he picked up from being in all their ears. So I could get back to the whole purpose of the trip—hunting a flippin' wampus cat.

Now wampus cats are more than just the monster with maybe the coolest name in creation. They're fast, deadly ambush predators, *and* they have the coolest name in creation. There's never been a recorded case of a captured wampus cat, which is why some reports say it's the size of a bobcat or a Maine coon cat on steroids, and other reports say it's the size of a mountain lion. If you aren't up on your North American predators, that's roughly the difference between a big terrier and a Great Dane, so there's a little bit of a discrepancy there.

They're also supposed to alternately be great swimmers, great climbers, incredibly fast with six legs, possessed of a long prehensile tail, and/or able to mimic human voices with their cries, luring unsuspecting hunters into the wilderness by pretending to be their wives or children. That last bit can't possibly be true, because most of the hunters I know go into the woods to escape their wives and kids, so why the hell would they follow the ankle biters anywhere? I don't have kids, so the motivations of breeders are often beyond me.

But since nobody really knows what a wampus cat looks like, and there aren't any reports of one in captivity anywhere, me and Skeeter have spent years talking about being the first people to catch a real, live wampus cat. It would make us legends in the cryptid hunting community, no matter how many damn YouTube followers Mason Dixon has. I'm not jealous. Really, I'm not. But I might be a little tired of getting compared to him just because he's the one all over the internet. I was here first, dammit.

So as I stomped through the woods, I was actually paying attention to my surroundings, not just tromping off in a huff. I remembered that the most recent sightings had all been down in valleys or hollers, and west was the more remote direction, so it made sense to head west. And since I had my earwig in, I could talk to Skeeter and he could keep track of me in case anything went sideways.

"They still arguing back there, Skeet?" I asked.

"Not as much," he replied. "Father Matthew seems to be more educated on the ways of Bubba whispering, and they're starting into the woods to follow you."

"Bubba whispering?" I asked.

"You know, when we make you think something is your idea so you'll quit bitching and go along with what needs to be done?"

"Oh yeah, that. I didn't know y'all had a name for it."

"Amy works for the government, dude. She's probably got an acronym and letterhead for it."

He wasn't wrong. My fiancée had really embraced the bureaucracy since getting hired back by the feds. And Director Pravesh was doing nothing to stem the tide of her paper-pushing, with more reports and budget forms than I'd ever seen all cascading across the top of my dining room table. I don't mind the clutter, but if the table's covered with paper, I have to find someplace else to put my empty beer cans before they go to the recycling bin under the sink, and that's a pain in the ass.

"Okay, are they following my trail, are you guiding them to me, or are they just saying 'screw it' and going off in a completely different direction?" I asked, realizing that I was standing in the middle of the woods at sunset talking to thin air. If I was hunting crazy people and came across me, I'd think I'd just bagged my limit.

"A little from column A, a little from column B," Skeeter replied. "If they stay on their current heading, they oughta catch up to you in about fifteen minutes."

Fifteen minutes? I guess I stomped off through more woods than I remember. I found a fallen tree that was kinda leaning in the crook of another pair of trees and sat down on it, testing it with my weight before finally settling all my bulk onto it, listening to the creak of the protesting wood as I did so. Everybody's a damn dietician, even in the middle of nowhere.

About ten minutes later, I heard something coming through the woods and stood up to have a look around. "Skeeter, you suck at estimating time," I said. "I can hear 'em coming through the brush already."

"Uh, Bubba," Skeeter replied. "I'm watching all four of you on my monitor. Your trackers are still half a mile apart. I don't know what's coming through the woods to you, but it's not our team."

Well, *that* got my damn attention. I looked around for cover, but it was getting hard to see in the gloom. It was dusk when I stomped off, and down here in the valley, it got dark faster than up on top of the hill. I had my pistol out, but I had limited faith in my ability to hit anything with it. It was a new gun, one that I'd only put a couple hundred rounds through, and it was coming on full night with no moon, so if I was really lucky the big boom would scare off anything coming through the woods with bad intentions. If not, well it was at least a really heavy pistol, so I could beat the shit out of something with it until they bit my arm off.

"Skeet, can you see down into this holler I'm in?" I asked.

"Not a bit," he said. "Only way I'm able to see your location is the tracker in your earpiece. Your phone isn't pinging anything, and neither are the trackers in your knives and guns."

"Well, shit," I said, then paused. "Wait, what trackers in my guns and knives?"

"The ones I planted there after you cut the tracker out of your arm." Skeeter did not sound nearly as abashed by this revelation as I wanted him to. "Oh, don't act like you give a shit about your body autonomy, Bubba. You let somebody shave a number three into your leg hair when Dale Earnhardt died."

"Yeah, but there was consent involved, Skeeter," I said. "You don't just go planting bugs in a dude's weapons. That's a serious breach of trust."

"Is it?" he asked. "How many cell phones have you smashed, thrown out of truck windows, hurled off mountaintops, chucked in lakes, or dropped in mailboxes on the side of the road, just so I'd stop bothering you?"

I thought for a second, counted on my fingers for a couple more, then said, "I don't know, ten?"

"Try thirty-seven."

"You keep count?"

"Me and Geri have a running pool each year whether you'll destroy more phones or throw more away in irritation, so I have a running tally."

"Who's winning so far?"

"Bubba, it's February."

"I know. Who's winning?"

"So far, you've only smashed one phone on the concrete this year, which is lower than your usual pace. But you also flushed one down a toilet at a rest stop, threw one off your back porch, and left one on the roof of the truck when you pulled out of the parking lot of a Buc-ee's."

"Does that count as destroyed, or lost?"

"Half credit to both," he said. "Which puts me at two and a half to Geri's one and a half."

"I reckon I better break some shit so it stays interesting."

"Bubba, if there's anything life with you can be called, it's interesting. Speaking of interesting, do you still hear something coming through the woods?"

I turned to where the sound had been coming from. "Nope," I said. "Ain't nothing coming."

"Oh, good."

"Because it's here."

"That's probably not good."

"Probably not." I looked down into the beady black eyes of one of the most dangerous predators in North America. "Skeeter, is it against the law to shoot a wild hog in Tennessee?"

This was a big pig. Like, a *big* pig. Its shoulders probably came up to my waist, and it had a pair of short tusks sticking out of its lower jaw, with a little sliver of meat still hanging from one, left over from its last meal. I was hoping that there wouldn't be little Bubba chunks hanging from it in a couple minutes.

"It's a hog?" Skeeter's voice told me that he understood exactly the danger involved. Wild hogs aren't just mean, they're mean *and* smart, with big-ass knives sticking out of their mouths. Nobody in their right mind messes with a feral pig if they've got any other choice. Unfortunately, this pig was ten feet away and glaring at me like it could smell the bacon I had for breakfast. To be fair, I went back for seconds, so maybe it *could* smell the bacon I ate fourteen hours ago. I don't know how pig noses work.

"Yeah, it's a hog," I said. "Big, bristly hair, tusks, beady eyes, looks like it wants to eat my kidneys, that kind of thing."

"You want to move very slowly," Skeeter said. "Don't startle it, but draw your pistol. If you get a chance, don't aim for the head. The skull is really thick, and I think your new hand cannon would make it through, but if you ain't dead on, it could deflect and not do anything but piss the critter off." I've noticed over the years that Skeeter sounds more country when he's scared. Which does not do wonders for the blood pressure of whoever he's on comms with when he starts to sound like a Clampett.

I did what he said, sliding my hand across my chest to pull out the massive revolver tucked under my arm. I swung the pistol around like I was moving through molasses, finally lining the front sight up with the hog's forehead. I pulled the hammer back, sending a loud *click* through the hushed wilderness, and just as I did, another three, smaller hogs came out of the underbrush.

"Well, shit," I said, decocking my gun. "Skeeter, it's a mama pig with three little babies. The babies are kinda cute, in a psychopathic, eat your innards kinda way."

"Bubba, get up a tree. Now." Skeeter's voice was tight with worry, the kind of fear I hadn't heard from him in a long time. I opened my mouth to ask him what had him so freaked out when I was forcefully reminded of exactly how intense a mother animal's instincts to defend her young could be.

Miss Piggy lowered her head, let out a snort, and charged me, her tusks aimed right at my favorite part of my anatomy. So I did what any reasonable human being would do when a wild hog charged straight at their junk.

I ran like hell.

8

I'm not sure what made more noise crashing through the underbrush—me or the giant, murderous, ball-devouring swine. Probably me, since I was the one breaking the trail. I'm also a lot taller and a good fifty pounds heavier than the pig that was in hot pursuit. I justify my abject terror and rapid flight through the dense sticker bushes, low-hanging branches, and thick carpet of kudzu by the fact that the hog, while outweighed and outgunned, was not unarmed, as it had those razor-sharp tusks waving around in front of its face. If I had to admit my own shortcomings, I'd probably also own up to the fact that the hog might have been the smarter participant in this chase, just based on the fact that I was the one running through the woods like my ass was on fire, and the pig was the one doing the chasing.

Given that this was not the time to be contemplating my poor life choices or evaluating whether or not I was smarter than a Tennessee wild hog, I just ran like hell. I stomped down saplings as I encountered them, hopped over a couple of fallen trees, vaulted a narrow creek that sluiced its way through the red dirt hillside, and finally found what I'd been desperately searching for ever since I first took flight—a climbable tree.

When you're as big as I am, you can't just climb any tree. You ain't shimmying up any narrow-ass loblolly pines once the needle crosses three hundred pounds. For one thing, you'll probably bend the whole tree slap over, which puts you right back on the ground. For another, you can't exactly wrap your legs around the trunk and dry-hump your way to safety like you're back under the bleachers with Mary Jane McGillicutty at the homecoming game, on account of you being too damned heavy. And because humping a tree hurts your nuts. Trust me. It's a long story involving Robitussin, college, and a fairy tale about dryads, but I know of what I speak.

So I needed a big tree. A *really* big tree. Preferably hardwood, and it needed to have decent-sized branches close to the ground. My vertical leap ain't what it once was, and it was barely eighteen inches before I blew out my knee. So I ran through the woods, getting my face slapped silly by branches and my clothes picked and snagged by thorns until I found a massive oak with branches both low enough and thick enough to hold my fat ass. Then I jumped for it, hauled myself up out of tusk range, and extended my middle finger to the hog, who slammed into the trunk of the tree again and again, either in frustration or in a futile effort to shake me loose. Even if the tree moved a little, I was locked onto the trunk like a tick on a hound dog, and I wasn't going any-damn-where.

The pig glared up at me again, its beady little black eyes radiating rage and hatred, then it turned and waddled off back the way we came, its bristly little butt wagging like a happy puppy at the knowledge that it had scared me off and treed me, and I wouldn't be coming back to bother its piglets. Or maybe I'm giving the pig too much credit and it didn't give a shit about me one way or another. But you spend as many years as I have running through the woods in search of things that want to murder you, and you'll anthropomorphize a little, too.

"Skeeter, do pigs hate people?" I asked the air. The air didn't answer, which was odd. That was a silly enough question that I expected Skeeter to reply almost instantly.

"Skeeter?" I called, then reached up to tap my ear, just in case a branch had somehow reached all the way inside my ear canal and turned the communicator off. My finger met nothing but flesh. Okay, flesh and a little bit of ear wax, but either way there wasn't a comm in there.

"Shit." This time I knew there wouldn't be a response, but it made me feel a little better to have my assessment of the situation out there for everyone to understand.

"SHIT!" This time I yelled it, but apparently the therapeutic effects of swearing only stretch so far, because this time I didn't feel any better. Bummer.

"GODDAMMIT!" That one was for science. I still didn't feel any better, so now that I had definitively determined that I had reached the end of profanity-based healing, I started to pat myself down and take stock of my supplies and situation.

Gun? Check. I still had the cannon in my right hand, but I paused my inventory to yank a slender pine branch out of the barrel. I slipped the pistol under my left arm and fastened the holster, then patted my right armpit and confirmed the pair of speed loaders were still there.

Backup gun? Check. My Taurus Judge revolver was nestled in the small of my back, having been clipped securely inside the waistband of my jeans. I felt some nasty scratches right where my tramp stamp would be if I had one, but my gun was still there, and I wasn't bleeding too much, so we counted that as a win. My phone was gone, having fallen out of my shirt pocket at some point in my mad dash for safety. I reckoned that might have tied up the contest Skeeter and Geri were running.

My knives were still strapped to my belt, but my caestae were gone. That one pissed me off. Amy had given me those metal-banded gauntlets for Christmas a few years back, and we'd made some improvements to them over time, adding screw-in spikes of silver, cold iron, and regular steel to handle different kinds of monsters. I kept them fastened to my belt using Velcro straps, but I must have snagged them on something as I ran, because they were nowhere to be seen. And it was getting dark, so it was getting harder and harder to see anything. I reached in my shirt pocket to turn on my phone's flashlight, then remembered that my phone was lying somewhere in a piggy footprint behind me.

"Shit." This one was more muttered than shouted, and still had absolutely no positive effects on my mental health, but at least I wasn't shouting anymore. That had to count for something, right?

I looked back up the trail I'd blazed through the forest, and started trudging back toward where I'd left the others. It was getting dark, but if I didn't lose the trail, I should be able to make it back to the rest of the team before total nightfall. I might even be able to get a spare comm from Amy, if I was lucky.

I wasn't lucky.

I not only lost the trail, I wandered so far off anything resembling a trail I couldn't swear I was still in Tennessee. I couldn't even blame it too much on the darkness, as the full moon blazed down upon me as I stood in a little clearing turning around and around trying to figure out which way might lead me back to me team and our vehicles. There was a narrow path leading off to my left, and a wider, more defined track through the woods to the right. I weighed the options and chose the right-hand path, deciding that even if I wasn't going in exactly the right direction, moving was better than sitting still where nobody had a clue how to find me, and if the way was even remotely clear, then it probably led to something resembling civilization.

Spoiler alert—it didn't.

I rumbled and stumbled through the woods for a solid hour after I lost the trail completely, tripping over vines, snapping fallen branches, and generally sounding like a grizzly bear rampaging through a Victoria's Secret. Don't ask me how I know what that sounds like—it involves a very bashful werebear and a faulty dressing room latch. Let's just say that Geri is never allowed back in the Mall of Georgia.

I finally burst out into a small clearing, just an open circle in the trees, about ten feet across. I looked up at the big old moon, shining down on me just like I was some lovestruck teenager holding hands with his sweetie, instead of a pissed-off middle-aged ex-football stud with no damn idea where his sweetie was or if he was going to be able to find her again before he rotted away in the woods forever.

"Halle-friggin'-lujah," I muttered as a shape materialized out of the gloom ahead of me. I was trying hard to rein in my potty mouth, on account of my time with Quincy Harker making me drop F-bombs like they were commas and Amy starting to make noises about meeting parents. I asked her if I could just go back to Fairyland and fight my psychotic grandparents again, but the look she gave me reminded me that Queen Mab wasn't the only terrifying woman in my life.

Standing on the far edge of the clearing was a wall. And not just a random wall, like that weird staircase in the woods on *Wynona Earp*. No, this wall was attached to other walls, and a roof, which meant there was almost certainly a whole damn building sitting there in front of me! A building that had a wisp of smoke coming up out of the chimney, a little bit of a glow peeking out through the curtains, and a damn power line running straight into it!

Yeah, in hindsight I probably should have been looking up for things like power lines instead of looking down trying to retrace my steps like I was some kind of tracker, which I ain't. My idea of hunting has always been more the "sit in a tree stand and drink beer until it ain't safe to climb down under your own power, so you spend the rest of the day just peeing on the deer rather than actually trying to shoot anything" type than the "track things through the woods like you're a mighty woodsman" type. So

I didn't immediately think to look for power lines to lead me back to civilization. Not that much in that part of Tennessee was really "civilized." But I live on a mountain in Georgia, so who am I to judge?

Anyhow, this little cabin looked like it might have been the answer to all my prayers, and I was grinning like a possum as I took my first step in that direction.

That grin fell away at the unmistakable sound of somebody racking a shell into a twelve-gauge shotgun less than ten feet behind me. I turned to see a gaunt old man, shirtless, with a pair of baggy overalls swallowing his narrow frame, holding a shotgun trained on my sizable midsection. Even if I was a normal-sized person, there was no way he could shoot at that distance and not cause some serious damage.

"Who the hell are you, and what the hell are you doing skulking around behind my shitter in the middle of the night?"

That's when I noticed the man was framed in the door of a ramshackle shed. A door that stood wide open with a little crescent moon carved into it. A door that let the unmistakable aroma of outhouse waft through the crisp night air and assault my nostrils with its funk.

Well, at least the old fart had pulled his britches up before threatening to kill me. I raised my hands up over my head and uttered the words that so many men have uttered, and so few situations have been helped by.

"I can explain."

9

It didn't take much more explaining past "I'm lost as shit" before the old guy took the shotgun off his shoulder and pointed toward the back wall of his house.

"Come on, let's at least have a drink while we figure out where you think you're trying to be, and how that dragged your sorry ass to my back yard where you interrupted an old man and his nightly constitutional."

I noticed he didn't throw the scattergun over his shoulder, just pointed it less directly at me. He could still swing it up and cut me in half in a fraction of the time it would take me to charge him and steal his...I dunno, outhouse? But I went where he pointed, being the one without a gun in my hands at the moment.

He guided me around the back wall to the front of the cabin, a small place maybe thirty feet on a side. Not much by city standards, but if it was just me living way out in the woods, I could totally see living in something that size. Skeeter wouldn't survive. He takes up more space than that just with comic books and vintage toys.

The old man directed me up onto the porch, where a mini-fridge sat between two rocking chairs. I took one, slowly settling my weight into it until I was sure it would hold. That's something you learn being one of the biggest people you know—most things aren't built to accommodate you. I've never had a shower in a hotel bathroom that I didn't have to bend down to wash my hair in, I've turned more than one plastic lawn chair into shrapnel, and the last time I was on a commercial airplane, there were multiple seat belt extenders required for me to comply with FAA regulations. There are some issues that go along with being a big dude, but as long as I'm willing to stay fat, I can eat all the cheese I want, so I reckon I'm just going to pay attention to the weight limit stickers on ladders forever.

"Now what the hell are you doing wandering around out here in the Tennessee mountains in the dark?" he asked, reaching into the mini-fridge and pulling out two cans of Budweiser. I usually prefer something ever so slightly higher shelf than Bud, but crappy beer is better than no beer, and it wasn't Milwaukee's Best, so I kept my mouth shut except to drink.

I pondered how much to tell the old guy. I'm pretty open about my career to most folk. Either they don't believe me, so they just think I'm making something up and can't talk about whatever secret crap I'm doing, or the believe me and can't wait to tell me about that time their Great-Aunt Lulabelle saw a ghost flitting around in her laundry one night, but it turned out to just be the perky gym teacher peeping in their cousin Clarabelle's window while she put on her pjs.

"If you're taking all this time to make up a lie, it better be good, son," he said after a long slurp of his beer.

I figured I might as well tell him the truth, or at least part of it. "I'm out here hunting a wampus cat," I said. "I work for the government, and we've gotten reports of the creature damaging property and maybe endangering people, so we need to see if it really is a cryptid, and if so, whether or not we need to rehome it or put it down."

"Rehome? Put it down?" The old man looked at me with wide eyes. "Boy, are you saying that the United States Government—" except he said it more like Youuuunited States Gubmint "—has a whole department dedicated to hunting down monsters?"

"A couple, actually," I said. "I work for the Department of Homeland Security, and we handle most domestic cryptic and paranormal threats, but there are also departments that handle strictly international issues, as well as one division within the National Park Service that takes care of any incursions into our parks and monuments. They also manage Jurassic Park."

"They what the what?"

"It's the nickname we have for the Cryptic Preserves the government has scattered around the country. You know, Area 51, Area 52, Area 69, those places."

He looked dubious. "I've heard of Area 51, but them other two..."

I laughed. "Yeah, okay, I made up Area 69. The cryptic preserves started numbering with 50, but there's only 15 of them, so there is no Area 69." *That I know of*, I mentally corrected. The federal government has a lot of money, and a fetish about secrets, so for all I knew there was an Area 69 out there somewhere, I just didn't know shit about it.

"So you're some kind of federal agent?" I nodded. "You got ID?"

I reached in my back pocket and pulled out my credentials. He leaned over and took them from my hand, then fished a pair of reading glasses out of the bib on his overalls. He peered through the cheaters at my badge, then passed it back.

"Says you're a contractor," he said. "That like Blackwater for monsters or something?"

"Nothing like that," I said. "I mean, I'm a government contractor, but not a psycho like those guys. I also work for the Catholic Church. Kinda double-dipping, really, since the same jobs often end up doing work for both groups, but a man's gotta make a living, you know?"

He relaxed a little when I mentioned the Church, which was good. It was always a little dicey, mentioning Catholics in the rural South. It certainly isn't the predominant denomination down here, and the less people are exposed to other groups of people, the more their ignorance tends to bubble up. This old guy was either progressive for a hermit, or he just didn't have a problem with Catholics. Either way was fine with me.

"You got ID for that, too?"

"Nah, the Vatican doesn't send out badges. I think they want us to be more incognito."

"They might wanna think about hiring somebody that don't blot out the whole damn sun when they walk through a clearing, then." He laughed and pulled out another pair of beers. I chugged the last of mine and took the proffered can.

We sat there in a companionable silence for a while, just listening to the cicadas and the trickle of water from a creek off to our left. After I finished my second beer, I stood up. "I think I gotta go borrow your outhouse, friend."

"Oogy," the old man replied.

I stopped, my bladder completely forgotten in my concern that this old hermit picked now to have a stroke. "Excuse me?" I asked. "Are you alright?"

"Yeah, I'm fine," he said. "Why wouldn't I be?"

"You just made this weird noise. Sounded like you said 'boogie,' apropos of nothing at all."

He threw his head back and laughed, which, while confusing, was a little comforting, too. If he was *compos mentis* enough to think I was an idiot, he was probably not having a stroke, or at least not much of one. "Boy, you make me laugh like that again, we gonna be racing for that shitter. My name's Oogy, not 'boogie.' You called me friend, so I figured I might as well tell you my name so you could just use that instead."

"Oh," I said, feeling about as stupid as he must have thought I was. "Well...Oogy, my name's Bubba."

He raised an eyebrow. "Bubba? Your ID says Robert. What's the matter? Your kid brother couldn't say 'Bobby' when he was little?"

Well, that was a kick right in the junk. Because Oogy was right. I went by Bubba on account of some speech issues my kid brother Jason had when he was growing up. He had issues with 'y' sounds, so he called me Bubba. It stuck, even after me and Jace grew apart. And it doesn't grow much further apart than one of you being on the right side of the dirt, and the other one buried in it. I killed my brother Jason when he went nuts and tried to raise a cryptid army to take over the world. If he'da just wanted Georgia, we might could worked something out, but the whole world? Nah, that didn't fly.

So yeah, my younger brother, who was now dead by my hand, was the reason I was called Bubba, and out here in the middle of nowhere, Tennessee, separated by my team and my loved ones, was not where I wanted to be when it was time to dredge all that up and sift through it. So I didn't. I just got up without answering, walked around to the outhouse, relieved myself of some Bud Light, and came back a few minutes later, hoping Oogy would have forgotten about his queston or taken the hint that I didn't feel like answering.

I rejoined Oogy on the porch and said, "Think I can use your phone to call my team?"

"Sure," he said. "Soon as the battery's charged enough to make a call. Been dead a few days." He held up an ancient flip phone. "Only damn way I can get the telemarketers to quit calling me for a free estimate on new siding for my house!" He cackled with laughter, and after a moment, I joined in. The cabin was full-on log construction, without any place to put siding. This thing had obviously been built decades ago, when people were way more concerned about protection from the elements than about being able to get the perfect shade of eggshell on their siding to go with their royal blue shutters. Geri's been on an HGTV kick, so I've gotten a lot of strange additions to my vocabulary lately.

I looked around the porch and didn't see any outlets, which surprised me not a bit. My own cabin is at least half a century newer than this one, and I don't have receptacles on my front porch, either. If I put in places for people to charge their phones, they might stay longer. And there ain't many people that I want at my cabin at all, much less for a protracted stay. "You need me to go inside and plug it in for you?" I asked.

"Nah," he said. "Lost the charger about six months ago. Ain't made it back to town to get a new one yet."

I stared at him, open-mouthed, for at least a minute before the old bastard threw his head back and laughed that big belly laugh again. "I got you, son! You probably believe the check really is in the mail and that she'll still respect you in the morning."

I had to laugh along with him. "Nah," I said, mimicking his earlier response. "I ain't lookin' for respect, just somewhere warm to lay my… head." I gave him a conspiratorial wink, and we both chuckled.

Oogy stood up, stretched, and opened the door into the house. "Come on in," he said. "I didn't lose the charger, but the phone *is* deader than hell. Might as well stay warm while we wait for it to get enough juice to make a call. Besides, I could go for something a little more stout than beer."

"As long as it ain't peach schnapps," I said. "I think I got a little PTSD from the last time I drank that shit."

"Son, I got a little PTSD just thinking about drinking that shit," the old man said with a laugh. Then we went into his cabin, where the real drinking started.

10

"Bubba, how the ever-loving hell do you manage to find a way to get drunk no matter where we go for a case?" Geri asked the next morning.

I held up a finger. "One, I am a very talented man, and finding booze where there should not be booze is but one of those talents. Two, please stop shouting. I have a little bit of a headache."

"He means he's hungover as a dog," Oogy said from where he puttered around the small kitchen, then cut loose one of those laughs that felt so light and fun the night before, but felt like someone driving a spike right through my left eye this morning.

"We know what it means, Mr. Pierce," Amy said, giving me one of the death glares she's perfected in the years we've been together. I'm pretty sure she didn't even have an "injure" glare, or a "severely maim" glare before we started dating, but now she's working her way past death glare and all the way to a "murder you and everyone you've ever spoken to" glare. I bring out the best in people.

"Please, sweet cheeks, call me Oogy," he said as he deposited a plate full of bacon with four slices of buttered toast in front of me. I put a light sprinkle of garlic salt on the toast and tucked in with gusto, ignoring the stunned looks from everyone in the room. A lot of people don't want to eat when they're hung over, but I've always found that recovery meals are important for Olympic-level drinking, just like any strenuous exercise.

My recovery meal just involves fried pork products and garlic. I mean, I was sweating cheap domestic beer and Wild Turkey, so it ain't like I was smelling fresh as a daisy in the first place.

Amy was standing frozen by the old man passing out food and calling her "sweet cheeks." I knew what happened to the last guy who called her that, because I *am* the last guy that called her that. She beat my ass in unarmed combat practice, then took over our cardio workouts and ran me until I puked every other day for two weeks. And that's not even counting how long I slept on the couch. But Oogy was an old man, and a little bit charming, in a backwoods, crotchety kind of way, so maybe she wouldn't put him in traction.

"Oogy," she said, her voice so sweet butter wouldn't melt in her mouth. "If you call me sweet cheeks, dumpling butt, cutie pie, or any other comment on my appearance or femininity again, I'm going to have the IRS crawl all over your existence for the rest of your life. I will have them audit you within an inch of your life, then put a lien on any assets you have, had had, or will ever have. Are we clear?"

Oogy gave her a rakish grin. "One hundred percent, apple bottom. I will not make any comment about how you're almost as hot as Raquel Welch, or that your bulletproof vest does nothing to hide the fluid dynamics experiment you got going on under that t-shirt. I won't even talk about how cute the dimples are on your cheeks, and I certainly won't make any assumptions about any dimples you might have on your other cheeks." Then he set a heaping plate of eggs and bacon down in front of her, along with a tall glass of orange juice, and turned back to the stove.

Amy was, in a word, speechless. It was the first time I'd seen her like that in a long time, and it took everything I could do, including shoveling bacon into my face as hard and fast as I could, to keep from falling out of my chair laughing. Even Geri grinned as she leaned over and said in a whisper loud enough to be heard halfway to Florida, "I think he's fucking with you, Boss."

Amy just grinned and took a sip of her OJ. "Yeah, and I think he won that round, too. Mr. Pierce, did Bubba tell you anything about why we're here, or did he just get drunk on your porch?"

"Yeah, he said something about hunting a wampus cat. Sounded like a crock to me, but we was already drinking by that point, so I let it slide. So what are y'all doing up here? Revenuers don't come down from old Rocky Top, you know."

"Despite the song, Mr. Pierce, we aren't revenuers. We work for the government, but we could care less about any stills we might find."

"Hold on now," I said. "I'm real interested in stills."

"We aren't robbing bootleggers, Bubba." Amy didn't even look at me, just threw that one out without missing a beat. "Mr. Pierce, we've had reports of wampus sightings in the area, and they're not only increasing, but moving closer and closer to populated areas. While we don't have any direct experience with wampus cats ourselves, we have far too much experience with what happens when cryptids meet up with humans without any protections for either group."

"A lot of people or critters end up dead," I said.

"So what do you want from me?" Oogy said. He gestured to a massive gun safe. "I got my shooting irons all cleaned and ready to go, but I ain't as young as I once was. Might not be the best choice for a local guide these days."

I could tell that admission pained him a little. Some men don't take to aging well at all. My grandfather was like that. He hunted until the day he died, finally falling to a nest of vampires when I wasn't good enough to save him. He was first on the list of family members whose deaths were my fault. I wished his name was the whole list, but it wasn't even close.

"Honestly, we were just hoping to retrieve Bubba and get him out of your hair," Geri said. "The fact that you made breakfast is a huge bonus. *Somebody* booked us at a Fairfield, completely ignoring the fact that their idea of a Continental breakfast is a cup of yogurt and stale bagels."

Father Matt at least had the good grace to look ashamed of his choice of hotels. I kinda wished I'd been able to sleep in a Fairfield in bed the night before. All Oogy had was a hammock strung up between a couple of the posts on his porch. Better than nothing, but still pretty damn sketchy when you're as big as I am and as drunk as I was when I finally tried to situate myself for sleeping.

I never did make it work and ended up just sleeping on the grass with the hammock bunched up under my head for a pillow. Not even in the Top Ten worst places I'd ever slept.

"But if you have any information on the wampus and its movements, we would, of course, appreciate it," Amy said, sliding that in there all smooth like a real government official. Look at my girl, sounding all professional and shit. She totally didn't learn any of that running around with me and Skeeter.

"I reckon if y'all were really interested in finding a wampus cat, you could go check out where them city boys are building a new theme park about five miles northeast of here. I hear tell there's been some equipment getting wrecked, and even a couple of night watchmen getting mauled by mountain lions they ain't never seen."

"If they were ambushed by a mountain lion, it's more likely they would have been found in pieces, not in a hospital," Father Matt said. "They're frequently the apex predator of any environment they're found in, and they do not take kindly to having their habitats disturbed. I can't imagine two attacks both leaving survivors." That fit with what I knew about mountain lions, so I let the skinny new priest keep going.

"From the reports we have been able to verify, wampus cats are smaller than mountain lions, a little larger than the average bobcat, and much less likely to continue to attack humans once they no longer pose a threat to their environment," he continued.

"What he means is, a wampus cat ain't gonna drag your carcass home to its den and feed your kidneys to its kittens," I translated, just in case Oogy didn't deal well with the pontificating Father Matt was doing.

"I got that, son," Oogy replied. "I went to college before you was even born. Just because I live back in the woods don't mean I've always been a backwoods redneck."

"If only the same could be said for everyone in this room," Geri muttered under her breath.

"I heard that," I grumbled at her.

"I meant for you too," she replied.

"Anyway," Amy cut us off before we could start into "she's touching me" and "I wanted the window seat." She glared at the two of us, to no effect, then turned her attention back to Oogy. "Could you show me on a map where this construction is taking place? I expect we could find it, but with Bubba in the driver's seat, the more specific we can be, the better."

She pulled a tablet out of her backpack and plopped it onto the table. I rescued the last of the bacon from the ignominious fate of getting cold and being ignored by popping it into my mouth and crunching it down with a contented smile.

Geri glared at me. "You know that was my plate, right?"

"Key word there is 'was,' young Paduan," I replied.

"Don't try to get all Jedi master on me, Bubba," Geri said. "You might have the beard turning gray, but the only thing strong with you is gas."

Before I could formulate a decent comeback, Amy straightened up and tossed a wadded-up bundle of fabric to me. I shook it out and a black t-shirt unfurled, with a stick of deodorant clattering to the table. "I brought your truck, so go out and put that on," she said. "I don't want to ride anywhere with you smelling like cheap beer and bad decisions."

"God, Boss," Geri said, laughing. "Cheap beer and bad decisions is practically Bubba's natural musk. If you don't want him smelling like that, he's gonna have to ride in the bed of his own truck."

Deciding that everyone was a damned comedian this morning, I took my faded Giggletime Mountain Amusement Park t-shirt and my Old Spice out into the morning sun to wipe away at least one layer of yesterday's funk. I had peeled off my dirty shirt, admitting to myself that it didn't exactly smell daisy-fresh, when I heard someone clear their throat behind me.

"What is it, Padre?" I asked.

"I just wanted to make sure we're all on the same page, Bubba," he said, his voice a little tenuous.

"We hunt monsters, the Church pays me a bunch of money," I said. "I don't know as how there's many more pages to be on, are there?"

"I'm not trying to replace Father Joseph—"

"Don't worry." I cut him off with a wave of my hand. I turned back and looked him in the eye, only possible because he was standing on one of the porch steps. "Ain't no chance of that." I turned back to the new liaison. "Look, Father Matt. I expect you're a good dude. Dedicating your life to the service of something bigger than you is a good thing, and being willing to go out in the woods with a bunch of heavily armed government contractors to hunt down monsters that most folk don't even believe exist says that you've got a pair of brass balls to go along with that good heart. But you ain't family."

I kept going. "Joe was more than just Skeeter's adopted uncle. He wasn't much older than we were, so he was as much a big brother to us as anything. He looked out for us when we were little, he taught me how to smoke cigarettes we stole from my daddy's dresser, he even helped me pass freshman algebra. Ain't no way you can fill the hole in our lives that Joe left. That don't mean we can't make space for you on our team, or in this weird-ass little family we done built here. But you're gonna have to do it your way. Not Joe's way, not the Church's way, and sure as hell not the federal government's way. Just…relax a little bit. You're here, and we ain't tied you up and thrown you in the back of the truck for three days like we did the one 'interim liaison' we had for a week the one time Uncle Joe went on vacation and we had to hunt down a pack of were-donkeys in

Alabama. Just give us some time and we'll probably come around to accepting you. You ain't ever gonna be Joe, but if you work at it, you might be a pretty damn good Matt."

The little priest looked at me for a long minute, then nodded and stuck out his hand. "Thanks for that. I'll work on it."

We shook, and he nodded toward my torso. "But you should put a shirt on. I think I did hear a mountain lion as we were looking for you in the woods last night, and with as hairy as you are, I'd hate for one to mistake you for a possible mate."

I laughed and finished changing, and the others joined us at the trucks to continue our hunt. Oogy said goodbye to everyone, then stood by the door of my pickup with his hand out. "I like you, kid. You remind me a little bit of my grandson. You don't have an unhealthy obsession with old video games and NASCAR, do you?" he asked as I clasped his hand.

"I still play Mario Brothers on my original SNES, Oogy. If it's got more than sixteen bits, I ain't interested."

"Yeah, that's like my boy. Y'all got a lot in common. Good kids, but y'all need a shave. You take care now, alright?"

"You too, old man," I said, smiling as I slid behind the wheel. "You too."

I looked at the team, gathered around Amy's Suburban and my F-250 and said, "Let's go do what we do."

"Get shitfaced drunk and beat up rednecks in bars?" Geri asked as Father Matt looked horrified.

"Nah, that's Tuesdays. This is Thursday. That's hunt monsters *then* get drunk and beat up rednecks in bars," I said.

Geri and I high-fived as Amy grinned and Father Matt gave us yet another "what have I gotten myself into" stares. It was wampus-hunting time!

Another day, another hungover monster hunter rolling up to a construction site that's the likely cause of a bunch of cryptid or paranormal crap. One of these days, I'll learn to just start my hunt at the nearest cluster of bulldozers and dickheads with hardhats. And sure enough, I had just put one foot down on the red dirt outside the largest and least rundown trailer on the site when a young guy with a white hard hat and a paisley necktie came rushing up to the side of my truck with his hands waving over his head like he was trying to direct flights at LaGuardia.

"You can't be here!" he hollered, despite being less than ten feet away from my damn face. "This is a closed site, and no one is allowed here without the proper permits. Now turn this hunk of junk around and get to steppin'!"

Now I'll put up with a lot in my line of work. I've traipsed through cow pastures dodging bovine land mines at three in the morning. I've almost burned down a shopping mall lighting fairies on fire. Shit, I even went to a ballet once on a hunt. But I will not stand idly by while some snot-nosed pencil neck who only has to shave every third day insults my truck.

But I had promised Amy that I would do everything in my power not to get arrested this time. So I didn't slap the little weenie into the middle of next week. I just reached in my back pocket, held up my credentials, and said, "I think this counts as my permit. Now you apologize to my truck before I start looking for OSHA violations."

I gave him my best "don't mess with me" glare, which was pretty good now that I was out of the truck and able to stretch to my full height. He was a tall drink of water himself, only a couple inches shorter than me, but about a foot less in diameter, and I did have a very large fashion accessory hanging from a holster under my left arm, an accessory that Foreweenie definitely noticed, based on how big around his eyes got. He almost skidded to a stop, he halted his power walk toward me so fast.

"Um, uh, I…"

"It's okay, Mr.…?" Amy slid out of her Suburban and walked around to the now-frozen foreweenie. "We're with the Department of Homeland security and wanted to come check out some reports of vandalism to nearby businesses. We want to see if any of your equipment has been tampered with while the site was empty."

Foreweenie now looked more confused than terrified, which I didn't think was an upgrade. He turned around in a complete circle. "Nearby businesses? What kind of fake news revenuer bullshit is that? There ain't so much as a gas station for five miles in every direction. Now how about you tell me why you're really here, Missy. And don't give me none of your deep state propaganda, neither. I want the real truth!"

Wow. I just spent the night with a geriatric mountain man who looked like he should be singing "God Bless the U.S.A." at the top of his lungs at a political rally, but he was as mellow and pleasant an individual as I could have hoped to meet. Now here I was, just a few miles away, staring at the Great White Hope - Conspiracy Theorist Edition. I almost wanted to hold him down and vaccinate him, just to see if he'd burst into flames.

Amy, however, was slightly more mature than me. Slightly. Because she did have buttons, and apparently an officious little prick calling her "Missy" at ten in the morning pressed a lot of them. She walked up to Foreweenie and put a hand on his shoulder. She leaned in close, until they were almost touching foreheads, and said, "I'll tell you this, you inbred, backwoods piece of shit. If you ever want to get on a female Deputy Director of Homeland Security's good side, and trust me, that is the side you want to be on, calling her 'Missy' is not how you get there. Now let's start again, and I'll pretend I wasn't just insulted by a misogynistic putz and you'll pretend you *aren't* a misogynistic putz. How does that sound?"

I gave my best stage whisper, which is only about five decibels below my maximum shouting voice, and said, "I'd take her up on that, pal. I can see three different violations from here that'll get you shut down for at least a week, and I ain't even started looking."

He spluttered, looking from Amy to me, then back to Amy, and after a long moment where I wondered if I was going to be called upon to back up my totally fabricated accusation of OSHA violations with fact, he deflated. Like, almost literally. His puffed-up little chest sank in on itself, his face fell all the way to the basement, and he even shrank a couple inches in height, like if he was using pump up lifts in his shoes and they just had a blowout. Now I want to market a new kind of shoe that pumps up to make you taller. I bet Tom Cruise would buy the patent for a billion dollars.

Anyway, Foreweenie shrank in on himself at the sight of a strong woman with a badge and gun, and said, in a meek voice, "What can I do for y'all today?"

"That's better," Amy said, folding her badge wallet and tucking it away in a back pocket. "Now—"

"Hold up," I said, taking my life in my hands by interrupting the woman who knew both where I slept and where I kept all my knives. "You still owe somebody an apology." I nodded toward my truck.

Foreweenie gaped at me. "Are you serious?"

I glared down at him, a lot easier since he shrank even further. He kept this up he was going to be short enough to audition for that new *Lord of the Rings* show. "Do I look like somebody who ever jokes about my truck?"

He gulped and said, "I'm sorry, truck." It obviously pained him to say it, like the words stuck in his throat a little. I thought about continuing to screw with him, making him do it again and again until I was satisfied that he was appropriately penitent, but a look at Amy's expression put the brakes on that idea. So I just waved at her to continue.

"As I was saying," she said, in a tone that promised at least a weak on a lumpy couch or in Skeeter's guest room, "we have had reports of wild animal attacks in the area, and we wanted to see if you've had any strange occurrences here at the site."

Foreweenie looked around, like he was now afraid to be seen talking to us. He didn't have much to worry about, since there were only three vehicles in the parking lot: my truck, Amy's Suburban and his white Prius. Seriously, a Prius? He was talking shit about my truck, and he was driving a *Prius?* Nobody was ever going to take this dude seriously on a construction site with those wheels. Hell, I had enough trouble getting them to listen to me, and that's just because I drove a truck that wasn't generic contractor white.

"Come into the office. I don't want to talk about it out here. The guys might be back from lunch soon." He turned and practically scurried up the steps to the job site trailer. We all exchanged confused glances and followed him. I brought up the rear so I could take one last look around, just in case there happened to be a wampus cat wandering through the middle of a wide-open construction site in the middle of the day. There wasn't, but there did seem to be a narrow trail winding its way through the woods off to the east of the site.

We crowded into the small office at the back of the trailer, with Foreweenie sitting behind the messy desk in a rolling chair that had the arms held together with silver duct tape. Pretty easy to see where this guy lived in the corporate power structure. Geri grabbed a folding chair from around the folding "conference table" that took up most of the main part of the trailer, and planted herself behind and between Amy and Father Matt, making a little triangle while I leaned against the far wall. I picked my spot both on account of there not being but two guest chairs and on account of wanting to keep glaring down at this dude a little longer.

"Is the door closed? Would you lock it, please?" Foreweenie looked up at me with something like actual fear in his eyes.

"No," I said, my voice flat. "Now what the hell has got you so shook? You came on like a house afire, all regulations this and closed site that, but the minute the Deputy Director mentioned weird critters, you started looking like a long-tailed cat in a rocking chair factory." Yeah, I know my metaphor fell apart a little with the modification, but I was trying something new.

He slumped back in his chair and let out a long breath, redolent of onions, oil, and vinegar. I could see the telltale sub sandwich wrapper sticking out of his wastebasket, with what looked like a dab of mayo on one corner. Ugh. Mayo's disgusting, and I can't fully trust anybody that would pick that to go on a sandwich in a world where mustard and hot sauces exist. That long sigh moved some papers off a stack at the front of his desk, and as Amy reached out to save them from cascading to the floor, I noticed one of those gold desk nameplates that bankers and officious construction foremen have on their desks.

Anthony Gerald Cooper. That was Foreweenie's real name. I don't think it was noticeably better than "Foreweenie," but I tried to make it stick, at least until I could get out of the trailer and forget this idiot ever existed. "There have been some strange occurrences on the site. Equipment being damaged, strange tracks around the trailer after it rained, weird sounds coming from the woods at night. I went through five different security guards, but none lasted more than two days. I finally started spending a few nights a week out here myself, and there's definitely something in those woods, and it does *not* like us being here."

"When did the trouble start, Mr. Cooper?" Amy asked. I looked around for a second to see who she was talking to, then remembered that Foreweenie's name was right there in front of me. Guess I was faster at forgetting him than I expected to be.

12

Tony, which was what Foreweenie preferred to be called, told us his tale of wrecked equipment, strange noises, and tracks that looked like no animal he'd ever seen. I traded glances with Amy and Geri, thinking that this city slicker probably hadn't seen much of anything past the tracks of the wild Nike and Reebok, but I let it go. Then he walked us out to a shed behind the job trailer and unlocked a heavy padlock.

He looked around again, making sure the whole site was deserted before pulling open the door and showing us a mangled mass of steel and aluminum. Before I could even start to decipher what the mess started life as, he gestured to it, his voice going up an octave in his excitement or terror. I couldn't really tell which.

"See?" he said, pointing all over the inside of the shed at twisted bars, pretzeled wire mesh, and snapped chains. "This thing has destroyed every trap I've set for it!"

Okay, now that I knelt down and got a good look, these had been traps at some point in their life. A couple looked like the humane catch-and-release traps that animal shelters and vets loan out for people to trap stray dogs and cats and have them neutered. One looked like a homemade rabbit trap, but big enough to hold a German Shepherd, and another chunk of twisted wrought iron was unmistakable once I saw the massive spring and the nasty jaws.

"You used a bear trap? In public woods?" I turned on the little foreman, ready to punch his lights out. He could have seriously hurt an innocent person walking through the woods, or worse, snapped an animal's leg and left it out there to suffer. I might be a hunter, both of monsters and meat, but I've never been into making animals suffer. That kind of crap gives rednecks a bad name, and we don't need any help.

"No." Tony held up both hands and took a step back. "I used a bear trap on land that was clearly marked No Trespassing, far from any houses or businesses, where the only thing close was our job site and whatever was wrecking our stuff." He pointed to a pile of shredded hoses, shattered glass, and other detritus piled in a corner of the shed. "That's what's left after the thing got hold of my pickup. Busted every piece of glass on the thing, slashed all four tires, ripped off the tailgate, and twisted the hood up into a ball."

Now that I shone my flashlight onto the pile of crap farther back in the shed, I could make out the beginning of the word "Toyota" on a twisted white rectangle. I let out a soft chuckle. Next time he oughta buy a Ford.

"Let me take a look at this," Father Matt said, slipping past me into the small room. He picked up the twisted mesh that had once been a humane trap and turned it over in his hands. He plucked a few strands of hair from it and passed it over to me. "What do you think this looks like, Bubba?" he asked.

I took the little ball of fluff, which was way softer than I expected from a horrific forest monster with the strength to tear metal apart. It was gray and downy, like a dog's undercoat, or like…

"Holy shit," I said, looking at the priest.

"Yeah, that's what I thought," Matt replied.

"You wanna share with the rest of the class?" Geri asked from outside the shed.

"Just a sec," I said, kneeling by Matt's side and looking where he pointed. There were little flecks of a dark brown substance that could only be dried blood, and bigger drops on the barely recognizable bear trap. "They caught something," I said, looking at Matt.

"A couple of somethings," he agreed.

"And Mama got *pissed*."

"Mama?" Amy's voice had a little more behind it than just a question, because if this wampus cat had wampus kittens, our job just got a lot harder and a *lot* more dangerous. As I learned again last night, nothing will fight harder than a mother defending her babies, and when that mother has claws, maybe a spiked ball on her tail, and the strength to bend steel…well, let's just say stepping up to a pissed-off Mama Wampus was not at the top of my bucket list. It was even further down than getting chased through the woods by a pissed-off Mama Boar, and I knew intimately how much fun that wasn't.

Matt and I stood and turned back to the trio waiting for us outside the shed. Matt looked at me, but I waved for him to go on. After all, he figured it out, so he oughta get to share the good news with everybody.

"Bad news," he said. "It seems that our wampus cat has at least one kit, probably more. The fur we found caught in the cage was very soft, like a baby animal's first coat. And there was a little blood on the remnants of the cage, which may have come from the kit injuring itself trying to escape, or it may be from the mother rescuing its baby."

"Who could blame her?" Geri asked, shooting a dark look at Tony. She liked all animals, and not many people, so the use of a bear trap had left a nasty taste in her mouth where the little foreman was concerned. Tony wisely kept his mouth shut.

"How long ago did you find this trap all jacked up?" I asked.

"About two weeks ago," he replied.

"Great. That means that Mama Wampus is probably all healed up and rarin' to get her revenge on the nasty two-legged hairless cats who hurt her baby and her leg. Fantastic." I tapped the comm unit in my ear. "Skeeter, you got any reports of other property damage within a two-mile radius of this site?"

"Bubba," Skeeter came back seconds later. "There ain't even any property within two miles of this site. If it wasn't for this amusement park, there wouldn't be any people for ten miles in any direction."

Now it made sense, in a greedy robber baron asshole kind of way. I could see it now—this wasn't about building an amusement park; this was about building a whole town. The developer probably bought up all the woods for miles around, and was planning on cutting a bigger road, adding hotels, apartments for staff, restaurants, and shopping for visitors and employees. Owning a piece of all that would give him a nice diverse investment opportunity for venture capitalist assholes to chop down a bunch more trees for yet another friggin' water slide. I hate water slides. There was an unfortunate swim trunk incident at Elizabeth Bruno's tenth birthday party that left me a little hydrophobic. And not the kind you get when a stray bat bites you, which happens way more often than you want in my line of work. Lucky for me, my part-fairy blood keeps me from getting most mundane diseases.

"So how big are the plans for the rest of the site?" I asked. "Show me."

Tony opened his mouth to protest, but I tapped the butt of my pistol at the same time Amy cleared her throat and held up her badge wallet, and all his arguments were suddenly invalid. He locked up the shed, then led us back into the trailer where he opened the bottom drawer of a flat file cabinet and pulled out a set of blueprints with CONFIDENTIAL stamped on the cover sheet in huge red letters. "Please don't tell anyone I showed you these. I could lose my job and be sued over breaking my NDA."

"National Security, Mr. Cooper," Amy said. "My badge trumps any NDA you've ever signed."

So does my gun, I thought. But for once, I managed to avoid saying it. I'm trying to learn to take the win with my mouth shut. It ain't easy.

Tony laid the massive sheaf of papers onto the top of the flat file and started flipping through. There had to be two hundred plates in that stack, more than I'd ever seen on a set of construction documents before. Admittedly, the blueprints I'm used to looking at are either stuff I drew on the back of a napkin to explain how I wanted to rebuild my bathroom (Amy wouldn't let me, no matter how many times I promised her an indoor jacuzzi), or they're plans for a building I'm trying to break into, and I usually just make Skeeter steal those so he feels like he's got something to do. We all know I'm just going to kick the door down anyway, no matter what the plans say.

"The initial scope of the project is the park and the access roads, but the plan is to lay in the infrastructure for a much larger community, including homes, retail, and other entertainment options. Our vision is—"

"Tony, we don't give a shit," I interrupted the little dude before he could get going. "We just need to see the big site plan. What I think you middle management nerds call the twenty-thousand-foot view."

Tony's face fell, and you woulda thought I'd just insulted his truck. But since his truck was a twisted pile of metal, and a Toyota, there wasn't a whole lot left to insult. "Oh. Right. Sorry, it's just been a while since I was able to talk to anyone about the scope of the project."

He flipped a few more pages, then stepped back and gestured to the cabinet. "That's the overall site plan, showing the boundaries of the park, with retail and restaurants centered around the southern edge, hotels along the northern side, and housing to the west. We plan to construct a six-lane highway leading directly from Pigeon Forge to here, passing through all the shopping areas en route to the park."

I pointed at several of the locations to the west, then tapped my comm again. "Skeeter, you still got that camera hidden in the butt of my gun?" I asked.

"Yeah, that's one of them. I've got a cam in Amy's necklace, too, so I've got a pretty good view of the plans," he replied.

I tried hard not to think about all the other places he could have planted cameras. Not only did he have a key to my cabin, he had more access to it than I did. He set up my whole smart home system, so if Skeeter wanted to take control of my house, he wouldn't even have to leave his recliner. "Do the places I'm tapping on this blueprint line up with that arc of confirmed sightings Father Matt showed us?"

"Gimme a second," he said. I could hear tapping as he did some kind of computery thing I neither understood nor cared about. "Yep," he said after a few seconds. "Those housing areas are exactly where the earlier wampus sightings took place."

I looked up at Tony. "Lemme guess. Y'all already started building temp housing for the crew, and they're all staying right around here, aren't they?"

Tony looked confused. "Yeah, but how could you tell that?"

"Because I'm a Hunter, dumbass. Not just monsters, but deer, rabbit, squirrel, and anything else that'll go in a pot. When y'all started building housing, you disturbed the wampus cat's natural habitat. So it ran away from the noisy humans and their noisy machines. Then you followed them, chasing them from spot to spot as you graded sites, dug sewer lines and septic tanks, and all that shit. They kept running east, and y'all kept getting closer."

I leaned in and pointed to a line of blue running along the eastern edge of the development site. "That's your boundary, isn't it? That river?"

"Yeah, that's where our project stops. The final plan is luxury river homes, once we've made the whole area a destination." Tony's chest puffed out a little. He was obviously proud of his work.

I almost hated to deflate him, but I did it anyway. "Yeah, and in the meantime your project has displaced a family of cryptids who are now wrecking your shit and posing a danger to people in the area. You've chased them until they ran into a natural boundary—this river. Maybe the kittens aren't big enough to get across it yet, or maybe Mama just decided to make a stand at the water. But whatever made her stop, she ain't running no more."

"Yeah," Geri said, her voice dark. She *really* didn't like bear traps, and I could tell she sided with the monsters a little on this one. Hell, I did too, and I figured Matt and Amy probably felt the same way. "Y'all done messed with Mother Nature, and Mama Wampus is gonna kick your ass for you."

"Fortunately for you, Tony," I said, clapping the small man hard enough on the shoulder to nearly buckle his knees. "We're from the government, and we're here to help."

13

Tony wasn't going anywhere near the woods with us, and I couldn't really blame him. If Geri was looking at me like that, I wouldn't want to intentionally go somewhere with a lot of places to hide a body, either. So me and the rest of Team Bubba (I kinda like the sound of that. Maybe I'll get t-shirts made.) walked across the muddy job site and headed into the woods.

The trail was narrow and hard to see, but we managed okay for the first few hundred yards, heading almost directly due east. But after we crossed a little stream, I couldn't find anything that looked like a path. Father Matt kinda slid past me and knelt down on the ground, looking at a branch or something.

"You gonna tell me you're a priest *and* a tracker, Padre?" I asked, half-joking.

He wasn't joking when he looked up at me and said, "Actually, yeah, I am. I was an Eagle Scout before I went to seminary and have spent a lot of time teaching wilderness survival classes at summer camps since I got my collar. The creature that made these tracks definitely has paws like a big cat, but they're slightly different from most American large felines. The prints are symmetrical, with the toes fanning out evenly from the center of the paw, not like bobcat or cougar prints. And there's an extra toe."

"Like Hemingway's cats?" Amy asked. I raised an eyebrow at her, and she shrugged. "Ernest Hemingway's cats had six toes, and it's a mutation that has passed down to their descendants. I spent some time in the Key West Field Office, and there wasn't much to do except read about the touristy stuff."

"Yes," Father Matt replied. "Like Hemingway's cats, if they were huge. Judging by the width and depth of these tracks, I'd estimate the wampus cat to be somewhere around three to four hundred pounds, and at least four feet high at the shoulder, judging by the height of broken branches I'm seeing."

"Three *hundred* pounds?" Skeeter's voice was shrill in my ear, and I winced. "Bubba, that's twice the size of most mountain lions, and a good foot or two taller! I thought these things were supposed to be the size of a bobcat."

"Yeah, bud," I replied. "I think we're hunting the Big Show of bobcats here."

"What's a big show?" Father Matt asked.

"Oh god, we're never leaving these woods," Geri muttered.

I gave my new Church liaison a pitying glance. "The Big Show is only the greatest big man in pro wrestling since Andre the Giant. He's seven and a half feet of big, bald badass, and he's a Southern boy to boot. He makes me look tiny, and that ain't the kinda thing I get to say very often. So if this wampus cat is way outside the normal size for a big cat in this part of the world, then we oughta call it Paul when we find it."

"Paul?" Father Matt was obviously woefully out of touch in his pro wrestling viewing, and I made a vow to myself to get him to watch a whole lot of "big meaty men slapping meat." If this skinny little preacher was gonna be part of the team, he was gonna have to develop an appreciation for huge men in tiny spandex.

"Paul Wight is The Big Show's real name. It'd be kind of an in joke, us calling the big-ass cat by the real name of the World's Largest Athlete."

"Why would we call it anything?" Matt asked. "Aren't we just going to rehome it or kill it?"

Geri drew in a breath, and I knew she was about to go off on the padre, but I held up a hand. "We're gonna do everything we can *not* to kill the wampus cat. It ain't the cat's fault people are screwing with its habitat. Paul's just trying to do what animals do—hunt, eat, screw, and roll around in a sunbeam. As long as we can come up with some kind of non-lethal way to relocate the cat, we're going to."

Father Matt looked perplexed. "I was warned that you were a blood-thirsty, possibly psychotic, half-monster that needed a firm hand holding your leash. But you seem like anything but that. How did the Vatican get it so wrong about you?"

"They're not all that wrong," Geri said. "Bubba is at least half psycho most days."

"But he already has a firm hand on his leash," Amy added. "Mine." She reached out and put a hand on my forearm. "Right, honey?"

I just nodded and said, "Yes, dear."

"Plus it ain't like the Church has the best track record on who they trust," Skeeter added.

I shook my head at my best friend's version of a defense for me. "Truth be told, Matt, the Church's assessment ain't far off some days. If anybody hurts my people, they get to see how bloodthirsty I can be. I will bring down my own version of a righteous smiting on somebody's ass if they harm so much as a hair on any of these people's heads. But I try to save my real ass-kicking for them critters with coherent thought and intention. This wampus is just operating on instinct, doing what its nature demands. I can't want to kill something for doing what God intended it to do, can I?"

Father Matt shook his head, a rueful smile spreading across his narrow features. "No, you can't. And I should know better than to judge a book by its cover."

"I don't know about that," Skeeter said. "There's plenty of books where the cover sucks, and you know good and damn well that's because the book sucks."

"It's a metaphor, Skeet," I said. I might have given myself a couple of mental pats on the back for remembering the different between "metaphor" and "simile."

Skeeter's only response was a heavy sigh, then he said, "The biggest problem with having a dumbass for a best friend is that your sarcasm gets lost."

"Or does it?" I asked, feeling one corner of my mouth twitch up into a smirk. There was a tiny *beep* in my ear as Skeeter snapped off his mic in frustration. I licked my finger and made a little invisible mark in the air. One for me. I don't get too many of those, so I revel in them when I do. "Alright, Padre. Where do the tracks go from here?"

Matt pointed in a direction that was a good forty degrees off from where I thought we oughta go, so I reckon it was a good thing I wasn't leading this parade no more. I let the priest take the lead, and we slipped back into the underbrush, heading more southeast this time.

It only took us a few minutes to get to a large clearing with a ten-foot circle of disturbed dirt, scattered rocks, and lengths of heavy chain fastened to chunks of rebar sticking up out of the ground. I walked over to the nearest one and saw the chain, which looked like a logging chain with links bigger around than a bratwurst, had been snapped in two. I picked up the end and looked closer, finding telltale signs of dried blood on some of the links. "I think we found where the foreman set out his traps. There's blood on this chain."

Matt walked over, looked at the snapped chain, and went a little pale. Paler, really, since this looked like the most time he'd spent in the sun in a decade. Poor little guy had led a cloistered, sheltered life. We were throwing that right in the dumpster and lighting the whole thing on fire. "That's...incredible. Whatever was captured here snapped this chain like it was..."

"Dry spaghetti?" Geri supplied.

"A twig?" Amy suggested.

"Your leg if it gets hold of you." Everybody looked at me, but I just shrugged. "Let's put things in a framework we can all understand. This thing's sex organs are obviously in its mouth."

A trio of perplexed looks came back at me, and I barely held my giggles in as twelve-year-old me finished the joke. "Because if it gets its teeth on you, you're screwed."

A withering glare from Amy was cut short by a rustling in the trees just outside the edge of the clearing. I slapped my hand to the butt of my pistol as we all turned to see...nothing. There was nothing there. At least, not at first. We all stared off in a roughly easterly direction for a long moment, almost holding our breath waiting to get set upon by a ravening wampus, but after about thirty seconds of highest alert, I let out my breath in a long sigh.

"Well, that was a whole lot of nothing," I said, letting my hand drop from my gun.

"Umm...not exactly," Geri said, pointing. I adjusted my gaze to follow her arm, and looked a lot lower than I'd been focusing. A tiny little gray ball of fluff took a tentative step over a fallen branch, then tumbled ass over teakettle into the clearing, letting out a soft *mew* as it came to a stop, shaking dirt and leaves off its head.

"Oh my god that's thecutestthingI've*everseeeeeeeen!*" Geri's voice went hypersonic at the end as she squeed over the little furball that had somersaulted into view. I thought she was going to start hyperventilating, then the stakes got even higher as three more little fluffballs came into view.

"Oh, son of a *bitch*," I said in a low voice. "We are so screwed."

"Oh my god, they're the cutest thing *ever!*" Geri took four quick steps forward and dropped to her knees right in front of the first kitten, scooping it up and hauling it to her chest, nuzzling the baby wampus cat with her cheek and cooing at it. Cooing. The tough-as-nails monster hunter who legit tried to hunt me down and murder my ass for being part fairy (and for getting her sister killed, which was a much more reasonable motive for murder than my mom being a fairy) was now on her knees in a forest where we were pretty sure there was a giant cat that would eat our kidneys as appetizers, and she was *cuddling baby wampus cats.*

I couldn't really blame her, though. The little fur balls were adorable. They were larger than normal kittens, but not by a ton. They stood maybe six inches off the ground at the shoulder, with short, mottled coats that seemed to shift in color depending on what they were near. Some sort of natural camouflage, apparently. They were base gray, with darker and lighter spots like a sun-dappled stone floor, and they all had little balls on the end of their tails, which the lead kitten was using to thump Geri on her shoulder, eliciting giggles.

Giggles. I didn't know Geri *could* giggle. I'd been in combat with this woman, shared a house with her for the better part of a year, had seen her in the morning before coffee, watched the sun set on my back deck with her—everything. But I had never, *ever* thought I'd ever hear her giggle. And yet here we were, with her scooping up kittens in her arms, burying her face in their fur, and giggling like a kindergartener. It was frickin' adorable.

Until the fat redneck with the hunting rifle stepped out of the woods and pointed it at me. "I'm gonna need you to tell your daughter to step away from the monsters before somebody gets hurt."

Daughter?!? Oh, somebody was getting their ass beat for that one.

14

———

y *what* now?" I asked.

"His *WHAT*?!?" Geri asked, her tone possibly even more affronted than mine, which I thought was a little unneces-sary. I agree that I'm not really "dad" material, except for the belly, but she didn't need to sound quite so unbelieving.

"Whatever," Dipshit the Gun-Toting Dingelberry-apotamous replied, jerking the barrel of his rifle in Geri's direction. "Daughter, niece, girl-friend, whatever. Put the creatures down and get over there with your sugar daddy." As he waved the gun in our direction, a handful of other guys, all in jeans, work boots, and orange vests that marked them as part of the construction crew, came out of the woods, all toting rifles or shot-guns. That's one downside of living in the South—*everybody* owns guns, no matter their job or politics. So you just gotta assume that anybody you piss off has a 50/50 chance of going out to their truck, grabbing some-thing persuasive off the gun rack, and coming back to continue your argument with additional persuasion.

Oh, there was no question I was going to wrap the barrel of that .308 around his goddamned neck. Geri put the kits down and stepped over to stand next to me. Amy and Father Matt made a line on my other side, with Amy looking up at me, questions written all over her face. Questions like "are you going to do something stupid?" Or "is this going to get really,

really messy?" Or even "am I going to have to cover up multiple felonies this afternoon?"

The answer to all of those would have been a resounding "yes" had a deep growl not emanated from the edge of the woods right about the time I decided that I could snatch the rifle away from the lead dumbass before he could shoot me or any of my people too much. Dipshit turned to look, and the trio of morons he was rolling with followed suit, so Geri and I just nodded at each other, took three steps forward, and decked the nearest pair of dumbasses.

Dipshit was a little out of reach, so I focused my first punch on the guy I assumed was Dipshit's kid brother, because they looked a lot alike, but relatively close in age. I mean, we were out in the woods, so it could have been a brother, a cousin, a nephew, or some very hillbilly combination of the three. Either way, he quickly shifted from "problem" to "unconscious" as my fist slammed into the hinge of his jaw and he kissed the dirt. His shotgun hit the ground but fortunately didn't go off. Especially since it was kinda pointed at my junk when it landed. That would have been awkward.

Geri was just as direct, if a little more *Road House* in her approach. She kicked one toothless methhead right in the side of his knee, and he went down just like Sam Elliott told us he would. Then she planted a knee in his nose and left him rolling around spewing blood all over the dirt. Amy was half a second behind us, but more official, yanking out her badge and yelling for Dipshit and his minions to drop their weapons.

Spoiler alert: they didn't drop their weapons. They did focus their attention on Amy, though, which allowed Father Matt to bend down, scoop up the discarded twelve-gauge, and point it at the remaining rednecks. "You should really listen to the lady," he said in a voice colder than the Bud Light waiting for me in the mini fridge on my back deck.

Dipshit didn't drop his rifle, but he stood there kinda wavering, looking back and forth between Amy with her badge and service pistol pointed at his skull, and me, with his buddy's blood on my knuckles and a big grin on my face. He had a decision to make—drop his weapon and look like a pansy in front of his friends, most of whom were too jacked up to notice that he was surrendering, or get his own ass beat and maybe shot by resisting.

He chose poorly. Dipshit focused his attention on Amy, and as he brought the barrel of his rifle up, I reached down with my right hand, grabbed Geri by the back of her belt, and flung her at him.

Yeah, I used my sidekick as a missile weapon. It happens. Not often, and not with most normal humans, but I'm a long way from normal and only part human, as the federal government has been quick to remind me. So I channeled my rage into strength, something Amy and I have been working on in training, and focused all my latent fairy power into chucking a human being at another human being. It worked. Geri flew across the twenty feet separating us from Dipshit, crashed into him, and took him down before he got a shot off.

But I might shoulda warned her that flinging was an option, because as soon as she left her feet, a nonstop string of profanity flew from her lips that didn't stop until she disentangled herself from the prone Dipshit, dusted herself off, and stomped back over to where I stood grinning at her.

"You son of a *bitch*," she said, kicking me square in my left shin. "That was *not* funny!"

"Tell that to them," I said, pointing at the kittens who were no longer huddled up in a terrified ball of fluff, but were now tumbling over one another playing some weird King of Cat Mountain game that only they knew the rules to.

"Awwwww," she said, her anger melting away in the face of all that cuteness. But her adoration was quickly replaced by worry as another low growl split the clearing. "Bubba, I think Mama might be home."

"Yeah, and she might not approve of this play date," I said, staring into the woods trying to get a peek at the wampus cat. I thought I saw something moving in the underbrush, but I couldn't be sure, and if Mama shared the kittens' coloring and adaptive camouflage, I wouldn't get a good look at her until it was too damn late.

"Too damn late" came about three seconds after the thought crossed my mind, as a mottled gray-and-brown cat the size of a small panther slipped out into the clearing, barely even disturbing a branch. Mama Wampus was a magnificent creature, all sinewy muscle and glass-smooth movements. Her gaze swept the assembled humans, then locked onto her babies. She let out another little growl, and before I even saw her move, she was standing over her tumbling balls of fluff, glaring around at the humans as if daring us to touch her. I did not take up the challenge.

"Good kitty," Geri said, moving forward slowly with one hand extended. She was careful not to meet the wampus's eyes, worried it might take that as a challenge. Mama Wampus didn't pounce on her and rip her limb from limb, so I thought that was probably a good sign.

Geri eased her way across the clearing until she was almost close enough to touch the wampus, then knelt down with her hand out, palm down. Mama Wampus sniffed her hand once, twice, then kinda butted her palm with her head, and Geri responded by scratching the massive kitty behind the ears.

And that's when a giant cryptid that could have turned her entrails into outrails with one swipe of its massive claws, dropped on her belly in the dirt and started to roll around with my junior sidekick, filling the clearing with loud purrs.

"I think they like each other," Amy whispered.

"I didn't know Geri could smile that big," I replied. "Or at all."

Geri, for her part, didn't stop petting the big kitty, just reached back with her other hand and flipped me off. "I think she's calm enough not to murder anyone at the moment. Maybe you should take this chance to hogtie those assholes and relieve them of their weapons."

Seemed like a good idea to me, so Father Matt and I zip-tied the construction idiots' hands behind their backs, emptied their guns, and flung them deep into the woods. It was technically littering, but I really didn't feel like toting any extra firepower. The hand cannon dangling under my left arm was enough extra weight. I endured several minutes of lurid description about exactly what they were planning to do to me when they got loose before I smacked Dipshit upside the back of his head. That shut him up for a few seconds, but as soon as he opened his mouth again, I yanked him to his feet and spun him around so he looked right at me.

I held up another big zip tie right in front of his eyes. "You see this, asshole?"

"Yeah, I see it. You already got me tied up. What you gonna do with that?"

"Well, there's a lot of really nasty stuff I *could* do with it, but I don't wanna touch your balls. So if you don't shut the hell up right now, I'm gonna cut a hole in your top and bottom lips with my pocket knife here —" I drew one of the silver-edged kukris from my belt and held it up next to the zip tie. "And I'm gonna zip tie your goddamn mouth shut. How fun does that sound?"

He opened his mouth to reply, but I just waggled the knife and plastic tie in front of his eyes. He closed his mouth with a "snap."

"Good call," I said, patting him on the cheek. Maybe a little harder than necessary, but not harder than I *thought* was necessary.

I turned my attention back to Geri and Mama Wampus, who were now literally rolling around on the ground play-fighting like kittens. It was a little disconcerting, seeing something so lethal playing like a little kid. A little weird seeing the wampus cat do it, too. "What's the plan? We've got these assholes sorted out, but we still ain't got a solution to the real problem—development."

"He's right," Amy said, and I made a mental note of the date and time, since those words didn't get uttered often. "As long as Mama and her kits are in the path of the development, we're going to have more run-ins between wampus and humans. And those run-ins are going to get more and more dangerous until someone gets badly hurt or killed."

"Or Mama Wampus gets killed and her babies are sold off to some shitty zoo like that douche in Florida had with the were-gators," I added.

Father Matt cleared his throat. "There is someone the Church has a tenuous connection with, out in the Midwest. He runs a nature preserve for cryptids, after a fashion."

"Oh yeah," I said. "I met that guy. He's a friend of Mason's, right?"

"Yes," Father Matt replied.

"What's the Church's connection with him?" It's not that I distrust everyone associated with organized religion, just almost everyone.

"He sometimes provides a safe refuge for cryptids that must be rehomed because one of our Hunters has found them too close to humans. There's no official relationship, but sometimes we will do favors for each other. I feel like housing a mother wampus cat and her litter would be right up his alley."

"Sounds good," Amy said. "Can you call him? I can get everything arranged for transport, but before we go trying to tranq Mama and get her into a cage, I'd like to know we definitely have a place for her to go."

"Yes, I can make a call," Matt said, stepping off into the edge of the woods and pulling out a satellite phone I didn't know he'd been carrying. I might have to start paying attention to this dude if he kept on being useful. Especially if the check cleared *and* he wasn't completely dead weight in the field.

Matt punched in a few numbers, then froze as I heard a branch snap off in the woods just outside the clearing. I whirled around, looking in the direction of the sound, but Mama Wampus was way faster than me. She was on her feet and putting herself in between the sound and her babies before I'd even locked in on where the noise came from. That low growl was back, but this time her ears were flat, her tail was extended low behind her, and I could see the corners of her mouth creeping up in a snarl. She made a low sound, and her kits all huddled up together behind Geri, peeking around her legs as she got to her feet with her pistol drawn.

Mama Wampus let out another growl that grew until it was a kind of yowl that sounded like a cross between a cougar and a freight train, and took a couple of steps toward the edge of the woods. Another rustling crack came from off to our right, and we all turned to look that way, Mama included. This time she let out a serious *roar*, a full-throated cry of challenge and rage that someone interrupted her playtime and may have threatened her babies. Mama was *pissed.*

She spun her head back around to face the original source of the sound and bunched up her legs as if ready to pounce. There was another, much louder, *crack*, this one followed by two more, and red blossomed on Mama Wampus's sides as three large-caliber bullets ripped into her. She whirled around, crying out in shock and pain, looking for what hurt her, and I watched in horror as her back legs gave out, then her front, and she collapsed to the dirt.

Geri rushed over to her and dropped to her knees, trying frantically to put pressure on the wounds, but the big cat was already gone. She was dead before her head hit the ground. Geri sprang to her feet and turned in a circle, rage mottling her face. "Who's out there? Show yourself, you son of a bitch!"

"Okay," came a voice from the woods. "But we've got all of you covered, so please don't do anything stupid. I'm mostly talking to you, Brabham. Your reputation precedes you."

The voice belonged to a muscular man carrying a military-looking rifle with a grenade launcher slung under the barrel. He was a little over six feet tall, with dark skin and a neat goatee. His brown eyes were cold as ice chips, and the look on his face was not that of a man one should screw with. He wore black tactical gear, and there was a Velcro label on the front of his flak jacket that read "PEST CONTROL."

Two others in similar garb stepped out of the woods on either side of us, covering us with guns of their own. They all wore "Pest Control" on their vests, and they all looked way too comfortable with the idea of shooting us all.

"What the fuck was that? Who the fuck are you? What are you doing out here?" Geri shouted, tears streaming down her face. Her hand twitched, and I could see the effort she was putting into not drawing down on the man who had an assault rifle pointed right at her chest.

"Same as you, cookie," the man said. "My job. Only difference is, I'm good at mine. Now all y'all drop your gear and go sit in the dirt where you can't bother anybody. Get in the way, and I'll put a bullet in your face. There's plenty of space here for me to dig graves."

For once, we did as we were told. I sat down at the base of a tree and watched as the Lead Asshole waved his Hench-Assholes over. One was a white woman, stocky and muscular, with short blond hair and an acne-speckled jawline that screamed steroid abuse. The other was a thick-necked Asian man who looked like a powerlifter or college wrestler, and he carried a massive machine gun instead of an AR-15 or whatever the other two dickheads were toting. It wasn't the ridiculous minigun the genetically altered half-cryptid freaks I'd run into with Harker carried, but it was about as big a damn weapon as I could imagine a human being carrying. This dude was *stout.*

We sat there for a couple minutes before the roar of engines came to us through the trees. A quartet of ATVs crashed through the brush, breaking their own trail where none existed, and pulled to a stop. My blood started to boil even more when I saw the collapsible cage on a small trailer behind one of the four-wheelers. They weren't just murdering assholes. They were murdering, *kidnapping* assholes. I swore to Mama Wampus's spirit that I'd get justice for her, no matter what it took. I felt a little tingle run through me, and it felt like my fairy magic considered that kind of promise very serious. That was fine by me, I was pretty serious, too. Seriously *pissed.*

We sat in the dirt as the Pest Control pricks loaded all the kits into the cage, and all our weapons into a duffel one of the Hench-Assholes opened up.

"I'll be coming for that stuff," I said.

The Asian man grinned down at me and patted the barrel of his machine gun. "Come on, redneck. I'll be waiting."

I'm used to being the guy with the biggest gun in the room, and I don't like it when somebody threatens me, so I smiled back at Asian Hench-Asshole and said, "Good."

He looked a little disturbed at me not being afraid of him, like that didn't happen much with this bunch, and took a couple steps back toward where his pals were loading the four-wheelers. A couple minutes later, and they were gone, along with all our weapons except for pocketknives. I mean, I assumed everybody else carried a pocketknife. Everybody but Amy, because she was raised civilized.

We got up and all just kinda stood there for a moment, the rest of my team as surprised as me, then I walked over to the dead wampus cat. I knelt by her body and patted her head. "I'm sorry, Mama Kitty. But I promise you this, we will save those babies." Then I stood up and turned to my team—Amy, furiously tapping on her sat phone looking for answers, Matt, swiping his finger across the screen of his phone trying to get a signal, and Geri just standing there, fury and sorrow radiating off her in waves as she stood with tears streaming down her face.

"I've just got two questions," I said. Everyone turned to me, and I continued. "Who the fuck is Pest Control, and where do we go to kick their ass?"

***

Thirty-plus thousand feet overhead, a monitor flickered to life. A shadowy figure appeared on the screen, bathing the cabin of the Gulfstream in bluish light. "I trust everything went according to plan?" the figure asked.

"Yes, Director," said one of the men sitting in plush leather seats. He held a flute of champagne in one hand and an unlit cigar in the other. A proud smile split his square face, and he said, "The redneck and his people didn't know what hit them."

"Do not underestimate Brabham and his associates. They have surprised us in the past," the figure said.

"Don't sweat it, Boss," said an Asian man with bulging biceps from another chair. "If he comes for us, we'll take him out. No big deal."

"Others have tried, and failed," the figure said. "Do not provoke them directly, or I will not be there to bail you out when it goes poorly."

"I'm not worried about that moron," the Asian man replied with a snort.

"But we do have a healthy respect for the abilities of his associates," said the first man. "His tech officer is first rate, Deputy Director Hall is a formidable adversary in the field and in the office, and the woman Geri is…unpredictable."

"And that makes her dangerous, we know." This comment came from a stocky woman sitting near the back of the plane. "Come on, we got the kitties, killed the mother, sent a message to Bubba and his cronies, and got away without a scratch. Let us have the win, Boss."

The figure's shoulders bobbed up and down as if in unheard laughter. "Of course, Karen. Celebrate your victory. Enjoy the mini bar, and there will be a car at the airport to take you to a fine victory dinner when you return to base."

Smiles and high-fives circled the cabin. When the boss bought dinner, it was usually at a place that made Morton's look like McDonald's, and nothing was off limits, even the stuff on the tippy-top shelf. "But Chad?" The figure spoke again, and the crew fell silent.

"Yes, Boss?" the first man replied.

"Be in the office at eight tomorrow morning or I'll cut off one toe for every member of your team that's late." Then the figure leaned forward to press the "OFF" button on their computer, and as they did, a curl of blond hair peeked out from under the hood they wore to obscure their features.

The team exchanged worried glances. This was the first identifying feature the Boss had allowed any of them to see in the nine months since Pest Control had been founded to eradicate all cryptids and protect humanity from the growing threat of human-cryptid breeding. The Boss had been incredibly private up to this point, and the last thing they wanted was to be on their...*her* bad side.

As the screen went black, Chad stood up and faced his team. "Nobody saw what we saw, okay? There was no lock of hair that slipped free, and nobody got a look at the back of her hand, right?"

One by one, every member of Pest Control shook their heads. No one had seen anything. Chad nodded. "Good. We all remember what happened to Chavez, right? I still don't know what he saw, but I know what he's seeing now—nothing. So we do our job, we hunt monsters, and we beat the shit out of anybody who protects them. Especially any fat, tattooed rednecks from Georgia." Chad reached down and patted the orange "T" on his forearm. "But when we finally get the green light to take his mongrel ass down, Bubba Brabham is *mine*. He might not have recognized me back there in the woods, but I remember him. Me and Bubba have got some catching up to do, and this time I plan on him being the one leaving in an ambulance."

He finished off his champagne, then looked around at his team. "Or maybe he leaves in a hearse."

TO BE CONTINUED

CHURCH ON TIME

1

It was a beautiful place for a wedding—gently rolling hills leading to a rustic-looking pavilion that was still modern enough to have LED lighting overhead, a full sound system cleverly disguised as boulders around the seating area, hanging choir mics so the audience wouldn't miss a word of the lovely hand-crafted vows, and a set of low, wide steps leading up to the stage, almost impossible to trip on no matter how long the train. It was almost perfect, and with a few modifications to suit our particular needs, it would be the absolute ideal venue for us.

"This place looks great," I said. "My only concern is that the wide open spaces means we're gonna have to bring in a metric buttload of salt to sprinkle around the perimeter."

"Not to mention probably a quarter ton of cold iron filings for the fairy barrier," Amy agreed, her finger tracing an imaginary line around where the guests would sit. "Should we only run the cold iron around my half, just in case some of your extended family show up?"

"Well, I didn't invite any of those relatives, and I haven't heard so much as a whimper out of any of 'em since we got back this side of the Veil, so I don't think it's real likely," I replied. "But maybe we leave a path to the front row just in case Mama and my sister pop in at the last minute. I'd hate for them to feel left out."

"I'd hate for them to feel left out and *pissed*," Skeeter chimed in from a few steps back. He looked over at the confused venue manager, whose eyes darted between Amy and me like she wasn't sure which of her newest and most psychotic clients was the bigger danger, the giant redneck or the slender blonde with the pistol on her hip. I could answered that for her in a hot second—Amy.

"Yeah, all we need is one of my pointy-eared relatives taking offense at something and putting a hoodoo on the whole shebang. Maybe we go without the cold iron altogether? Or like you said, only put it around the seats on the bride's side."

"Um…Mr. Brabham?" The venue lady interrupted us. "We don't allow any import of outside flora or decor, unless it's provided by one of our approved contractors."

Amy turned, as if suddenly remembering that we had a mundane in our midst. "I'm sorry, Margery. It was Margery, right?"

Maybe-Margery nodded.

Amy went on. "Margery, we have some very specific security needs for our ceremony, due to my position with the Department of Homeland Security. I'm afraid that supersedes your normal policies. We will, of course, pay extra for any cleanup required."

And that was apparently the magic word. Or magic phrase, I reckoned. As soon as Amy said she'd pay extra, Margery stopped worrying so much about us bringing in anything extra. And really, the iron filings would be the easy stuff to clean up. Just walk around with a couple big magnets and you're done. As long as she didn't think too much about what putting a big-ass salt ring around the property was going to do to the lawn she spent so much money maintaining, we oughta be okay. And if Margery's manicure was any indicator, she didn't spend enough time messing around in the dirt to know that we were probably gonna kill anything growing wherever we salted the earth. I felt a little twinge in the butt cheek where I carried my wallet, wondering how the hell I was gonna pay for re-landscaping a couple acres of Georgia mountaintop.

"So what about snipers?" Geri asked from where she sat on the edge of the stage, and I saw Margery turn a whole new shade of pale.

"We'll have to see where we can put some counter-sniper positions," Amy said with a glance at me. I looked away. Sniper was Joe's thing, but Joe wasn't gonna be with us on the most important day of my life, and the reminder stung. It had been more than a year since he died saving the world for the umpteenth time, but every once in a while it felt like yester-day. My friend Karla down at the comic book shop once told me that grief was like a weird roommate—you could go weeks without seeing it at all, but then there it was again, sitting on your couch eating all your Cheetos and being right in your face. She was pretty spot on, I thought.

"I think this place looks pretty much perfect, Margery," I said to the terrified woman. "Now you said something about a rain venue?"

Margery perked up like a geranium that somebody had finally poured a little bit of water onto, and the plastic smile that had slipped away at all the talk of defensive positions and salt lines popped back into place like it had never left. "Yes, certainly. Our indoor venue, which is where we would hold the reception, is also where we would move the ceremony in case of inclement weather. If you would just follow me…" Her voice trailed off as she hustled back toward the main entrance to the property, her heels sinking a little with every step. I thought to myself that I'd never seen a woman who could more stand to invest in some decent footwear.

"You had to bring up snipers?" Amy asked Geri. "That poor woman is already terrified. I really don't want to have to find another venue. Bubba's already been barred from half the churches in the county, and the ones that will let him through the front door won't allow a wedding there if Skeeter participates, and all the other places to host a wedding are either booked for the whole summer or don't hold enough people for a decent keg party, much less a wedding!"

Now lemme be clear, Amy was no kind of Bridezilla. All told, she'd been pretty chill with the whole idea of marrying a tattooed, overweight, part-fairy redneck from the mountains of North Georgia. She'd even been okay with the idea of bringing all her family down to my part of the world instead of trying to do some location closer to where she grew up in Kentucky, or some destination wedding thing that woulda required plane tickets for everybody. Which would have been even harder, since some of our wedding party, like the groom, were on No-Fly lists, and others weren't human enough to have Social Security numbers, much less any ID the airline would accept.

But she was pretty damn firm on the idea of wanting a nice, big wedding, in a beautiful place with a lot of flowers and as many friends and family as we could cram into the place. And this joint, the Rolling Clover Event Venue and Soiree, was pretty much perfect. And it had an opening pop up suddenly when one of the upcoming brides found her husband sleeping with her Maid of Honor. And his Best Man. At the same time. I'm not gonna judge what anybody else is into, but it sounded like somebody missed the "communication and consent" parts of the story.

That meant a couple things. First, it meant that we needed to kick our wedding planning into high gear after it had been idling in neutral for a couple years, because the opening in the venue's schedule was in six days. Next, it meant that we needed to not piss off Margery or give her any clue exactly how weird we really were, because the second she got any idea that the Homeland Security Deputy Director she was trying to rent to worked in the Paranormal Division and was usually tasked with hunting down myths, legends, and monsters…well, there was a long waiting list for this place, and she wouldn't have any problem filling our spot with some normal level of bridal insanity and a wedding party with no Sasquatch in it.

We followed Margery up the hill to a big-ass prefabricated metal building with a whole lot of frou-frou and geegaws hanging off it, enough to make a normal human being think that it was something nicer than a redecorated tractor shed. But I'm a hillbilly from generations back, and we know a Butler building when we see one. But they'd cleaned the place up nice with some stone cladding and color-changing LED lights pointing up at the "architectural features," which were really just the beams holding the roof up, only wrapped in sheetrock and painted white, so I bit my tongue while Margery gesticulated this way and that way to point out some "feature" or another. I'll be honest, I zoned out a little. As long as Amy was happy with the place, I didn't give a shit if we got married in an active minefield. Hell, given the groups of people we were likely to have at the reception, a minefield mighta been safer.

"This is where we will plan on the reception, and in case of rain, we can hold the ceremony here, move everyone to the pre-function space during photos between the ceremony and the reception while our crew resets the interior, lays down the dance floor, and sets up the rounds and chairs," Margery said with many a flourish and gesture. I didn't hear anything past "dance floor" because I was hit with a sudden moment of abject terror. I was going to have to dance. In a tuxedo. In front of people. Some of whom I gave a shit about their opinions. Most of whom my soon-to-be-wife cared about their opinions.

Now let's be real, this wasn't gonna be the first time I've danced in public. It wasn't even gonna be the first time I danced in public with a lot on the line. But there's a whole world of difference between busting out a Macarena in front of a psychotic fairy monarch so you and all your loved ones don't get murdered by a bunch of critters out of a storybook, and trying not to break your wife's foot on the dance floor at your wedding while your newly minted in-laws looked on. If I was given the choice, I'd do The Worm nekkid across the fifty-yard line at Soldier Field in the middle of a snowstorm before I tried to cut a rug at my wedding. But that wasn't an option. A life goal, maybe, but for the moment, not an option. So, when Margery mentioned dancing, my brain kinda vapor-locked on me, and I didn't snap back to the conversation until Skeeter smacked me on the shoulder.

"I'm sorry, I was mentally rehearsing my dance moves," I said. "What was that last bit?"

Amy glared at me, Skeeter snickered, Margery gave me the sympathetic eye of a woman who has seen literally thousands of petrified grooms, and Geri did what Geri does, which is usually look at me like I'm an idiot.

"I was just saying that all we need to do to lock in the venue is handle the deposit. Usually, we require a fifty percent payment up front, but with the date this close, we will need seventy-five percent. And that is non-refundable," Margery said.

"Any chance we can use some of the deposit them other folks put down, since it sounds like they ain't gonna be using it?" I said with a grin.

Margery gave me a pitying smile. I'm used to those. "I'm sorry, but no. That has already been applied to other operating expenses and fees."

"Like the pita tax," Geri muttered.

"Pita?" I asked. "What do those little flat bread thingies have to do with a wedding? I mean, I guess there could be hummus at the reception, but…"

"P.I.T.A.," Geri replied, making sure I understood it was an acronym. "It's a pain in the ass tax. When somebody does something stupid, you charge them more. Customer Service 101, Bubba."

"My only customers are the federal government and the Vatican," I said. "I don't get to change my rates." I pulled out my wallet. "What's the damage?"

Margery quoted a number that cost more than my first pickup. And my second pickup, although the second one was kind of a piece of crap, and I handed over my credit card. I gave Skeeter the "are you sure you got all my money shit sorted out?" look, and he nodded while Margery pulled out a little electronic doodad from her purse and ran my card.

She tapped on the screen, printed a receipt, and gave us a sunny smile. "Thank you for choosing the Rolling Clover Event Venue and Soiree. If there is anything else I can do to make your special day extraordinary, please don't hesitate to call. I believe you both have my cell number?"

Amy nodded. I looked over at Skeeter, who nodded, so I did too. I don't even bother trying to keep numbers in my phone, given my unfortunate tendency to either break cell phones or throw them into bodies of water. In my defense, if people weren't irritating as piss, I wouldn't feel like I needed to throw my phone in a lake on the regular. But we got finished with Margery and headed to Amy's DHS-issued Suburban, ready to head into town and grab lunch at a little meat and three that opened up a few months back.

"Mother*fucker*," Amy said, looking at her phone.

"What's wrong?" I asked, barely stopping in time to keep from knocking my fiancée ass over teakettle on the white-stone gravel path leading to the parking lot. Amy is not one to throw around f-bombs without good reason, and I was suddenly wishing I hadn't left Bertha in the truck, civilian wedding planner or no civilian wedding planner.

"My family's arriving early," Amy replied. She looked as rattled as I'd ever seen her, and this was a woman who had literally stared down *demons*.

"Well, that ain't a big deal, right? We can handle an extra day or two with the kinfolk. Worst case, we'll all go fishing or something, and if your weird racist uncle starts spouting off some kind of obnoxious crap, we just make him swim home." I didn't see the big deal. But I'd never met any of Amy's family, and I was starting to wonder if it wasn't me she was embarrassed by, but them.

Amy turned her gaze on me, and I honestly wasn't sure if she was going to puke or pass out, she was so pale. "They're not coming a day or two early, Bubba. They're at your house right now."

Suddenly "motherfucker" seemed like the perfect word for the situation.

2

We rolled up my driveway to a sight I never expected to encounter in the backwoods of North Georgia: an invasion of the carpetbaggers. I tried to be kind, I tried to be gracious, but god*damn* it looked like a twenty-first century version of Sherman's March, except instead of the noble cause of freeing the slaves and beating the racists into submission, they were marching to build a Starbucks on every corner and make sure every square inch of woods was manicured, sanitized, and purified.

There was a Mercedes SUV parked in front of my house, blocking my F-250 in and making sure that it was gonna be inconvenient as hell if I needed to go save the world during their visit. It was gleaming black with tinted windows befitting a rock star, or it probably was before it turned off the main road and drove up the half-mile winding gravel road that led to my house. Now it was splattered with mud, dust, and bug bits that made it almost look like something a body could go off-roading in. The poor Jaguar convertible next it, though… Well, let's just say it had been a rough day for the little two-door coupe.

You don't drive sports cars back in my neck of the woods. For one, you're liable to strip the gears just trying to get up my driveway in one, and even more likely to lose hold of the car around one of the switchbacks going back down. For another, it's a solid half mile up an unpaved road that I get scraped once a year or so and get re-graveled maybe every ten. There's mudholes deep enough to send a submarine down into and ruts in the road that would make the Donner Party proud. I shook my head at the ridiculous little car sitting on my lawn, marveling at the fact that the whole undercarriage hadn't gotten scraped off halfway down the mountain.

Leaning on the front quarter panel of the convertible was a guy I assumed was Amy's brother, since there was another grumpy-looking man in his sixties sitting behind the wheel of the Mercedes. Little bro looked like an absolute douchebag with his tie artfully undone and hanging loose over his dress shirt with one button unbuttoned and his sleeves rolled up exactly twice to show how casual he was being. He had on khakis and dress shoes, and his sunglasses probably cost more than my whole outfit.

Of course, since it was Saturday in the Georgia woods, I was wearing my Timberlands, jeans, and a *Baldur's Gate 3* t-shirt, so my whole outfit barely cost more than a hundred bucks, and only that because good boots are expensive. I hate paying good money for clothes, especially since in my line of work they usually make it one good wearing before they're either in tatters or covered in blood—human or otherwise. Except shoes. Terry Pratchett built a whole economic theory out of shoes, but what I took from it was—buy the best damn boots you can afford and you won't have to buy boots as often. So I pay good money for my boots. Everything else? Total thrift store chic.

Amy threw the Suburban into park and slid out of the driver's seat, moving fast. The only time she put on that kind of speed was when there was an immediate threat, so my heart beat faster and I reached for the center console, ready to grab Bertha II.

Geri put a hand on my wrist. "It's not that kind of danger, Bubba," she said, her voice low like we were trying not to be heard by a hungry cryptid.

"What are you talking about?" I asked.

"It's family dynamics stuff," she said. This I could relate to. My family history was almost *Game of Thrones*-level complicated, except without the incest. Plenty of murder and mommy issues, though. "She needs to preempt their attack on you and your home to keep you from throwing her brother off the back deck, and she needs to prep them for encountering a wild redneck in his natural habitat."

"What about prepping me? I coulda used a little heads up on the way back from the Soiree," I said.

"There's no prepping you for meeting the potential in-laws. I remember when Britt brought you home to meet our parents. Do you?"

I did. It hadn't gone well. My girlfriend, Geri's sister Britney, had spent two weeks trying to get me to act like less of an uncouth hillbilly, or at least to eat my French fries with a fork, but it all fell apart within ten seconds of me stepping through their front door, bumping into a side table by the door, and knocking an antique vase to the floor. Spoiler Alert: her parents weren't predisposed to like the giant Cro-Magnon that was sleeping with their daughter, and they certainly weren't going to like me when I knocked over Aunt Doris's vase to shatter on the tile entryway.

It got way worse when I realized it was actually Aunt Doris's *urn*, and now somebody had to sweep Aunt Doris up and pick the leaves and ceramic out of her cremains. Seemed like I should probably wait in the SUV until Amy gave me the all clear.

Except she was waving for me to follow her, so I reluctantly did as I was told. The chorus of *thump-thump* from behind me clued me in that Skeeter and Geri were also hopping out of the car, so I had some backup, even if it wasn't in the lead-slinging variety. At least, mostly not. I would have bet my house and all my acreage that Geri had a hideaway piece tucked somewhere on her person. It's just kind of who she is.

Amy blew right past her brother, who was staring at his cell phone and frowning. We did have cell service up on the mountain, thanks to Skeeter's technical know-how, some creative wiring, and a few pieces of communications gear that probably weren't exactly legal for personal use. But we worked for the government, so that made it okay, right? So I knew little bro had signal and hoped he wasn't losing too much money trying to short stocks or something else men with more money than sense did on their phones.

The doors on the Mercedes opened, and her parents stepped out. I steeled myself for the inevitable disapproval. I've met rulers of magical kingdoms and not been intimidated. I spent weeks running around North Carolina with friggin' *Dracula* and didn't get ruffled. Hell, I'm technically part of the Fairyland royal family, but a pair of yuppies boomers from Kentucky had me shaking in my Wranglers. Love makes idiots of us all, and I don't need the help.

"Mr. Hall," I said extending my hand to the older man. "I'm Bubba. It's good to finally meet you."

"Wilson Hall," he said, staring at my hand like I'd just pulled it out of a cow's ass. "Amanda told us your name was Robert."

"Robert's my given name," I replied, leaving my hand floating in midair. If he was going to be an ass, I was going to make sure it was obvious which one of us was the rude one. "I go by Bubba. Ever since my brother was little and couldn't say his 'R' sounds."

"Oh," Amy's dad said, still staring at my hand like it was roadkill. "I suppose we all make accommodations for our relatives. Will your brother be in the wedding party?"

"No, sir," I replied. "He passed away a few years ago."

"I'm sorry to hear that," my future father-in-law said, with an odd glint in his eye. "What happened?"

Something clicked in my head right then. This son of a bitch knew exactly what happened and was trying to get a rise out of me for some reason. I ran over everything I knew about Amy's father in my head and remembered that she said he had worked as a government consultant of some sort and was tight with some people high up in a bunch of alphabet agencies. Well, whatever test he was trying to put me through, I was about to either pass with flying colors or flunk like some of my old D-line buddies at Georgia trying advanced calculus.

"He went nuts and I shot him. A lot. But you knew that already, didn't you?" My voice was low, and I'm pretty sure the look on my face was the same one that had sent Sasquatch running away rather than step to me in that kind of mood.

"What makes you say that?" He was smooth, I had to give him that. A prick, but a smooth one.

"Because no reasonable person asks about somebody's dead brother ten seconds after meeting them. So you knew what was up and assumed that killing Jason would be my biggest regret, and mentioning it would throw me off guard and give you some kind of edge in whatever stupid verbal pecker-measuring contest you think we're in. But it ain't. I've done a lot of stuff in my life I regret, but putting down my batshit baby brother ain't on the list. Neither is putting a bullet in my daddy, in case that's where you wanted to head next. Now I don't know what kind of game you think we're playing, but you ain't at home in your fancy house, or even in Washington where you've got some swanky office to work out of. You're in *my* front yard, on *my* mountain, and if you can't act like you've got some damn raising, you can turn your overpriced hunk of German steel right back around and take your sorry ass back to where you came from."

I put my hand down then and turned back to Amy's Suburban. "Babe, that's about all the surprise family I can handle in one shot. If y'all need me, I'll be on the back deck cleaning my guns." I fetched Bertha II out of the console and stomped up onto my porch, then let the screen door slam behind me as I went into the house, grabbed a twelve-pack of Stella out of the fridge, and headed out the sliding glass doors on the side of the den. I set Bertha on the table, cracked a beer, and started field-stripping the Desert Eagle to clean. I keep a gun cleaning kit on the back porch, since I like to sit out there and watch the sun set while I have a couple cold ones, so I got to work at calming myself down.

The gun was spotless, since she hadn't been fired since the last time I cleaned her, but there's something about the ritual of breaking down a weapon, oiling everything, wiping away any excess, and putting it back together that I've always found soothing. My therapist would probably say it has something to do with my need to impose order on a life that is inherently chaotic. If my therapist hadn't retired after one session with me.

"Nice weapon," came a female voice from the doorway. I looked up and saw Amy's mother standing there in a perfectly pressed pantsuit and a thin smile.

"Thanks," I replied, turning back to my work. "She gets the job done."

"She? I thought men only called their cars and boats 'she.'"

"I don't know about that. Only boat I've got is a little fishing boat too small to carry a name. But I've always called this one Bertha. Well, the first one was Bertha. This is Bertha II."

"What happened to the first Bertha?"

"She got blown up on a case a while back." I didn't mention that Bertha wasn't the only, or the most important, thing we'd lost on that case. Mrs. Hall hadn't shown any signs so far of being a Grade-A asshole like her husband, but I wasn't rolling out any red carpets just yet.

"I'm sorry about Geoffrey," she said. "He can be a real prick some-times. I'm Leigh, and I'm glad to meet you. Can I have a beer?"

I nodded, and she sat across from me, twisted off the cap and tossed it into the recycling bin by the door. She drained half her Stella in one long pull and plopped it on the picnic table with a long sigh. "Thanks. It was a long ride, made longer by having to listen to my husband argue with talk radio the whole trip."

"You're welcome. But why are you here early? We weren't expecting y'all until closer to next weekend. If we'd known, we could have made arrangements for y'all to have a place to stay."

"Oh, we aren't staying the whole week, don't worry," she said, then laughed at the sigh of relief that escaped from me. "We're going to Atlanta for a few days, then we'll be back for all the festivities right before the wedding. I wouldn't dare leave my Amy to fend for herself on this massive undertaking."

Yeah, because Deputy Homeland Security Director Amy Hall, the woman who had literally traveled across dimensions for a case, needed help making a wedding happen. Oh, this woman had *no* idea what she was dealing with.

3

Supper was about as tense an affair as you'd expect, given the personalities involved. Amy's dad and I sat about as far away from one another as two people can get and still be at the same table. The conversation mostly centered on lighter stuff—weather for the weekend's festivities (we'd paid off a couple of elementals Quincy Harker was buddies with to make sure that no matter what was going on anywhere else, the wind and rain wouldn't screw up our party), the guest list (we didn't mention anything about salt rings or potential fae-blooded wedding crashers), and band for the reception (there wasn't going to be one since Skeeter had more DJ equipment than David Guetta).

There were a few conversational detours we had to navigate as Amy's mama took every opportunity to criticize my cabin and the decorating Amy had done since moving in. And let's face it, everything on the wall that didn't somehow relate to UGA football or pro wrestling was one hundred percent Amy's. I tried to keep my cool, but Geri definitely had to stomp on my foot to keep my mouth shut when Mama Hall got all snarky about the dishware. My own mother picked out the china we were eating off of, and she was a goddamned fairy princess, so talking shit about her sense of style kinda flew all over me. But I held it together and redirected the conversation back to the weekend's events, excited to share the style of service we'd finally settled on.

Turned out that wasn't the light, airy topic I expected it to be, given our choice of ministers. It's not that Amy and I aren't religious. You can't see the shit we've seen and not understand that there's too much weird shit in the universe for it to happen randomly. There was some higher power out there, we just weren't convinced humans, *any* humans, had figured out what it was. So I guess you'd call us agnostic. But Skeeter's cousin Wardell had gone to Clemson with a football scholarship and NFL dreams, and like someone else I know and love, had come home from college with a knee that never worked quite right again. But Wardell had the grades to stay in school and a calling to keep on going after that, so when he finally came back to the holler he grew up in, it was as a full-blown Baptist preacher.

Now there's a lot of different kinds of ministers in the world, but Wardell was not what you think of when you imagine a Baptist preacher in the backwoods of Georgia. For one thing, he grew up with a Black adopted first cousin that was as queer as a football bat, so any inherent homophobia got drummed out of him before he could drive. Skeeter's family was an enlightened bunch of hillbillies, at least as far as LGBTQ+ issues went. Some of them still wrapped their heads in tin foil to keep the "gub'mint" from sending them subversive liberal signals while they slept and refused to pay income taxes as "sovereign citizens," but they didn't have any racist or homophobic tendencies.

Wardell was a progressive Baptist preacher from the Georgia backwoods, and he was gonna be sharing the pulpit with the Archbishop of Atlanta, the big high muckity-muck of Georgia Catholicism. My family's worked for the Church for a long time, and even after they decided they couldn't officially have someone in their employ who was only part human, they kept Uncle Father Joe around as our liaison, and even appointed us a new one, Father Matthew Ortega, who was turning out to be okay, for a priest. And apparently when your family works for the Catholic Church hunting down monsters for more than a century, you get an important dude in a funny hat to come preach at your wedding. I was just hoping he didn't make us kneel too much. Some of my kinfolk are still pissy about taking a knee at Appomattox, and I'm just too damn old and fat to be getting up and down too often. Unless I'm drunk, in which case my brain forgets to tell my knees that I ain't twenty-five anymore, or I'm in a fight, in which case my adrenal system tells my brain to shut the hell up and whoop that dude's ass.

I ain't right sure whether Amy's pops was getting bent out of shape about there being a Baptist preaching his daughter's wedding, or if he was getting bent out of shape about a Catholic priest preaching at it, but I was about half a second away from calling in a friendly rabbi from Greenville for some religious reinforcements when her brother, whose name was Jarvis, said, "Dad, why do you care? You've been saying for years that since she waited until she was past thirty to get hitched, you didn't care what she did for a wedding because you weren't paying a dime for it."

The silence that dropped over the table was like a heavy blanket. Amy flushed a bright crimson, her mother gasped and downed the dregs of her fourth glass of wine in a huge swallow, and Papa Hall just sat there with his mouth gaping open like a fish on a pier. You coulda heard a pistol cock, and would have in about another half a second, except Geri stood up, looked around the table, and asked brightly, "Who wants dessert?"

You know it's a bad night when the psychopathic assassin with an explosives fetish is the one defusing the situation. Skeeter and Amy ran into the kitchen with her to see what we could scrounge up for an unexpected dessert for eight, and I sat glaring down the length of the table at her father.

He looked at me with the expression of a man who knew he was standing in quicksand, and the only way he was ever getting out of it was to tap-dance. "You know that was just my frustration talking, right?"

I didn't respond, just stared at him.

"A father wants his children to be happy, to be successful, to be loved. And when their child doesn't find that love, he gets frustrated. You understand. You must have had similar conversations with your..." His voice trailed off.

"I shot my father dead because he was a psychotic murderer who gutted my first fiancée. Then I blew my baby brother straight to Hell because he was even more nuts than my daddy and was responsible for just about every bad thing that ever happened to me off a football field, including my father's killing spree. My mother left when I was in high school, my grandfather died in my arms, and last year one of the three people I was closest to in this world bled out in front of me on a mission. The three people in that kitchen are the people I love the most, and I would walk through fucking *fire* for each and every one of them. So let me be very goddamn clear, Mr. Hall. If I hear another word come out of your mouth, or your son's mouth, that is intended to cause any of those people, or any guest at our wedding, the slightest hint of embarrassment or pain, I will Fucking. End. You. Do you understand?"

He opened his mouth to bluster, and I reached behind my back and put my Taurus Judge on the table. Then I slid my right hand under my left arm, drew Bertha II, and put her on the table. Then I unclipped the knife from my right front pocket and set it down with them. Then I drew the stubby little last-resort knife from my belt buckle and dropped it with a *thunk.*

"Do. You. Understand. Me?"

He nodded, and I turned my glare on Jarvis. "How about you?"

He drew a breath, and I held up a finger. "Before you protest that all you were doing was informing Amy of something she needed to know, understand that while I might live in a cabin in the woods, I'm not some dumbass hillbilly. I've been educated in a lot of ways over a lot of years, and I've seen and lived through shit your puny little yuppie mind could not begin to comprehend. So yeah, I might look and talk like a refugee from *Duck Dynasty* most of the time, but don't ever mistake an accent for an IQ test. Now. Do. You. Understand. Me?"

"Yes."

"Thank you both. Mrs. Hall, I apologize for threatening extreme violence upon your family, particularly in your presence."

"You are totally forgiven, Robert," she said, slurring surprisingly little. "In fact—"

I held up a finger. "But don't think you get off free and clear, either. I haven't missed a single one of your little digs about Amy's decor, or her wardrobe, or her hair, and that shit stops right damn now. Because while I might have been raised not to hit a woman, and I would never disrespect my future mother-in-law by slapping the taste out of her haughty goddamn mouth, Geri has neither the upbringing or restraint I do, and she loves your daughter like the big sister she lost. So you need to button up your shit, get your drinking under control, and mind your manners, or I guaran-damn-tee you will find yourself dangling off my back deck by your ankles before the night is through. Is that clear?"

She straightened up in her chair and fixed me with a glare that probably wilted a thousand peckers, but I was unimpressed. Her daughter's death glare was more impressive, and usually backed up with an ass-whooping. The worst Mama Hall was gonna do to me was bitch me out, and when Queen Mab is your granny, it's real hard for a human cussing to even register. But I still wasn't in a listening mood, so I held up a finger to stop her.

"Don't," I said. "Just. Don't. Don't equivocate, don't prevaricate, and don't sit there at my dinner table, piss on my leg and tell me it's raining. If y'all can't show your daughter the respect she deserves and let a modicum of that spill over onto the rest of us, then you can get the hell off my mountain right now. Or we can have dessert and pretend this conversation never happened. What's it gonna be?"

They looked at one another, then at me, then at one another, and finally after a long moment, Jarvis leaned over and said, "That's a really big gun. Can you teach me to shoot it?"

And just like that, the Bro Code was observed, a non-apology apology was issued, and we could all have dessert.

4

I didn't know you even knew words like 'equivocate' and 'prevaricate,' Bubba," Geri said as she stepped through the sliding glass door onto the back deck.

"I'm an onion, Donkey," I replied, quoting that great piece of philosophical cinema, *Shrek*. "I got layers you ain't even seen yet."

"Let's keep it that way since your metaphor is about to verge into creepy territory."

"Fair enough. Beer me?" I didn't turn around, just kept looking out onto the moonlit valley below us. Geri slapped a Stella into my hand, and I popped the top off on the edge of the porch railing.

She stepped up beside me and leaned on the railing. "I guess now we know why Amy never brought you home to meet the family, huh?"

"Yeah, she was afraid I'd do something like I did at dinner." I was embarrassed about losing my temper. I've been called worse things by better people and should have been able to keep my cool. I've fought monsters of almost every type imaginable, including a dragon, but I lost my cool when a bitchy Karen insulted my living room décor. That was even less restraint than I was typically known for.

"More like she was afraid *they* would do something like they just did," Geri corrected me. "You know, Britt was worried about the same thing before you met our parents."

I looked over at her a little. We never talked about Britney. Her sister, and the first woman I fell in love with. The woman who died because of me, at the hands of my psycho father, at the urging of my even more psycho brother. The reason Geri got trained in how to fight, how to hunt, and how to kill—all so she could hunt down and slaughter the asshole responsible for her sister's death. Me.

We've mostly gotten past the point where she wants to kill me. I don't even padlock her in her bedroom at night anymore, and I deactivated the motion sensor in the hallway months ago. But we still never talked about Britt. It hurt us both too much, even all these years later. "I got along fine with your parents. At least I thought I did." It had been a long time since I spoke to Britney's family. I'd forgotten Geri even existed until she showed up on my porch, all grown up and packing enough firepower to take over a small country.

"You did fine, and Britt had told them to be on their best behavior because she loved you and would pick you over them if they made her choose," Geri replied.

I stood there with that for a long moment. "I loved her, too. More than I had anybody in my life up 'til then. My mama broke something in me when she left, and she broke something in Pop, too. We were already the poster boys for toxic masculinity, but it got even worse after Mama left. I don't think we said a word to each other that wasn't some kind of insult from the time she left until..." I trailed off because the only thing that followed that "until" was "I killed him."

"I know," Geri said. "I didn't believe it for a long time. After she died, when you weren't around anymore, I just thought she...*we* didn't mean anything to you after all. That everything you said about her was bullshit, and you were just another dude chasing the pretty blonde and not giving a rat's ass about anything but football, beer, and babes."

"To be fair, that did describe the first nineteen years of my life pretty well," I said, taking a long pull of my beer.

"Then I get here, and you're with another blonde woman? Dude, it was all I could do not to shoot you the second I laid eyes on you."

"Yeah, you were pretty angry. I'm glad you didn't shoot me. I don't need any new scars."

"Bubba, have you ever known me to shoot anybody and leave them alive to worry about scars?" She seemed a little insulted.

"Fair enough." She did have a good point. Geri was a crack shot when she first got here, and then Joe spent time teaching her some of the long-range rifle stuff he learned in the service. So now she was lethal from hundreds of yards away with the right weapon. "Why didn't you? Shoot me on sight, that is."

"I'm not really sure. I think part of me wanted answers more than I wanted to see you dead. It was a small part, to be sure, but it was enough to keep me from killing your ass."

"Well, that is now officially my favorite part of you, kiddo," I said, pulling her into a rough side hug. "The teeny tiny part that doesn't want to murder me."

"Y'all look all cozy," came a slightly slurred voice from the doorway. I turned to see Jarvis leaning on the jamb holding a beer.

"Come on out, Jarvis," I said, gesturing around the porch. "The stars are out, and the night is beautiful."

"I see that," he said, leering at Geri. "Lots of beauty in these mountains."

"Dream on, douchecanoe," Geri said, slipping past him to go inside and help Amy and Skeeter with cleanup. I'm as useful in the kitchen as a bull in a china shop, and about as destructive, so I was off dish duty any time we ate off breakable plates. I'm perfectly capable of loading a dishwasher with our normal cheap shit cutlery and dishes, but when we move to the nice stuff, I head out to the porch for some drinkin' and thinkin' time.

"I don't think she likes me very much," Jarvis said, grinning up at me.

"What's not to like, Jarvis? You drive a sports car, you dress like a stockbroker, you look down on everything around you, and you talk to everybody like they're low-grade morons. How could anyone not realize that you're an absolute peach of a human being?"

"Whoa whoa *whoa* there, big fella," Jarvis said, holding up his hands in mock surrender. "My folks are already back down the mountain headed to whatever Airbnb they'll be leaving a one-star review for next week. I'm still here because I wanted to get to know my soon-to-be brother-in-law a little better."

"You're still here because Amy took your keys an hour ago and told you there was no way in hell she was going to let you drive off the side of the mountain trying to get to a hotel, so you're spending the night on my couch," I corrected.

"Okay, that too. But I would like to get to know you, Bubba," he said, weaving his way through all kinds of imaginary obstacles to get to a seat at the picnic table on my back deck. "I know you played college football. No chance to go pro?"

This was safer conversational footing. It was hard for even me to get in too big a fight over my college football career. It wasn't distinguished enough to get that pissed off over, honestly. "I blew out my knee on a play that went sideways. I didn't have much real chance to get drafted anyway, but that ended it for sure. I was a second-stringer playing behind some future NFL studs, so I didn't see the field much. Then when I did, I got hurt. So that ended that. You do any sports in college?"

"What makes you so sure I went to college?" he asked with a smirk.

"Besides the car, the suit, and the tie that cost more than a meal at Morton's? Maybe the family dynamic of valuing higher education pretty strongly such that, despite any teenage desire to rebel, would never allow you to not go to college. Or it could be the University of Kentucky ring on your right hand," I said. I was showing off a little, but I didn't like Jarvis very much, so I wanted to play a little Sherlock Holmes on his ass.

"Guilty," he said with another pull on his beer. He waggled the empty at me. I took it, replaced it with a full one, and he just stared at the cap for a minute. "Um, this doesn't twist."

"Shit, son. I thought you went to college," I said. I took the bottle back from him, laid it against the porch railing and slapped the top, ripping the cap right off. I gave the bottle back.

"Thanks. Yeah, I went to Kentucky for undergrad. Vanderbilt for my MBA. Now I work in commodities trading. Do you know what that is?"

"Moving around fake money for products that don't exist?" I asked.

He stopped for a second to consider that. "You know, that's pretty damned close. We can just go with that. So, what are your intentions regarding my sister?"

I gaped at him for a second, then we both broke out laughing. We finished our beers in a companionable silence, and I was happy to realize that there was at least one future in-law that I didn't want to dump in a holler for the bears to gnaw on. For the moment.

5

I woke up sprawled out on the picnic table, covered in dew. I shook the fuzz from my head and the water from my beard and thought back over the night. Dinner sucked. Arguing with in-laws sucked more. Drinking with Brother Jarvis sucked less than I expected it to. Then we broke out Skeeter's stash of his uncle's peach pie moonshine and everything got fuzzy. I vaguely remembered something about Amy telling me she was not cleaning up my puke from the bedroom the week of her wedding, so I could sleep outside or in my truck.

Apparently I decided that puking was definitely on the menu and that I didn't want to scrub vomit out of my pickup, so I slept outside. Not the first time it's happened, but the first time in a long while. As I rolled to my feet and put a hand out to make the porch stop spinning, I remembered exactly why it had been a long time since I drank that much. Hangovers *suck*. I heal a good bit faster than a normal person, on account of being part fae, but it doesn't mean I skip out on any of the suffering associated with my bad decisions. And I was definitely suffering.

I heard the rumble of the sliding glass door loud as a freight train behind me, and I turned around slowly. It was either someone bringing me coffee and Advil, or it was a monster come to take me out for good. Either way, I was in no shape to argue, so it was a good thing all I saw was Geri in sweats and a New England Patriots Super Bowl LI Champs t-shirt. I'm pretty sure she thought buying that shirt and living in Georgia would get her some heat, but she underestimated exactly how little most rednecks care about pro ball. Now if she was wearing Auburn gear around my mountain, that might get her shot, but nobody outside of Metro Atlanta cared about the choke job the Falcons performed.

She handed me the largest mug we had, filled to the brim with coffee, five sugars, double cream, and a peppermint stick. I don't like coffee, so when I need it for medicinal purposes, I do everything I can to make it not taste like coffee. I sucked down about half the mug, scorching my throat to basically glass, and held out my hand, palm up. She dropped four ibuprofen and two Extra-Strength Tylenol in it. I slammed all six pills down, then chased them with the rest of the coffee. Feeling closer to human, if damp, I nodded my thanks and passed her the mug back.

"You got shitfaced last night," she said, dropping down into one of the faux Adirondack chairs.

"I got a decent buzz," I protested.

"You were singing," Geri replied.

"I like to sing!"

"You were singing Beyoncé."

Okay, she had me there. My usual karaoke failings were more in the Chris Stapleton or Waylon Jennings catalog. "Yeah, I mighta been pretty lit if I was getting all bootylicious out here."

"You were getting something, alright. It wasn't delicious or anything anyone would consider a variant of delicious, but it was definitely something. Just be glad you don't have social media."

"Why?" I had a sinking feeling growing in my stomach, and it wasn't caused by the 'shine.

"Let's just say that Skeeter's Insta has gone viral and leave it at that."

I had no choice but to leave it at that, since I had no damned idea what she meant, so I jerked my head toward the doors and asked, "Jarvis awake yet?"

"Oh, yeah. He was up and raring to go by seven, and by seven-thirty he was halfway down the mountain."

"Shit," I said. "What time is it now?"

"Nine-thirty. Amy left an hour ago to go look at flower arrangements, and we've got fittings at eleven for tuxes. Time for you to try and scrub some of the disgusting off, use some of that beard oil you got for your birthday, and maybe we can get down to town in time. I do not want to be responsible for you showing up to your wedding in overalls and Timberlands."

"I can't wear my boots to my own wedding?"

She didn't smile at my feeble attempt at humor, just pointed at the door. "Shower. Now."

For once, I did as I was told.

The men's shop on Main Street in Dalton was a musty old joint where generations of teenage boys had gotten their prom tuxes, and for most of them gone back a couple years later to get fitted for their wedding uniforms. I hadn't followed the traditional North Georgia path of peak in high school, flame out at twenty-five, and come home to settle down in a trailer park with the girl who used to cheer for me on Friday nights. For one thing, I played on the defensive line, and we don't usually get the cheerleaders. For another, while I did blow out my knee in college and come home to recover, I never really settled down, despite living in the house I was raised in.

All that combined to mean that I hadn't set foot in Jacobs' Menswear in a couple decades. Nothing had changed. It still smelled a little like old pipe tobacco, the tiny bell over the door still jingled to announce our arrival, and the stooped old man who shuffled out from the back even looked like the same guy who'd wrapped a tape measure around my neck my junior year and pronounced me "impossible to fit in anything other than a gunny sack."

"Well, well, well, if it isn't little Robbie Brabham," he said in a voice that sounded like creaking doors. "I never thought I'd see you back in here after how high you jumped the first time I asked if you dressed right or left." The little old bastard cackled, his voice high and thready, turning into a rattling cough that culminated in him hawking something vaguely luminescent into a hanky and stuffing it into his pocket for safekeeping. I had a moment to wonder if old man Jacobs was some flavor of cryptid, but then the door jingled again and a form blotted out the sun as Barry entered the shop for his fitting.

Barry, more accurately named Brar'kan, was a Sasquatch. Yes, an actual Bigfoot. We'd become friends on a case a few years back and I'd helped him free his family from my brother's influence. We'd kept in touch ever since via email, not that I understood where a Sasquatch kept his wireless router, and every once in while he'd Nair his entire body and come visit for a few days. I'd had an unfortunate experience with the foaming depilator many years ago as part of a University of Georgia football hazing ritual, and I understood the sacrifice Barry was making on my behalf. He did keep the most obscene handlebar mustache in the free world, though, convinced that it made him somehow less noticeable. I didn't have the heart to break it to him that being seven and a half feet tall and built like he could bench press Andre the Giant meant that some people couldn't even see all the way up to his face, much less remember it. They'd just remember the giant in the room.

"Holy moly, Robbie, what in the free world is *that?*" Mr. Jacobs said, pointing at Barry.

"That's Barry," I replied. "He's one of my groomsmen."

"He's a monster!" the wizened little tailor replied. "What am I supposed to make a tux for him out of, a circus tent?"

"I am very sensitive about my height," Barry said. "Please refrain from further inconsiderate comments." He leaned forward just a little and put not an ounce of intentional menace into his tone, but when you're a walking eclipse, you don't have to work very hard to intimidate most humans, much less an octogenarian tailor.

Mr. Jacobs backed up, his hands held high in surrender. "Anything you say... Barry, was it?"

"Yes," Barry rumbled.

"I'm just going to go into the back and get a stepladder. And my grandson. It's going to take both of us to measure you two." He shuffled off toward the back room, where I could hear a sewing machine running faintly. Mr. Jacobs stopped and turned back to me. "Your order said five groomsmen. Are the rest...?" His question trailed off like he wasn't sure how to ask the question.

"Giants?" I finished for him. "No, it's Skeeter, Geri here, and my future brother-in-law, who's running late."

"Nope! I'm here," Jarvis said, coming out from behind a rack of clothes holding two neckties. "Do you like the blue one or the red one?" He held them up to me.

"I hate neckties, so my answer would be 'no,'" I said.

"What about you, big guy?" he asked Barry.

"I also have little need for neckties in my line of work," the Sasquatch replied. I realized we'd never come up with a cover story for Barry. My in-laws knew that Amy and I worked for the Department of Homeland

Security, with her holding an impressive position and me getting a gig as a contractor based on nothing more than my size and connection to their daughter. I was fine if they thought I was just a hanger-on. They didn't need to know anything more about my real work, or my real heritage, or really anything about me. They thought Skeeter worked in some kind of mysterious internet startup streaming thing that no normal person could comprehend, and that Geri was Amy's assistant. We conveniently left out the trained assassin part of her job description, just like we didn't mention my fairy blood.

"And what line of work is that?" Jarvis asked. Because of course he would. It was the next logical question. I was slapping myself silly for not planning ahead. I'd gone on enough guys' trips to strip clubs to know the deal. You always made up a fake name and occupation, and made sure your bros knew the lie. That's how I got my buddy Dave a free lap dance in Greenville, North Carolina, one night. I backed up his lie that he was a professional hot air balloon pilot to a blonde with a face that vaguely resembled John Elway and an ass that had fewer curves than a North Texas highway. Still not sure I did him any favors, but he seemed to enjoy himself.

"I am the manager of Bubba's CrossFit gym in Atlanta, and I bounce at the Pony on weekends," Barry replied without a moment's hesitation. I was impressed, not just with the speed of his reply, but with his obvious preparation. I mean, I did own a gym in Atlanta, one that catered to shifters and cryptids and had super-heavy weights available for those clients with superhuman strength. And Barry certainly looked like some-body you'd see guarding the door of a strip club. I didn't expect him to have a cover story planned when he walked in, but my buddy had his shit down cold.

"Sounds like fun," Jarvis said, his tone holding only a hint of conde-scension. I was starting to think that he might be the least douchetastic of my new family. "Can you get us two-for-one dances for the bachelor party Friday?"

Barry opened his mouth and closed it again, not prepared for this line of questioning. Fortunately, I had plenty of experience in navigating the sometimes murky waters of gentlemen's lounges. "Nah, that takes money out of the girls' pockets, figuratively speaking. We'll definitely hit up some clubs, but we'll pay full freight for any entertainment. The girls deserve all the money they make."

"Fair enough," Jarvis said. "I didn't even think about that part of it.

We'll have a killer time, and maybe your big pal here can get us a break on drink prices instead."

"That I can do," Barry replied, fist-bumping Jarvis. I had just seen a douchebro fist bump Bigfoot in a tuxedo shop in Georgia. My life was *weird.*

6

After we finished up at the men's shop, we strolled down the quiet Main Street to a little cafe run by my retired seventh-grade shop teacher and his wife. Mr. Norton stood behind the counter taking orders and yelling back at the kids in the kitchen just like he'd bellowed at me and Skeeter goofing around with the power tools back in school, and it brought back a wave of nostalgia that almost had me itching to build a birdhouse. Almost. And given that the birdhouse I built in Norton's class had held together just long enough for me to get it out to my car after school the day of the final, almost was close enough for me. A carpenter, I am not.

"Bubba!" Norton yelled as the five of us came in. Every head in the place turned to look at us—two locals, a young woman in combat boots with pink streaks in her dark hair, a giant with muscles on top of his muscles, and a Jarvis.

Jarvis grinned up at me like Ryan Gosling in the Barbie movie and said, "Dude! This place is awesome! Totally rustic. Like Cracker Barrel decor without the gift shop."

"Or history of homophobia," Skeeter muttered.

"Don't count on that, Skeet," Geri said, her voice just as low. "We're getting some awfully strange looks."

"Oh, that ain't because they all know I'm gay," Skeeter said. "Those are racist glares, not homophobic glares. You live in a small town in the South long enough, you can tell the difference. These crackers are just scared I'm gonna want to sit at their lunch counter or something terrible like that."

"I do not like racists," Barry said. Unlike Geri and Skeeter, Barry did nothing to keep his voice down, so everybody in the diner heard him, and it was like one of those moments in a movie where time stops. The place went dead silent except for the soft strains of Mr. Norton's Lord and Savior George Jones, who was always streaming from the speakers, no matter what time of day or night you entered his restaurant. But all the little conversations, the murmurs, the whispers, even the clink of silverware on plates and the rattle of ice in glasses halted like a switch had been thrown.

"Me neither, Barry," I said, also not keeping my voice down. Barry was the biggest guy in the place by a wide margin, and while I wasn't even close to his size, I was still the runner-up, albeit a distant one. There were a few good old boys clustered around a table near the kitchen that looked like they might want to object to Barry's proclamation, but when I brushed my aloha shirt open to reveal my shoulder holster, they thought better of it and wordlessly stood up, dropped a stack of bills on the table, and hustled out the back door.

"Good," the Sasquatch replied, walking over to a table set up for six and lowering himself down into one of the chairs. The metal creaked, but held, so I felt confident taking the other end of the table for myself. If it was Sasquatch-rated, it would definitely hold my ass.

A sprightly woman in her seventies bustled over to the table, all smiles and lavender hair rinse. "Hey Robbie! How are you? You getting ready for the big day?"

"Yes, ma'am, Mrs. N," I replied. Mrs. Norton had been the nurse at the middle school when me and Skeeter went through. I always assumed she hadn't wanted to work at the high school on account of how many injuries came straight from her husband's classroom to the nurse's office, but she certainly bandaged up more than one set of scraped knees and bloodied knuckles for me in seventh and eighth grade. "We get hitched on Saturday up at the Rolling Clover. Amy's family's already started coming into town. This is her little brother Jarvis." I gestured at him. "You know Skeeter and Geri, and this is my friend Barry. He works with me in Atlanta."

"Well, ain't you a tall drink of water?" she asked Barry. He looked a little confused by the colloquialism, but Mrs. N was already running her fingers through Jarvis's short blond hair. "And you were just the cutest thing! If I was thirty years younger, I might make a run at you myself."

Jarvis blushed and looked around the table for a rescue. I studied the menu, even though it hadn't changed since the day the place opened fifteen years ago. Mrs. N flirting with you was sort of a rite of passage in Dalton. If she didn't, you'd probably come off as a complete putz the first time she met you. If you got offended, she'd never flirt with you again, but your refills would also be a little slower in coming to the table. If you played the game with her and steadfastly refused to remind her that even if she was thirty years younger, she'd still be a good fifteen years older than Jarvis, then she'd move on to another target in about thirty seconds, less if she could get a good blush outta you, which she had managed with Jarvis in a heartbeat. That poor boy's ears looked like they were carved out of a tomato, they were so red.

"Now, what can I get y'all? Our special today is meatloaf, but it kinda sucks, so I wouldn't eat it if I was you."

"Chicken livers, mashed potatoes, collards, and sweet tea," Skeeter said, drawing a look of horror from Jarvis, who had probably thought chicken livers was a dish people only ordered on TV shows where they want to show how redneck the town is. Little did he know that Skeeter and I could have *written* most of those shows.

"I'm gonna do the quarter chicken, white meat, fried squash, fried okra, and sweet tea," I said.

"You know they don't count as vegetable if they're deep-fried, right, Bubba?" Geri asked before putting in her order of hamburger steak—no onions—fries, and tea. Barry got the veggie plate with broccoli, sweet corn, and carrots, and Jarvis got a cheeseburger.

I raised an eyebrow at Barry as Mrs. N walked away. "You gone vegetarian on me, old buddy?"

"Not at all," Barry replied. "But it is very difficult to get meat in your establishments that is as raw as I prefer."

Jarvis looked up at the denuded Bigfoot. "How raw do you prefer your meat?" he asked.

"Still warm from the slaughter, preferably," Barry said, baring his elongated canines. I'm not gonna say he looked like a shaved Wookie, but if he'd let out a growl, I'd ask him how fast he could do the Kessel Run.

Jarvis's blush faded instantly as he went paper-white. "Oh." My new brother-in-law was learning some shit this week. Just wait until he saw the wedding reception. If any of my relatives showed up, it could get downright magical.

We stuffed ourselves full of meat and fried goodness, then walked back out onto the sidewalk to head home. We hadn't made it ten feet before a ruckus from across the street drew my attention. Something was going on in the window of the men's shop, and as the person with the only need for group formalwear in the county this week, I figured the commotion probably had something to do with me. Or my future in-laws, more specifically.

"Oh shit," Jarvis said under his breath as he followed my gaze.

"You see something I don't?" I asked. My eyes followed his finger as he extended one arm in a silent motion, pointing out the black Mercedes SUV parked in front of the fire hydrant just outside the front door of Jacobs' Menswear. "Well, shit," I said, echoing Jarvis's sentiment.

"Yeah, this isn't gonna go well," my future brother-in-law said. "Dad's…pretty particular about his tuxes, and he wanted to bring his own and just rent a cummerbund or vest or whatever to match the rest of the wedding party. Mom wouldn't let him. She said he was going to wear the same weak-ass rented tuxes as everybody else because it's Amy's day and neither of them were going to show up their daughter by wearing couture to what we sure to be an off-the-rack wedding. Her words, not mine." He held up both hands in front of his face like he expected me to punch him.

It wasn't an unreasonable fear. Hearing his mother's opinion of my lifestyle and home town wasn't surprising, not after the way both her parents had behaved the night before, but it still pissed me off. It wasn't even very inaccurate, which might have been what pissed me off the most. But now it looked like I had a couple of situations coming to a boil very quickly. The first, and probably worst, was whatever was going on in the men's shop. I could see Mr. Jacobs waving his arms through the big picture window, and if the old dude got too wound up, I was worried he might have a heart attack or a stroke. I could also see Amy's dad gesticulating wildly, but I didn't have the same high hopes for his imminent hospitalization. He seemed to be in better shape than Mr. Jacobs, and more used to yelling at people. It was doubtful he'd stroke out in the middle of the store. Not out of the question, but doubtful.

The second problem was the grinning buffoon strutting down the sidewalk with a huge grin on his face and a ticket book in his hand. It seemed our local deputy, Randall Williams, had spotted Mr. Hall's car parked in front of the hydrant and was gleefully preparing to write a ticket. This might be the first piece of law enforcement Randall had done all year, since he got taken off speed trap duty when it became widely known around town that two doughnuts with pink icing and sprinkles from the QT on the bypass would get you out of any ticket. Randall wasn't exactly the Barney Fife of North Georgia, but that was only because Barney actually solved a crime once. A low bar, but it was one Randall hadn't managed to clear yet.

"Goddammit," I muttered as I crossed the street. "Skeeter, you got a badge of some sort on you?"

"I got about six," my buddy replied. "Which one you want?"

"Let's use the real one this time, just for kicks," I said, then yelled across the street, "Cut it out, Randall, he's with me. Official DHS business!"

I saw the confusion run across Williams's face as he tried to figure out what DHS stood for. His pondering gave me time to make it across Main Street to stand in front of him. "Randall, you know I've been working with the Department of Homeland Security for a while now. The guy inside is my boss on an investigation, and he's in Jacobs' on official business."

"He's parked in front of the hydrant, Bubba." Randall was always a man of few words. This was a bonus most of the time because he was also dumb as a box of hair, but right now I needed to make sure he understood me.

"I know he's parked in front of the hydrant, Randall, but he's working for the government and needed a place to park close to the store in case there was an emergency."

"What kind of emergency?" Randall asked. "Is Mr. Jacobs a terrorist? I always wondered about him. He's…" He looked around, then leaned in a whispered the next word. "Jewish. Did you know that?"

I blinked a couple times. "No, he ain't," I said. "He's Methodist. Hell, Randall, you go to church with Mr. Jacobs, don't you?"

Randall looked even more confused, if that was possible. "Yeah, but he might be a Methodist Jew. That's a thing, Bubba. I seen it on the TV."

"You think that Mr. Jacobs, who's owned this shop longer than either one of us has been alive, has been going to the Methodist church for fifty years to hide the fact that he's a secret Jewish double agent? What do you think he's trying to do, Randall? Help aim the space laser?" I tried to pretend like I wasn't talking to the guy who got held back in elementary school so often that by the time he made seventh grade he could drive himself to middle school, but I didn't quite keep the "Are you stupid?" out of my voice.

"I ain't stupid, Bubba. I know you can be Jewish and not religious at all, so why couldn't Mr. Jacobs be Jewish and Methodist all at the same time?" Randall raised an eyebrow at me, and I let out a sigh.

"It doesn't matter whether or not Mr. Jacobs is Jewish," I said. "He's not who my boss is investigating. And why did you think he was Jewish in the first place?"

Randall looked confused at the question. "Well, he's a tailor. Ain't all tailors Jewish?"

I blinked, slowly, hoping that if I did, that the world would come back into focus and whatever alternate dimension I was obviously in would disappear. It did not. "Randall, being a tailor has nothing to do with being Jewish. And being Jewish has nothing to do with tailoring. I need you to not write this car a ticket because the driver is on official Department of Homeland Security business. Business that is Top Secret and has nothing to do with Mr. Jacobs. Now," I lowered my voice so Randall had to lean in to hear me, "can I count on your discretion in this matter?"

I was pretty sure Randall had no goddamned idea what the word "discretion" meant, but he nodded and put his ticket book away. Then he straightened, *saluted*, and walked off down the sidewalk, whistling an off-key but jaunty tune.

"Not bad, Bubba," Jarvis said, walking up beside me. "But I think you're about to go from the frying pan right into the fires of Hell." He pointed through the window, where I saw my future father-in-law choking the only man within fifty miles who might possibly be able to get tuxes in mine and Barry's sizes before Saturday.

"Well, shit," I said. "Skeeter, get your phone out and have Amy on speed dial. I might need backup."

"Oh, you're definitely gonna need backup," Jarvis said. "Like maybe a bazooka."

"I can help with that," Geri said, looking through the plate glass window. "I think I've still got that grenade launcher under the back seat of your truck."

Jarvis looked terrified, but I actually considered it before I put my hand on the door and pushed my way into the fracas.

7

I charged through the front door of the shop, the merry tinkling of the bell in direct contrast to my mood and the scowl on Mr. Jacobs' face. "Looks like you met my future father-in-law," I said, my voice low and menacing.

Amy's dad didn't take the hint. "Robert, this man is providing me with drastically inferior service, and I demand that we take the entire wedding party's business elsewhere!"

Mr. Jacobs looked up at me, bushy gray eyebrows quivering with rage. "Robbie, you need to get this arrogant piece of crap out of my shop before I put my shears somewhere that will make him very uncomfortable on his drive back to wherever he came from!"

I stepped between the men and looked down on them. They were a study in contrasts. The florid, sweaty face of an irate Mr. Hall looked even rounder than usual when compared the nearly skeletal mien of Mr. Jacobs, who was old when the War Between the States ended and now looked positively mummified. Looking at the wires of muscle wrapped around his forearms, I had no doubt that he could stick his scissors so far up Mr. Hall's ass that he'd cut his fingers on them when he flossed. Mr. Hall had the fleshy, red-faced look of a man used to yelling until he got his way, while the tailor looked like he'd just cut you from nose to nuts, roll you up in a bolt of spare suit fabric, and toss you out with the garbage.

I gently pushed each man back a step, so they would at least have to work a little harder to stab one another. "What's wrong, guys? I'm trying to get married in a few days, so I kinda need y'all to behave." I turned to Amy's father. "Mr. Hall, there ain't another person in all of North Georgia that can get a tux in my size for this weekend. Now if you want to be responsible for me showing up to my wedding in a black t-shirt and jeans, I'm fine with that. But I expect your wife, and more important, your *daughter*, might have something to say about it."

I turned to look at the tailor. "Mr. Jacobs, my family's done business with you since along about when they invented clothes, ain't we?"

The little man nodded, keeping his rage-filled eyes focused on Mr. Hall. "Good," I continued. "I wanna keep that tradition alive a little longer by getting all the tuxes from my wedding here, then getting started on making little baby Bubbas who can come in here and get their prom tuxes from you for years."

I heard a soft gagging sound and turned to give Geri a nasty look. She stopped fake-puking at the thought of me having kids, and I turned my attention back to the feuding men. "To do that, I need to get married this weekend. And to do *that*, I gotta have my tux. And my wedding party's tuxes." I now turned my attention back to Mr. Hall. "Now, I don't give a flying rat's butt if you want to walk your daughter down the aisle in a tux you rent from Mr. Jacobs here, or in a tux you had hand-spun out of an artisanal silkworm's butthole directly onto your body. But you *will* walk your daughter down the aisle on Saturday, and you *will* behave like you have an ounce of respect for my friends, family, and neighbors until you leave Dalton Sunday morning, or I *will*—"

"You will what, exactly?" Amy's dad sneered up at me, and I could tell this was a guy who left a penny tip in his water glass at restaurants. "You'll hit me? I doubt it. Beat me up? I'd sue you within an inch of your life."

"I'll do way worse than that," I said, my voice low and threatening. "I'll tell your daughter."

And just like that, all the air went out of the man. I've met men with daughters before, and they are universally wrapped around their little girl's finger. I knew my future father-in-law was no exception because I knew how totally wrapped around his daughter's finger *I* was, and she'd had more time to work on him. He deflated like a quiche at a Limp Bizkit concert, and I could see all the fight leave his body. "Fine," he said after a long moment. He turned to Mr. Jacobs. "What do I need to do?"

"You need to get the hell out of my store and drive back to wherever *your* tailor is. I'm not dealing with you," the wiry little tailor said.

"Oh, come on," Mr. Hall whined, even adding a little foot stomp at the end. Unfortunately, decades of dealing with high school boys taught Mr. Jacobs how to deal with whiny little shitheads.

So he ignored the pouting red-faced man and looked to me. "Robbie, all the tuxedos for the polite members of your party will be here Friday morning. We can do a final fitting, then you can get married. But him? He can kiss my ass. He gets nothing from this store, ever. I reserve the right to refuse service, and I am refusing service. Get him out of my sight."

I looked down at the chastened man who I was going to have to share a lot of Thanksgiving dinners with and said, "Come on, Mr. Hall. Let's head back to my place and see what we can do to rustle up some lunch."

"Bubba, we just had lunch," Geri reminded me.

"Yeah, but what about second lunch?" I said, shooting her a "shut the hell up and let me get him out of here" glare.

"I could eat," Amy's dad said, slouching his way toward the door. He left, and even the tinkle of the bell over the door seemed dispirited. I turned back to Mr. Jacobs to apologize, but he waved me off.

"Don't worry about it, Robbie. He's not the first new-money carpet-bagging assclown to try and play 'do you know who I am?' with me in my own shop, and he probably won't be the last. I'll take care of you boys, even the giant. Never seen a shaved Sasquatch before. That's a new one on me. One of these days, you'll have to come back down here and tell me how you ended up with a Bigfoot groomsman."

I goggled at the little tailor. "How did you know…"

"That your friend Barry is a 'squatch? It's obvious if you've ever spent any time around them. It's the way the eyes are set in the face and the shape of the jaw. I couldn't let on before that I knew what he was, on account of my idiot grandson Henry working in the stockroom. Didn't want him overhearing anything. He's on lunch now, probably asleep in his Prius or something."

"You have been among my kind before?" Barry asked, amazement in his voice. "Very few of your people have ever been allowed close enough to one of us to see our faces that clearly."

"Not only have I been among your kind, big boy, I once got shithouse drunk with this one's grandfather and a Sasquatch while we all played poker with a golem and a vampire who claimed he was Count Dracula! I didn't believe him, but he played a mean hand of cards," Mr. Jacobs replied. He waved us out. "Now go. I need to get these orders in, or you really will be walking down the aisle in crocs and heart boxers!"

Not wanting to look like some nerdy cosplayer on my wedding day, I turned and left, filing Mr. Jacobs' words away for the future. I was one hundred percent going to need the details on that poker game. Seemed like there was more to the town tailor than I ever imagined.

***

We made it back to my place just in time to pull waaaayyyyy off to the side of the road to let Amy's mama and daddy inch past us on my narrow gravel driveway. I parked the truck and got out, raising an eyebrow at Geri in hopes that she'd go in first and maybe save me from the ire of a fiancée whose parents have just been run out of town a couple days before the wedding.

"Not a chance, big guy," she said, interpreting my glance perfectly. "I'm not sleeping with her, so I'm not apologizing to her. That's my standing rule—I only apologize if it affects me getting paid or laid. This one's on you." She turned to Amy's brother. "Come on. I'll teach you how to clean a machine gun."

Jarvis looked at me in confusion, and I chuckled as I answered him. "Go on," I said. "That ain't a euphemism for anything. The shed out back is the armory, and there's always something that needs to be cleaned, sharpened, or zeroed in. Geri won't let you shoot your foot off."

"Which is more than I can say for your sister if you go in there with Bubba right now," Geri said.

"Barry, let's you and me go take a walk in the woods," Jarvis said.

"I live in the woods," Barry said. "Why would I want to walk in them for pleasure?"

"Because neither one of us wants to be in the room when my sister rips into Bubba for getting our parents so pissed off they went back to Atlanta just a couple days before the wedding," Jarvis replied. It was the smartest thing I'd heard him say since we met.

"That is logical," Barry replied, half-convincing me that I had the Bigfoot version of Mr. Spock in my wedding party. The pair of them walked off around the other corner of the house, leaving Geri to go clean guns all by her lonesome and me to trudge up the front steps of my cabin and face the fury of my fiancée without any backup. I wondered how fast

Harker could get to Georgia and maybe blow me up, thus saving me from the inevitable ass-chewing I was walking into.

I opened the door, fully expecting to find Amy standing in the middle of a storm of broken crockery or whatever else she felt like destroying, and really wishing they made Kevlar vests for your face, and stopped dead at the scene I walked in on. My fiancée wasn't screaming, wasn't crying, and wasn't throwing things. She didn't seem to be depressed, frantic, panicked, or even angry.

Nope. She was sitting on my couch with her feet up and a glass of red wine in her hand. Admittedly seeing her drinking wine on the couch at two in the afternoon wasn't exactly normal, but it was a far cry from the rage and devastation I'd been expecting. "Um…honey?" I called from the doorway. "You okay?"

"Better than I have been in about thirty-six hours," Amy replied.

"You know your parents just hauled ass down the mountain, right?"

"Oh yeah, and I don't know what you had to do to make that happen, but it's definitely upgrading your honeymoon experience, baby." She gave me a sultry smile that warmed certain parts of my anatomy but confused the larger head significantly.

"And you're not pissed at me for running your daddy off this close to the wedding?" I asked, trying to find the land mine I was sure was right in front of me.

"Daddy was being a dick to the tailor, wasn't he?" Amy asked.

"Yeah, in a big way. Almost got our whole order thrown out by Mr. Jacobs, and he's the only place in town that could fit me and Barry on short notice."

"Well, that goes right along with how Mom was talking to the caterers and the florists all morning, until I revoked her cell phone privileges in a very Bubba fashion." She took another long drink of wine, then refilled her glass. The hollow *thunk* of the bottle landing on the side table told me this was not the first, or second glass.

"What does that mean, exactly?" I was pretty sure I knew, but not one hundred percent.

"I tossed her phone off the back deck."

Yep, exactly what I thought she meant. Somebody with a little gumption could probably recover at least two dozen cell phones from the woods below my deck. I had a bad habit of flinging them off the porch when somebody irritated me. Which is basically anybody calling me on a

Saturday afternoon from September through December. You do not call a man during college football season. It just ain't right.

"Are they coming back?" I asked. I was hoping they would return, for Amy's sake. None of my family would be at the wedding, which was fine. They were all dead, not human, or psychotic. Or some mix of the three. It would be nice to have Amy's family around, since as far as I knew, she'd never had to murder any of them. Strangle them a little, maybe, but not outright slaughter.

"They'll meet us at the wedding venue at ten o'clock the morning of the wedding. And they found an Airbnb in town where they'll stay after the wedding before returning to Kentucky the next morning. Daddy was furious at the tailor, and you, but Mom just said that whatever mess I wanted to make of my life, I was the one who had to live with it. I told them I was fine with that and that I'd see them Saturday morning." She took another sip of wine.

"I guess that wasn't the answer they were expecting?"

"Not a bit," Amy replied, killing her glass. She picked up the bottle for another refill, but it was empty. "Why is the wine gone?"

"You drank it."

"Yes, but *why* is the wine gone?"

"Okay, Captain Drunken Sparrow," I said. "Are you okay with this? I know women like to have their mothers around them while they get ready for big events."

"Normal women with normal mothers," Amy said. "Neither I nor my mother could be considered even remotely normal. Besides, this way we don't have to worry about hiding who and what everyone around here is." She flashed me a grin.

"What about Jarvis?" I asked.

Her face stilled. "Oh yeah. Jarvis. He's still here?"

"And apparently planning to stick around. He and Barry are on a hike right now."

"Oh, *that* should be interesting. Well, he either figures out that we're more than meets the eye, or he doesn't."

"Did you just jump from referencing *Pirates of the Caribbean* to *Transformers?*"

"I'm multi-faceted, Bubba. Keep up. And while you're standing there, will you get me another bottle of wine?"

8

A few hours later, I was on the couch next to Amy watching the sixth episode of *Gilmore Girls* in a row, thinking I'd seen the guy playing Dean, the boyfriend, in something else somewhere, but I was at least nine beers into my afternoon and I couldn't place the kid. Amy was out cold, the second bottle of wine proving more than she could handle solo, and I couldn't move because she was laying on my arm, so I couldn't even reach the remote to change the show. Not that I wanted to. *Gilmore Girls* was oddly fascinating, somehow. Beat the hell out of learning about Rob Lowe's skin care regimen on *9-1-1: Lone Star.*

I was just starting to nod off, the stress of the morning and the dozen beers taking their toll, when I felt a disturbance in the Force. Or at least what I figured that would feel like. The air in the room suddenly felt heavier, and more than a little bit colder, as if someone materialized an iceberg in the middle of my living room.

Shit. I knew what was up without even looking around. "Hey, Mama," I said, not taking my eyes off Rory Gilmore's latest monologue.

"Hello, Robbie," my mother said as she stepped into view, perfectly positioning herself between my eyeballs and the television. I'd seen her pull this move on my dad a bunch when I was a little kid. It was funnier then. "Did you forget something in all the rush of your long-postponed wedding?"

I furrowed my brow and adopted an expression that I hoped conveyed my deepest concentration for a moment before I replied, "Nope, not a thing."

Mama's eyebrow arched up so high I was afraid it was going to get lost in her scalp, and she gave me the kind of glare that melted a normal man's testicles and turned his bowels to ice water. But me? Nope. I am a rock. I am an island. I am the walrus, goo goo ga-choo. I am also very accustomed to getting the ol' hairy eyeball from a woman who carries a gun and knows how to use it, so my mother's glare had less effect on me now than it did when I was a child. I had also consumed the better part of a twelve-pack along with my six episodes of *Gilmore Girls*, perhaps adding to my bulletproof feeling.

Amy, however, was awake now, and I could feel her tense up, then stretch and rouse herself, looking at my mother through a cascade of tumbling blond hair. "Hello, Mrs. Brabham," she said, getting to her feet in what was nowhere near her most steady move ever. An hour asleep on the couch did nothing to erase the effects of two bottles of wine and a morning with her mother, so Amy was still hammered. She lurched off to the bathroom, providing me with no help at all. I was going to have to deal with my mother alone.

"Alright, Mama," I said, dragging myself to my feet. "Lay it on me."

"Why is it that every time I come visit you, you're drunk?" she asked. I blinked twice, trying to clear my head. This was not how I expected this conversation to go. Admittedly, she was right. I got hammered the last time she popped in on me, and I was hammered now. This time there was no connection between my drunkenness and her sudden appearance. This time.

"I reckon you bring out the best in me," I said. "But seriously, what's up? You just here to give me shit for not telling you about the wedding? Because if I recall, we decided it was for the best if we didn't see each other a whole lot, given the whole bit about Granny Mab being batshit crazy and homicidal, and Papa Obie being batshit crazy and, well, also homicidal."

My mother looked like she was trying very hard to not laugh at my assessment of her parents. I guess it's not often that anybody calls a couple of fairy monarchs out on being absolutely around the bend crazy. "We did decide that, Robbie. And it still stands. But someone out in the multiverse is talking about your wedding, and if word got to me and Nitalia, you can bet my parents heard about it, too."

"Well, shit," I said. I stomped off toward the fridge. "You want a beer,

Mama?" I asked, in perhaps the single most redneck sentence that had ever crossed my lips.

"No, thank you, but if there is any wine left..."

"Not a chance," I replied. "Amy's parents are in town for the wedding. Or they were, until today."

Mama had a pained expression. I guess when your parents are Queen Mab and Oberon, you know a little about psychotic parental units. "Was there a fight?" I caught her eyes flickering down to my hands, looking for bloodied knuckles.

"Not in the usual sense," I said. "I didn't beat the shit out of her daddy, although I thought about it. And as far as I know, she didn't beat her mama's ass, although I'm sure she deserved a solid whoopin'. No, we just had some very spirited discussions, and they decided to head back to Atlanta for a couple days of sightseeing before the wedding on Saturday."

"You bought them aquarium and World of Coke tickets?" Mama asked, an amused smirk on her lips.

"I didn't buy them a damn thing," I said. "They ooze new money with every step they take, so they can afford whatever tickets they want. I was just happy to have them out of my hair."

"And then I show up," Mama added.

"I wasn't going to say that," I said.

"I might have," Amy chimed in as she padded barefoot back from the bathroom. She'd also taken the time to pull her hair back into a loose ponytail and put on sweats and a baggy Stone Cold Steve Austin t-shirt. Of course it was baggy on her, it was my shirt, and I'm about seventeen sizes bigger than Amy. She still looked good, though.

I gave her a quick kiss and said, "Good morning, Sunshine."

"Where's the rest of the wine?"

"Whatever you didn't just flush is still in your belly, babe."

"Dammit. Nothing stashed?"

"Honey, I don't hide wine in random places all over the house," I said.

"Why not? There are pistols in cereal boxes. I wouldn't put it past you to hide literally anything."

"You found a gun in a cereal box? Which gun? And more importantly, what cereal?"

Amy looked puzzled. "It was a little .380 in a box of Lucky Charms. Why?"

"Dammit," I said. "Was it new in a box? I think that was supposed to be Geri's Christmas present from last year. I hid it there because she was on some anti-refined sugar kick and I knew she wouldn't look under all those marshmallows."

From the looks both Mama and Amy were giving me, I could tell they were having trouble unpacking everything going on in that sentence, so Amy just waved a hand at me and moved on. "My point is, with your tendency to hide stuff all over the house, how is there no wine stash?"

"Oh, that's easy," I replied. They both just stared at me until I shrugged and said, "I don't like wine. Since I don't like it, I don't think to stash it for a rainy day because if it ever rains so much I want a nice glass of Pinto Noir or whatever it's called, I'll just throw myself off the back deck."

Amy walked over to the cabinet by the sink, pulled down a tumbler, dropped a few ice cubes in it, then stomped over to the bar. She poured herself a very large bourbon on the rocks, then turned to my mother, apparently now fortified enough to face her soon-to-be mother-in-law. "So why are you here, Mrs. Brabham? Are you mad Bubba didn't invite you to the wedding and now you're going to turn us all into frogs?"

"No, not at all," Mama replied. "As I said to Robbie, I completely understand why he didn't invite us. It isn't safe for word of your impending nuptials to make its way to Faerie. That's why I'm here—someone has been making sure that word *has* reached the Fae. And that means…"

"That Granny Mab probably knows what's up," I said.

"And is probably pissed off that *she* wasn't invited," Amy added.

"Despite the fact that she threw me in a dungeon and threatened to have me executed," I said.

"My mother is known for many things, Robert," Mama chimed in. "But stability and logic are nowhere on the list."

"So, what do we do?" Amy asked. "We can't live our whole lives avoiding having a celebration just in case Mab learns about it and gets pissed off." She took another slug of her bourbon and cracked her knuckles. I didn't know what kind of weird drunk we were gonna get with her pouring whiskey on top of wine, but I really hoped I didn't get Drunk Fighty Amy, who'd want to storm Fairyland and kick my grandmother's pointy-eared ass. Mostly because I wasn't sure we could pull that off even if we tried. Mab was the Queen of Winter, after all. Her very thought was *law* in her realm, and while I didn't know how strong she would be on this side of the mushroom ring, I didn't feel any overwhelming desire to test her.

"I will help you lay on extra security at the wedding venue, and I have a few contacts that are still in this realm who will be willing to lend a hand as well," Mama said.

"I'm pretty sure we've got security covered," I said. "We do have all the resources of the Department of Homeland Security at our disposal."

"And yet I walked in through your front door, completely bypassing a lock, a deadbolt, four security cameras, three magic wards, and an infrared tripwire," she replied, arching that damned eyebrow again.

I paused. "A tripwire?" I asked.

"Wards?" Amy asked. We exchanged a look. "I had Skeeter put in the tripwire a couple weeks ago. He ringed the whole property with them, just as a boundary defense," she explained.

"I did the same thing with wards, about a month ago. I had Madame Wanda come down and smudge sage over the whole place and lay in some magical stuff that was supposed to repel supernatural creatures."

"That's why it didn't work on me," Mama said. "Fairies are not supernatural. We are extra-dimensional, which is different."

That made absolutely no sense to me, but I let it go. "So, none of our locks, wards, or tech will keep Granny away from the wedding, got it," I said. "But you have some ideas to keep the festivities free from any in-laws who want to do worse than show off middle school class photos?"

"I do," Mama replied.

"Then I reckon we'll gladly take any help you offer," I said, looking to Amy for agreement.

She nodded. "Thank you, Mrs. Brabham," she said. "We really appreciate the help, and I hope you know there was no slight intended—" She stopped as Mama raised a hand.

"Think nothing of it, my dear. Just get a quick start on making me a grandmother, and all will be mended."

As my mother stood in my den with a beatific smile, I wasn't sure who blushed more, me or Amy. Probably me.

9

It was a brightly smiling but perplexed Margery who met us at the wedding venue the next morning. She looked Mama up and down, obviously well-versed in handling bridezillas and their mothers, but I don't think anything prepared her for the two emaciated black-robed wizards standing off to one side, seemingly mute. Mama had introduced them as Sunil and Christo, but so far, their only response to anything had been a nod or an almost imperceptible shake of the head. Their robes dragged the ground, had big bell sleeves that extended past their fingertips, and sported deep hoods that completely shrouded their faces in shadow. I was pretty sure they weren't going to look much like me if and when we got shed of Margery and they exposed their countenances, but I've gotten pretty used to hanging around non-humans since I realized I was one myself.

"I'm not sure I understand," Margery said for about the fourth time in the ten minutes since we arrived. "I have an event setting up at ten for a ceremony today at two. I can't just—"

"That leaves us forty-five minutes to do our security sweep, identify any weak points that need shoring up, and be out of your hair before the first catering van arrives," Mama said, breezing past Margery like she owned the place.

I followed Mama, leaving Amy to deal with the flummoxed event planner. Sunil and Christo fell into step behind me, silent and creepy as hell. I waited until we were out of earshot, then hissed at my mother, "What are these guys, Mama? Pallbearers? They're freaking me out a little bit."

"A little bit?" Skeeter said over comms. "Bubba, your blood pressure is so high I'm afraid you're gonna bust a gasket any second. You need to exercise your chill, my brother."

Yes, we had our comms going for this excursion to the wedding venue. I learned a long time ago that anything involving my family in any way could be...eventful, so I'd geared up before coming on this little trip. Bertha II was in my shoulder holster, my Judge backup piece was tucked into a paddle holster in the small of my back, and my black hoodie hung open and loose to allow me access to my weapons if I needed them, but still kept things out of sight so as not to freak out the mundanes. Although when Mama showed up with the friggin' Grim Reapers, I reckoned that ship had sailed.

"Skeeter, shut the hell up," I replied, trying to keep my voice down.

Mama's ears were sharp, and I don't just mean the pointy bits. "Be nice to Skeeter," she said. "He's been a good friend to you."

"He's my brother in all but blood, but that don't mean he ain't a pain in my ass," I replied. "Now don't duck the question, who are these goobers?" I pointed at Heckle & Jeckle, standing like two gangly crows on the rolling lawn.

"Sunil and Christo are master magicians, and some of the most skilled ward crafters I have ever encountered. They will encircle the entire property with defensive spells designed to warn you of any threats that arise, and deal with those threats."

That sounded good, until I got to the last part. "What do you mean 'deal with those threats'?" I asked.

"Destroy them," Mama said, just like she'd say "no, thank you" if I offered her marmalade for her toast.

"And what if you get it wrong, and someone these guys pegged as a threat is just a drunken wedding guest looking for a quiet spot to take a leak?" I asked.

Mama looked at the Spooky Twins, as I'd come to think of her pet magicians, and they shattered the scary image they'd concocted by shrugging in unison. She turned back to me with a slightly sheepish expression. "Oopsie."

"Oopsie?" I asked. "You're talking about vaporizing an innocent person and your best response is 'Oopsie'?"

Mama looked a little offended as she said, "Humans breed so quickly, they're easy enough to replace. If we kill one or two of the spares, it won't affect the overall population. As long as you two are safe, that's all I care about."

I had to appreciate the honestly, if not the Machiavellian philosophy. I took a deep breath and counted to ten. Then backward. Then to ten again. "Mama, you cannot randomly obliterate human beings. That's not good."

"I wouldn't *randomly* obliterate anyone, Robbie," she said, her tone making it clear that she felt me to be the least mentally competent member of our family, including the dead ones. "We would only destroy anyone who strays into unauthorized areas or threatened anyone we care about."

"Which is me and Amy," I said.

"And Skeeter," Mama added quickly. "I love Skeeter."

"So, me, Amy, and Skeeter would be safe. Everybody else is fair game?"

She thought for a long moment before replying, her expression saying that she knew I was setting a trap, but she couldn't quite figure out how. "I suppose we could come up with some type of wardstone that you could provide to guests, staff, or members of the wedding party that I don't consider relevant enough to warrant exclusion from the defensive spells."

I didn't push too much on whether or not Amy's parents would be "relevant enough." And frankly, depending on their behavior, I wasn't sure whether or not *I* would think they were worth saving, much less what Mama thought. She was a pretty normal Southern mother when I was growing up, but being back in Fairyland for more than two decades had sharpened her less human instincts to a razor's edge. "Let's plan on that," I said. "We can give them out as party favors. Maybe a cute necklace or bracelet?"

"I will work with Christo and Sunil to develop something appropriate to the decor," Mama said, then walked off toward the stage where we'd be holding the ceremony.

A big chunk of the pavilion was currently occupied by a cherry picker and a young technician working on lights. I couldn't tell if they were a man or a woman from the ground, and the string of creative profanity wasn't narrowing the field of available genders, either. If I've learned anything from being around my fiancée, it's that eloquent swearing is not the exclusive province of the male of the species. Although I've yet to meet anyone that cusses as prolifically or poetically as Quincy Harker.

Thinking of the surly wizard, I made a mental note to text him and tell him he was invited to the wedding.

Then I had a better idea. "Hey, Skeet?" I asked the air.

"Yeah, Bubba," Skeeter's voice came over my comms.

"Will you text Harker and invite him and his crew to the wedding? I don't know if they can make it on short notice, but we should probably invite him." I was kinda proud of myself for having a thoughtful moment.

Until Skeeter blew it out of the water. "Dude, they were all on the first guest list we sent out. We even have a designated Team Harker table at the reception. You think Amy wouldn't invite her *boss* to the wedding? And before you ask, yes, we invited Director Pravesh, too." Keya Pravesh was the Director of the Department of Homeland Security, Paranormal Division. In short, she was Amy's boss. And mine, most of the time. Deputy Director Rebecca Gail Flynn was our direct supervisor, and also Quincy Harker's main squeeze. I'd heard a rumor that the two of them were also engaged, but Harker was even better at delaying his inevitable nuptials than I was, so no telling when that was gonna happen.

In a slightly deflated voice, I said, "Oh. Thanks, Skeet."

"No problem, buddy. You need anything else? There's a kickers *Real Housewives* marathon running on Lifetime, and I'm missing a cat fight with every minute we're on the line."

"Go ahead and enjoy your surreality television," I replied, and tapped my earpiece to end the conversation.

I turned my focus back to Mama and her magical weirdos, only to find them already up on stage, with one of them unscrewing the legs on the cherry picker and another taking up position to push the thing off to the side of the stage.

"Hey!" came a shout from the basket, some twenty feet above us. "HEY!" came a louder shout a few seconds later. "You wanna cut that shit out, or you want me to start dropping wrenches on your heads?"

"Sorry!" I yelled up at the pink-haired person scowling down at me. I turned to Mama. "Tell them to cut that shit out. They're working up top!"

"Well, Sunil and Christo cannot properly ward the space with this massive hunk of cold iron in the center. It will disrupt their magic and make any spell unreliable at best, and explosively dangerous at worst. Well, that's probably not the worst. Let's say 'apocalyptic' at the worst. Regardless, they cannot do their work with this monstrous machine in the way."

"And I can't do my work with some jackass screwing with my lift while I'm twenty feet off the ground!" the person leaning over the basket yelled down. "Hey you, big guy?"

"Yeah?" I asked.

"Reach behind the main mast of the lift and pull that red handle. That'll bring me down and we can talk about what you're doing and see if I can hold off on my decorating until you get done with your…wards or whatever."

"You can't come down?" I asked.

"I could, if your buddies hadn't unscrewed the feet and turned off the safety sensors. Now the bucket won't move until they're screwed in again or unless you use the emergency release. So get me down and we can talk about this. I'd rather not climb down the mast if I can help it." They paused, and I could have sworn I heard them say "again" after they finished their sentence.

I walked over to the lift, shouldered one of the wizards out of the way, and pulled the little red handle. The hydraulic lift let out a hiss and the basket lowered, bringing me face to face with a slim person in slightly ragged jeans, a t-shirt with a union logo on the front pocket that said "*Les Misérables* Local Crew 2022" and work boots. They had a tool belt around their waist, an orange safety harness on top of their pants and shirt, and a long orange tether hooked to the bucket of the lift. A long telephone cord was clipped to the wrench in their hand, and it hung down and looped to the tool belt.

"So, I guess the threat of dropping a wrench on my head was pretty empty?" I asked, pointing at the tether.

"I can go back up and show you how quickly I can unhook this, if you like," they said, giving me a sideways grin. The tech was clean-shaven, with high cheekbones and a half-shaved head. The other side of their scalp was covered in a mop of bright pink curls that flopped down over one green eye. They held out a hand, wrapped in a thick leather glove. "I'm Ash. I'm the venue's lighting and sound tech. Are you Mr. Brabham?"

"Bubba," I replied, shaking the proffered hand. "This is my mother and her two…associates, Christo and Sunil." I gestured randomly at the two mages, since I had no friggin' idea which was which. Maybe if they cut out the Ghost of Christmas Yet to Come cosplay, I could learn who was who.

Mama came over and looked at the diminutive technician. Ash was slender, about medium height, with lean muscle corded all up and down their heavily tattooed arms. I recognized symbols from a couple of comic book franchises, and at least three different anime. "Hello, my dear… I apologize, how should I refer to you? Are you a man or a woman?"

I cringed internally. Mama had missed a few cultural shifts since she'd left this dimension, it seemed. Ash didn't seem bothered, however. "I'm nonbinary. I don't really identify as specifically one gender or the other. I prefer they/them pronouns, but you can also just call me Ash."

"Ah, yes. We have this in my society, as well. Our word for it is 'univ.' As in 'universal,' because existence is universal, not tied to the masculine or the feminine. It is a pleasure to meet you, Ash. How long before you are finished here?"

That's my mama. Nothing getting in the way of her plans. "What my mother is trying to say—" I tried to butt in, but Ash and my mother *both* raised the "shut up, Bubba" hand to me.

"It's cool," Ash replied. "I've got about another two hours of work here, stringing all the Christmas lights overhead and testing the mics and speakers. The grounds guys are bad to cut through speaker wire when they mow the grass, so that's what'll take me the most time. I could go do that while y'all finish smudging the stage or whatever you're doing."

I cocked my head at the tech. "You know about smudging?"

Ash laughed. "Dude, it's the twenty-first century. This is a non-denominational event venue, with clients ranging from Southern Baptist to Hindu to Buddhist to pagan. I've seen smudging, blessing, baptisms, and all sorts of blessings. I will admit, I've never seen a client bring their own witches before. And I've sure as hell never seen an honest-to-whatever faerie before."

Everyone froze, even the normally stoic Christo and Sunil. Every eye focused on Ash, who just looked back at each of us in turn. "What did you just say?" Mama said, and there was enough of Queen Mab in her tone that I knew Ash's fate, and maybe the structural integrity of the entire building, hinged on their response.

"I said you're faeries. You are, right? I've never seen full-on fae here at the Soiree. Don't worry, I've got no problem with faeries. Not metaphorical or legitimate." They chuckled at the joke, but stilled when they realized no one else was laughing. Ash held up their hands. "Look. I'm not gonna out you. That's not my vibe. I just think it's neat. A little cross-species outreach is good, right? Got to keep relations between the mundane and the magical copacetic, right?"

I looked at Mama, who seemed to be backing down from Defcon Mab, and gestured for Sunil and Christo to back off a little bit. I leaned in toward Ash a little. "That's right, Ash. We need to keep our true identity as secret as possible. A lot of people wouldn't think very much of our presence here, and I'd like to get married without a big fight over species. That sound cool with you?"

They gave me that little smirk again. "Dude, I'm a pink-haired enby stagehand in Georgia. I learned discretion before I learned the vocabulary for who I am. I'll keep your secret. But you gotta lemme watch. I won't get in the way, I promise. I just think it's probably the coolest thing that's ever happened around here."

"You think that's cool, wait until you meet the wedding party," I said. Images of Barry danced in my head. If they thought Mama and her weird twins were cool, they were really gonna flip out over Bigfoot in a tux.

10

A sh finished their work, then trailed along after Mama and her twins specters of faerie intimidation as they cast wards, scattered salt and iron filings, and generally made most of the entrances and exits from the venue inhospitable to the fae folk. Mama warned me that it wouldn't stop anyone truly powerful, or truly determined, but she deemed it likely good enough to deter any minions Granny Mab might send to pee all over my parade, and I trusted her.

Our cotton candy-haired stagehand trailed along behind the cavalcade of weirdness, keeping their mouth mostly shut, except to whisper a few "whoas" every now and then whenever Mama or one of her pet wizards did something that make a sparkle. I suspected them of making their magic especially visible on account of having an audience, but I knew better than to mention it. The last thing I wanted to do was piss off the person trying to help me safeguard my wedding.

"I have set a timer on the wards," Mama said as we walked back to my truck. "They will become active thirty minutes before the scheduled ceremony and will deactivate four hours later. If your reception runs too deep into the night, you will be on your own for protection."

"The guest list has a few people on it who should be able to help out if anything goes sideways after the wards go down. I just hope they aren't too lit to be able to shoot straight," I replied.

"You have mages coming to the wedding?" Mama asked.

"Well, I invited Quincy Harker, but I don't know if he'll show."

"You invited the *Reaper* to your wedding?" Mama's face looked horrified, like I'd just told her our wedding bands were made from cold iron. They were, but they were a stylish blend of cold iron, silver, and blessed gold. And there was zero chance I was telling my faerie mother about that.

"He kinda hates that name," I said, then went on at the glare Mama shot me. "Look, Harker and I work together. Sometimes. We're not… *friends* per se, but his fiancée is Amy's direct supervisor, and we've done a few gigs together and they went pretty well, so in the interest of corporate bonhomie and not pissing off someone who legit lives next door to Count Dracula, I invited him. But he hasn't RSVP'd, so I have no idea if he'll come or not."

"Oh, he RSVP'd," Skeeter said in my ear. I'd turned my comms back on as we headed to the truck, a decision I regretted almost instantly. "He's coming, and bringing Becks, Glory, Faustus, and someone called Nameless. I don't know if that's a nickname for Luke or what, but he did request finely diced tuna at the reception for Nameless."

"Nameless is Harker's cat," I said. "Can't understand why he'd be bringing a cat to a wedding, especially an outdoor one, but somebody needs to tell him to get a pet sitter."

"I think his pet sitter is Dracula," Skeeter replied. "He might be better off bringing the cat with him."

I had a mental image of the legendary vampire sitting on Harker's couch with a cat on his lap and couldn't suppress a chuckle. "Yeah, you might be right. I can't really see Luke as the nurturing type."

"He raised Harker, didn't he?" Skeeter asked.

"And look how that turned out," I replied. "The man is essentially feral, a ball of poor impulse control with almost immeasurable power, all wrapped in a meat suit of anger and hair gel."

"That is why I would hope you would not invite him to your nuptials," Mama said. "The man is insane, and has been insane for a very, *very* long time."

"Mama," I asked, staring at her. "Do you *know* Harker?" The look in her eyes told a lot of stories, and not all of them were the kind of stories a son wanted his mother to share. A very loud refrain started going around in my head of *Please do not let my mom have banged Quincy Harker.*

"We…met near the end of your Second World War," Mama replied. "Harker was suffering the loss of someone he cared very deeply about, and he was nearly mad with grief and rage. I encountered him in Eastern Europe as he was hunting Nazis for sport. The bloodshed surrounding that man was something I had never encountered before, in your world or in mine. He was death on two legs, a walking storm of pain and chaos, and he cut a swath through the ranks of the Germans in Hungary that more resembled a tank division than one man."

"So how did you run into him?" I asked, now more intrigued by this insight into one of Mama's prior trips to our world than terrified at the thought of her making the beast with two backs with Harker. That concept still grossed me out, but it seemed a lot less likely given the circumstances of their meeting.

"I was in Hungary rescuing children whose families had been killed. That's what most changelings were, by the way. When a child is orphaned, if there is a faerie family that wants a child and has been unable to conceive, sometimes an ambassador comes into this world to give the child a chance at a happier life. Or a life at all, given what the Germans were doing to any child they deemed 'unclean' at the time. There was a city called Szeged, near the Romanian border, and Germans were systematically herding Jews into a ghetto there, then murdering them. I was there rescuing what children I could find with even a drop of fae blood that would allow them to live in our world long-term, and Harker was there painting the streets with Nazi blood."

"Yeah, the man can drop some bodies," I said, my tone muted at the thought of what they had both seen.

"I'm not being metaphorical, Robert," Mama said. "When I met Quincy Harker, he literally had several buckets of blood and a paintbrush and was painting the walls of the SS headquarters with the blood of Nazis he had killed."

"Holy shit." I'd known Harker had a serious beef with Nazis, having heard a little of the story of his first serious girlfriend, who was murdered in front of his face in the mountains of France. But I didn't know he had it in him to go full on horror movie justice on their asses.

"Exactly," Mama said. "I saw him as an even greater threat to the safety of the region than the Nazis, because while he was only targeting evil men with his power up until that point, I could tell he was riding the ragged edge of sanity, and one small push could turn him into a merchant of death the likes that Europe hadn't seen since…"

"Since Count Vlad Tepes?" I asked.

"Something like that. I...persuaded him that he should relocate his efforts to the American West. Once I had him safely deposited on another continent, I returned to trying to rescue as many children as possible. I did not save them all, but some lived out full and happy lives in Faerie."

I raised one eyebrow. "How exactly did you manage to 'convince' Harker of anything? I've always known him to be pretty hardheaded."

"Convinced might not have been the right turn of phrase," Mama admitted. "I bespelled him into slumber and shoved him through a mushroom ring with a note pinned to his chest. My friends in Faerie carried him to another ring that opened into New Mexico, dropped him there without waking him up, and when he came to, he was in the New World. And, apparently, healed of the worst of his madness. That was a side effect of my sleeping spell, but not at all an unpleasant one."

"So, the first time you met him, you knocked him out and teleported him like ten thousand miles across the globe? No wonder you don't want to see him again anytime soon."

"He may hold a grudge," Mama admitted. "And I would prefer not to sully your wedding day with bloodshed."

"And you aren't quite sure you can beat him on this plane when he's in his right mind and expecting you to try something," I added.

Mama looked affronted for a few seconds, then got over it. "Yes, that too."

"Well, if he shows up, let's count on him not remembering you the better part of a century later. I mean, he was delusional and psychotic when you last met, so there's hope, right?"

Mama didn't look hopeful. "Of course, Robbie," she said with obviously fake enthusiasm. "It's entirely possible that he has forgotten what my aura looks like after all these years. After all, how often does anyone encounter the same Princess of Faerie twice in one lifetime?"

"That's what we're gonna hope for, anyway. Now let's get back to the house. I have a bachelor party to get ready for, and you have...whatever mothers of the groom do the night before a wedding. But it is *not* joining me for the bachelor party."

Mama looked a little green around the gills at the very thought. "Oh, worry not, sweet child of mine," she said, and I managed not to reply with "whoa-whoa-whoa-whoa" in an homage to GnR. "I have no intention of participating in, observing, or even ever hearing the stories of your bachelor party."

"That, Mommie Dearest, will be the safest decision for all of us," I said, putting the truck into gear and heading home for my last night as a single man. As excited as I was to get married, I was at least that much terrified about whatever my friends had planned for my evening's entertainment.

11

Out of all the things I expected Skeeter and my friends to pull off for my bachelor party, an independent wrestling show at the National Guard Armory was nowhere on the list of things I expected. A nice dinner, maybe. A strip club, almost certainly. More alcohol than a human being could safely consume, definitely. But sweaty mostly naked dudes slapping the piss out of each other and executing some of the sloppiest top rope suplexes in the history of Georgia? That one I didn't see coming.

But there we were, a monster hunter, his technical ninja, his future brother-in-law, an Episcopalian priest, and a Sasquatch, all watching dudes beat the ever-loving piss out of each other for probably less than Brother Jarvis spent at the concession stand buying the horsepiss that counted as beer for all of us. In short, I was loving life. It got even better when one of the wrestlers, a chunky brown-haired guy with more tattoos than me got slammed into the guard rail right in front of me, and I got a face full of sweat and hair.

"Get off me, you bum!" I yelled at the wrestler, who was selling the impact like he'd just been in a car crash. "Get back in there and kick his ass! Do I need to get up there and show you how to whoop that skinny bastard's butt!" It was all intended to be part of the show, but the wrestler apparently didn't get the memo that heckling was more than just a wrestling fan's birthright, it was more than half the reason anybody went to indie wrestling matches in the first place. He whirled around and cocked his fist back like he was going to slug the jerk who was giving him crap, but he stopped cold when he had to look up a good six inches to see my face.

"Go for it, dipshit," I said, the grin never leaving my face. "I'm just as happy to kick your ass myself as to see this douchebag do it." I pointed to the ring, where his opponent stood on a turnbuckle flexing for the crowd.

The battered wrestler slunk back into the ring, got a few more kicks and punches from his opponent, and finally missed a dropkick and got pinned for his efforts. This was the last match before intermission, so we got up and headed for more beer and to look at the t-shirts. I walked up to the guy I'd just insulted and stuck out my hand. "Sorry if I was a little too much, pal. Just trying to have a good time."

He shook his head with a grin. "No worries, bro. I get that crap all the time. I just wasn't expecting it to be somebody quite as big as you when I went for the fake punch. The name's Zane." We shook hands, and I bought a baseball cap, a cool little military styled cap with a red star on the front, the logo of his faction, The Revolt. "You ever think about getting in the ring? You've got the size for it."

"Nah, I never trained," I said. "I get in there, I'm just gonna have to beat somebody's ass for real, and that's not what anybody came here to see."

"I dunno," Zane replied, shaking his head. "There's a tough man segment right after intermission where people from the audience can try to stay in the ring three minutes with The Beast." He pointed at a massive blond wrestler standing behind another merch table. This dude was *jacked*. He had muscles on top of muscles, and Norse tattoos covering almost every inch of his torso. He saw me staring and pointed across the room at me.

"You! Fat boy! I want YOU to fight me in the tough man contest! If you've got the balls." He laughed, a loud cackle that told me he'd watched the old *Master of the Universe* movie was too many times. His gimmick was pure Skeletor, in Thor cosplay. I looked at the rest of my wedding party, thought for a minute about how pissed Amy would be if I showed up for my wedding with a black eye, and decided it wasn't worth it.

Until Skeeter did what he's been doing since we became friends in middle school—opened his big mouth and got me in a fight. "Dude, Bubba would wipe the ring with your big Aryan ass. You couldn't hold his jock, let along beat him in a fight."

Then of course my future brother in law decided to help. "Yeah!" he yelled. "I just heard him say how much of a pansy you must be, since the only fight you can win is one of these fake ones."

And there it was. The dreaded "f-word." Not "fuck." Nobody cared about that one. In pro wrestling, there's only one taboo word that starts with the letter "f." Fake. Wrestlers hate the use of the term fake. And I get it. They're athletes, putting their bodies on the line every time they get in the ring. The injuries are very real, and the danger with the moves they perform is very real, even if the outcome of the match is set ahead of time. So when Jarvis called it fake, any chance of me not getting in the ring with this massive assclown went right out the window.

"Hey, Jarvis?" I said.

"Yeah?"

"Stop helping." I walked over to the giant, who was at least as tall as me, and in immaculate shape. They looked a lot like gym muscles, rather than hard work muscles, but since all my muscles are carefully hidden under layers of beer and nachos, he still seemed pretty formidable. "So you wanna do this?" I asked the guy. "I'm no wrestler, but I've been in my fair share of scraps. So if you wanna go, we can go."

He leaned in to me, dropping the bombastic act. "The tough man segment is legit. If you can stay in the ring with me for three minutes, you get five hundred bucks. If nobody can stay the three minutes, I get the five hundred. But it's a shoot, not a wrestling match. You sign up for this, I'm gonna try to beat your ass as hard and as fast as I can."

"So if you lose, you're working for free tonight? That doesn't seem fair," I replied, also keeping my voice down so the crowd milling around didn't hear the details.

"It's cool," Norseman said. "I'm also the promoter, so I'm getting paid no matter what. So you in? If we give them a good show, more people will sign up, thinking they might have a chance. I'll let you go first for free if you want. I think it might really get some good action. Usually I charge twenty bucks to fight me."

"Making it a lot more likely you won't lose money," I said.

"Just because I've got muscles doesn't mean I'm an idiot."

"No," I replied, raising my voice to make sure everybody around me could hear. "Wanting me in your little tough man contest means you're an idiot. I tell you what, big boy. I'll take you on and I'm walking out of here with your five hundred bucks. And after I whoop your ass, I'll take on any other sumbitch in this arena that wants to dance!" I looked back at the giant and said in a stage whisper, "That cool?"

"Perfect," he whispered back to me. He raised his voice. "Okay, dumb-ass. Go hit the bathroom so you don't crap yourself the first time I body slam you in the center of the ring. Then meet me backstage and you can sign the medical waivers. Maybe notify your next of kin while you're at it. Because in five minutes, you're taking the Beast Challenge and I'm gonna break bones you didn't even know you had!"

12

Now I've watched "rasslin'" since I was an almost normal-sized toddler, but actually getting into a ring in front of people? Nah, that was a new one for me. I didn't mind getting into a scrap. Hell, it's pretty much my raison d'whatever the hell that phrase is. But I prefer to do it either in private, or at least away from a bunch of cell phone cameras. So what the hell was I doing stepping through the ropes into a sixteen-foot raised square surrounded by steel cables wrapped in electrical tape? Trying to win enough money to cover my bar tab because once I got finished with this silliness, I was getting *drunk*. I also thought if we wasted enough time here and stayed all the way to the end of the show, I might get out of my bachelor party without ending up in a strip club. Not because I have any moral objection to naked women, but more because Jarvis had been pounding beer since we left my house and had "I'm going to get you in a fight on my behalf" written all over himself. So the farther I kept my soon-to-be brother-in-law away from any naked women and irritable bouncers, the less likely I was to have to get in a fight.

Another fight, I mean. His big mouth already had me stripped to the waist, showing off my impressive physique and tattoos to the crowd as I waited for The Beast to make his entrance. I didn't get entrance music. The condemned never do. I just walked out from the "locker room," which was actually a deserted science classroom, complete with lab tables and Bunsen burners. Pro tip—do not put a bunch of wrestlers, professional or amateur, in a science classroom with no adult supervision. I learned a LOT about the proper way to light a fart without burning your nut hair off in the three minutes I was back there ditching my shirt and emptying my pockets.

The Beast had an entrance befitting his ring name. Black Sabbath blasted out of tinny, overworked speakers as the gym lights went out, leaving me in a solitary pool of light. Then my opponent burst through the black curtains to an explosion of small pyro and strobe lights. I flinched a little when the pyro went off, not because I hadn't seen the flash pots on the floor as I walked past, but because in my line of work, when you hear an explosion that you didn't cause, you should probably duck. My flinch got a laugh from the audience, so it was worth looking a little silly, I figured.

The Beast walked up to the edge of the ring and jumped straight up, grabbing the rope and hopping the three feet straight up to land on the ring apron. Pretty impressive for a human. He stepped through the ropes and stomped right over to me, bumping chests and snarling the entire way. "You good for this?" he asked under his breath, his lips barely moving.

I didn't say anything, just reached down with both hands, grabbed him under his arms, and snapped my body backward, tossing him over my head. He managed to flip himself so he landed flat on his back with a resounding crash, and I spun around as he scrambled to his feet.

I grinned at the look of shock on his face. "Yeah, I'm ready."

He snarled at me for real this time, the half-smile he'd sported while he told me the rules of the fight backstage long gone. He barked at the timekeeper to ring the bell and lowered his head as he barreled toward me. I easily side-stepped him, adding a little shove to his back to increase his momentum as he hit the ropes, and clotheslined him almost completely out of his boots when he came back. I managed to hit the top of his chest instead of his throat, so he wasn't completely crushed, but his feet definitely didn't get the memo that his upper body was stopping, so he flopped back down onto the mat with another crash.

"Ease up a little bit, brother," he stage whispered. "The ring's a rental."

I had a brief thought that if the ring couldn't hold me slamming him down onto it a few times, that seemed a lot more like a him problem than a me problem, but I wasn't there to ruin anybody's livelihood, just blow off a little steam and have fun before I got hitched in the morning.

Remembering that, I leaned down and grabbed him by the hair. As I got close to his head, I whispered, "I won't break the ring if you don't leave any marks on my face. I'm getting married tomorrow, and I don't want to do it with a black eye."

Beast grinned at me. "Really? Congrats, man." Then he hit me in the breadbasket with a massive uppercut that threatened to paint his entire face with my dinner. I held my ribeye where it was supposed to go, but I dropped to one knee. That put my head at just the right level for Beasty Boy to wrap his massive arm around my neck and start to squeeze. I got one hand up under his elbow, but he had his choke cinched in tight, and it took just a few seconds for my vision to go sparkly.

But I wasn't quite out of tricks. In wrestling, a lot of times guys stomp on the mat when they punch or kick someone, just to make it sound more impressive. Well, I stomped the mat all right, but I made sure that Beast's foot was under mine when I did. Three hundred-plus pounds of redneck stepping on your foot by accident hurts like a sumbitch. Just ask Geri who had the unenviable task to giving me dancing lessons in preparation for the reception. But when it's done with intent, and heel-first, it hurts a whole lot more.

Beast let go of my neck and staggered back, wincing and limping. "Asshole!" he hissed. "You broke my toe!"

"But I didn't break the ring," I replied, backing up into the ropes to spring off with some momentum, and launching myself into a flying clothesline that would have gotten me benched and probably suspended if I'd tried it back at the University of Georgia. Division I football teams frown upon you actually trying to decapitate opposing quarterbacks for some reason.

Problem is, I haven't been a Georgia Bulldog for better than two decades, and I might have lost a little spring in my first step. Or my second. Or third, for that matter. And I definitely didn't get the kind of explosive leap that I used to get when I was headhunting University of Tennessee quarterbacks. So, I fell a little short of my flying clothesline. Like several feet short. Like, I belly flopped in the center of the ring short. At least the crowd got a good laugh out of it.

Beast took advantage, running over to me and flopping down on my back in a huge diving splash. "You gonna roll out of the ring now, or am I gonna have to break a sweat?"

"If you're not already sweaty, why do you smell so bad?" I hissed back. He froze, and I could feel him twisting around to give himself a pit check.

When he did, I bucked him off me like a bronco and hauled myself to my feet with the ropes. "How much time?" I asked. I didn't really want to take this dude's money. Indie wrestling isn't making a lot of money to start with, and I wouldn't feel right taking away this guy's livelihood, but I at least wanted to look good losing.

"Thirty seconds," he said under his breath as he buried a shoulder in my gut.

"Okay," I replied, doubling over to hide my mouth from the audience. "Gimme a couple more good shots and I'll let you throw me through the ropes. I won't even try to get up. Will that let you win and still look good?"

The Beast stood upright and gaped at me. He legit looked like I'd just told him Santa Claus was real after all. "This is a real fight, dipshit. You need to try to kick my ass." He didn't even hide the fact that we were talking, not that any of the fifty or so people in the armory had any illusions about how wrestling works.

"Dude, if I wanted to kick your ass, you wouldn't have made it past the first minute," I replied. "I fight monsters for a living. The kind that don't fight fair, and the kind that can take way more of a punch than anybody in this building." I didn't mention Barry, because he didn't need to know Barry's more hirsute side.

"Oh, you think so?" Beast said with a snarl.

"No, pal. I know so. And you've got fifteen seconds to really knock me out, or I get five hundred bucks off you."

He immediately saw the truth in my statement because he hauled off a swung at my jaw with a roundhouse that would have taken my head off if it had landed. Too bad a couple decades of performing for an audience taught him to telegraph his moves. In a wrestling match, you want your opponent and everyone in the arena to know what you're doing, so nobody gets injured and you get a better reaction from the crowd. That means if you're going to knock somebody's block off, you draw back and swing in with everything you've got, then either miss or pull your punch so you don't do any damage.

That's not how it works in a real fight, which he had obviously decided we were in, since despite promising not to leave any visible marks, he was throwing a haymaker right at my face. In a real fight, you keep your movements small and quick, like a short step inside the big, looping right hand your opponent is throwing, a sharp headbutt right to their nose, then a swift kick in the jewels to take every last bit of fight out of the other guy.

So that's what I did. I stepped into his punch, slammed my forehead into his nose with a cartilage-splintering *crunch*, then stepped back and punted his gonads up into the vicinity of his nostrils. Then the bell rang, signaling time, and I hopped out of the ring, collected my cash, and walked over to where my groomsmen were all high-fiving each other.

"Let's go before he gets up," I said to the boys.

"What happened?" Skeeter asked. "I thought you were just gonna play with him and then let him win to save face."

"I was, until he got all offended that I was going easy on him and took a shot at my moneymaker." I stroked my cheeks with the back of my hand. "You try to damage my pretty face the night before my wedding, I'm gonna have to leave you laying in the middle of the ring. It's as simple as that."

Making our escape was just as simple, since none of the guys helping The Beast back to the locker room looked like they had any interest in stopping us, particularly after Barry stood up and they realized I wasn't the biggest member of our crew. We got out to the parking lot, where Jarvis waited beside a stretch Hummer that looked cool, but couldn't make it up the mountain to my house, forcing us all to meet up at Skeeter's place for our pickup.

He turned to me and clapped his hands together loudly. "Okay, boys! It's time for the most sacred of bachelor party traditions—the strip club!"

"Are they human strippers?" Barry asked, disappointment evident in his voice.

"Are they women?" Skeeter sounded equally uninterested.

"Is there beer?" I asked. I didn't care much for strip clubs, having largely left that recreation behind me when Amy and I got together. But I had worked up a powerful thirst opening up all that whoop-ass on The Beast.

"Yes, yes, and a resounding yes!" Jarvis yelled, and threw up his hands like he'd just scored a touchdown. "Now let's *really* get this party started!"

He jumped in the car, and I gestured to Father Matthew. "After you, Padre," I said. "Maybe mine ain't the only soul you'll get to save tonight." And off to the land of body glitter and bad decisions we went.

D alton has a strip club?" I asked as we pulled into the packed parking lot of a strip mall sporting a check cashing place, a pawn shop, a liquor store, and a comic/card shop. All the way down at the end of the row of stores, tucked into the last spot right beside the liquor store, was a row of blacked out windows and a neon sign that simply said "GIRLS."

"They don't call it a strip club," Skeeter said. "Something about zoning. It's a 'private club.' There are memberships and everything."

"I have to buy a membership?" I asked. This was way more dubious than any of the sketchy clubs I'd been to before. Well, maybe not the one in Atlanta with the Skittles dispenser in the handicapped stall, but definitely sketchier than all the rest. Okay, maybe not the one outside of Greenville, North Carolina, that was in a double-wide trailer at the end of a gravel road that wasn't shown on Google Maps. But definitely sketchier than the rest. I'd done the "membership" thing at clubs in the past, usually when they had to skirt the booze laws in a particular town. But this place was fifteen miles from my house and I'd never heard of it. My strip club game was definitely rusty.

"No, you're good," Jarvis said. "I got memberships for everyone the other day when I first got to town." He handed out little cardboard rectangles with "GIRLS" on the front in the same pink script as the sign over the door. On the back it just said "MEMBER" in big block letters. I guess they weren't wasting their budget on the membership cards.

Or the building maintenance, since the door stuck and almost came off in my hand when I gave it a good yank. But after showing our ID to the mountain standing just inside the door, we passed through the second doorway into a dimly lit, yet tastefully elegant room fit for a quintet of refined gentlemen such as ourselves. The entire place was subtly furnished in mahogany and leather, with plush couches and muted music. It seemed more suited to contemplation of Kierkegaard than appreciation of boobies.

Nah, I'm full of crap. We opened the inner door and got blasted in the face by cheap cigar smoke and the ear-splitting tones of the late, great Jani Lane shrieking, "She's my cherry pie," at the top of his tortured lungs. The carpet was actually crunchy under our feet, and I was very happy that the place had adhered to the universal shitty strip club decor of very dark carpet shot through with Day-Glo squiggles and lines reflecting the ubiquitous blacklight. There was one main stage with a couple of smaller satellite stages scattered throughout the converted warehouse, with a bunch of surplus restaurant furniture dotting the landscape.

The dancers I could see were pretty, with good bodies and most of their teeth, at least as far as I could see. They were working mostly topless, with the stereotypical stripper heels omnipresent, a fact I reminded Jarvis of as I pulled his head back from getting clocked in the temple by a girl spinning around the pole on one of the satellites. "Head on a swivel, dude," I said.

He grinned up at me. "My head is on a swivel, that's how I almost got clobbered. I was looking at *her*." He pointed to a statuesque brunette on the main stage.

I nodded in agreement. She was the hottest woman in the place, by a wide margin. Even Skeeter seemed taken with her, and he makes Jim J. Bullock look straight. She was tall, curvy, and gorgeous, with perfect makeup and plump lips that made every man in the room think evil thoughts. She moved across the stage like a python, wrapping every guy in the building up in her sensuality and squeezing all the oxygen out of us. The only people I saw that were unaffected were Father Matthew and the other dancers. I gave myself a shake and leaned over to Skeeter.

"Something's up with that dancer," I said in his ear.

"Yeah, she's amazing," he replied, his voice dreamy.

"Skeeter, you aren't even into girls," I said.

"I'm into that one," he said.

"Dude, she's mine," Jarvis said. "I'm younger, and I'm straighter."

Skeeter actually bowed up at him. Skeeter, my best friend who hasn't thrown a punch at another human being since he got his ass beat in ninth grade, balled up his fists and took a step toward my future brother-in-law, who raised his own fists and stepped in, ready to throw down.

Father Matthew got between them, breaking their attention and snapping them back to reality. "There's an open table," he said, pointing to a corner of the room farthest from the main stage. "There's plenty of space for all of us there. Why don't we head that way and see if we can maybe each get a dance from her when she's done on stage?"

Both our hotheads nodded vigorously and followed Matthew to the table. I positioned myself and Father Matt so Skeeter and Jarvis had their backs to the stage, with me on one side of Skeeter and Barry on the other side of Jarvis. My Sasquatch buddy seemed a little smitten with the dancer, but less than the other two chuckleheads, so I hoped whatever mojo she had didn't work on Bigfeet.

A cocktail waitress appeared out of thin air with a smile and a drink tray. "Are y'all the bachelor party? My manager told me to keep an eye out for y'all and to make sure you have a good time." She was cute, a twenty-something bottle blonde with the thick accent that marked her as a local. It took me a few seconds, but eventually I recognized her.

"Sandy? Is that you?" I asked, leaning forward.

She blushed and waved a hand at me to shut me up. "I'm Pepper when I'm working. How are you, Bubba? How's that pretty fiancée of yours? She know you're here?"

"If she doesn't, she's gonna know in the morning when he shows up for his wedding covered in glitter and reeking of cigars and cheap whiskey!" Jarvis said with a laugh, punctuated by a slap on Sandy's butt.

I followed up his slap on her ass with one of my own across the back of his head, Leroy Jethro Gibbs style. "Keep your hands off her, dipshit," I said. "I've known Sandy since she was a little girl. Her older brother went to school with me and Skeeter." I didn't bother to say that her older brother Randall was a moron and a shithead, tortured Skeeter all through middle school, and found himself on the wrong end of my fists a few times after using either racial or homophobic slurs toward my buddy. He learned, though, and eventually cut all the nastier words out of his vocabulary and grew up to be a pretty decent local cop, if he did have a reputation for being one of the laziest men to ever hide in a speed trap, and was easily dissuaded from writing parking tickets if you spun a wild enough tale.

"Sorry," Jarvis said. He looked at Sandy. "Sorry. That was uncalled for."

"Then the first round is on you, and it's gonna be the top shelf," Sandy replied. "Course, top shelf around here is Absolut and Wild Turkey, so it ain't gonna hurt you too bad." She smiled at the table. "What'll it be, boys? Let's get this party started *right*!"

We ordered a round of Wild Turkey for the table, with a glass of red wine for Father Matthew. I gave him a little side-eye, but when he said that brown liquor made him a mean drunk, I let it go. The last thing I wanted to deal with was a feisty Latino priest in a Georgia titty bar.

We spent the next couple of hours at the club, fending off overzealous dancers that I either recognized from high school, recognized them as the younger sisters of women I went to high school with, or was pretty sure they had been my substitute teachers in high school. Jarvis kept buying Skeeter lap dances because he thought it would be funny to make the gay guy uncomfortable, but Skeeter just kept striking up conversations with the girls and making friends, so it kinda backfired on my douchetastic in-law. He tried to order one for Father Matthew, but one look at his collar and the girl did an about-face, muttering something about not looking for a confessional, just a trip to the VIP room. The brunette who had so captivated everyone didn't do the traditional lap around the room after her stage set, she just vanished into the dressing room. The boys were disappointed, but there were plenty of naked women in the building, and not that many men who didn't reek of diesel fuel or body odor, so we were never lonely.

We all had a pretty good buzz going and were having fun listening to Barry's running critique about how strange all the hairless females looked. He was really having a hard time figuring out our attraction to anything that would be so defenseless. Having seen female Sasquatches, there were *plenty* of noticeable differences, and the lack of body hair was just the first. Female Bigfeet were also usually better than seven feet tall, with rippling muscles under their fur. It was kinda like if Hulk Hogan didn't wax himself and had boobs, only even taller. The women in the club were fragile by comparison, but most creatures, and all humans, were fragile in comparison to Barry. Needless to say, he passed on every lap dance, which only made the next girl try harder. Every time. He was the forbidden fruit, or the unobtainable apple, and that made him into some weird form of stripper catnip. Oh well, the rest of us got extra dances on his behalf.

Then about midnight, the lights in the place got even lower, and all the LEDs in the ceiling went blood red. A voice came on the PA system, and the DJ in perfect carnival barker form said, "Please welcome to the main stage, for her second set of the night, the spectacular, the sensual, the steamy mistress of the mountains… Delilah!"

Madonna's cover of the Peggy Lee stripper theme song "Fever" came on, and the smoking hot brunette who had been on stage when we first walked in kinda *oozed* out from the curtain. I could almost see smoking footprints on the stage with every step she took, she was that hot. She was wrapped in a floor-length black evening gown with a plunging neckline and a slit in one leg that went all the way up to caress her left butt cheek, playing peekaboo with her everything when she strode across the stage. She walked straight down the runway, arresting every man in the place with her confidence, her poise, her beauty, and some other ineffable quality that made my stomach just the tiniest bit queasy. There was magic afoot, I just couldn't tell what type. But I knew it was potent when I watched Father Matthew walk straight up to the stage with a five in his hand and slide it under her garter.

Yeah, when the priest starts rubbing a stripper's thigh right out in front of the whole club, there is definitely something more than pheromones in the air. I looked over at Skeeter and Jarvis, who both sat with their tongues literally lolling out, and Barry, who just looked confused. "You don't think she's hot?" I asked the Sasquatch.

"Still no fur," Barry replied. "And she's much less attractive than the rest of the girls here. Why are all of you looking at her like she is the last steak on the grill?"

I looked back at her, trying to make Barry's comments jibe with the phenomenal beauty that I saw right up on the stage, and blinked as something *wrong* stared back at me, just for an instant, before the image of the beautiful brunette returned. For barely half a second, I saw the face of a hideous hag, with gnarled hands, sagging skin, and a wart-riddled, wrinkled face. There was lank, stringy black hair hanging down over hunched shoulders and cascading down past one of the most impressive turkey necks I've ever seen on anything without feathers. Then, in a blink, the image was gone and we were back to seeing a hot stripper that made Salma Hayek in *From Dusk til Dawn* look like a bag lady.

"Shit," I whispered. "She's got a glamour."

"What does that mean?" Barry asked.

"It means she's a faerie. It also means she's dangerous as hell. We gotta get out of here before the real shit starts," I said.

Except the real shit started right then, as some dude by the stage yanked on Father Matthew's belt to get him to sit down, and the priest spun around, cold-cocked the guy, and turned back to the faerie before him. Of course, the guy wasn't alone, and his friends took exception to Matthew laying him out like that. And if the leather vests with the top and bottom rocker panels they were wearing meant anything, they were all in the same biker gang, along with half the guys in the club.

"Come on, boys," I said, standing up. "We've got to go rescue our priest from the strip club's resident biker gang or there ain't gonna be no wedding tomorrow."

"Woo-hoo!" Jarvis shouted, springing to his feet. "I never been in a bar fight before!" He ran toward Matthew, tripped over a chair, caught his forehead on a table, and fell to the floor, out cold before he even threw a punch.

"And now you never will be," I said as I walked past his unconscious body. "Skeeter, make sure nobody steps on him, will ya?"

Then the Sasquatch and I stepped to half a dozen bikers in the middle of a North Georgia strip mall topless joint, and shit got really real.

14

I looked at the faerie, who had stopped dancing when Father Matt decked the first biker and gave her a "you stay out of this" point to the back wall. I don't know if she got my exact meaning, but she scooped up her discarded evening gown and scurried back to huddle against the mirrored back wall of the stage. I had to give it to the owners. For a titty bar built out of a repurposed doublewide, it was pretty swanky, and the floor didn't sag nearly as much as most mobile homes did when I walked across a room. I guess they had to reinforce things to get more people inside.

But they didn't reinforce *everything*, a fact made very clear to me as Father Matthew grabbed one of the oncoming bikers, did some kind of aikido or judo twist-toss-flip thing, and sent a dude my size crashing through one of the cheap tables. Father Matthew isn't tiny, but he's not a big dude by any stretch, so him bouncing a three hundred-plus pound man around the room gave the other guys a half second's pause. Which was just enough time for me and Barry to get to the party.

I grabbed the biggest dude's shoulder and spun him around. "You got a problem with my priest?" I asked, my voice low and grumbly as I considered how pissed Amy was gonna be if any of us showed up with black eyes, split lips, or busted noses. A shitstorm was pretty unavoidable at this point, what with the massive goose egg Jarvis was gonna have on his forehead, but maybe if I could keep my face from looking like raw hamburger meat in the wedding photos, I'd actually be able to spend the night in my wedding bed, instead of on the couch.

The big biker still had to look up at me a little, but he was obviously a man who'd seen some shit in his time. Maybe fifty, he was a big man, with deep gray muttonchops and a long handlebar mustache. He had full sleeves of tattoos, and more ink crept out of the neck of his black t-shirt and wrapped around his neck. He just exuded the aura of a man who could beat your ass and not even spill a drop of his beer. "He knocked out Spider. That can't go unanswered. Not in Devils territory."

The Georgia Red Devils were in fact the local "outlaw" biker gang. Their outlawry wasn't much, mostly ferrying cigarettes down I-85 from North Carolina, where the taxes on tobacco were lower. But I think they profited maybe a nickel a pack, and they weren't into any harder crimes, as far as I knew. I'd been drinking with a few of their guys in high school, but never paid them much attention. Until I noticed the pistol wedged into the waistband of the man standing in front of me. "This ain't no more Devils territory than my living room is Death Valley, you dumbass," I said. "This is Sean Conley's granddaddy's vacant lot with a trailer parked on it and a bunch of half-naked women packed inside. And last time I checked, Sean couldn't ride a ten-speed, much less a Harley. So why don't you chill out, sit your boys down, and I'll buy y'all a round. What are you drinkin'? Bud? Bud Light?"

"We drink Coors," he growled, like that was a more masculine beer than Budweiser somehow. I waved Sandy over and ordered a round for the bikers, and suddenly they didn't want to bash anybody's head in any more. It's amazing how often a round of drinks will deescalate a situation. I should try it on the next monster hunt. The drinks came, we all toasted each other, and I hauled Father Matthew back to our table, almost having to pick him up at one point. He didn't stop arguing with me until I pressed my pocketknife into his hand.

Suddenly his eyes cleared, and he looked around, befuddled. "What happened? Why was I up at the stage? And why am I holding your knife, Bubba?" He moved to hand my Buck folder back to me, but I waved for him to keep it.

I pointed at Skeeter, who had one of those spiked kubaton keychains in his left hand, and held up my left hand, showing him the knuckle duster in my palm. "Cold iron, Padre," I explained, gesturing at the items we held. "It breaks the glamour and protects you from faerie magic. Take a look at the hottest dancer in history over there." I pointed at the faerie

347

stripper, and Father Matt's brownish face turned very green at the edges. "Yeah, that's whose thigh you fondled, buddy. Welcome to the concept of coyote sex."

"When you'd rather cut off your arm than wake up whoever you woke up beside," Skeeter explained. "We've all been there."

"I sure have," Jarvis groaned from the floor. I looked down, and he had one hand wrapped around the metal post in the center of the table. "Sounds like I should hold on to this iron? Is that what I need to do?"

"Well, that, and put ice on your forehead. That's gonna leave a hell of a bruise," Skeeter said.

"Now that you know what I am, is this going to be a problem?" came a voice from behind me. I tried to casually reach around to the small of my back where I had a Judge revolver with at least one shell of mixed silver and cold iron shot tucked. "Please don't do that, My Lord," she said, and my hand froze.

"Your what?" I asked, turning around to look at the hag. This close, she was truly horrifying. An absolute cliche of scary, gnarled witchiness.

"My Lord," she replied. "You are fae royalty and must be addressed as such. I would never dream of offending either of your grandparents by showing you disrespect."

"Oh yeah," I said. "I guess I am kind of a fairy prince or something."

She looked skeptical. "Definitely 'or something.'"

I looked her up and down, a far less appealing prospect now that she looked like a bag of yarn dropped on top of a rag bag wrapped around a quartet of broomsticks with a saggy flesh hanging off them. The worst thing about the visual image of a several centuries old hag standing in front of me wasn't that she looked like literally the oldest person or creature I'd ever seen, it was that she looked that ancient and wrinkled and was wearing nothing but a sequined thong. Apparently, the glamour couldn't extend to her clothes, so this horrific creature with boobs hanging down past her navel was actually stripping.

I looked very pointedly in her eyes, mostly as a self-defense mechanism, and said, "We won't have a problem as long as you go in the back and stay there for the rest of the night. It seems like you ain't really doing anything that bad, just humping rednecks for their paychecks and making them do what the good Lord and Jack Daniels intended—blow their paychecks before they make it home. So long as that's the case, you won't have any problems out of me and mine. But you start any shit around my home town, and I'll happily be the one to finish it. We clear?"

"Yes, My Lord," she said, and curtsied. Now, usually a naked woman curtsying does all sorts of pleasant things to the jigglier parts of her anatomy, but when said anatomy has varicose veins that resembled a map of the Rocky Mountains, "pleasant" is not a word I'd use to describe the jiggling in question.

The faerie turned and started walking off back toward the dressing room, only to be cut off by some Poindexter in an honest-to-God plaid polyester sports coat. I could see the sheen on the fabric from ten yards away, which is how far she'd gotten before this short round man who resembled nothing more than Jason Alexander cosplaying Herb from *WKRP in Cincinnati*. He grabbed her arm and pulled her down into his lap, earning himself a ringing slap and gaining the attention of every biker in the place, as well as my team.

"Man, just when I thought we were gonna get out of here without breaking any furniture," Skeeter said from the chair next to me.

"Any *more* furniture," I corrected. "Maybe we can manage to stay out of it?" I asked, trying to infuse a hope I didn't feel into my words. Even the feigned hope vanished as Baldy stood up and slapped the faerie back across her face. Yeah, that wasn't gonna stand, not with me, not with Barry, and certainly not with the Devils. About a dozen guys started converging on Baldy, including the slowest-moving bouncer I think I've ever seen, a massively corpulent man with a long gray ponytail and a limp. I thought we'd all just stroll over, instruct Baldy in the error of his ways, and go back to enjoying the boobies, but fate had other plans.

Fate, in the guise of half a dozen of Baldy's friends, all younger, slimmer, and generally more fit than their less-impressive leader. The biggest one didn't even try to speak or calm things down at all; he just threw a right cross at the lead biker that dropped the older man with one punch. A shower of silver sprinkled out of his hand as the roll of dimes in his fist exploded, and the melee was well and truly on.

I felt more than saw Skeeter moving off toward the side of the room, pulling Jarvis with him. Good. One civilian I didn't have to worry about. Barry and I split, me going right and him going left as we moved in a pincer formation toward the asshole who started this mess. Father Matthew positioned himself a few feet in front of where Jarvis and Skeeter were working hard to stay clear of the fray, giving them a little bit of cover. Skeeter could handle himself in a fight, if by "handle himself" I meant "stay under furniture and don't get killed," but I really didn't want to return Jarvis to his sister in a pizza box, so having two people protect him seemed like the best plan. And it left more room for Barry and me to have fun and punch out some douchebros. Or bikers. I didn't really care. It had been a confusing, frustrating night, and I wanted to punch someone.

So, when one of the bikers staggered into my path and raised a fist in my direction, I popped him in the nose with a quick left jab, bloodying his face and dropping him to the increasingly stained carpet. It only took a few seconds to get to the section of the room where Baldy was still grappling with the faerie, surrounded by scrapping bikers and bros. I grabbed one of each by the neck and bounced their heads off each other, letting them collapse to the floor as they watched the pretty birdies and stars float around their vision.

I was about to grab Baldy's shoulder when he whirled around and punched me in the gut so hard I almost puked right on his little bald head. "Piss off, Hunter," he growled. "This one belongs to Pest Control."

Pest Control? *Those* motherfuckers? We'd encountered a team of rogue monster hunters calling themselves Pest Control a few months ago on a wampus cat hunt, and they'd murdered a mostly harmless cryptid and stolen her cubs for who knows what purpose. Since then, I'd had Skeeter trying to dig up anything her could find on them, to no avail. It looked like other than one website where people could hire them to "eradicate cryptids, ghosts, fae, and monsters of any ilk," that they didn't exist at all.

Except for the fact that the five guys I'd thought were just average douchebros now shed their polos and short-sleeved Madras button-downs to reveal black tactical tees and ripped physiques. Baldy grinned at his team. "See, boys? I told you Brabham lived around here and if we lay in wait at the only strip club within twenty miles of his house, eventually he wouldn't be able to resist the lure of lousy beer and floppy boobs. Now we don't just get to bag a quarter-fae mongrel, we get a full-blooded faerie and a Sasquatch, too!"

"You're missing just one thing out of your plan, little buddy," I said, looking down at the fat man.

"What's that, asshole?" he asked me with a curl of his lip.

"You ain't bagged shit yet," I replied. Then I laid an uppercut on the button of his chin that lifted him off the ground and deposited him flat on his back, unconscious. I turned to the douchebros, cracked my knuckles, and grinned. "Let's dance, bitches."

15

I knew I wasn't getting out of my bachelor party without at least one bar brawl. Pretty sure Amy knew it, too, if the amount of cotton balls, antiseptic, and Advil on the kitchen counter at home was any indication. All she told me when we left was "try not to get any injuries we can't Photoshop out of the wedding photos."

She really gets me.

Unfortunately, at the moment, a posse of dickhead corporate monster hunters were busy trying to get me, too, and their plans for what to do with me were way less likely to be fun and way, *way* less likely to involve whipped cream, cherries, and sprinkles.

Don't ask.

No, really. Don't ask.

While Baldy sprawled napping on the floor, his four buddies all pulled stun guns out of various pockets or orifices and fanned out to try and get a better angle of attack on me. They were stymied by the natural layout of a strip club, which doesn't have tables in organized rows. The whole point of strip club furniture is to create winding routes that the dancers meander through while separating morons from their lap dance budgets. The place just isn't designed to make for a great fighting bar. But I was willing to work against type and fight both the architecture and Pest Control.

And I had backup. Barry stepped up to my right shoulder, Father

351

Matthew stepped up to my left, and Skeeter dragged Jarvis farther back out of the way. I'll give my soon-to-be brother-in-law credit, though. He was trying to get into the fray, despite Skeeter working hard to steer him out the front door. They struggled for a few seconds before Skeeter sighed and shoved Jarvis into a passing biker, starting a whole new mini-skirmish behind us.

"Not sure that's helping, Skeet," I called over the pounding beat of the 90s classic "I Wanna Sex You Up" by Color Me Badd. Not exactly the best fighting music, but not the worst, either. You try beating some troll's face in while a string quartet plays "Rite of Spring" sometime. It'll put you right off your game. One of the Pests stepped toward me, his stun gun held out ahead of him like a wand.

"You gonna cast a spell or try to poke me with that thing?" I asked the sweating twenty-something. He looked like the youngest one there, with his bulging muscles and blond crew cut, but everything in his manner told me this was his first field op. He was tentative, nervous, and he had no idea how to approach an opponent both larger than him and completely unafraid. He took a little stutter-step forward, then flicked out a snap front kick toward my face. I moved my head to the right an inch, making his foot fly by my chin, and I snatched his ankle out of the air. I pulled straight up, and he went ass over teakettle, taking out a table, two chairs, and the nearest Pest as he tumbled.

With two temporarily out of the fight, I turned to see how Father Matt and Barry were doing. I shouldn't have worried. The Padre was ducking, weaving, and generally being impossible to hit as his much larger opponent tired himself out punching air. Barry took the complete opposite approach, letting his Pest walk right up and jam his stun gun into the Sasquatch's side. Sparks flew as the metal prods pressed into the cloth of Barry's shirt, but that was the only effect.

Barry just looked down at the stun gun pressed into his belly and said, "Ouch. Please stop that." When the guy didn't stop, Barry backhanded him lightly. Well, lightly for a bitch slap from friggin' *Bigfoot*. The Pest twirled around twice and just sat down on the questionable carpet, his eyes unfocused. Barry looked at me and shrugged. "I asked him to stop."

"Fair enough," I replied, then staggered forward a couple steps as something slammed into my back. Fire erupted from my left kidney, and I heard the tell-tale crackle of electricity, and my muscles seized up. I dropped to my knees, struggling to turn around and see which dickhead zapped me.

Baldy grinned down at me, albeit not that far down. Even on my knees, I was almost the same height as this clown, who reminded me an awful lot of the clown in that old movie *Spawn.* Only less handsome. "Not so tough now, are you, asshole? Your fat carcass is going to make for a nice Christmas bonus for old Tony."

"Tough enough, prick," I said, as I mustered all the strength I could to raise my right arm to chest level. My fist snapped up, connecting with Baldy's nutsack, and his eyes bulged out like the wolf in a Tex Avery cartoon. He dropped the stun gun, clutched his balls with both hands, and toppled over, gasping for oxygen. I pulled myself up using a nearby chair, only to go right back down as the Junior Pest I'd laid out earlier got to his feet and shocked the ever-loving shit out of me.

"Stay down, monster!" he yelled from above me. A pain grenade went off in my shoulder as the little bastard kicked me when I was down. Did he not get that memo in elementary school? This little shithead wasn't fighting fair.

Good thing neither was Team Bubba. "I am the monster here," Barry's voice rumbled over the pounding bass of early 90s dance pop. I managed to lift my head enough to see Barry thump Junior on top of his head like he was bopping Little Bunny Foo-Foo, dropping the Pest and turning to see what the next challenge would be.

I dragged myself up, quite a bit the worse for wear after two shots from a stun gun and a hellacious kick to the shoulder. Father Matthew was still playing with his food, making his Pest look like the loser in a Three Stooges fight scene, while Skeeter and Jarvis were trying to talk the Devils out of beating them to a bloody pulp. One Pest still stood, and he had a stun gun in one hand and a Taser in the other. Tasers are very different animals than the little stun guns you can buy at the convenience stores. Tasers put out a ton of power and can drop a huge man with one zap. I'm pretty stout, but I can't stay on my feet after a Taser shot at my best, and I definitely wasn't at my best. I had my doubts about even Barry handling one of those without ill effects.

"Put the Taser down, dipshit," I yelled. "There's too many of us, and we've already beat the shit out of your friends. Just get them out of here and stay the hell away from me."

"Piss off, Brabham!" he yelled. "You're an abomination, and we're gonna rid the world of your kind!"

"Wow, Bubba," Skeeter yelled from somewhere behind me. "That's usually how they talk about me. How does it feel to get called an abomination?"

"Doesn't really bother me," I replied. "I'd feel a little worse if this idiot could spell abomination."

The Pest glared at me, then raised his Taser. Barry sidestepped right in front of me, taking both prongs right in his chest. I guess I was about to find out if Bigfoot could handle a shot from a Taser. Spoiler—he can. The prongs didn't even penetrate his thick hide, bouncing off and *plinking* off a cocktail table as they fell to the floor. I took advantage of the stunned Pest's moment of distraction, stepped up, and laid him down with an open-handed slap. My hand covered the entire half of his face, and he looked like a comic book panel as his whole head turned around.

The Pest recovered in a blink and spun back to me, jabbing his stun gun toward my ribs. I wasn't in the mood for another full-body muscle spasm, so I slid to the side and punched him in the nose. I didn't hit him all that hard, but with a punch to the nose you don't have to. One good boop on the snoot and your eyes water, snot runs all down your face, and you can't see worth a shit. Which is really bad when you're trying to keep from getting your ass kicked. One more good punch, this one a massive right hook that came from my shoelaces, and the last Pest was down.

Or so we thought. Just as the last dipshit dropped, the door crashed open and another trio of massive men in full tactical gear stepped in, firing tear gas canisters and flash-bangs and terrifying those few patrons that hadn't already run for the hills. This was enough to unite Team Bubba and the Devils against a common enemy, so me, Skeeter, Jarvis, an Episcopal priest, a Sasquatch, and a biker gang all descended upon three completely overmatched SEAL Team cosplayers.

The only surprise was that nobody died. Not for lack of trying, but Skeeter managed to talk Sandy the cocktail waitress out of slitting Baldy's throat with a box cutter she pulled out of her corset top. Apparently, she'd been raking in record tips all night and was less than pleased about Pest Control showing up and cutting off her revenue stream. She got a little happier after I emptied all their wallets and told her to divide the contents between all the bar's employees. Judging by what was in there, being a privately contracted monster hunter paid better than working for the government. Or maybe being a dick paid better. Hard to tell with those guys.

I stood in front of Baldy, who was tied to a chair. The fluorescent lights were on, casting a hideous brightness across the room and bathing it in more light than a strip club should ever be seen in. "Okay, asshole. Who sent you?" I asked.

"Nobody," he replied. "We're just freelancers out hunting assholes. And we found the jackpot."

"You understand that you assaulted a federal agent, right?" Skeeter asked, pointing at me. "We could have you sent to Gitmo!"

"He's not a federal agent," Baldy said, spitting a gobbet of blood onto the floor. "He's not even human! We can do whatever we want to him, and nobody can touch us."

"I think you will find that we can absolutely touch you," Barry said, looming over Baldy's shoulder. He put a hand over the man's entire skull as an example.

"Who else knows where I live?" I asked.

Baldy looked at me like I was the stupidest man alive. Which, given his answer, I might actually be. "Everybody knows where you live, dipshit. You're still listed in the phone book."

Skeeter glared at me. "I told you to fix that. All the government contacts you've got, *plus* a super-hacker best friend, and you're *still* listed in public records. Goddammit, Bubba. Why do I even try?"

"I've had that same phone number since I was a kid," I protested. "I'm sentimental."

"You don't even have a phone in your house!" Skeeter protested. "You hate talking on the telephone more than anyone I've ever met!"

Okay, he had me there. On both counts. "If we let you go, will you pack up, get the hell out of town, and promise never to bother me or my people again?" I asked Baldy.

The weaselly little asshat grinned up at me. "Of course, Mr. Part Faerie Abomination, we will treat you with the respect you are due as a sentient being and honor all our agreements with you just like the federal government has always done." The last time I saw a smile less sincere than that, it was when Amy's dad said he was happy to meet me.

With visions of gift blankets dancing in my head, I turned to Father Matthew. "Does the Church have a Gitmo?"

"Bubba, are you asking me if there is a black site owned by the Catholic Church where we can imprison these men unlawfully and in violation of their civil rights?"

I thought about my answer for a couple seconds, then nodded. "Yeah. Just for like two days. Once the wedding is over and my in-laws are gone, they're welcome to release the assholes. I just need tomorrow to go off without a hitch."

"You mean today," Jarvis said.

I stared at him, and he shrugged. "Dude, it's like, a quarter of two. It *is* tomorrow."

Sonofa*bitch*. I was getting married in twelve hours. And I was still pretty drunk. And now I had these assholes to deal with. I turned my attention back to Father Matt, who was already tapping on his phone. I opened my mouth, but he held up one finger and pressed the device to his ear.

"Yes, sir. It's Ortega. We need a temporary contain on some hostiles."

Pause, then, "Human, sir."

Another pause. "Yes, sir. I said human." Matthew sighed. "It's a long story, sir. But we have eight hostile humans that we need tucked away in a secure facility for forty-eight hours, or we may lose Brabham as an operative. Yes, sir. It is that serious. Thank you, sir."

He tapped the screen and put his phone in his back pocket. "A retrieval team will be here in thirty minutes. Can we land a helicopter in the parking lot?"

Sandy piped up. "It ain't so much a parking lot as it is a clear patch of dirt with some gravel on it, but yeah, there oughta be enough room out back."

Jarvis stood, looked around the room, and said, "Well, since we've got a little time before they get here, and these dickheads are all tied up good and tight, sounds like it's time for shots!"

16

For the record, whenever someone more than a decade your junior calls for shots, it's probably in your best interest to say no. Sometimes it's in your best interests to say, "Hell no." But it is never, *ever*, in your best interests, especially if you need to be vertical in less than twelve hours, to say "Hell yeah!" and spend the next two hours slamming tequila with bikers and Bigfoot in a doublewide titty bar while your best friend and your priest forcibly abduct more than half a dozen men and turn them over to a shadowy religious strike team.

But my best interests are sometimes boring, and tequila never is. Which is why I found myself staring up at a pink-haired masochist way too early in the morning with a colossal hangover, what felt an awful lot like a new tattoo on my right butt cheek, and an incredible need to pee, puke, or poop. Not necessarily in that order. Or in any order whatsoever.

"Bubba, I am not holding your hair back while you vomit, so you'd better get yourself under control and into a shower pronto, or I will not be responsible for whatever Amy tells me to do to you. But you are *not* going to be late for this wedding, no matter how hung over you are," Geri said, glaring down at me.

That put everything into perspective for me. It was my wedding day. The single most important day of my life, when I was about to make a final, formal commitment to the woman I loved. In front of my friends, my family, and a bunch of other people Amy decided we should give a shit about. Or at least a bunch of people Amy decided we should feed for free. I rolled over, expecting to throw my feet out of the bed and kinda roll to my feet, only my feet didn't drop like they were supposed to. Instead, my feet thumped into wooden planks, and I realized I was outside. On my deck. *Flat* on my deck, where I'd apparently spent the night. Or the morning. Again.

"What time is it?" I croaked. Something in the back of my mind made me think two o'clock was important.

"It's almost eleven," Geri said.

"Does that mean I have to get up now?" I asked. "I'm pretty sure I didn't get to bed until…not long ago."

"I'm pretty sure you didn't, too," Geri agreed. "But now you have a hair over three hours to scrub the stench and body glitter off, sober up enough to say 'I do' at the appropriate time, and haul ass to the church. Or your fiancée, who I love dearly, will probably shoot us both. And I've seen her shoot. She can dot the eye on a quarter from fifty yards with a pistol."

She wasn't wrong. I groaned again and rolled over, then used both hands to push myself up to my hands and knees. Fighting back another wave of nausea, I reached out for the porch railing and hauled myself to my feet. "Oof," I said. "I think that last round of shots was a mistake."

"I think the first round was probably a mistake, too," came Skeeter's voice from the top of my picnic table. He was laid out flat on his back, eyes squeezed tightly shut and both hands pressed to his temples.

"If the first round wasn't, the second definitely was." Father Matthew opened the sliding glass door and stepped out, looking rough but holding two steaming mugs. He handed one to me. "Coffee."

"God bless you, Padre," I groaned as I slurped the lava-hot black liquid.

"Pretty sure that comes with the collar," Father Matt said with a half-smile. "I've already had my shower, so the bathroom is free."

At the word "bathroom," both my stomach and my bladder reminded me of their existence, so I staggered into the house, then down the hall to relieve myself. I hung a towel over the mirror so I didn't have to see the evidence of my bad decisions, then carried my coffee back out to the den, where Geri and Matthew stood watching as Skeeter rattled around pots and pans in my cabinets.

"Bubba, where the hell is that big cast iron skillet your mama used to use?" he asked, his head half-buried in the warming drawer under the oven.

"I don't have any idea," I replied. "You know I don't even heat up Pop-Tarts. Did you look in the dishwasher?" The looks I got from the three of them would make you think I told them to shoot the Pope right in front of the Vatican.

"You're joking, right?" Father Matt asked.

"He's not that funny," Geri said, opening another cabinet and pulling out the frying pan. Skeeter pulled a dozen eggs out of the fridge and starting cracking them into a big mixing bowl.

"Where's Jarvis?" I asked, looking around. The door to the guest bedroom had been standing open, so he wasn't in there. Nobody was on the couch, and I hoped to everything holy he hadn't decided to crash in my bed. Of course, I couldn't really remember anything after the fifth round of shots and the impromptu wrestling match between me and three of the bikers. To be specific, I didn't remember anything after the three of them body slammed me through a table.

"He slept in the truck," Skeeter said.

"In the truck?" I asked. I didn't have any real objection to somebody sleeping in my truck, but we'd had a lot to drink, and I had some serious objections to anybody puking in my truck.

"In the bed," Geri said. "He's alive. I checked his pulse as I walked past."

"Okay, good. Then I'm gonna go take a shower," I said, heading back toward the bathroom.

"Good call," Geri said. "You all smell like cheap booze and cheaper strippers. And Bubba?"

"Yeah?"

"Clean underwear. With no holes. This is your wedding."

I turned around and grinned at her. "If there ain't no holes in my underwear, how am I supposed to put 'em on?"

Twenty minutes later, I smelled better, which was something of a double-edged sword. On the one hand, I didn't smell like dollar store cigarettes and bad decisions. But on the other hand, I could smell the rest of my bachelor party, and they were *ripe*. Barry walked in as the platter of bacon hit the table, looking fresh as a daisy and smelling like pine trees.

"Where did you sleep?" I asked. "Or were you Jarvis's big spoon in the bed of the truck?"

He chuckled. "Bubba, I live in the woods. I did what I always do—I slept on a bed of moss at the base of a big oak tree, then bathed in the stream down the hill."

"Doesn't that creek run right behind a housing development?" I asked.

Barry actually blushed, something I'd never seen before. Admittedly, his face was usually covered by a buttload of hair, so it was pretty hard to see normally. "There may have been an unintended audience to my ablutions."

"Well, once we get some grub in us, let's get all gussied up and head to the church. We can still get there a little early if we don't screw around too much," I said, piling enough bacon on my plate to give a normal human a coronary right there at the table. Since I'm neither normal nor completely human, I counted on that to save me.

It took another hour and half to get everybody scrubbed down and headed to the venue, but we were still on track to be there half an hour before the ceremony, which I figured was plenty of time. Amy must have thought the same thing, since after a couple of reassuring texts from Geri, she stopped calling. Father Matthew and Skeeter rode with Geri, and Jarvis and Barry piled in my truck to get going.

We pulled off the main road onto the long driveway leading up to the Rolling Clover Event Venue and Soiree, and a familiar-looking black Suburban slid in right behind us and blinked its lights. "Harker's here," I announced to the truck.

"Who's Harker?" Jarvis asked from the back seat.

I looked at Barry who shrugged. How to explain Quincy Harker to a mundane? "You ever watch *Supernatural*?"

"Yeah, why?"

"Well, Harker is kinda like the short brother on that show, only more sweary," I said.

"*More* sweary? Dean was pretty profane," Jarvis said, his skepticism evident.

"Quincy Harker is the only person I've ever heard use the word 'fuck' as every part of speech," I said.

"I know a lot of people who do that," Jarvis said.

"In one sentence?"

"Oh."

"Yeah. He kinda works with us. Sometimes. He's engaged to Amy's boss, so be nice." I left out the part where he also throws fireballs and might roast Jarvis from the inside out if he said the wrong thing, but hoped that was understood.

I saw another compact SUV pull into line behind Harker as we drove up the winding gravel road, then pulled into the wide parking lot and slammed on the brakes, almost causing Dalton, Georgia's first ever pileup. "What the hell, Bubba?" Jarvis cried, throwing out a hand to keep from slamming his face into the back of Barry's seat.

I ignored him, flinging my door open and sprinting up the hill to the venue. Seconds later, I heard a chorus of other doors open and slam shut, and a series of pounding feet behind me. I stopped at the base of the steps leading into the main building, and everyone else stopped a few steps behind me.

"What the fuck?" Harker asked, perfectly encapsulating everything I was feeling.

"Bubba?" Skeeter's voice was thin and worried.

"Yeah, Skeet?" My own voice sounded small, like a frightened child. Which made sense, as that's how I was feeling right then.

"Where's the building?" Skeeter asked.

"Skeeter," I replied. "I have no goddamned idea."

Where the Rolling Clover Event Venue and Soiree had stood just twenty-four hours earlier, now nothing but an empty patch of bare earth remained. A few pipes stuck up from the red dirt, and I saw a black snake slither along, unconcerned about the vanishing architecture. The wedding venue, and everyone belonging to the cars in the parking lot, had simply vanished.

"Um, dude?" I turned to see Ash, the stagehand from the other day, standing next to her car in the black pants and white dress shirt of cater-waiters everywhere. "Does this have anything to do with my gig and everyone in it disappearing?"

I looked where they were pointing and saw a mushroom ring right in the center of the dirt. I walked over to it and stared down, feeling the fear and rage begin to crystallize in my gut. "Shit," I said as I recognized a pattern in the center of the ring. Four rows of mushrooms, all perfectly arranged to form a capital "M."

I looked at the rest of my assembled friends and family. "Mab," I said, unable to keep the dread out of my voice.

"What?" Harker asked.

"Queen Mab, my psychotic grandmother and the Winter Queen of the Fae, kidnapped Amy and the whole damned wedding party," I said.

"Holy shit," Geri said.

"Holy shit is right," I replied. "Because now we have to go to Fairyland to get them back."

NOT THE END

ACKNOWLEDGMENTS

As always, I have to thank my wife Suzy, for putting up with my shit. I want to thank Melissa McArthur and Natania Barron for making this and all my series look as good as they possibly can. Any complicated grammar things that I get right are because of Melissa. Any typos are my fault. Natania brings so much to the table as a cover designer and handling the overall branding of the series, I can't thank her enough for making me look way classier than I am.

Thanks to my team of misfits at Falstaff, especially Theresa, Katie, and Erin, who struggle valiantly trying to keep my ADHD-addled brain at least a little focused. And thanks to my "younger" sister Bonnie, who has dived right into this odd world of ours and become an integral part of our team.

But most of all, thanks to you for continuing to read the ramblings of a redneck about an even bigger redneck. When I started publishing over fifteen years ago, I had no idea I'd ever sell a single book, much less be able to feed my family off of this silliness. So thank you for reading, and thank you for sticking around.

This also means you can't kill me for the cliffhanger at the end of this book, because if you do, you'll never figure out what happens. :)

JGH
April, 2025

ABOUT THE AUTHOR

John G. Hartness is a teller of tales, a righter of wrong, defender of ladies' virtues, and some people call him Maurice, for he speaks of the pompatus of love. He is also the award-winning author of the urban fantasy series *The Black Knight Chronicles,* the Bubba the Monster Hunter comedic horror series, the Quincy Harker, Demon Hunter dark fantasy series, and many other projects.

In 2016, John teamed up with several other publishing industry professionals to create Falstaff Books, a small press dedicated to publishing the best of genre fiction's "misfit toys." Falstaff Books has since published over 300 titles with authors ranging from first-timers to NY Times bestsellers, with no signs of slowing down any time soon. He is also the founder of the SAGA Genre Fiction Writers' Conference, where students hone their business and craft skills to write better books and make more money.

In his copious free time John enjoys long walks on the beach, rescuing kittens from trees and playing *Magic: the Gathering.* John's pronouns are he/him.

ALSO BY JOHN G. HARTNESS

THE BLACK KNIGHT CHRONICLES

The Black Knight Chronicles - Omnibus Edition

The Black Knight Chronicles Continues - Omnibus #2

All Knight Long - Black Knight Chronicles #7

Lady in Black - Black Knight Chronicles #8

BUBBA THE MONSTER HUNTER

Scattered, Smothered, & Chunked - Bubba the Monster Hunter Season One

Grits, Guns, & Glory - Bubba Season Two

Wine, Women, & Song - Bubba Season Three

Monsters, Magic, & Mayhem - Bubba Season Four

Blood, Sweat, & Tears - Bubba Season Five

Shinepunk: A Beauregard the Monster Hunter Collection

QUINCY HARKER, DEMON HUNTER

Year One: A Quincy Harker, Demon Hunter Collection

The Cambion Cycle - Quincy Harker, Year Two

Damnation - Quincy Harker Year Three

Salvation - Quincy Harker Year Four

Carl Perkins' Cadillac - A Quincy Harker, Demon Hunter Novel

Inflection Point

Conspiracy Theory

Comes a Reckoning

Lost

Histories: A Quincy Harker, Demon Hunter Collection

Histories II: A Quincy Harker, Demon Hunter Collection

SHINGLES

Zombies Ate My Homework: Shingles Book 5

Slow Ride: Shingles Book 12

Carnival of Psychos: Shingles Book 19

Jingle My Balls: Shingles Book 24

Snatched: Grandma Annie and the Cooter of Doom: Shingles Book 29

Deader than Hell: Shingles Book 40

NSFW - The Shingles Collection

OTHER WORK

The True Confessions of Fandingo the Fantastical (with EM Kaplan)

Queen of Kats

Fireheart

Amazing Grace: A Dead Old Ladies Detective Agency Mystery

From the Stone

The Chosen

Genesis

Hazard Pay and Other Tales

Have Spacecat, Will Travel

Identity Theft

Unforgiven

FRIENDS OF FALSTAFF

Thank You to All our Falstaff Books Patrons, who get extra digital content each month! To be featured here and see what other great rewards we offer, go to www.patreon.com/falstaffbooks.

PATRONS

Dino Hicks
John Hooks
John Kilgallon
Larissa Lichty
Travis & Casey Schilling
Staci-Leigh Santore
Sheryl R. Hayes
Scott Norris
Samuel Montgomery-Blinn
Junkle
Vickie DeSantos
Quincy J. Allen
Allison Charlesworth

Thank You for Supporting Independent Publishing!

We believe that you should be able
to read your books, your way.
That's why this Falstaff Books
print edition includes a digital copy
at no additional cost!

Just scan the QR code with your device,
follow the directions on Prolific Works,
and enjoy!
You can also join our newsletter when prompted,
and never miss an awesome Falstaff Release!